1

Computers Don't Work That Way

"*Now* what is it doing?" Granny cried impatiently.

I ran into the front room of our little cabin home and found my grandmother and my father bent over the newest addition to the decor: a bulky, secondhand computer sitting on a polished pine desk.

Out of all four hundred Indian reservations in the US, Nettlebush was probably among the very last to get with the 21st Century. At the start of September, the tribal council had announced--kind of gleefully, I thought--that we were finally getting internet service.

Predictably, reactions were a mixed bag. My best friend, Annie Little Hawk, had serenely stated she'd use the hookup to find more recipes and sell her crafts online. Her boyfriend, Aubrey Takes Flight, had squawked and squeaked like an excited prairie chicken and spent countless hours talking about the metaphysics of cyberspace and the liminal ramifications of such a thing and William Gibson and--well, at that point, I'd kind of tuned him out. Sorry, Aubrey. No offense.

Really, the old folks had had the best reactions. Imagine a bunch of little old Plains People who have never seen the inside of a car, much less the upside of a computer. Now imagine trying to explain to them what a search engine is. For bonus points, make sure you're talking to the ones who don't speak English.

I joined Dad and Granny by the computer with an amused, inquisitive smile. Their identical, water-gray eyes were fixed on the dully glowing monitor. Dad's raven-black hair fell smoothly over his shoulders, his hands on his knees.

"It's booting up, Mother," Dad explained stiltedly. He had a profile like a sad, chubby hawk, a straight nose and a wobbly chin. He was turning forty soon--sometime in January, Plains People don't traditionally celebrate birthdays--and his stomach had accumulated an indicative paunch.

"I don't see what I need this rickety-rackety nonsense for," Granny said severely. I think she must have been a beautiful woman in her youth, but in old age, you couldn't really tell what she looked like beneath all those heavy, leathery wrinkles. Her snow-white hair, braided, was Rapunzel-length; she wore a simple trinket around her neck, a glass gem on the end of a willow string.

I don't look anything like Dad or Granny, except for my nose, maybe. My hair's a crazy, curly blond and my eyes are a plain brown. I've got freckles all over my arms and stomach, and until I learned how to cull oil from lavender spikes, I used to burn in the sun. I inherited all my looks from Mom. I inherited her last name, too: Plains People are matrilineal, so the kid always belongs to the mother's clan. We were Paul Looks Over and Catherine Looks Over and Skylar St. Clair. Nothing out of the ordinary here.

"To keep in touch with your friends outside the reserve," Dad said. "Solomon set up a tribal website. You--"

"A what?"

"A website. Now you can talk with the Northern Shoshone whenever you want. You don't have to wait for the winter pauwau."

"That's what the postal service is for!"

I hid my smile. Granny was set in her ways. No amount of arguing would ever change her worldview.

"Skylar," Granny said. "What is it doing?"

I bent over the desk and peered at the computer screen. It wasn't actually doing anything, unless you count sitting still as doing something.

I shook my head. *Nothing, Granny*, I meant to say, but couldn't. I've been mute since I was five. My vocal cords never healed correctly after--well, there's no reason to dwell on the past.

"Then make it do something! I didn't let the Gives Light boy put all those wires around my house for nothing!"

What did she want the computer to do, shawl dance? Granny looked at me sharply, accurately surmising my thoughts. I grinned sheepishly. Granny wasn't a lady you wanted to cross.

"Here," Dad said wearily. He took the mouse in his pawlike hand and clicked around on the screen. A blank window popped up. He typed on the keyboard, and a big orange website flooded the screen.

The website read, "WELCOME TO THE HOME OF THE PLAINS SHOSHONE." I winced. I wouldn't have chosen bright red text for an orange background.

"Hmph," Granny said noncommittally. She sat down on the stiff wooden chair. Then: "Quiet," she ordered, though no one had said anything. "I'm reading."

Dad and I exchanged sideways smiles, his wry, mine endeared.

The website had a neat little history blurb about the Shoshone tribe: how we had originated in the Sierra Nevada but migrated to the Plains, where we bonded with the Paiute and fought bloodless battles with the Lakota; how our Lost Woman had led Lewis and Clark in making the first real map of America and our benevolent chief, Shoots Running, had taught the white men to ford the rivers and survive in the wilderness; how a small band of Eastern Shoshone had fled south to Arizona after the harrowing Bear River Massacre, where Dad, Granny, and I lived today.

"I don't see anything about Bear Hunter," Granny said. Granny was very hard to please.

"There's a chat room, Cubby," Dad said. "You can check and see if any of your friends are connected."

Granny waved at us dismissively. She rose from her chair and shuffled off to the kitchen for a cup of roasted acorn tea.

"Or Eli's boy," Dad said meaningfully.

I didn't look at him. I took Granny's seat, my face burning with embarrassment.

Dad chuckled, low but audible, and went upstairs.

I looked again at the website, squinting to shield my eyes from the red-and-orange onslaught. There were a whole bunch of tabs on the side for tribal resources, including a map of the reservation and an event calendar. I found the button labeled "Chat," clicked on it, and typed in my name.

Mercifully, the bright background faded to an off-white chat room window.

```
ZEKE: AHAHAHAHAHA IM TYPING THE FASTEST
William Sleeping Fox is idle.
stu stout: Why are you typing in all capital
letters?
matthew: i dont wanna go to church 2day
Annie: Hi, Skylar!
Skylar St. Clair: :)
prairierose: me neitherrrrr
ZEKE: WHAT
HollyAtDawn has entered the room.
stu stout: Never mind.
ZEKE: OKAY
Aubrey TF: hi skylar!!!
Aubrey TF: how are you??
Skylar St. Clair: hey holly :)
Annie: Hi, Holly
```

Skylar St. Clair: hi aubrey. not bad, thanks
HollyAtDawn: ugh
Skylar St. Clair: you?
ZEKE: OH ITS YOU
ZEKE: I MEAN SKYLER
ZEKE: SKYLAR WHATEVER
dosabite: sk,hdksh,f
ZEKE: I DIDNT NO YOU COULD TALK
HollyAtDawn: stop yelling...
dosabite: hinni
Aubrey TF: well, a little confused, really!

He sure wasn't the only one.

dosabite: ekkesah
dosabite has left the room.
HollyAtDawn: good riddance
Annie: That's not nice.
ZEKE: I NO RIGHT SHES SO WEIRD
Aubrey TF: was that imaculata?
ZEKE: LOOK I AM TYPING
stu stout has left the room.
Annie: Yes, that was Immaculata.
ZEKE: FINE
William Sleeping Fox is no longer idle.
Aubrey TF: wait, the shaman has a
computer??????
Skylar St. Clair: ;) he keeps it in his tipi
next to the travois
rafael has entered the room.

Oh, boy, I thought. If there was anyone I didn't trust with
technology, it was Rafael.

ZEKE: HEY DUMBASS GET OUT CAN;T YOU SEE THE

```
SIGN THAT SAYS COOL GUYS ONLY (JUST PRETEND
ITS THERE)
Skylar St. Clair: hi rafael :)
HollyAtDawn: stop yelling, stop yelling,
STOP YELLING!!!
Annie: In that case, Zeke, what are you
still doing here?
Aubrey TF: eek.......
rafael: hi
rafael: huh
HollyAtDawn has left the room.
Siobhan Stout has entered the room.
ZEKE: WHAT AWWWWW WHAT THE HECK FINE IM OUTA
HERE IT'L GET BORING WITHOUT ME ANYWAY
prairierose: SIOBHAN
William Sleeping Fox is idle.
rafael: sleeping fx
ZEKE has left the room.
rafael: fk you
Skylar St. Clair: rafael :(
Siobhan Stout: this is cool heh
Skylar St. Clair: hi siobhan :)
Siobhan Stout: whats up?
Annie: u r all losers
Skylar St. Clair: hi lila ;)
Annie: hey baby
Aubrey TF: where did annie go??
rafael: how you gtthe thing to stop blinking
rafael: huh
Aubrey TF: ???
```

The computer screen was starting to give me a headache. I said a quick goodbye to the chat room--although it probably got lost in the flood of textual chaos--and turned off the monitor.

I went outside the house, sat on the porch, and breathed in the fresh morning air.

The Nettlebush Reserve was the most beautiful place I'd ever been. A very vocal part of my heart wished that I had grown up here, but you know what they say: Better late than never. An early blue sky of pale pastels hung high above the bull and pinyon pine trees. The fervor of a sweltering August, mercifully, had yielded at last to a cooler September. It would be autumn before long. The oak leaves would turn color, then tumble to the ground. I couldn't wait to see it.

The door opened, then snapped shut again. Granny climbed down the porch steps, Dad following her.

"Come, Skylar," Granny said sternly. "It's time for church."

The three of us walked down the dirt path together, Granny leaning heavily on my shoulder.

"Skylar!"

A family of five was traipsing down the path toward us: two men, one of them elderly, and three children. I grinned at Annie Little Hawk. She was a very small-statured girl, and very pretty--or I thought so, anyway, but I was way too biased. She ran to me, her short hair bobbing around her chin, and took my hand.

"So how do you like the internet?" she quipped.

I smiled. *Pretty cool*, I signed. Annie's whole family knew sign language. Annie's little brother, Joseph, had been born deaf.

"Yes, did you see the history section? Mr. Red Clay wrote it, he's got a mind as sharp as a tack. Listen, I won't be around later. We're visiting family in Tucson today. Will you tell Aubrey? And Rafael, if he asks, but I doubt he will."

I'm sure he will, I signed. Annie scoffed. She kissed me on the cheek and ran back to her family.

"Don't miss me for too long, sweetcheeks," shouted Annie's

eleven-year-old sister.

I couldn't help laughing, though it was soundless, like all my laughs were. I waved wide to Lila Little Hawk. That little brat was one of my favorite people on the planet.

The Little Hawk family trekked south. Granny nodded curtly after them and we went on to the church. I caught the hint of a smile on Dad's face.

The church in Nettlebush was nothing more than an old white building with polished pews of gleaming wood. It wasn't very remarkable to look at.

But the services themselves--now those were crazy. I don't mean that disrespectfully. I just mean to say that they were incredibly diverse. The preacher was an old man named Reverend Silver Wolf, and he was the sort of guy you couldn't help but like. His hair was long and silver with age, and he never went anywhere without a bashful smile on his face. He reminded me of a little kid at times. He read from the Bible with loving zeal, but the Christian proverbs were always bookended with traditional Plains parables.

Granny, Dad, and I arrived at the church just as Reverend Silver Wolf took his place at the pulpit. Granny led Dad to the very front row and took a seat. Reverend Silver Wolf was soft-spoken, and not very good at projecting his voice; to remedy this, Granny preferred to sit as close to the altar as possible. I would have followed her, as I did every Sunday, except that someone sitting in the back row captured my eye.

I smiled at the preacher and slid into the back pew.

"Let us remember," Reverend Silver Wolf said meekly, thumbing through his Bible with aged brown fingers, "that the Gray Bear, too, showed us the way to eternity. He left his white trail in the sky for us to follow."

The hulking boy sitting to my left was probably the largest boy in all of Nettlebush. He was seventeen, with thick, muscular arms and long, muscular legs. His hair was lank and black, some of it braided, most of it loose; it lay flat over his left shoulder, providing me with a pretty good view of the iron earring dangling from his right ear. On his exposed right arm was a tattoo--self-drawn, as I knew from experience--in the shape of a winding blue chain.

I elbowed Rafael. He started and turned toward me.

Rafael Gives Light was my other best friend, and I'm not kidding when I say you'd be hard pressed to find a friend more loyal than him. Sure, he had the occasional attitude problem, but I didn't mind those so much. I couldn't keep the smile off of my face. I surveyed Rafael, his strong, square jaw and flat nose, the dimples set low in his cheeks, the blue eyes dark and turbulent beneath brushstroke black eyebrows.

That's new, I thought. I stifled a laugh. He was wearing a pair of wiry blue eyeglasses, the frames rectangular and small. He looked kind of bookish now--and if you know Rafael, you know he's constantly reading novels--but no less imposing.

"Shut up," Rafael hissed. I swear he would have blushed if his complexion had allowed it. "Uncle Gabe made me get 'em."

The unique thing about Rafael was that he always--or almost always--knew what I would have said had I had the voice to say it. It had unnerved me, at first, but in a good way. With a connection like that, we'd practically had no choice but to become friends.

I gave him a simpering pat on the shoulder. He took a fake swing at me. Luckily, Reverend Silver Wolf had his face buried in the Bible and didn't notice us; he was a nice guy, and I would have felt bad about interrupting his sermon.

Reverend Silver Wolf read to us about the Garden of Gethsemane. Rafael, surly, slouched in his seat. I side-eyed him with disapproval. He folded his arms, pointedly ignoring me, and loudly snapped the gum in his mouth.

Not on my watch, I thought. I stuck my hand in front of his face, palm open. He gave me a disgruntled look, but obediently spat the wad of gum into my hand. That his spit swimming in my palmlines didn't bother me in the least probably says much more about me than him.

We were the first two out the doors at the end of the service. I tucked Rafael's gum, now dry, into my pocket. The rest of the congregation flooded out the doors after us, a few of Granny's friends waving to me in passing.

I tapped Rafael's shoulder and tilted my head. What was he doing at church? He'd never gone to Sunday services in the past.

Rafael scowled. "Rosa," he said shortly.

My head tilted in the other direction.

The church doors opened again. A young woman with a very round, very honest face came ambling outside. She tucked her arm around Rafael's, maternal and sweet.

Rosa Gray Rain was in her mid-twenties. She worked at the reservation hospital as a nurse. I knew her. I just never realized she knew Rafael.

Rafael shot me a pleading look. I raised my eyebrows.

"Uh," Rafael said. "This is my uncle's girlfriend."

I grinned impishly. A long-standing point of contention between Rafael and his uncle Gabriel--the uncle who had raised him--was that Gabriel was nearing thirty and had yet to settle down. I guessed the pattern was finally broken. Go Gabriel.

"Shut up, Sky."

Rosa's face drooped into a frown. She wasn't a very vocal woman.

A lot of Shoshone are reticent, to varying extents. It's a cultural thing. Maybe it's because I'd grown up mute, relying on body language and facial cues to get my point across, but I found that I could read Rosa's face like an open book. She didn't approve of the rough way Rafael addressed his friends.

It's okay, I wanted to say. I smiled placidly. Rafael didn't mean to come across as harsh. Most people didn't realize, for example, that his usual smoldering expression wasn't borne out of hostility. His face just happened to look that way.

"Uh," Rafael said again. He coughed. He turned to Rosa. "Can you go home without me?"

She chewed uncertainly on her lower lip.

"It's okay. Just tell Uncle Gabe I'm with Sky. He knows him, he won't mind."

The heavy expression cleared from Rosa's face. She smiled sweetly and nodded in concession. She released Rafael's arm, gave us both gentle pats on the head, and bustled away. I knew she was headed north. Rafael lived as close to the badlands as humanly possible without actually sitting on top of the canyons.

I smiled warmly. Cute as a button, that Rosa. Rafael gagged.

"Wanna go into the cupola?" Rafael asked.

The church had an open, room-sized cupola above the steeple that was meant to house a bell, but never had. Rafael and I had secretly taken to using it as a private hangout over the summer. It was easy to get into, too: All you had to do was climb the ladder behind the apse wall.

Someone had propped open the church doors. I glanced inside. Reverend Silver Wolf was still standing by the pulpit. He was deep in conversation with a friend of Granny's, Hilde Threefold, a garrulous lady who wore sunflower-shaped earrings. Granny, too, lingered by the altar, because she liked to argue with her friends. Dad, looking awkward, stood sullenly at Granny's side.

I pulled back and quirked the corner of my mouth. Mrs. Threefold could talk for hours. There was no sneaking past them any time soon.

"Damn," Rafael muttered. "I don't wanna go home. I hate being indoors."

Do you want to go to the grotto? I signed. *Annie's not going to be there, though.*

Rafael didn't actually know sign language. He knew the alphabet, though he sometimes got A and E confused, and a few words I'd taught him over the summer, like "race," "grotto," and "father." I was still working on teaching him more.

"Annie's at the grotto? What?"

I smiled wryly. Close enough. Then I remembered something I'd forgotten to do. *Wait*, I signed. I knew Rafael was familiar with that word, at least; the finger wiggling is kind of distinct.

I went around the church to the square, compact graveyard and pushed open the black iron gate.

The headstones were small, uniform, and pristine. I had visited the graveyard many times over the summer, seeking my mother's burial place as a source of solace.

It wasn't my mother's grave I was looking for this time. I walked slowly up and down each row until I had found it--a tiny, out-of-the-way mortuary on the east side of the graveyard.

"Julius Looks Over," the headstone read. "1966 - 1971. Our children have a wisdom all their own."

My father's brother--my uncle--had died in childhood. I hadn't even known about him until this summer. In fact, I still didn't know whether his death had been an illness or an accident. Like many things, it was a topic neither Dad nor Granny was keen to discuss.

I knelt in the dirt; I read and re-read the words engraved in stone. It was surreal to think that Uncle Julius should have been a thirty-four-year-old man--maybe he would have had my Dad's winter-gray eyes--but instead lay sleeping undisturbed beneath the soil, an eternal child.

I'm sorry, I wanted to tell him. Because he had an amazing brother, an incredible mother, and he couldn't enjoy them the way I could.

I promised, silently, that I would enjoy them for the both of us.

I kissed my fingertips and touched them to the smooth headstone. I stood up, a smile on my face, faint and content. I turned to leave.

Rafael had followed me as far as the fence. I hadn't realized it. In hindsight, I find that curious: Bulky and sluggish, Rafael wasn't the sort to tread lightly.

I smiled, quizzical. Rafael gazed at me intently. He looked as though he desperately wanted to say something, but couldn't find the right words. I found that sort of funny, considering which of us had the busted vocal cords.

I crossed through the gate and closed it behind me; it creaked with weary protest and old age. I touched Rafael's arm, gently, prompting.

"Nothing," he grumbled, and turned pointedly away.

He was embarrassed about something--that much, I could tell, but whatever had embarrassed him, it was a mystery. Much of Rafael was a mystery, a mystery I was constantly chipping away at, constantly trying to solve. I was proud to have solved at least half of the enigma: No one would have guessed it by looking at him, but underneath his gruff exterior, Rafael's innermost nature was shy.

My smile softened, then faded. My fingers trailed their way up his arm to his shoulder, where my hand came to a rest. He followed my hand with his eyes--until I touched my fingertips to his face. His eyes jumped and met mine.

I'd never seen a blue like the blue in Rafael's eyes. Like indigo and oceans and hot summer storms.

His lips crashed down on mine. My lips parted and I tasted the sugar in his mouth, on his tongue, our tongues brushing together, his hands possessively biting my hips and the black gate behind me bumping hard against my spine. I ghosted my fingers down his strong profile and his square jawline, and he liked that, I think, because he kissed me even harder, and my fingers wandered, sinking into his coarse hair, twisting around his braids--

His glasses bumped into the bridge of my nose.

Ow, I mouthed, surprised. We broke apart. Stumbling, Rafael looked dizzy, like someone had bopped him on the forehead. And technically, someone had; my nose had knocked his glasses, hard, into his brow. He swore loudly, confused. I won't repeat the word here. I'm a gentleman.

"Cubby?"

Heat flooded my face with embarrassment. How long had Dad been standing there? He approached us from the back of the church. I couldn't make out the expression on his face--but then I never could. He always looked somber. His face didn't come in any other variety.

Rafael, oblivious, rubbed his brow in pain. He took off his eyeglasses and squinted at them like they were his mortal enemy.

"We have to go to the doctor's, remember?" Dad said.

Oh. Right. Turns out I was missing a few immunizations I needed for the start of school. I should have gotten them years ago, but it's not exactly Dad's fault. I'd imagine raising a kid on your own is hard enough for anyone, let alone a guy.

"You're leaving?" Rafael said. There was an earnest expression on his face, the sentiment mirrored in his tone.

I smiled at him. Much as I didn't like the prospect of Dr. Stout poking me with needles, it wouldn't take long. Rafael seemed to come to the same conclusion. He nodded and replaced his glasses.

My heart swelled with familiar warmth. He looked good in glasses. He looked good in anything.

He looked away from me, embarrassed again. But I thought I saw the hint of a shy smile playing at his lips.

Dad and I walked through the reserve together--without Granny; she had gone west to play cards with Mrs. Threefold and Mr. Marsh. A silence settled between us. That wasn't particularly unordinary; Dad was prone to bouts of pensive silence. I looked sideways at him and tried to glean the thoughts from his bear trap mind. Nothing. On the other hand, it seemed like he was pointedly avoiding my eyes. I was certain, suddenly, that he had seen me kiss Rafael. Maybe he was more comfortable with it in theory than in practice.

That made me feel pretty lousy.

The hospital was at the southern end of the reservation: one story, because it only serviced Nettlebush, with solid caramel walls and wood floors. Dad signed us in at the front desk, and we sat together in the waiting room.

He still wasn't looking at me.

This is ridiculous, I thought. I jostled his shoulder.

"Cubby," he started, mid-thought. "Sorry. What?"

I gave him a pointed look. *You know what.*

He looked me dead on, his eyes like still water beneath a midwinter sun; muted, slate-gray, revealing none of the thoughts hidden beneath. Finally, he sighed.

"I told you I don't mind," he murmured, his mouth barely moving. "I do mean that. But it's still a shock."

I raised my eyebrows.

"...To see my only son kissing another boy."

Poor Dad; I wished I hadn't made him say it out loud. He was such an awkward guy, the kind who stammered whenever he had to talk to an unfamiliar woman. I reached sideways and cupped his shoulder. He smiled at me fleetingly.

The nurse called my name and Dad and I rose together, edging out of the waiting room.

"It's just," Dad went on, as we walked down the narrow hallway between examination rooms. "It's more than that. Considering the history between our families--"

I swallowed.

Rafael's father was a serial killer, and the reason I didn't have a voice. The reason Dad didn't have a wife.

The nurse led us into a blinding white room and checked my weight and my blood pressure. I wished he wouldn't. Rosa had already done all that in August.

"I've been wondering..." Dad said. "How exactly did the two of you become friends?"

I sat on the exam table while the nurse shunted out of the room to fetch Dr. Stout. I regarded Dad thoughtfully. He sat on a chair by the scales, fumbling with a keychain in his hands, his eyes downcast, his face as serenely somber as an ancient statue. We were completely different from each other, he and I, even down to the shapes of our fingers: his short and stubby, mine long and thin.

I took a folded sheet of paper out of my back pocket. Peripherally, I saw Dad's eyes raise. I unfolded the paper, smoothed it out, and handed it to him. He took it delicately, surprised, and perused it.

For once, I saw a real expression on his face. The problem is, I couldn't read it.

"Did Rafael draw this?" Dad asked.

I nodded.

Rafael was an amazing artist, the kind who could capture the heart and soul of a moment with nothing but charcoal.

The drawing depicted my mom as she had been in life: bushy, curly hair pulled back in a ponytail, freckles running up and down her arms, her teeth poking innocently out of her mouth in a rabbit-like underbite. I knew because I had studied it again and again by lamplight, in the privacy of my bedroom, overwhelmed by emotion.

Dad lowered the paper. He met my gaze, the still water of his eyes wavering.

"He's a good boy," he said quietly.

I could only smile.

Dr. Stout came into the room at last and chatted with Dad for a few minutes while he picked his way, awkwardly, through the conversation. I looked away when Dr. Stout uncapped a plastic syringe and filled it with whatever Godforsaken vaccination I should have had years ago. I practically broke my neck, straining my head away from her gloved hands. And then she stabbed the needle in my arm and *Ow, holy crap!*, and I must have been making a really weird face because Dad struggled not to laugh.

It was around noon when Dad and I left the hospital, my arm smarting and my ego bruised.

"That's a very nice bandaid, Cubby," Dad said gently. I gave him a sulky look. He *would* say that about teddy bears.

We went home for lunch, after which Dad said he had to leave for a visit with Meredith Siomme. Ms. Siomme was a member of the tribal council; she and Dad had been friends since before I was born. I waved goodbye; and then, when he was gone, I set out for the grotto.

Years and years ago, when Annie was a little girl, she had found a natural rock cave in the woods, a grotto flanked by a creek and a weeping willow tree. I hadn't known Annie back in those days; but she'd decided to share the grotto with me last summer, and it quickly became one of our favorite spots. Aubrey and Rafael used it, too, but never without Annie. Not usually.

The dense forest overgrowth was shadowy and cool. I heard the bubbling of the creek long before I saw it, a cascading, iridescent sliver as smooth as a jewel. The drooping tendrils of the willow tree swayed with even the faintest breeze; glass windchimes tied high around their boughs clinked together musically. The mouth of the cave was decked in a colorful mural of hand-painted stars.

I saw Rafael sitting on the other side of the creek, his head bent, his face buried in a book. Lost in the literary world, as always.

I had an idea. I smiled to myself, a secretive, impish smile. He was distracted. Could I sneak up on him? If I went around the other side of the willow tree, maybe I could approach him from behind. I like playing jokes on people. Maybe that's not very nice of me, but the world's never at a surplus of laughter.

I crept up on the willow and hid behind the thick trunk. I watched Rafael through the curtains of the hanging boughs. Man, was he involved in that book. I could have just run up in front of him and he probably wouldn't have noticed. But where was the fun in that?

I slithered around the tree trunk. I wedged myself between the open mouth of the cave and Rafael's broad back. He looked nice in that lightweight gray jacket. I wouldn't have worn it, though. It was still pretty hot outside, September or not.

Rafael turned the page.

Just a little closer, I thought. I inched forward. I extended my arms, my hands like claws. Muahahaha--

"I can hear you, dumbass."

I deflated. I slumped across Rafael's back and draped my arms over his shoulders. He dropped his book and turned his head, scrutinizing me mercilessly.

"You'd think a mute guy would be stealthy."

I showed him my best imitation of Lila Little Hawk's bratty, insouciant pout. He rolled his eyes. I flicked his earring for revenge.

He rolled me to the ground and pinned me down.

Suspended above me, dark hair falling around our faces, he looked like a reward, a secret gift I wanted to take and keep and hide away from the world. I saw his rare grin swallow up his face, the one that set my heart ablaze, boyish and bright, all his sharp, sharklike teeth and the tooth missing at the back of his mouth.

"Big damn elephant," he remarked.

I dragged my fingers up and down Rafael's sides. Predictably, he burst into uncontrollable laughter. Ha, I thought, triumphant, and slid out from beneath him, running to the shelter of the willow tree. Nobody messes with Skylar St. Clair.

I sat under the shade of the willow tree. Rafael lumbered after me and spilled to the ground at my side.

"You're an ass," he told me, grinning brightly.

From Rafael, I considered that a compliment. Smugly, I kissed him on the nose. His eyes crossed when they followed my lips--probably unconsciously--and then, with what I thought must have been contentment and peace, he lay back on his elbows, watching the creek run by.

"I can't believe it's the last day of summer vacation," he said distastefully.

Me neither, I thought. Summer had been like a whirlwind fantasy, and now it was over. It was bittersweet, in a way. I felt wistful that the lazy days were gone, but excited at what the rest of the year might bring.

I thought: Annie and I had spent most of our summer mornings cooking dinners for the reservation. I wondered who was going to pick up the slack while we were in school.

"Where are Annie and Aubrey, anyway?"

Annie's visiting family, I signed. I couldn't remember whether I'd taught Rafael how to say "family" in sign language. I paused. That accounted for Annie, but what about Aubrey? He always joined us at the grotto in the afternoons.

I shrugged, nonplussed.

"Huh. Guess we'll find out tomorrow."

I nodded, satisfied. I lay on my back, hands folded atop my stomach, and gazed up at the thick, tangled tree limbs and the gnarled leaves that hung like wet linens. I watched the windchimes, glass butterflies, dancing in the shade. It was perfect here. It was easy to forget about time, about the outside world.

I felt a pair of soft lips brush against my cheek. Surprised, I turned on my side.

Rafael lay in a position mirroring mine, determinedly silent. I could tell from the way his eyes moved, roaming without purpose, that he was flustered.

Poor Rafael. It must have been hard, having all those emotions battling for dominance in his head. I felt a smile, involuntary, affectionate, stitch its way across my face. I reached for his hand and took it for my own, gently weaving our fingers together.

He shifted on his side, facing me. His eyes danced with light amid a dark face. Slowly, his free hand settled on the curve of my cheek. The calloused pads of his fingertips brushed over my skin, over my curls, exploratory, reverent. Maybe it's crazy; but I felt like the luckiest guy on the planet.

"Why are you wearing a teddy bear bandaid?"

An irrepressible grin spread across my face. I shoved his shoulder. He shoved me back.

We spent the next hour practicing sign language together. Rafael was getting better at identifying hand signals, I thought, but he was a very slow learner, the kind who needs everything repeated two and three times before it sinks in. Not that there was anything wrong with that. Actually, it was kind of endearing. At the end of the lesson, Rafael asked me to play him a song on the plains flute. I realized I'd left my flute in the cave a few days ago, so I got up and went into the cave to retrieve it. I knelt and pushed aside bowls of beads and willow baskets. I spotted the flute hanging by its leather cord on one of Aubrey's prayer sticks--no idea how it got there--I picked it up and hung it around my neck.

I went back outside the cave and found Rafael standing by the creek, stock-still. I drew closer. He brought his finger to his lips, silencing me--ironic, I know. He pointed.

There was a coywolf pup rummaging around a pale yellow creosote bush.

Rafael and I exchanged a look. Coywolves aren't solitary creatures. Half-coyote, half-wolf, they're supposed to live and travel in packs. More pressingly, creosote leaves are really bad for consumption. The petals are okay, though. They make a good remedy for snakebite and chickenpox.

"Hey," Rafael said. "Wasn't that coywolf hanging around here a couple of weeks ago?"

Rafael was right, I realized. I looked back at the coywolf. The little guy was skinny and gangly, with big, round ears, his sandy coat interspersed with gray. Too skinny. He was hungry. My heart wrenched. Why was he foraging on his own? Where had his pack gone?

I ran back to the cave. We kept a store of chokecherries in there, in the event that one of us got hungry before dinnertime. I found the chokecherries next to the candles and scooped them off the smooth cavern floor.

Rafael had followed me to the mouth of the cave. He glanced in dubiously. "Don't," he warned. "If he starts relying on humans, he'll never fit in with his pack."

I gave Rafael a questionable look. It was pretty obvious to me that he already didn't fit in with his pack.

I emerged from the cave with an armful of chokecherries. I set them down beneath the weeping willow and took a cautious step back. Rafael joined me, a heavy hand on my shoulder, frowning, unsure. The coywolf's head shot up eagerly; he sniffed at the air, no doubt picking up the sweet, distinct scent on the lush breeze. He ran from the creosote bush on clumsy little legs, skittering alongside the creek, and dove beneath the willow tree.

"His mom might have abandoned him," Rafael said haltingly.

I looked at him, alarmed.

"Coywolves are monogamous," Rafael said. "If his mom mated with a coywolf who wasn't her rightful mate, she might have abandoned the litter to avoid conflict within the pack. Don't know how he survived without her milk, but it happens. Animals aren't all that different from people. Don't forget that we're animals, too."

A mother should never abandon her child, I thought, weighted with sadness.

"Don't be like that," Rafael said, his tone unexpectedly soft. "The gray wolves might adopt him. Full-blooded wolves are good like that. They'll take in any lone wolf they find wandering around."

I watched the pup, his head bent over his dinner, his tufted tail wagging with happiness. I sure hoped someone would take him in. It wasn't like he could change who his parents were.

It was three o'clock in the afternoon when Rafael and I gathered our belongings--his book under his arm, my flute around my neck--and made our way west through the woods, heading back to the community. Rafael ranted about the girl in his book, the main character, I think, and how she was the only girl on a cargo ship in the 1800s and how she became a sailor after one of the crew members died. "That chick is awesome," he swore. I nodded politely. I was happy to listen to him, but I didn't like books all that much.

We barely had time to say goodbye when a loud crash captured our attention. Rafael jumped. We looked around, disconcerted, for the source of the sound.

Someone had thrown their computer through the window of their home, and the monitor had landed on its side next to the tribal firepit. The screen was shattered, the cables split, like the whole setup had been yanked unceremoniously out of the wall. The culprit, a little old man in a Panama hat, stood outside his house, pointing at the machine as though it were the devil himself.

Rafael and I looked at each other, slowly.

"I don't think the internet's going to catch on," he said.

Probably not.

2
Balto

I like mornings. Dawn is my favorite time of day, when the sun hasn't risen just yet, but its errant light has already escaped into the sky. You don't see colors like those anywhere else in nature. It's like a song all its own.

One of these days, I thought, watching the sunrise from my bedroom window, I was going to capture that song and play it. But I doubted I would ever do it justice.

I shut my alarm clock off before it had the chance to bang and clang all over the bedside table. I dressed quickly and went downstairs for breakfast.

Granny attacked me with a comb before I even had the chance to sit at the kitchen table.

"It's your first day of school," she said imperially. "You *will* look decent."

I cringed and grimaced and recoiled as she dragged the comb's sharp teeth through my floppy, unruly curls. "Stop making those ridiculous faces," she insisted. I purposely crossed my eyes. She hit me with the broad side of the comb.

"Mother, that's child abuse," Dad said from behind his coffee mug.

Granny pulled back and observed me. She sighed through her tight lips. "It's impossible," she said. She waved a dismissive hand in my direction and hobbled away to tend to the stove.

I sat down with Dad and he raked his pawlike hand sympathetically over the crown of my head. Granny gave the both of us stacks of sweet frybread and blueberry wojapi.

"Meredith will want to talk to us eventually," Dad murmured, distracted.

"What on earth for?"

"It's about Cubby."

I sat bolt upright, worried. Dad glanced at me--no expression--and broke his bread into tiny square pieces. "It's nothing troubling," he said. Whether he was speaking to me, or to his dish, I didn't know. "We've just got to figure out how to make this living arrangement...permanent."

"Of course it's permanent," said Granny, puzzled. She sat down with a cup of roasted acorn tea. "I told that Officer Whatsit that I'd be willing to take him in until they found you."

The unspoken understanding was that the police were never going to find Dad. A loophole in the Constitution meant he couldn't be arrested if he stayed in Nettlebush. Reservations operated off of their own individual governments--and the crime Dad was wanted for had happened in Wyoming.

"Yes, I know. But you're his foster parent, not his legal guardian," Dad explained. "The only way we can guarantee he stays in Nettlebush is if you adopt him."

"Well, then," Granny said, and sipped at her tea.

I waved goodbye to the both of them when I left for school--books in my backpack, springy hair defying Granny's obstinate orders-- but I felt kind of nauseous. I loved Granny more than anything. I was grateful beyond words that she had given me a home. I just didn't like the word "adoption." I was Dad's kid; I had been Dad's kid all my life. It unnerved me to consider a reality where, at least legally, I wasn't Dad's kid anymore.

The school building was a couple of yards away from the church. I hadn't paid it much attention over the summer, except for the playground between the red pines out back; I'd taken Annie's brother Joseph to play on the rope swings a couple of times.

Now, coming up on the schoolhouse, I saw that it was only one story, red brick, with an uncommonly flat roof and old windows on its sides. The double doors stood open, preceded by a small flight of stone steps.

It looked colonial, I thought. Probably it was the exact same school our ancestors had attended in the 1800s.

I climbed the steps and went through the doors. I stopped, caught off guard.

The room was big and wide with a low ceiling, a chalkboard at the far end and bookshelves sitting between the windows. Nothing peculiar, I guess--except that there were about fifty kids in the room at the same time, some of them my age, some of them as young as six. I saw Joseph Little Hawk sitting in the very front row, Lila several benches behind him. Lila spun in her seat and blew me a kiss. I waved back, confused, smiling.

"Move, please," someone said behind me.

I went into the classroom. Annie, Aubrey, and Rafael were sitting on a bench toward the back. Aubrey had all his pencils arranged on the long, wooden table in perfect organization. I had to wonder what one guy needed with so many pencils. I scrunched my way into a seat between Aubrey and Rafael. I dropped my schoolbag below the bench and playfully tousled Aubrey's short hair.

"Ah, Skylar!" Aubrey said. He caught his Coke bottle glasses before they flew off his face. "I was just telling Rafael how nice it is that he and I finally match!"

In the vaguest sense of the word, maybe. No one would have looked at Aubrey, tall and weedy and bright as a lightbulb, and mistaken him for the darker, skulking Rafael.

Rafael scowled.

"You know...the glasses? Oh, well, anyway..."

Where were you yesterday? I signed.

Aubrey was Rafael's polar opposite; he had picked up on two hundred or more hand signals over the course of summer vacation. This was one of those rare occasions when he didn't understand what I was saying. He peered at me, polite but bemused. Annie intervened.

"Mr. Takes Flight had to visit the hospital," she filled in. "It was all very sudden."

I felt my eyes widen. Oh, no, I thought. I was surprised I hadn't run into them when Dad took me for immunizations. *Is he okay?*

"He's always had a bit of a heart condition," Aubrey said uneasily. "But he'll be fine. We checked him out the same day and Mom's monitoring him with hawk eyes."

"I just remembered," Annie said, "I brought back a gift for you from Tucson--"

Annie and Aubrey chatted between themselves. I smiled slightly at Rafael. He knitted his eyebrows and buried his face in that Charlotte Doyle book. I guessed he wasn't in the mood to talk.

My attention wandered to the kids sitting on either side of us. Except for our happy little group, it looked like all the eleventh graders were staunchly determined to divide themselves by gender. On Annie's left were the boys; on Rafael's right, the girls. I spotted Zeke Owns Forty, a bony, egotistical guy with a frantic smile, half his hair shaved close to his head, the rest of it long and combed to one side. He blathered a mile a minute to the kid on his right, a boy I didn't recognize. I don't think Zeke noticed, but his friend was sound asleep, his wiry, curly-haired head still on the table and tucked between his folded arms. A lean guy with waist-length, auburn hair--probably one of the Stouts--was sitting as far from Zeke and his buddy as space would allow, teetering disdainfully on the edge of the bench. The girls weren't much better. The At Dawn twins sat with their heads bowed in private conversation. They were identical, those two, from their curved falcon noses to their wavy ringlets, except in demeanor: Daisy was bubbly and giggling, whispering behind her hand, while Holly looked like she wanted to throw herself into the nearest fire if it meant getting away from her sister. The two of them were completely excluding poor Immaculata Quick, the shaman's granddaughter--but Immaculata didn't seem aware of it. Her bushy hair stood unkempt, as though zapped by a livewire; her crazy eyes bulged with interest every time she caught a word of conversation from either of the twins. Not that she knew what she was listening to. Immaculata didn't speak English.

"I hate school!" shouted a chubby little boy in Joseph's row. "I'm bustin' outta here!"

And he might have done it, too--except the doors snapped suddenly closed. Everybody turned in their seats, me included.

"Really, Mr. Nabako? You think *you've* got it rough?"

I could hardly believe that this guy was Mrs. Red Clay's son. Mrs. Red Clay had heavy jowls and a face as impassive as a bas relief. She wasn't what you would have called a classical beauty. There was no other word for it; this guy was handsome. He was middle-aged, about forty or so, but the years had distinguished his looks rather than diminished them. His cheeks were high and strong, his jaw perfectly angular, his mouth full, his nose sharp. His sleek black hair was tied in a long, loose ponytail. He moved from the doorway to the front of the room, calmly, effortlessly. Rafael glowered at me. I must have been staring.

Mr. Red Clay took his place before the chalkboard, his hands on the lectern. He raised a single eyebrow as though daring his pupils to challenge his authority. A total silence fell tangibly over the room. Maybe Mr. Red Clay didn't look like his mom; but he had definitely inherited her ability to command a crowd.

"Want to know who really had it rough?" Mr. Red Clay asked-- gesturing in sign language with every spoken word. That had to have taken a lot of concentration. I guessed it was probably for Joseph's benefit. "The kids who went to Carlisle Indian School."

Notebooks flew open on my left and right. I took it as a cue and retrieved a notebook of my own.

"Who can tell me what Carlisle Indian School is?"

Hands shot into the air, younger and older alike. This lesson was really baffling so far. How could Mr. Red Clay teach all twelve classes at the same time when we didn't have the same curriculum?

"Miss In Winter?"

"A boarding school?" said a breathless ninth grader.

Mr. Red Clay lifted his eyebrows. "Is that all?"

More hands raised.

"Miss Two Eagles?"

"A boarding school run by the white settlers," said a seventh grader. "They rounded up Native kids and forced them to go to boarding schools. To learn how to be white."

"Picture this," Mr. Red Clay said. He leaned across the first graders' table, signing impeccably while he talked. "You're living peacefully with your tribe. Your family. Your brothers and sisters are a pain in the neck, but you love them anyway. Your elders are your teachers. You help your father catch game; you help your mother take care of the home. For most of you, that's true even today. What if a total stranger showed up on your doorstep tomorrow morning and took you away from all that? Can you imagine what that would feel like?"

There was silence.

"That is precisely what happened in the 1800s. A group of white men who called themselves the 'Bureau of Indian Affairs' forced thousands of Native children to leave behind their homes, their families, and their traditions. The children who attended Carlisle Indian School were not allowed to wear their own clothing. The teachers forced them to eat lye soap whenever they were caught speaking their Native languages. If your teachers caught you praying to the Wolf or the Great Spirit, they beat you until you bled. Many times they beat you for less than that."

I saw Annie clasp her throat, something she only ever did when she wanted to hide her discomfort.

Mr. Red Clay stepped back from the table. "One by one," he said, "the Native tribes were forced to relinquish their children to these dehumanizing boarding schools, often with no guarantee that their sons and daughters would make it home alive. Regardless of their desire to resist, all tribes ultimately complied. They had to. The BIA weren't above retaliating with brutality in the event that their orders went ignored. However, despite the greater danger of disobedience, one tribe ignored the BIA's orders. One tribe clung steadfastly to their children and protected them. Who can tell me the name of that tribe?"

Aubrey's arm shot into the air, nearly decapitating me in the process.

"Yes?"

"The Shoshone."

"The Shoshone," Mr. Red Clay said. "We refused to send our children to these boarding schools. We knew our children were safer with us, where they could express their identities however they wanted, where they could learn at their own pace. When the BIA finally grew tired of our defiance, they sent armed soldiers to our settlements. The soldiers literally had to pry the children out of their parents' lifeless hands. This is where the phrase 'over my dead body' comes from."

I felt a little ill.

"We lost everything during those days. Our land, our freedom, even our children. Our children faced death if they didn't become Christians. They were even forced to give up their names. Little boys and girls named White Elk and River Runner and Gives Grain were given brand new 'white' names by their teachers-- Charlie, Sarah, Emily. They were taught to hate everything Native American. Everything about themselves. They were destroyed from the inside out. The children who graduated from Carlisle Indian School suffered from severe psychological trauma. Many of them committed suicide.

"But," said Mr. Red Clay. "The spark of defiance was smothered, not extinguished. In one small, yet very profound way, the defeated Shoshone held onto their heritage. Charlie and Sarah and Emily all grew up. They married and had children of their own. They retained their old names as family names and passed them down to their children. That's how most of you got your last names."

The whole classroom began applauding. I'd never experienced that kind of enthusiasm in a school before. I started to join in when Mr. Red Clay glanced impassively over the student body, cutting short the response.

Mr. Red Clay took a stick of chalk and began writing instructions on the blackboard. *Grade 11 - History - Pg. 44*, he wrote. I dug my history book out of my backpack. He turned around when he had finished writing multiple sets of instructions--I don't know how he managed to recall all those page numbers by memory alone--and wiped the chalk residue from his hands. "If your grade is on the blackboard," he said, "start reading. If you're not on the board, talk quietly among your friends. I'll be with you in a second."

He went over to the first graders' table and bent his head toward them in conversation. I tried to read his hand signs, but Autumn Rose In Winter's long, bobbing ponytail was blocking my view.

"Well?" Annie said. "What do you all think?"

I read the question at the top of page 44. *How successful is forced cultural assimilation? Explain.* Oh, boy. I hated questions like those.

"It didn't work," said the auburn-haired boy at the end of the bench. "We're still living on a reservation, aren't we? And we've got our ancestors' given names as surnames, as Mr. Red Clay said."

"Nah," Rafael said, "I think it worked. We wear jeans and speak English."

"You're cheating!" Zeke said. "You read all this stuff last year."

"You wanna say that again?"

"You wanna hit me again?"

I waved my arms. I didn't know how else to get them to shut up.

"Everything alright here?" asked Mr. Red Clay, approaching our table.

The wiry-haired boy lifted his head from the table at last. Had he been sleeping all this time? His eyes were a blue-green, his face dusted with freckles. He looked exotic, in a way, three different ethnicities rolled in one.

"Rafael threatened Zeke," he said.

I gazed at him in disbelief. I shook my head.

"He most certainly did not!" Annie burst out at the same time.

"Mr. Sleeping Fox," said Mr. Red Clay, "how old are you?"

"Seventeen," said the wiry-haired boy.

"Then I suggest you act it. Turn in your summer book reports, please."

I hadn't actually written a summer book report, but Rafael had put my name at the top of his. He opened his folder, took out a thick leaflet, and handed it to Mr. Red Clay. I touched Rafael's arm as Mr. Red Clay collected the papers and moved on to the twelfth graders. The look on Rafael's face was scalding, but I knew it wasn't meant for me. I smiled at him. His anger visibly melted away. He closed his hand over mine and gripped it, his thumb running over my knuckles.

It was about noon when the school day ended. If this was indicative of a regular school day, I thought, I might finally become a fan of the education system. I went home for lunch, then out to the grotto. I didn't know whether that coywolf pup was still hanging around; I left sandwiches for him underneath the willow tree, just in case.

Annie, Rafael, and I went to Aubrey's house in the afternoon for homework. I really liked Aubrey's house, an old-fashioned farm manor with dark walls and ceiling fans. His bedroom window overlooked the cultivated fields out back, the leafy shoots of the autumn crops already poking out of the ground. Aubrey played bluegrass on his portable radio and we sat beneath the sloping ceiling while we read sleep-inducing history passages, Annie on the bed, Aubrey on the windowsill, Rafael and me on the floor.

Happily, not all of Mr. Red Clay's assignments were lengthy chapters from the history book or inundating math problems. Sometimes he took us out to the woods, where he showed us the plants that were centuries old and the newer ones that the European settlers had brought over, and the hybrids born when the two interbred. He took us into the badlands and we sampled the tent rocks to find out how long ago they had formed. He showed us the hidden seams in the gorges where our ancestors had mined coal and Zeke Owns Forty swore he found a dinosaur fossil, but it was only the remains of a big-horned sheep.

Sometimes, after school, Annie and Aubrey and I went back to Rafael's house to study, and Rosa, sweet-faced and eager, came in and out of his room with peanut crackers and cactus fruit jelly for us to eat. Quietly, Rafael sulked. I guess he thought she was treating him like a baby. I thought she was just being nice.

"I wanna get out of here," Rafael said one afternoon.

Rafael was the kind of guy who lost his temper if you tried to keep him indoors for too long. At the very least, he needed to be near a window. His room didn't have any windows; just layers and layers of sketches taped to unpainted walls. It had embarrassed me when I'd first seen my own face reflected on those walls.

Annie dog-eared her page and closed her book. "Shall we go to the grotto, then?"

Rafael's reply was cut short by the sound of smashing glass. All four of us looked toward the door, alarmed. Rafael looked at me, rare fear on his face.

"The hell was that?"

We got up and went out into the narrow adjoining hallway. From there, we went into the sitting room, its ceiling rafters exposed, its grand window facing the blue-gray badlands to the north.

A picture frame had fallen off of the tall mantelpiece; it lay on the floor, broken, in glass shards. Rosa, round-faced, stood by the front door in her hospital scrubs. It looked as though she had just come home from work. Rafael's uncle Gabriel was in the kitchen doorway, light brown hair braided, tan arms folded, eyebrows raised politely.

"My bad," said a girl standing by the hearth, a cigarette hanging from her mouth.

I had seen this girl before--not in person, but in a handful of Rafael's drawings. She was about twenty, or maybe a little younger, her thick hair teased, her mouth and eyelids shaded in heavy, hyper-violet, day-old makeup. She was a lot skinnier than Rafael's drawings had depicted--deathly skinny--a shadow of herself. She wore black netting on her arms and a black corset in the place of a shirt. Just looking at her made me feel uncomfortable, and kind of itchy.

Rosa scurried to the closet and came back with a broom and dustpan. Gabriel put his hand on her shoulder; she halted. "Mary will clean it," Gabriel said. He sounded perfectly friendly, not at all as though his stray niece had just destroyed one of his treasured keepsakes. "Won't you, Mary?"

Mary puffed rings of smoke absently from the end of her cigarette. I wasn't sure whether she had heard Gabriel: Her hazel eyes were glazed.

"Put it out, Mary," Gabriel said.

Mary crushed her cigarette against the mantel.

The only way I can describe Rafael's face at that moment is to compare it to a fish out of water. He looked absolutely bewildered, like he couldn't figure out why the air was so dry, but his bewilderment belied what I took to be cautious hope. I remembered seeing a photograph of a younger Rafael with his arms around his big sister, matching smiles on their faces. Rafael had barely talked about Mary over the summer; now, I realized how acutely he must have missed her.

Rosa swept the scattered glass into her dustpan. Gabriel rubbed his face with a broad hand.

"We should probably get going," Annie said. Expertly, she wrapped her hand around Aubrey's arm.

Mary glanced briefly in my direction. She double-took and stared at me.

"Have a good day," Rosa called shyly after Annie and Aubrey.

I made to follow the two of them out the door. Mary stopped me in my tracks with a broad grin.

"Chrissy's kid!" she said. "Wow! I can't believe you're here... Oh, crap. Did you know my dad offed your mom?"

"Shut up in front of him," Rafael growled.

Mary shrugged. She searched her pockets for something, maybe for a second cigarette.

"Rafael," Gabriel said, as cordial as could be. "Mary's going to be living with us again. Isn't that nice?"

"Why's that?" Rafael asked scathingly. "Didn't she become a rock star?"

These weren't the loving brother and sister I had glimpsed in Rafael's favorite photograph.

I took Rafael's arm. Startled, he turned to me. I nodded toward the door. He shook his head and held my shoulder. *It's fine*, I told him with a placating smile. *I'll see you later.* I don't think he wanted me to leave; but he nodded, his jaw squared, and let me go.

I slung my bookbag over my shoulder and waved goodbye to the Gives Light family. I closed the door behind me when I left the house.

I breathed deeply in the cooling summer air. My legs carried me east to the woods--and from there, to the grotto.

I sat by the creek and set my backpack on the grass at my side. Annie and Aubrey rose from the mouth of the cave and sat next to me.

"Mary Gives Light," Aubrey said uncomfortably. "I thought she had left the reservation for good. I remember the time she dropped Stuart's cat down the water well, poor thing cried for who-knows-how-long before Reverend Silver Wolf found him..."

"She looks ill," Annie said. "I don't doubt she's fallen in with a bad crowd."

I didn't think it was right to talk about Rafael's sister behind his back--or hers, for that matter. I gave the two of them a small smile. Annie smiled back. I think she got the hint.

"A coyote!" Aubrey said suddenly. "Or--no, is it? I thought all the coyotes lived in the badlands?"

I followed his gaze to the opposite side of the creek. Soundlessly, I laughed. The coywolf pup was back, his snout to the ground, his bushy tail wagging fiercely.

Half and half, I signed to Aubrey. He looked puzzled. I unzipped my dingy green backpack and pulled out a stack of cream cheese and cherry sandwiches. The moment I unwrapped them, the pup came bounding over the cold creek.

"Is that a coywolf?" Annie asked. "Where's his mother, then?"

I shrugged. I laid the sandwiches on the grass. The pup attacked them with zeal.

"Ah, Skylar," Aubrey said gravely, "you'd better be careful, you don't want him to get too attached to humans. I don't know about wolf hybrids, but coyotes can become rather temperamental in their adult years."

The pup had a round and healthy little tummy; it made my heart sing to note that I couldn't count his ribs anymore. I crouched in the grass, arms around my knees, and watched him eat. He finished his sandwiches in messy gulps and drew closer, curious, looking for more food. He sniffed my hand and I held it out for him, flat, palm out. He gave my fingers a hopeful lick, his tongue like sandpaper. Sorry, little guy, I thought. I knew where I could get him some young ferns, but any fatter and he wouldn't be able to jump the creek anymore.

Apparently, he forgave me. He let out the characteristic yip that all coywolves use to greet one another, and then he charged around me in energized circles. Just watching him made me dizzy. I couldn't stop laughing. I toppled onto my back, gripping my stomach, and he nudged my neck, concerned, with his wet nose. I waved my hand to let him know I was okay. Satisfied, he trotted off to find something more interesting to do.

Annie and Aubrey went home before me. I stayed by the creek and the pup kept running back to me, delivering small trinkets of pebbles and forest twigs. I applauded with each present, inspiring him to yip and run victory laps around the willow tree. It was during his fourth victory lap that Rafael came walking between the beech trees and sat next to me, moody.

I touched his knee.

"Doesn't matter," he muttered.

I thought it mattered.

The pup came back to us and dropped a willow shoot at my side. I reached out and stroked him between the ears. Rafael glanced our way. He blinked rapidly behind his blue-wire eyeglasses.

"Are you keeping him?"

I'd never heard of anyone keeping a pet coywolf before, but it wasn't like the pup had anyone else to take care of him. He crept toward Rafael, sniffing inquisitively. Rafael held out his hand. The pup decided he was safe and rewarded him with a lick. I watched as Rafael struggled to smother his smile.

I'm calling him Balto, I signed.

"What the hell is a Balto?"

I looked at Rafael reproachfully. I'd forgotten he didn't watch movies.

All that running and jumping must have sapped Balto's energy. He dug himself a little spot by the creek, curled up in the fresh soil, and went to sleep. Rafael had brought a notebook and a pencil with him and sat sketching Balto's likeness. The sun dimmed overhead; Rafael put his pencil down when he couldn't see his sketchlines anymore.

"I'm sorry," he blurted out.

I smiled patiently. I had no idea what he was apologizing about.

"About...Mary," he specified, mumbling. "The crap she said to you."

I waved my hand. I didn't want him to worry about it.

"She doesn't think about people's feelings," he went on. "She's like a careless wildfire. She--" He faltered. "She and Dad were a lot alike."

I reached sideways until I found Rafael's hand. I held it.

"She was a daddy's girl. Until he... Dad's shadow followed us everywhere, but it hurt her the most. None of the girls wanted to be friends with her. She's not like me; she needs to be liked. She used to lash out all the time, claw up people's arms. Grounding her wasn't any good; she'd just claw up her own arms. Cut her nails and she'd bite herself instead. She always told me she had to leave the reservation or die. So...what? Did she come back to die?"

Maybe, I thought, she came back because she missed her family.

"Yeah, right," Rafael said. "Anyway, I'm sorry. Nobody should talk like that to you."

I gave Rafael a meaningful look. Why was he so loath to believe people cared about him? I knew I'd miss him tremendously if I woke up tomorrow and he was gone. And I hadn't known him for anywhere near as long as his sister had.

Rafael returned my gaze uncertainly. He had all the vulnerability about his face of a little boy who'd just been told Daddy wasn't coming home. His parents had left him, each in their own way. I wasn't leaving. He saw that.

He broke into a broad smile, the most impossibly beautiful smile, like sunlight at the end of a long storm, like a warm hearth on a desert night.

It's funny. I used to think his smile was rare. When did his smile stop being rare?

"You're nuts," he said. "Don't know why you hang out with me."

Because I was hopeless, I thought. Because I was helpless when it came to him. Because anything he said or did had the ability to make me smile, because I felt his pain for my own and wanted to wash it away. Because I had a voice when I was with him.

The smile slipped away from Rafael's face. I couldn't be sure--I wasn't the one with the crazy mind-reading powers--but I thought he could read each of my thoughts like written words on a sheet of paper; I thought he felt exactly what I was feeling. He always knew what I was thinking. His eyes dropped from my eyes to my lips. My heart forgot its own rhythm; it pounded erratically in my chest. In that singular, uncommon moment, I knew what he was thinking, too.

He set aside his notebook, his pencil tucked behind his ear. He put his hands in the grass and leaned closer. I rested my hand atop his and linked our fingers together.

It was soft when he kissed me, like homecoming, like summer linens on a taut clothesline, tossing in a summer wind. Our lips slid together, his lips warm, his breath warm, heat crackling its way across my skin. His glasses bumped against my cheek and we paused, for a moment, his expression sheepish, a laugh dancing at the corners of my mouth; but then he angled his head--just so--and it didn't happen again. I held the nape of his neck in the palm of my hand and felt his earring tickle my bare arm.

We held hands when we walked back to the reservation proper. Balto followed us as far as the forest's outer boundary before he yipped indignantly and ran back into the woods. I guess he only felt safe around the trees.

The bonfire flared brightly in the tribal firepit that night. Old men sat singing around a double-skin drum. Men and women handed out hotbread and sagebread. I sat down to dinner with Dad and Granny beneath the stars. Dad quickly hid his beer bottle; he didn't like to drink in front of me.

Soon after that, Ms. Siomme came over to talk to us.

Ms. Siomme was a pretty lady. I guess you could say her face was full of personality. She had a long nose and a strong chin, dark brown hair and dark green eyes. No matter what was going on around her, she exuded a calm energy. Seriously--you could accidentally set her hair on fire and she'd probably just put it out and make sure you weren't scared. Not that I'd ever tried it.

"Hello, Catherine," she said, smiling. "Hey, Sky. Paul said you've been talking about adoption."

My stomach turned. I smiled anyway. Don't be dumb, I told myself. You're still Dad's kid.

"Tell me I've seen the last of that fool social worker, at least," Granny said. "I don't understand why she keeps barging into my home."

"Actually, that's part of the reason why I think we should get the adoption out of the way as soon as possible," Ms. Siomme said. "As long as you're Skylar's foster mother, he's what they call a ward of the state. It's sort of like dual citizenship. He may be living on an Indian reservation, but in the state's eyes, he still belongs to Arizona. If they want to, they can take him away."

I looked quickly at Ms. Siomme. *They wouldn't do that*, I signed. *Would they?*

She looked at me with sympathy. She was one of the few adults around the reserve who knew sign language. "I can't say for certain," she admitted. "Law enforcement's pretty mad at us after that stunt we pulled in August. I don't know whether they'd take you away in retaliation, but I wouldn't put it past them."

"Living on a reservation is a bit of a risk to begin with," Dad said. "White families in America are constantly clamoring for children to adopt. When there aren't any, social services will sometimes take Native children from their homes and put them into foster care. The families who report the kidnappings often go ignored."

I looked at him. No way was that true.

"It's true," he said mildly. "It happens the most to Lakota children, I expect because there are so many of them."

"Of course," Ms. Siomme put in, "we're not concerned about that happening to you, Skylar. Nola's too aggressive of a prosecutor to look the other way when intruders break reservation laws. Besides, white families are almost always looking for cute little babies to adopt, not teenage boys."

"I think he's plenty cute," Lila Little Hawk said. She marched over to our spot on the ground and sat heavily at my side.

Right back atcha, sister, I signed.

She batted her eyelashes at me.

Ms. Siomme smiled at Lila. "Well, we definitely agree on that," she said. "Hey, can you show me what your jingle dance looks like?"

"You're not the boss of me," Lila said, but got up and danced over to the double-skin drum.

Ms. Siomme clapped appreciatively. When Lila's back was turned, she gave Granny a serious look.

"I've got the adoption papers ready for you. Nola's agreed to act as your attorney. But you're going to need to get that social worker to sign them."

I looked disbelievingly at Ms. Siomme. Ms. Whitler was the social worker who had called me a "little liar" only a month ago. To be fair, I *had* been lying--about Dad's whereabouts--but I'd walked away from the experience with the distinct impression that she didn't like me, or the Shoshone community on the whole. I wasn't at all certain she would sign off on letting me live with Granny permanently.

"Meredith," Dad said. I think he had picked up on my misgivings. "Isn't there any way to...work around her?"

"You mean get a new social worker? Sure, Nola can petition the courts for that. It will take even longer to get a brand new case worker, though, especially a case worker who knows sign language, so we have to try and work with the one we've got right now."

I smiled without any confidence. That was sort of like dropping a crab down your pants and asking it not to pinch you.

3
Lilith

It was chilly come Saturday morning. Granny made me put on a handmade sweater before she let me leave for Annie's house. I walked through the reservation, the weak sun still low in the sky, and saw the bergenias in bloom, their heart-shaped leaves a burnt and coppery red. I knew what that meant: It was officially the start of autumn.

I found Annie on her front porch, pulling laundry off of a clothesline. I climbed the short staircase and she smiled brightly.

"I've just been to the council building," she said. I wondered at that. It was only seven in the morning. "It looks like we're getting that radio station after all."

I grinned. Aubrey had come up with the idea for a Plains music station a while back. At the very least, I thought, it would probably help bring revenue to the reservation. Nettlebush had its own economy, a gift economy, but in the rare event that we needed something from outside of the reservation, we relied on the tribal fund.

I helped Annie gather the last of the dry clothing and we went indoors to fold it.

"Isn't it exciting?" she went on. "You could play a couple of pieces on the plains flute. You're quite good, you know."

Playfully, I stuck out my tongue. Granny had signed me up to play songs for the ghost dance over the summer, and I'd just about dropped dead from nerves. I wasn't too eager to replicate the experience.

Critically, Annie peered at my laundry pile. She pursed her lips.

"You may be a good flautist, but you can't fold for crap," she said evenly.

I tossed a sock on top of her head.

By afternoon, predictably, the autumn chill had dulled with the heat rolling in from the desert out west. I took off my sweater. Annie had baked bass for dinner. I hadn't been much of a help; I always get squeamish around dead animals.

We sat behind the house and watched Joseph playing on the rope swing. Annie pulled her knees to her chest.

"Mom was a good singer," she said distantly.

I wrapped my arm around her and pulled her against my shoulder.

"It's so hard to remember, sometimes," Annie said. "That she's gone. How do you stand it, Skylar? Your mother being gone?"

I didn't really know her, I signed. My mom had died when I was five. My memories of her were murky and incomplete. *It's different. It's harder for you.*

"Oh, I don't know... Let's clip some bergenias. I'd like a bouquet."

Every day after school we went out east and watched the men and women building the radio tower and its accompanying studio on the other side of the lake. I knew Dad was among them; he was good at building things, and he wasn't the sort to sit by and let others do all the work. It was fun when the four of us sat on the lakeshore, our schoolbooks on our laps, and watched the bare wood and latticed steel skeletons fill out slowly and climb into the sky. More often than not, Aubrey was so distracted by the sight of it that Annie had to hit him with her notebook and remind him we were supposed to be doing homework.

Come October, the oak trees bore new and grandiose foliage in shades of scarlet, persimmon, and gold. The midday air cooled to a tolerable seventy degrees. And the autumn crops the farmers had tended to so diligently over the summer finally emerged from the ground.

Suddenly the reservation was teeming with life. The farmers set up tables and stalls out on the country lane and loaded them up with kale and carrots and radishes and leeks. Families went out to the farmland with baskets for picking scallions and potatoes and blankets to sit on and spent the whole day chatting with their friends. Women plucked the fat, round apples off of the trees and lit pieces of charcoal to lull the bees into sleeping and husk the honeycombs from their hives. Aubrey threw open his family's farm gates and rolled enormous pumpkins out of the patch and onto the road and his two older brothers, Reuben and Isaac, brought out the fresh cheese and the fresh cream from the milkshed and started making cake. The old women shook their turtleshell rattles and the old men sang to the Great Mystery of the universe, the heart and soul of the living planet, and the children danced a harvest dance in looping, dizzying circles. I laughed to see Joseph Little Hawk, eager and dazed, spinning in the wrong direction.

Granny and Dad walked among the pumpkin crop--Granny, hard to please, couldn't decide which one she wanted--and Aubrey puffed and wheezed, catching his breath, leaning against the gate. Aubrey's three-year-old niece, Serafine, stood clasping his hand, her thumb in her mouth.

"They were a lot lighter going into the ground than they were coming out of it," Aubrey noted dolefully.

I laughed again and clapped him on the shoulder.

On the other side of the gate stood Mr. and Mrs. Takes Flight. From her Coke bottle glasses to her humble, boisterous face, Mrs. Takes Flight couldn't have looked more like Aubrey if she were thirty years younger and male. Mr. Takes Flight, wan and waxy-faced, leaned heavily on his wife's shoulder, his smile feeble.

Concerned, I nudged Aubrey. I nodded toward his dad.

"Ah..." Aubrey trailed off, discomfited. "At least he's getting his pacemaker soon. That should help..."

"Hello," Annie said pleasantly, tugging Lila along by her hand. To her credit, Lila resisted. "What are we talking about?"

"Annie!" Annie's effect on Aubrey was instantaneous; he lit up like a Christmas tree. "I put some apples aside for you--here--and a cake--well, it's not as good as yours--"

Annie was starting to blush. I took it as a sign to give them some privacy. I stole Lila's hand--not that Annie noticed--and we walked away from the gates to watch the harvest dancers down the lane.

We sat on the grass beneath an apple tree and Lila sighed.

"I wish I were pretty."

I looked at her in surprise. I'd never heard her say anything like that before.

I tapped her arm to get her attention. *You're the prettiest girl on the entire reservation*, I signed.

"Not like Mary Gives Light. She's the coolest."

I watched Mary prance around the harvest dancers in flamboyant circles. When she laughed, it was radiant and dark. I know that sounds like an oxymoron, but it's true. The rest of her body didn't match her Lilith-like countenance; she was so skinny, it was almost grotesque. Frail and brittle, with what I thought was self-neglect, her clavicle and scapulas and every bump in her spine showed through her paper-thin skin. Still, if you looked solely at her devilish grin, you couldn't see the ruin. I guess that was why Lila thought she was pretty. She chased Rafael, took his hands, and tried to get him to dance with her. Clumsy, startled, and protesting furiously, he stumbled after her.

I tapped Lila a second time. *I think you're the coolest.*

Lila gave me a wobbly smile that reminded me, for one winding moment, of my dad. "That's why I keep you around," she said.

Annie came to my house that evening and baked a pumpkin pie with Granny. Dad sat at the kitchen table and carved an oddly cunning face into the pumpkin's empty shell. Dad and jack-o-lanterns go way back. I asked Annie to show me how to make samosas and Granny brewed a strong draught of spicewood tea, and by nightfall, the four of us carried our covered pots and dishes outside for dinner.

Rafael dropped into a seat at the picnic table, closely scrunched in next to me, and started venting.

"She acts like she owns the ground she walks on. And she's always got to be the center of attention. And she won't stop making fun of my glasses."

I smiled angelically. Sometimes I was glad to be an only child.

"Shut up, Sky. Why did she have to come back here?"

I shot him a sideways look, concerned. I knew he loved his sister.

"It's not that. It's just... Never mind. Can I have a samosa? I like 'em."

It was some time later that Lila's friend Morgan Stout jumped from his seat and gasped.

"There's a wolf eating my dinner!" he cried.

That wasn't the sort of proclamation that could go ignored. Wolves usually keep a respectful distance from humans; whenever they cross that distance, it means danger.

Ten different people leapt up at the same time. A few shouted, paranoid. But then I heard Dr. Stout's voice rising above the crowd, reprimanding her son.

"It's just a coywolf, you loon!"

I thought: Now *that's* the pot calling the kettle black. Dr. Stout was as loony as they came.

Morgan's paper plate lay on the ground. Head bowed over the plate, Balto busily devoured the last of Morgan's jackrabbit.

"But..." said Morgan, distressed.

Coywolves will sometimes lurk around a human settlement looking for food scraps, but when there are a lot of people gathered in the same place at the same time, they typically stay away. I guess it was different for Balto. It wasn't like he had a pack to pick up normal coywolf behavior from.

Already the adults had gone back to their dinner, unfazed. Coywolves are like coyotes in that they really don't want to hurt humans. I clapped my hands twice, briskly, and Balto abandoned Morgan's plate and sprinted over to the picnic table. I bent over the bench to give Balto the rest of my pumpkin pie.

"He thinks you're his mom," Rafael said dryly.

I sat up straight and leveled Rafael with an unamused gaze.

"Seriously. He'll probably wanna follow you indoors. Are you gonna let him in bed with you?"

Rafael stopped and checked himself. He lapsed into an appreciative sort of contemplative silence I didn't know how to interpret.

Balto licked his plate clean and watched me expectantly, his tail thumping against the soil. I reached down and stroked the scruff of his neck. He curled up comfortably beneath the picnic table, and Dad came and sat opposite Rafael and me.

"Hello," Dad began stiltedly.

I waved and grinned. Rafael stared openly, like Dad was a ghastly apparition.

"It's nice out, tonight," Dad went on.

Really, Dad? I thought. You sound pretty uncertain about that.

I kicked Rafael under the table. He started.

"Uh," said Rafael. "Yeah. Yeah, it is. Sir."

It was impossible to tell which of the two was more socially stunted. I felt the strong urge to let my forehead fall into my palm. Instead I smiled, my chin on my hand, my elbow on the scrubbed table, and looked between the two of them.

"So," Dad said.

"Yeah," Rafael said quickly.

"Alright," Dad said. He nodded politely, rising from the table. "Have a good night, Rafael."

"Yeah. I mean, okay. Thanks."

Granny and Dad and I went home together after the bonfire had been extinguished. Dad lit the hearth for the cold autumn night. I caught Dad by the arm before he could retreat to bed.

"What is it?" Dad asked.

I lifted my eyebrows.

Dad coughed into his fist, stalling for time. I waited patiently.

"There's nothing wrong with trying to get to know my son's

boyfriend," he said sheepishly.

I didn't know whether to stare or hug him. I kind of wanted to laugh--because really, how amazing was my clumsy dad?--but I didn't want him to think that I was making fun of him.

"You're not really keeping that coywolf, are you?" Dad said.

Balto sat by the hearth on his scrawny legs and peered into the flickering flames like a sage old prophet searching for his future. Seriously, the little guy was mesmerized.

I showed Dad the most earnest, most piteous pair of eyes I knew how to affect.

Dad winced. "Okay, okay," he said. "Just remember that he's a coywolf, not a dog. You can tame him while he's young, but he's still a wild animal. When he grows up, and his wild instincts kick in, you'll have to let him go. And if he goes to the bathroom in the house...please clean it up before Mother notices. You know how she can be."

Dad's jack-o-lantern was sitting on the floor by Granny's loom. Dad picked up the jack-o-lantern and put it safely on top of the mantel. I guess he didn't want Balto destroying such a fine work of art in his childlike enthusiasm.

As a matter of fact, Balto *did* sleep in bed with me that night. He got his gold-and-gray hairs all over my pillow, too.

The real trouble started the next morning, when Balto tried to follow me to school. He made it as far as the front steps of the schoolhouse before Mr. Red Clay gave the two of us an appraising look.

"Sorry, Skylar," Mr. Red Clay said. "I only teach humans in this class."

It was heartbreaking to hear Balto whining and scratching outside the doors all morning. By the time class had ended, Balto was nowhere in sight. I had to track him down all the way back to Annie's grotto. The pattern repeated itself over the next few days until Balto finally learned to stay home in the mornings.

One afternoon, Balto and I came home from the woods to find Granny and Ms. Whitler sitting on the porch.

Ms. Whitler jumped out of her seat, her horn-rimmed glasses askew. "Oh, goodness, there you are!" she said. "I thought I'd be waiting out here all day for you!"

Granny shot her a furtive, disgusted look.

I smiled politely. Ms. Whitler presented as bubbly and ditzy, but she was a lot smarter than she was willing to let on. She liked to pretend she was your friend--while slowly gleaning whatever information she wanted from your defenseless mind. It seemed like a deadly combination of traits for a social worker to possess.

"Aw, is that your puppy?" Ms. Whitler bent down and reached for Balto's head. "Aww, aren't you so--"

Balto snarled, baring his lupine teeth.

"Anyway," said Ms. Whitler, standing quickly, "shall we go inside?"

I led the way into the house and kitchen and warmed some spicewood tea for Granny and Ms. Whitler. Balto scratched his nails along the seams in the cellar door. He constantly tried to open that door, but without any success. A good thing, too, or he would have eaten all the produce and left none for us. Ms. Whitler sat at the kitchen table with a sigh of contentment and kicked off her shoes.

The moment I sat down, I jolted. Where was Dad? The Major Crimes Act was the only thing protecting him from the FBI. If Ms. Whitler caught a glimpse of Dad... I didn't know what would happen. But I knew that I'd rather not find out.

I looked toward Granny for a visual cue. She didn't notice. She sat down, cleared her throat, and pushed a sheet of paper across the table at Ms. Whitler.

"Ooh," said Ms. Whitler. "What's this?" She adjusted her glasses and bent over to read it.

"I would like to adopt the boy," Granny said brusquely. "It's clear that his father isn't coming back for him."

"Mm, that's true," Ms. Whitler said. "And anyway, as a murder suspect, it's not like he's in a position to raise a kid on the run..."

Murder. I hated that word.

"Well, then?" said Granny. "Will you approve my request for custody or not?"

Ms. Whitler smiled tightly. She leaned back in her chair and crossed her legs.

"Mrs. Looks Over," she began. "I don't think I've had enough time to assess the long-term stability of this home. I don't know whether I could approve such a thing within good conscience."

"Not enough time?" Granny exclaimed. "He's been with me for four months!"

"Right, I'm glad you see it my way!"

"I absolutely do *not*!"

I stood quickly. I didn't want them yelling at each other.

"Mrs. Looks Over, I think you're raising a little liar. In fact, I think you're all a bunch of little liars! Either his father is right here on the reservation, or else Skylar knows where he's hiding. Heck, I'm just sure of it! When we let him keep that beeper--"

"Oho!" said Granny, enraged. "I think I want my attorney in the room for this one! Skylar! Go get--"

"No, no! That's quite alright; it looks like I've run out of time here. I'd better get going. I'll be back, though!"

We walked Ms. Whitler to the front door, her shoes in her hand, Granny livid.

"It's funny," said Ms. Whitler, just before she left. "If not for his birth certificate, I never would've guessed he's an Indian. He just doesn't look anything like y'all!"

Granny slammed the door in her face.

4
Ach'ii

Dad, Granny, and I sat down to a quiet dinner in Ms. Siomme's barn loft on Sunday. Balto sat on my lap, squirming, restless but compliant, and I fed him slices of ginger root from the table when no one was looking. A soft and hazy rain washed over the apartment's pasture-facing windows.

"I'm sorry to bother you with this," Dad said. "But I--"

"You're not bothering me. Go on."

"I don't think that social worker's going to cooperate with us," Dad said, resigned.

"Oh, you don't *think*, do you?" Granny snapped at him.

"Mother..."

"What exactly did she say?" Ms. Siomme asked. "When you brought up adoption?"

"Some nonsense about 'not having enough time,' " Granny reported. "As though four months' time isn't enough..."

"Then we'll definitely look into getting you a new case worker," Ms. Siomme said. "On the bright side, at least she didn't try to take Skylar with her when she left."

I didn't like this feeling. It was like sitting precariously on a bed of needles, tense, knowing you could never lie back and relax without fear of pain.

Granny tutted reproachfully. "If Christine were here," she muttered, "she would have decked that hussy straight across the face."

It took everything in me not to burst into laughter at Granny's language.

Ms. Siomme smiled nostalgically, her mug in her hands. "She did have a temper on her, Christine..."

I looked between Granny and Ms. Siomme with interest. It was rare that I heard anyone talk about Mom. The wounds were still sore, I figured.

"If Christine were here," Dad said, "we wouldn't be in this situation to begin with. There's no use thinking about it."

And there it was--the shut-down.

Ms. Siomme poured us cups of peppermint tea before we left for the remainder of the evening. Dad and Granny and I walked home together in the light rain, Balto trotting at my side.

As we were treading up the lawn, I took Dad's thick arm imploringly in my hand.

He knew what I wanted. Sometimes he knew what I wanted even before I knew it.

Can't you tell me about Mom?

"Not now, Cubby, please," he begged. "I'm tired."

We went into the sitting room and lit the hearth. I warmed towels over the wood-coal stove and we dried up, quickly, by the fireplace. Balto shook his wet mane all over the wood floor. Dad sneezed.

"Play something," Granny commanded me. She waved dismissively and went into the preceding front room to have another try at figuring out the computer.

I played a song called Heavy Fog on the plains flute while Dad sat on his rocking chair, gazing inexpressively into the fire. I heard Granny in the next room saying: "Hmm, looks like I've got an e-mail letter..."

"That was very good, Cubby," Dad said when I had finished playing.

I smiled wistfully. Dad went on looking at me and finally sighed beneath his breath, turning his head away so I wouldn't have to see a real expression on his face.

"It hurts to remember her. I wish you could understand that."

I'd been selfish, I thought. Of course I didn't want Dad to suffer.

An uncomfortable silence stretched between us.

"So," Dad said. "Are you going to the autumn pauwau? It's on the Black Mountain Reservation, I believe. I think you'll really enjoy it."

What did that mean? Wasn't he coming, too?

"I can't come," Dad said. "I'm sorry. The moment I step out of Nettlebush, the law stops protecting me. I know that sounds cowardly. But I..."

No, it didn't. I shook my head and touched his arm. The last thing I wanted was to lose Dad. Still, I thought, I wished he could join in on the fun.

Dad smiled, but he still looked like a flightless hawk to me. "Don't worry about me," he said. "I'll keep Balto company while you're gone."

In school, too, everyone was talking about the pauwau.

"The Hopi eagle dance!" Zeke shouted, dancing up and down the aisle between the tenth and eleventh grade tables. "Seriously, you've never seen anything so cool! It's like they're flying--" He stuck his arms out like airplane wings.

"And the corn dance," Stuart Stout said. "I suppose it's appropriate that they hold their pauwau in autumn."

"Don't forget the butterfly dance," Annie said dreamily.

William Sleeping Fox prodded the tattoo on my upper left arm.

"That's an atlas moth, dumbass," Rafael said darkly.

"Find your seats, please," Mr. Red Clay said. He rapped the chalkboard with his knuckles until everyone settled down, silent. At once, he broke into his fluid combination of English and sign language. "Who can tell me why we're called Indians?"

Almost everyone raised their hands.

"Impressive," said Mr. Red Clay. "We'll see. Miss At Dawn?"

"Because Columbus thought he'd landed in India, the crackhead," Daisy At Dawn said, snickering.

"Language, Miss At Dawn. He certainly did. But India was called Hindustan back then. If Columbus thought he was in Hindustan, why didn't he call us Hindus?"

Nobody raised a hand this time.

Mr. Red Clay's mouth curled in a half smile. "No one? Alright, let's try a different question. What was the name of the tribe Columbus first encountered?"

"The Arawak!" Jack Nabako shouted from the front row.

"Thank you, Mr. Nabako. Next time, I beseech you to raise your hand. The Arawak. Were the Arawak a peaceful tribe, or a warring tribe?"

Rafael raised his hand. I stared at him, my elbow on the table, smiling slightly. He'd never raised his hand in class before.

"Yes?"

"Peaceful," Rafael said. "Like, freakishly peaceful."

"Freakishly peaceful," Mr. Red Clay mused. "That's one way to put it. So they would have been welcoming toward Columbus?"

"I guess so," Rafael mumbled.

"So it makes sense that Columbus would call us 'a people of God.' Or," said Mr. Red Clay, "in Italian--his language of preference--'una gente in dio.' Indio. Indian."

Daisy At Dawn whistled.

"Pencils out," Mr. Red Clay said. "Time for a quiz."

The first graders filed into the playground after school. Jack Nabako shoved Joseph and Joseph wailed loudly; but then Lila shoved Jack and all was right with the world. Rafael and I watched Siobhan Stout pushing her brother on the rope swings. Rafael turned to me.

"Uncle Gabe says you and your grandma can come with us for the ride to Black Mountain."

I brought my hands together and pulled them slowly apart. *How far is it?*

"It's just a few hours away. It's in the mountains."

I shot him a quick and insolent smile. The name of the reservation had kind of tipped me off.

"Shut up," Rafael said, grinning, abashed. I wanted to kiss the grin right off of his face. "Anyway, it's cold there. So...there's that. Bring food. No, wait. Bring samosas. I like 'em."

I glanced quickly around the playground. No one was looking at us. I grabbed him by the front of his shirt, pulled him down to my height, and kissed his cheek. He looked dazed. I slugged him on the shoulder and started the walk home.

There wasn't any school on the day of the pauwau. By afternoon, Granny had me put on my green deerhide regalia and Dad embarrassed me by telling me I wore it better than he had at my age. We said our goodbyes, and Granny and I carried baskets full of samosas and apple pie and wojapi out of the house. I really wished Dad were coming with us. Actually, I considered staying behind with him. I'd just turned around to run back home when Granny rapped me sternly on the back of my head. Stars burst behind my eyelids. Ow. Granny wasn't a woman anyone in their right mind would want to cross.

The whole community of Nettlebush piled out into the parking lot between the hospital and the turnpike. I'd never seen the parking lot so crowded before. We were a mosaic of colors in traditional deerhide and elkskins, in overcoats and breechclouts and fringed sheepskin gowns.

I spotted Rafael's family standing by a big black SUV. Gabriel waved us over, a merry smile on his face. He wore tan trousers, a brown breechclout, and--not much else. Where was his overcoat? I guessed he was going shirtless. Considering our destination, I thought it a brave move.

"You're looking lovelier than ever, Catherine," Gabriel said.

Granny preened. She did look nice, actually, her white regalia fringed in royal blue, her painted glass necklace hanging around her throat. Gabriel helped her into the back of the SUV with a couple of her friends, the nattering Mrs. Threefold and the absentminded Mr. Marsh.

Mary Gives Light stood facing me in ornate violet regalia. A sudden and impetuous grin enveloped her face, and it was so sharklike and lupine, all at once, that it reminded me of Rafael's-- especially when her dimples showed. But it lacked his profound innocence.

"Hey!" she said. "It's my buddy!"

She snatched me into a deceptively strong embrace. She knocked the breath out of me and I probably would have coughed, except that I couldn't. I can't cough or hiccough--it's weird, I know. Your vocal folds need to close partway, and mine just don't.

I felt a hand on my arm, and then Rafael pulled me safely out of Mary's crushing grasp. "Would you let him breathe?" he said.

Rafael and Mary and I sat in the middle row of the SUV. Gabriel slid the doors shut when we had all boarded. Rosa, in the passenger seat, smiled meekly at me through the rear-view mirror. Her regalia was a soft salmon orange fringed with softer blues and greens, her leggings a pale yellow stitched from dried creosote petals. Her glossy black hair fell over her shoulders in the double braids characteristic of the Great Plains. Between her rich dress and her round, innocent face, she made me think of a child's cornhusk doll.

The car pulled out of the parking lot and onto the turnpike. Gabriel messed with the radio dial. "It'll be nice when we can listen to our own radio station, won't it?"

Rafael was wedged between Mary and me. I really liked his regalia, muted and gray; it matched the gray dove's feather knotted in his hair and lightened the dark blue in his eyes, reminding me of a cloudless sky.

Rafael reached beneath his seat, pulled out a wad of unwrapped, half-melted licorice, and offered it to me. I was very touched, but I could have puked on the spot.

"Who wants to play a road game?" Gabriel asked.

"When I was a girl," said Mrs. Threefold, fanning herself, though it wasn't particularly warm, "we played good old-fashioned shinny and made do with it."

"We have that now," Rosa said. "In February."

"Of course," Mrs. Threefold said. "But men weren't allowed to play back then." She stifled a sigh. "I miss those days."

I leaned against the window and watched the desert as it slipped past us, the lush brown hackberries and blossoming orange caltrops gritty but beautiful amid hills of burnt, bronze sand.

"You really like that desert," Rafael said, his chin on my shoulder.

I pointed at a caltrop bush close to the highway.

"I'll get you one."

I turned my head and grinned teasingly.

"I mean it," he said stubbornly. "After the pauwau, I'll go out to the desert. I'm not scared. I've been there before."

I might have kissed him if the car weren't crowded. The urge was incredibly strong.

"So weird," I heard Mary say in a mystified voice.

Rafael leaned back and tossed her a sour look. "What's weird?"

"That you're so buddy-buddy with each other. Our dad offed his mom. Right? Then his dad offed our dad--"

"I didn't just hear that," Gabriel said.

"Oh, sorry." But if she was sorry, it didn't last for long. "Hey,

Rosa, didn't Dad off your mom, too?"

Rosa's face took on several changes, one after the other; first, it was anguished; then, it was stone.

"Mary," Gabriel warned. For the very first time, I thought he sounded intimidating.

Sideways, I glimpsed Rafael, his jaw square and taut. Our hands were on the same seat, inches apart. Discreetly, I draped my fingers across his. He twined our fingers together firmly, chewing bitterly on a piece of licorice, but didn't look my way.

The long car ride took three or four hours. The journey was impeded with frequent restroom breaks, each one a request from Granny's friends. Stopping at greasy gas stations and ramshackle restaurants was a lot of fun, truth be told. I got a kick out of it whenever families put down their forks or tourists lowered their gas nozzles and they stared at us, slack-jawed, like we were from another world. I guess it wasn't every day that a group of Native Americans in full regalia visited their pit stops. At one point, I heard a snapping shutter and knew someone had taken our photograph. At another, a group of biker girls at the gas pump tried to touch Gabriel's shoulders until Rosa stomped her foot and showed them her meanest look, which wasn't very mean at all. She was precious.

We got into the car for the umpteenth time, Mary listening to her headphones, Rafael and me practicing sign language together, and finally, by early evening, we reached the mountain range.

I could see why it was called the Black Mountain Reservation. The mountain peaks, rounded and craggy, had a faint black undertone to them, foreboding in some way I couldn't define. A low wooden fence surrounded the settlement. From the fenceposts stood an aged wooden sign: In English, "Welcome to the Black Mountain Reservation!" and in Hopi, "Um Pitu?"

Gabriel parked his SUV with dozens of other cars on the dry

brown soil south of the gate. Granny handed me baskets to carry as we climbed out of the car. I saw thin white pillars of diluted chimney smoke still rising from the cottage roofs on the other side of the fence. Small wonder: It was chilly outside, and the stars had begun to appear above the twilight skyline of saffron and gray. Rosa gave Gabriel her pink shawl to wear around his shoulders for warmth. He laughed loudly, pulled her into a bear hug, and kissed her all over her face. He actually wore the shawl, too.

The area outside the reservation was filled with different tribes. I recognized the Pawnee, plain and understated, and the Navajo, flashy and bright in shining silks and weighted, feathery mantles tumbling down their backs. I spotted a tribe I didn't recognize by sight, dressed in shell jewelry and leather headbands, the men in beaded cotton shirts and the women in calico skirts. "Those are the Apache," Granny informed me. "Remember, your grandfather was White Mountain Apache."

"Okay!" shouted Cyrus At Dawn. He was a member of our tribal council, a huge guy with bushy hair and a booming, gravelly voice. He was carrying our tribal flag, a yellow banner emblazoned with an eagle and a pair of roses. "Everybody follow me!"

We went through the gates, the small city as empty as a ghost town. Mr. At Dawn led us past a police station and a small library and out to an enclosure wrapped in stone ledges, where fallen autumn leaves already decorated the ground, where tiny little huts decorated the base of the looming black mountain, and the Hopi-- well, they didn't cheer and greet us, if that's what you were expecting. I know I was.

If reticence is the Shoshone ideal, then solemnity must be the Hopi ideal. The Hopi were all dressed in dark, heavy layers fastened at the shoulder. Their cumbersome regalia reminded me much more of restrictive Elizabethan dress than the carefree clothing of the Plains. The women wore their hair in whorls shaped like butterflies and squash blossoms; the men wore kerchiefs. Altogether they were very solemn, very grave, as they welcomed their guests onto their homeland. I had expected the pomp and fanfare of the summer pauwau, when we had raucously greeted our sister tribes amid shouting and games. I guessed that this occasion was going to be a little more serious.

The visiting tribes planted their standards in the ground and the councils all went forward to shake hands. This part of the pauwau took way longer than it should have, because the Navajo had a council of twenty. The other tribes only had five or six. Ours had four. Mr. At Dawn and Mrs. Red Clay went forward and shook hands with the Hopi council, and after them went Ms. Siomme and Mr. Knows the Woods, a squat, shifty-eyed man who looked as though he spent most of his life suspecting his own shadow of treason. Ms. Siomme, who was half Hopi, spent longer talking to the council than the others did. It occurred to me that she might have had family still living on this reservation.

The Hopi opened the ceremony with their eagle dance. They performed a lot more gracefully than Zeke Owns Forty had done, but I still don't know how they managed to move around in all those layers. When their arms were outstretched, when they danced lightly in the direction of the wind, dancing against the hollow beat of empty drums, I could really believe they were soaring eagles, majestic and grave, searching for the skies they used to roam when once they were unfettered.

The eagle dance ended, and the mood of the pauwau relaxed. Suddenly the reservation was filled with the subtle air of competition. The Pawnee men showed us their pipe dance, which long ago had been danced to determine the princess of their tribe. Men and women laid blankets on the leaf-strewn ground and lit small fires to warm their food. Granny and I set out the wojapi and the pie. Rafael was content to eat his samosas cold. That kind of grossed me out. What grossed me out way more, though, was when the Navajo came walking among us with their delicacy--long ropes of twisted sheep intestines. This time, I almost did throw up.

"You don't like it?" said the girl holding the platter, peering at me with wonder.

I tried to figure out a way to apologize without words. Then I realized: I know this girl. How do I know this girl? She was dressed in red taffeta with lavender-gray accents, her hair tied tightly in the Navajo figure-eight bun, her winglike mantle hanging heavily from her shoulders.

She smiled mysteriously. I grinned. Now I remembered. We'd danced together at the summer pauwau.

Granny got up to dance with Reverend Silver Wolf. The Navajo girl took her seat. She scrutinized me shrewdly. "You still don't talk?"

I shrugged my shoulders and smiled ineffectually.

She smiled back and stuck out her hand. "I'm Kaya."

I shook her hand. I pointed at the sky above us--rich and blue with deepening dusk.

"Hello, Sky."

Rafael sat down on the blanket with a handful of samosas. He didn't bother trying to hide his glare, intensified as it was by the square lenses of his eyeglasses. Unperturbed, Kaya offered him her hand. Taken aback, he hesitated before he quickly seized it.

Kaya looked between us with recollection. "You two were together in July."

"Nah," Rafael said. "We were just friends."

A silence, indescribably awkward, settled over all three of us. Rafael seemed to realize his mistake. It was pretty impressive how quickly his face transitioned from its typically brutish visage to a sickly shade of puce. I shook my head and dropped my face into my hands. I was mortified, and yet I wanted to laugh.

Kaya beat me to it. I peeked between my fingers and saw her with her head back, her chest rippling with laughter.

"You're funny, Rafael."

Rafael gave her a perplexed look. "I didn't say my name."

"Your sister told me."

Kaya pointed to a group of Hopi who were generously giving out gifts of prayer sticks. Mary stood among them with prayer sticks in hand, bopping them on their heads.

It was Rafael's turn to look mortified. "Mary!" he shouted. He leapt up from the ground and ran at her.

"Charming family," Kaya said.

I tapped Kaya's shoulder and gestured between the two of us. I mimed writing a letter on my hand.

"You'd like to keep in contact?"

I nodded.

Kaya gestured for me to wait. She carried her platter of sheep intestines to a woman I took to be her mother, then returned with a notepad and a pencil. We wrote down our e-mail addresses and traded notes. She waved goodbye and danced away just as a man began to play the Apache fiddle.

By the time Rafael returned, he was thoroughly frazzled. His glasses were crooked, his dove's feather askew.

"I'll kill her," he swore.

I gave him a thumbs up.

"Where'd that girl go? I wanted some ach'ii."

I gave him a dubious look.

It was our tribe's turn to show off. Our elders gathered around the tribal flag and performed a wartime flag dance while Morgan Stout played Heavy Fog on his plains flute. Annie and the In Winter girls danced a shawl dance together, spinning and whirling like pinwheels in the autumn wind. Everyone laughed when Gabriel, still wearing Rosa's shawl, leapt into the fray. Mr. Red Clay led the first graders in a decorous grass dance, steps light, arms aloft. Jack Nabako kept abandoning his position and running at the girls. The girls shrieked. Morgan played the Shoshone love song, and the facade of competition dissipated. Misty-eyed couples from every tribe danced cheek-to-cheek; mothers danced with their babies. Gabriel wrapped Rosa's shawl around the two of them.

I got up off the ground and reached for Rafael's hand.

Rafael had promised back in August that he'd dance with me at the autumn pauwau. The thing is, Rafael hated dancing. He hated more or less anything that held the potential to bring attention to him.

I watched his eyes shift nervously behind his glasses while he chewed on the inside of his mouth.

Poor Rafael. I didn't want to press the matter. I reached down to pat him on the shoulder. He must have misinterpreted my intent, because he grasped my hand and stood.

"Now what?" he murmured, his mouth barely moving.

I could hear my pulse in my ears. Why was I nervous? I was supposed to be the confident one. No, I knew why I was nervous. I'd never danced with another boy before, much less in front of an entire reservation full of people.

An entire reservation full of people. That's right, I thought. They were all busy enjoying themselves. They didn't care who I danced with.

I took his hands and put them on my waist. I felt his eyes boring into mine; I didn't meet them. I slid my hands against his hips. His gray deerhide overcoat felt soft beneath my palms, his hips strong. Dizziness swarmed behind my eyes.

I felt his fingers crook beneath my chin and tilt my head up. Our gazes slid together and locked.

Forget dancing, I thought shakily. I wanted to kiss him. I wanted to pull him hard against me and devour him, body and soul; and then I wanted him to devour me.

His fingers sank into my curls. I felt the strength draining out of my spine. Maybe he noticed. His arm snaked around my waist. Our hips bumped together and I felt his chest against mine, his heartbeat against mine. His knuckles stroked patterns down my back. I felt his breath on my lips. His arms were around me, holding me. I smoothed my hands against his shoulders, rubbed the feeling back into my fingers.

I wasn't even sure whether we were dancing or not. I couldn't feel the ground beneath me, nor the autumn air on my face. I couldn't feel anything that wasn't a part of Rafael. I couldn't see save for Rafael's eyes in front of mine; the warmth that secretly hid there; the secret part of him that was mine.

He bent his head and buried his face against the crook between my shoulder and neck. His hot breath tickled my skin. He mouthed words against me, words I couldn't figure out.

The pauwau ended at midnight when the Hopi performed their corn dance, shaking their bells and their rattles in supplication to the four winds and the rain. They gave us presents of corn and piki bread as we walked back through the reservation to our cars. Mr. Little Hawk, his face long and childlike and his hair streaked with gray, carried a sleeping Joseph against his shoulder. I carried our laden baskets as Granny leaned on my shoulder, chattering animatedly. She was in an unusually bubbly mood.

Rosa was behind the wheel for the trip back to Nettlebush. Gabriel talked to her in hushed, light tones, his elbow against the passenger-side door. Mary and Mrs. Threefold both dozed off, Mary snoring loudly. At some point, I must have dozed off, too; I woke with my head on Rafael's shoulder, his arm around me, and pretended I was sleeping still, because I didn't want to move.

The car rolled to a stop. We were back in Nettlebush. I let Rafael jostle me--it amazed me, how someone so burly could be so gentle--and drowsily, the eight of us milled out of the car. It was three in the morning.

"I'm not going to school tomorrow," Rafael insisted. "Today. Whatever."

Before any of us could leave the parking lot, I heard Mrs. Takes Flight scream.

Rafael and I exchanged a look. I saw panic on his face and knew it was a mirror of my own. We ran to the Takes Flights' car, Mary following us.

Mr. Takes Flight was on the ground, convulsing.

"Get a doctor! Please!" Aubrey shouted, his face as gray as concrete.

Dr. Stout came rushing over to the car and knelt at Mr. Takes Flight's side. Morgan had followed her, his big eyes wide with fear. Dr. Stout bent over Mr. Takes Flight, her hands on his chest.

"Oh God," Aubrey moaned. "Oh God..."

"Shut up, Aubrey," said his brother, Isaac. "Mother--"

Annie and Lila and Grandpa Little Hawk edged their way through the crowd. So did Stuart and Siobhan Stout. Dr. Stout tucked her arms under Mr. Takes Flight's back and helped him to sit up. Rosa dashed over with a bottle of water while Dr. Stout fished medicine out of her purse.

"Do you--" Rafael faltered. "I can carry him--"

"No," said Reuben, Aubrey's oldest brother. He passed his sleeping daughter into Aubrey's arms and bent down to lift his father. Gabriel and Grandpa Little Hawk crouched on the ground next to Mrs. Takes Flight and put their hands on her shoulders, consoling her while she wept.

I stood by helplessly and watched as Reuben carried Mr. Takes Flight to the hospital. Rosa, Dr. Stout, and three other people I didn't know were quick to follow them.

"I don't know what happened," Aubrey said distantly, dazed.

Annie's hand on his shoulder was firm, her voice low enough not to wake Serafine. "It looked like a heart attack to me," she said. "But he's in good hands. You know that. He'll be fine."

"Mom's a pediatrician," said Stuart. "I don't know what she thinks she's doing..."

"Well, a heart is a heart," his little sister said.

If any of this was meant to reassure Aubrey, it didn't work. He moaned with anxiety. He might have spilled to his knees if not for the little girl in his arms.

"Aubrey!" Isaac scolded, starting up the hospital ramp. "Don't just stand there."

Trancelike, Aubrey followed him, absently patting Serafine's back. Mrs. Takes Flight wasn't far behind, dabbing the tears from her eyes.

"Damn it..." I heard Rafael say.

I heard a click and a hiss. I smelled smoke. Mary had lit a cigarette. She took a long, deep, toxic breath and released it.

"You should be in bed," she said.

"That guy just had a heart attack," Rafael said fiercely. "Do you even care?"

"What can you do about it? You're not a doctor."

"I never thought I'd say this, but your sister's right," Gabriel stepped in. "Bedtime. Come on, kiddo."

We said good night--Aubrey's dad still on my mind--and I followed Granny back home. Granny was silent and stoic as we walked arm-in-arm. The hearth in the sitting room was lit, and the faint smell of alcohol clung to the wood walls, but it looked like Dad had already gone to sleep. Balto ran at me with gusto as soon as we stepped through the front door. I pat him on the tummy and fed him a roll of piki bread when Granny wasn't looking.

"Pray for Martin," was the last thing Granny said before retreating into her room.

I sat in a rocking chair by the fireplace, wide awake. I left the front door partway open so Balto could run in and out. If Aubrey's father died... That didn't seem fair to me. Why did all of my friends have to become so acquainted with loss?

I still wasn't very tired, but I figured I'd better go to bed anyway. I clapped my hands and Balto came running in from the porch. I got up and closed the front door.

A thick book lay open on one of Granny's rocking chairs. Dad must have been reading before he'd gone to bed. Now that struck me as a curious thing. Dad's the kind of guy who doesn't like to read anything unless it's on the back of a ketchup bottle. Either way, I reasoned, it was none of my business.

The flames in the fireplace jumped--shedding light on the glossy pages. It was a photo album.

My heart pounded treacherously, my throat dry. I sat on the chair and scooped the album onto my lap.

The very first picture that attracted my attention was a photograph of my mother. God, was she young--about twenty-two, if my math was right. Her eyes were crossed, her tongue stuck out at the camera. Her arms were sleeved with freckles--like mine, I thought fondly--and her hair was curly and long. Her belly was heavy with pregnancy. I touched her swollen stomach with longing. It was strange to think that I was in there, that she had carried me safely inside of her, and without that, I wouldn't be here now.

I flipped through the pages. I felt the smile growing on my face. *Dad* looked young, almost unrecognizable without his paunch. There were various pictures of him sitting with Mom underneath a southern oak tree. I swear it was the same oak under which Gabriel would later build his house. Dad had his hand on Mom's belly in one of the photos. The pride on his face was glowing, palpable; his love poured out of the photograph and touched me, sixteen years after the fact. It was powerful and humbling. I swallowed. I was loved even when I was no more than someone else's thought.

Another page. Another set of photographs. Granny sitting under a winter sky, a curly-haired baby on her lap tucked tightly in her arms. She had wrapped me in a pendleton blanket to protect me from the cold. I realized, tremendously, that I still had that blanket. It was upstairs, in my closet; sometimes I threw it over my bed at night when I couldn't get warm.

I turned the page and felt my heart stop.

Two men were staring back at me from the glossy photograph, their arms tossed around each other's shoulders. Their smiles were identical; I almost took them for brothers--except that the rest of their features didn't match up at all. Dad's eyes were water-gray, his chin wobbly and round. His hair was lackluster and black. The other guy had black hair, too, but it took on a midnight-blue sheen under the light from the standing lamp. His jaw was square, his nose flat. He had the darkest eyes I'd ever seen on a human face: acrid and black, like infected blood.

A violent shudder shot through my body. The book fell out of my hands and slapped loudly to the floor. My throat felt tight and narrow, the scars on my throat searing with phantom pain.

Dad never told me he was friends with Mom's killer.

5
Caltrop

Autumn rendered the grotto picturesque. The beech trees showered the ground in falling leaves; the creek, clear and swift, carried them east.

" 'Name a prominent chieftain from each Shoshone band,' " Rafael read from his history book. "I got Pocatello, Bear Hunter, and Washakie. Are we supposed to count the Bannocks? What about the Comanche?"

"Do it anyway," Annie suggested, her head bent over her notebook. "Maybe he'll give you extra credit."

Annie and Rafael and I sat under the gray sunlight and helped one another with our homework. Balto hovered by the edge of the creek, his muzzle dipping under the cold water as he snapped at the minnows swimming past. My thoughts kept straying: to Aubrey's father, sick in a hospital bed; to my own father, hiding secrets from me. Annie, too, was distracted. On occasion, I saw her looking at her wristwatch, counting the minutes until Aubrey arrived.

Aubrey finally arrived, but he looked as though he'd just come back from visiting a ghost.

"How is he?" Annie asked softly.

Aubrey sank into a seat by the creek. "Heart transplant," he said faintly. "Dr. Long Way says he needs a heart transplant."

Annie and Rafael and I looked at one another.

"Does the tribal fund cover something like that?" Rafael asked uncertainly.

"I don't think we have $200,000, no," Aubrey replied. He sounded astonished, like he'd never heard his own voice before.

I was almost glad I couldn't speak; because I couldn't voice my inhibitions. Aubrey's father was kind of advanced in his years. Would a doctor really give him a new heart when they could give it to someone younger instead?

No, I didn't think it was fair.

Aubrey jumped up from the ground, surprising me. He paced frantically, pulling at his short hair. "A heart, a heart," he said. "Where am I going to get a heart?"

"We'll come up with the money on our own," Annie said with fire. "We don't have to wait for crafts month. We've got the internet now, haven't we? I can sell baskets and ornaments--dyes and paints--Skylar, you can make recordings--Rafael, you can draw portraits on commission--"

"I can make knives and spears and stuff," Rafael said. "I make all my own earrings. And Uncle Gabe showed me how to make bird bone flutes."

What about medicines? I signed. *A lot of the plants around here work better than antibiotics.*

"That's perfect!" Annie leapt up, invigorated. "Let's go to Mr. Red Clay's house this very instant. We'll ask him to put advertisements on the tribal website."

Aubrey didn't say anything. He stood by the willow tree, his hands tangled together anxiously. The expression on his face...I don't know how else to describe it except incredulous. It was like he couldn't believe one person, let alone three, cared so much about him. Annie shot him an encouraging wink. I don't know whether he noticed it, but he went on staring at her as though seeing her for the first time.

We spent the next few days hard at work, none of us harder than Annie. She wove baskets until her fingers splintered and smashed dyes from the forest plants until her hands stained purple and blue.

Rafael went into the badlands and came back with clay and goethite and made war jewelry--an inside joke, because Shoshone were historically the most peaceful tribe. He cut the branches from beech trees with his handsaw and carved spears from the wood; he fished smooth stones out of the bottom of the creek and knapped them into knives. I went into the cave because the acoustics were pretty good in there, and with my plains flute and Granny's old tape recorder, I played every Shoshone song I could think of. I scraped the bark from the willow tree and pulled the leaves from the low boughs. The bark's a decent remedy for joint pain, the leaves for fever. I went looking in the woods for elderberry and barberry and bitterroot and I clipped the creosote petals and the peppermint leaves. I tried very hard to find licorice ferns one afternoon, but couldn't. By the time I finally admitted defeat, the sun had already set.

"Caias told me what you're up to," Dad said one evening. "Is that why I hardly see you these days?"

I smiled fleetingly. The truth is, I didn't know how to approach my dad. I couldn't get that photograph out of my head; and when I looked at him, I imagined I could still see his arm around Rafael's father.

Annie's morale was very high during the first week of sales. By week two, it had plummeted. "At the rate we're going," she said, sitting in front of her computer, tears of frustration in her eyes, "he won't have his heart for another three hundred years!"

I rubbed her shoulders. *It's just a lull*, I tried to tell her, but she wouldn't be consoled.

Halloween crept up on me while my head was turned the other way. I took the bus out to the nearest city and bought face makeup, the cheap kind, and made my face up like a skeleton's. Halloween's my favorite holiday, so I make my face up differently every year. Last year I was a tiger. Probably not the wisest choice. I went back to Nettlebush and made pumpkin candy and maple candy with Granny while Dad surrounded the outside of the house with his weirdly cunning jack-o-lanterns. We concocted fake spiderwebs out of hot glue threads and strung them about the windows. Granny even consented to wear a witch's hat for the day.

Turns out people in Nettlebush don't celebrate Halloween. Total number of trick-or-treaters: zero. I brought the candy over to Annie's house, but Joseph screamed when he saw my face.

"What's the point, anyway?" Rafael asked gruffly.

It had taken a lot of coaxing and wheedling, but I'd managed to convince Rafael to let me paint his face. He'd agreed only under the provision that I make him up like a red wolf. I'd never done anything that complicated before, so I consulted one of the drawings on the walls. We were in his bedroom.

I pulled back and looked at Rafael reprovingly. Sometimes he acted like the word "fun" wasn't in his dictionary.

"I mean, the Celts, I get that. Fear of the dead and all. But I'm pretty sure Americans aren't Celts."

I penciled in his fangs.

"I know I'm not a Celt."

Really, Rafael? I never would've guessed.

"Are you a Celt?"

I chucked the makeup pencil at his head.

A grin flashed like lightning across Rafael's face. He grabbed my arm and yanked it. I toppled onto the bed. He gripped me by the shoulders. I didn't give him the chance to pin me; I picked up his pillow and smacked him across the face with it. He laughed and cursed at me and tugged the pillow out of my hands. A good half of his red-brown makeup was smeared on the pillowcase.

"So much for that," Rafael said.

He tossed the pillow to the floor and tucked his hair behind his ears, unveiling his square jawline and his dagger-shaped earring.

It was uncanny, how much Rafael resembled his father. Sometimes it halted me in my tracks. Sometimes it stole my breath away and made me think I could cry.

"What?"

I shook my head quickly and smiled.

"Don't give me that."

I sat up against the headboard, reluctant.

My dad knew your dad, I signed.

Rafael read my hands carefully. He bit his lip. His teeth were sharp, delectable.

"Your dad killed my dad," he said, in a very quiet voice. "I know."

I must have forgotten to teach him the sign for "know." My heart seized with pity. I couldn't honestly say that I lamented his father's death; but for Rafael, who had known him and loved him and been betrayed by him worst of all, I sort of did.

I tried again. *Our dads were friends.*

Rafael's blue eyes shot wide open, then narrowed.

"Are you sure?" he asked. "Because I knew I'd met your mom before. But that's... How the hell do you kill your friend's wife? Never mind that; how the hell do you kill anyone?"

I shook my head. I loved that about Rafael. For all his ornery, introverted ways, he had the kindest, most compassionate heart. I loved his heart.

"Are you okay? What are you smiling at? Oh, hey, I forgot."

He bent over the side of the bed and reached beneath the floor-length comforter. I didn't know what he was looking for. But then he sat up and presented it to me--an orange caltrop.

For the longest time, I could only stare at the caltrop in disbelief. I thought: When Rafael makes a promise, he keeps it. Really...what was I supposed to do with a flower? Wear it? I took the caltrop from his fingers and felt laughter flutter across my lips. I wasn't laughing at him. I would never demean his feelings like that. I couldn't. Not ever.

"You said you liked 'em," Rafael muttered defensively.

You silly boy, I thought. Thank you. Thank you. I tucked the stem of the caltrop safely between my fingers. I took his jawline between my hands. I kissed the corner of his mouth. I kissed his bottom lip. I kissed him again and again until I felt him responding, until he pressed his hands against my shoulders and my back hit the bed. I pulled him by the hem of his shirt and he straddled me, our mouths melded together. And when his hips fell down on mine, whether by accident or on purpose, I saw white.

A knock sounded at the door.

Rafael and I sprang quickly apart. He sat up and coughed. "C'min," he mumbled. I smoothed my hand over my heart and tried to think unpleasant, unappealing thoughts. Knives. I thought of rusty knives.

Gabriel stepped through the door, smiling amiably. His t-shirt and hiking pants were splotched with mutton blood. My stomach turned.

"Sorry, Skylar," he said. "I need Rafael to help me wrap the meat.

Come on, Raf."

Rafael groaned in complaint and rose from the bed.

Gabriel's face suddenly turned dark and cold. It scared me, in a way; I'd seldom seen him without a smile. What alarmed me the most was that his eyes, light brown, were directed at me.

"What were you two doing in here?"

My heart rose into my throat. Why was he suspicious? What had I forgotten to cover up? Self-consciously, I ran my fingers through my curls. Gabriel's eyes were on Rafael now, Rafael's expression uncharacteristically timid.

"What?" Rafael demanded weakly.

"Wipe your face," Gabriel said. He retreated from the bedroom and slapped the door shut as he went.

Nonplussed, Rafael fished the pillow off of the floor. He shucked off the pillowcase and used it to wipe away the remainder of his messy makeup. He handed it to me when he had finished. I flipped it over to the clean side and wiped my face.

Gray and white makeup rubbed off on the pillowcase. So did reddish-brown.

6
Shaman Sighting

Our sales were still looking pretty dismal by week three. Annie
and I carried our parcels to the hospital mail room--the reservation
didn't have a post office--and I knew that underneath her carefully
constructed veneer of resilience, she was just as disappointed as I
was.

"Siobhan started a donation fund," she said calmly.

She was a good actress when she put her mind to it.

We decided to drop in on Mr. Takes Flight. His hospital room was
airy, with a nice, wide window looking out on the pine trees. We'd
been to his room several times since the autumn pauwau, and no
matter when we visited him, he was never without a family
member: whether it was Mrs. Takes Flight, jittery and red-eyed, or
the stoic Reuben and his little daughter, Serafine, or Aubrey
himself.

Today it was Aubrey with a shaky smile.

"Should I get you some wojapi?" he asked his father. "A book to
read? Or--"

"All I need is this here radio, son," Mr. Takes Flight said. "I don't
see why you're all fussing over me. I feel fine."

I went home and found Balto chewing on a dead opossum by the
sundial. I grimaced, but pat him on the head. He'd grown rapidly
since August. Already he was starting to resemble an adult
coywolf in miniature, his torso and legs filling out. I guessed he
was about five months old.

I went up the front steps and found Dad and Granny sitting under
the porch eaves. Sitting with them was Officer Hargrove.

I hadn't seen Officer Hargrove since August, when the FBI took over the search for Dad. It was a shock to see her now, like stumbling upon an old photograph you've forgotten you took. She was a short woman, stocky, her hair pulled back in a tight bun. The ordinarily harrowed expression was missing from her face. Good, I thought. She deserved to relax.

"Hey, sweetheart," she said. She had the tendency to talk to me like I was a six-year-old. I couldn't blame her for it. A lot of people talked to me that way when they found out I couldn't talk back.

I started to smile, but stopped. My confidence drained. I shot Dad a hasty look.

"I'm not here to arrest anyone," Officer Hargrove said testily. "Couldn't if I wanted to. This is a reservation, isn't it? I'm a city cop."

Cautiously, I sat on the top step.

"Look," Officer Hargrove said. "I'm here on an 'anonymous tip.' Okay, that's bull. Your social worker complained about possible neglect toward a ward of the state and I'm here to check it out. You know it's not true. *I* know it's not true. I don't know what you did to piss her off, but you need to cut it out. The next cop who comes out here might not be me."

"If I may," Dad began, deliberating. Dad had a difficult time talking to women he didn't know. "My mother's been very cooperative. I think the real problem is that the state has no other way to...punish us, so to speak. We're trying to get that woman deposed. But..."

"I'll back you up on that one. She's crossing a professional line." Officer Hargrove pulled a harsh face. "I always hated that witch," she confided. "She's the same social worker Tyrone sicced on me during the divorce..."

"You're divorced, are you?" Granny piped up.

"Got two kids out of the deal. Want to see a picture?"

I thought about that picture tucked away in Dad's photo album. I thought about Dad with his arm around Mom's murderer.

I gave him a meaningful look and rose from the staircase. He followed me inside the house.

"Is everything alright...? Is Martin's condition any better?"

I delved into Granny's linen closet, where I'd stashed the photo album behind a stack of willow baskets. I retrieved the album, flipped open to the offending page, and showed it to Dad.

His eyes went from winter water to dead steel in record time.

With more patience than I really had, I waited for him to speak. Come on, Dad, I thought. It's up to you. You know what I want to ask you. You know I can't ask it.

"Yes," Dad said quietly. "We were very good friends."

Soundly, I closed the book. I tucked it under my arm, feeling, all the while, like my arm belonged to another boy's body.

My poor Dad, I thought. I touched the back of his hand.

"I'm so sorry," he said. The apology poured out of him like winter water through cracks in a dam. "I'm so sorry; I... I don't know when Eli became a murderer. Until the moment the hospital called me... Even then, I didn't know; I never suspected... Not him. Never him..."

I stirred. The hospital had called Dad? Hadn't he taken me to the hospital himself?

Dad shook his head. "I wasn't living on the reservation at the time. I suppose you don't remember how it happened. Somehow you got up and dragged yourself out of the house. I don't know where you thought you were going... Thomas Little Hawk found you wandering around. He brought you to the hospital, where they stitched you up."

My hand closed around my throat. I felt the rigid scars tighten beneath my palm.

Wait, I thought. Dad wasn't living on the reservation. Why wasn't Dad--

"Let's go back outside," Dad said. "I think it's a bit cruel to leave Miss Hargrove alone with your grandmother."

I took him by the wrist and shook my head. Not until he told me the truth.

Dad looked at me for one long moment, and his eyes were opaque, focused in instead of out. I didn't know whether he really saw me.

"We were separated," he said finally. "Your mother and I."

Oh.

The photo album lay on the floor. I don't remember dropping it.

Dad smiled without any sincerity. "Didn't I tell you?" he said. "It hurts too much to remember."

We went back outside to say goodbye to Officer Hargrove. I barely remember the conversation, except that Granny invited her to the solstice party in December. I was in a weird sort of limbo, wherein everything I'd always thought about my parents wasn't true. Once, Granny had told me that Mom and Dad were happy together. Not happy enough, I guess.

It was late in the afternoon when I went out to the woods. I clapped my hands and Balto loped at my side, his tail high in the air. We paid a visit to the grotto and I considered jumping into the creek, if only to get the feeling back in my legs. I decided against it. A light was glowing in the mouth of Annie's cave. Balto and I went inside.

The only person in the cave was Rafael, reading *Paradise Lost* by candlelight for the millionth time. He liked the part where his namesake, the archangel Rafael, came down from Heaven to teach Adam and Eve all about the cosmos. He said it was proof that he was a smart guy and that we should all shut up about his less than stellar grades.

He adjusted his glasses and looked up at me.

"Wanna talk about it?"

I shook my head. I sat heavily, listlessly, next to a bowl of clay beads. Balto stuck his nose in a basket full of sand. He sneezed.

Rafael closed his book.

"Uncle Gabe's not talking to me," he said. He tried to make it sound casual, but I could tell he was upset. "I thought he knew I was gay. I guess that time when I was ten and I told him I wanted to marry Chrestomanci never tipped him off."

I looked at Rafael sharply.

"Book character," Rafael said sheepishly.

Of course it was a book character.

"Seriously, you look pissed. I've never seen you this pissed. You sure you don't wanna talk about it? Or...uh, not talk. You know what I mean."

I started to calm down. Anger was an emotion I didn't wear very well. On principle, I thought it was a waste of energy. Besides, I didn't even know who I was supposed to be angry with.

I looked sideways at Rafael. I never would have expected there to be a rift between him and his uncle. Gabriel was one of the nicest people I'd ever met.

Rafael shrugged through his embarrassment. "I don't know that it's about us being gay," he said. "We were taught to revere the two-spirit. And Uncle Gabe's a hunter. He knows about the sheep and the buffalo and the dragonflies, the males that mate with males and the females that mate with females. I think it's more like... He raised me, so he should know everything about me. But then he finds out he doesn't. But I thought he did, so there's no way I'm taking the rap for that."

I smiled wryly. *Birds and bees*, I signed. I wondered how Gabriel had missed the clues during the sex talk.

Rafael snorted. "I don't know what you're thinking. The shaman's the one who explains that stuff to you. Except for girls. They build an isolation tent. Only women can go inside. I don't know what goes on in there. Always wanted to find out, though."

I tried to imagine the elderly and eccentric Shaman Quick counseling a twelve-year-old Rafael about his body. I immediately felt sorry for Rafael.

"Shut up," Rafael said, and tried to hide his grin.

I pushed his shoulder.

Rafael peered at me shyly. I gave him an inquisitive smile.

"When did you know you were...I mean, how did you figure out you were..."

Mr. Red Clay, I signed. I hadn't taught Rafael the signs for colors yet. I fingerspelled it for him.

Rafael had the good graces about him to look scandalized. "The hell?"

I grinned roguishly. I shoved his shoulder a second time.

November brought with it a unique kind of frenzy--the religious kind. On the walk to school every morning, I saw men and women in formal regalia marching in and out of the church.

"They're all getting married," Annie explained after school.

I gave her a weird look.

Annie returned it seamlessly. "We wait until autumn to marry, so the wedding coincides with a bountiful harvest. It's more auspicious that way."

Unless Mom had married Dad while she was still in college, I realized, I must have been born out of wedlock. Go Dad.

As the official Month of Weddings, I'm sure November was supposed to be a happy occasion for most of Nettlebush's residents. But there was one man who took great offense to the sacrament of holy matrimony.

In Shoshone, a man or woman who professes intimate knowledge of the spirit world is called a *natsugant*. In English, the best translation is "shaman."

Shaman Quick was the smallest, oldest living thing in Nettlebush, and as old people will do, he clung hard to the old ways. He dressed in breechclouts and moccasins and nothing else, no matter the weather. A real recluse, he lived in the heart of the badlands and came into the community so rarely that children had made a game out of spotting him. They called it "Shaman Sighting." He spoke Shoshone and sign language both beautifully, but alas, no English. So actually, while we all knew him as "Shaman Quick," he called himself "Natsugant Kitah."

Natsugant Kitah--or Shaman Quick--stood outside the church doors and wildly waved his arms. With his head tipped back, he yelled at the top of his lungs. I didn't know enough Shoshone to figure out what he was saying. His granddaughter stood at his side, her cunning eyes bulging with excitement. Immaculata was the sort of girl who smiled at mayhem. Instantly, I knew they were up to no good.

Reverend Silver Wolf ran out of the church, his silver braids flying, his Panama hat sliding off of his head. His face was splotched with a bashful blush. In Shoshone, he spoke back to the shaman; hushed and peaceful at first, but louder and louder, louder still, until finally, both old men were yelling at one another. The couple who had just married stood together in consternation, the lovely bride in carnation pink huddling behind her husband.

"Hahaha, they're really going at it!" said Zeke Owns Forty. He was kind enough to explain for me: "The shaman thinks he should perform weddings, not the preacher. He's calling it 'a betrayal to the true way.' "

A sizable crowd had amassed around the church. I saw Reuben Takes Flight with his daughter in his arms, staring blankly; and the identical spook fish eyes of my grandmother's friends that meant nothing short of disapproval.

"He should punch him," said William Sleeping Fox, in a vague, half-conscious kind of voice. "Either one of them. It would be fun."

Small wonder that he and Rafael had been left back for brawling.

The daily feuds continued well into the month. "Don't worry," Stuart Stout told me. "They go through this routine every year." Without fail, the shaman stood outside the church everyday and accosted the couples passing through its doors. Some of them, skittish, ran away. Others, won over by his arguments, followed him out to the badlands for a more traditional wedding. Others still argued right back, providing some seriously impressive cacophony. I'd never known church to be such a place of chaos.

I left the church with Granny on Sunday morning, and sure enough, Shaman Quick was still standing outside. He squinted his eyes at me in a shrewd glare. He was the sort of guy a rattlesnake had reason to fear.

I'd barely taken a step down the dirt road when the shaman stopped me with a raised hand.

Who do you know who is ill? he signed.

Granny looked on, baffled. To be honest, I felt just as confused.

Do you mean Mr. Takes Flight? I signed back. I'd thought everyone on the reservation knew about that. On the other hand, Shaman Quick spent most of his time in the canyons.

"What is going on here?" Granny asked impatiently.

The shaman said something to Granny in Shoshone. Granny tutted with dissatisfaction.

"Well, then," Granny told me, "you had better lead the way."

Lead the way to what? I looked between the two of them and hoped my bewilderment was apparent. Both Granny and the shaman stared at me unhelpfully. I assumed the shaman wanted to see Mr. Takes Flight. Feeling a bit silly, I started the walk to the hospital.

Both Mr. and Mrs. Takes Flight were bemused at our unannounced visit. We exchanged brief pleasantries before the shaman interrupted abruptly. The shaman held his hands above Mr. Takes Flight's bed and spoke to him in Shoshone. I didn't know what he was saying, but it sounded almost like a rebuke. Aubrey showed up in the middle of the visit and gaped. I wanted badly to ask him what was going on, but didn't think it proper to interrupt.

"He said, 'Go home,' " Aubrey told me later. " 'This hospital won't help you, and you'll die with the same wretched heart you were born with.' "

I couldn't believe the shaman would say something so cruel.

Aubrey was withdrawn and morose at dinner that night. The At Dawn twins played the double-skin drum, but he didn't dance. I sat with him and rubbed his back while he glumly sipped orange juice through a straw. Rafael came over and tried to make light conversation. He probably shouldn't have. Small talk was far from his area of expertise.

The music stopped. I looked around to see what was the matter.

Shaman Quick carried a large, square mirror over to the bonfire. Several men rose from their seats to help him. He yelled at them and they hastily sat down.

He smashed the mirror on the ground next to the firepit.

The whole of the reservation was dead silent.

Wavering, Aubrey got up from his seat. He walked over to the shining shards of glass and knelt among them.

"Tsikkinichi nukkatun," Rafael whispered to me.

Aubrey scooped a mirror shard off of the ground and stood. Stuart Stout had joined him.

"It's the prairie chicken dance," Rafael whispered, his mouth against my ear. "It's a healing dance."

The At Dawn girls pounded on the double-skin drum. Shaman Quick shook glass bells and sang in a voice pitched high in the back of his throat. Aubrey and Stuart danced around the bonfire in stomping steps, their waists bent, Stuart's auburn hair curtaining his face. They held their mirror shards aloft; and when the shimmering surfaces caught the light from the stars and the jumping flames, they flared like burning embers.

Ms. Siomme got up next. Then Mary. Then Reuben and Siobhan Stout and Rosa and Mrs. Summer Rose In Winter. Each one picked up a piece of the broken mirror. Each one danced around the fire with power and purpose. Granny joined them, too; and Dad, and Thomas Little Hawk, and Mr. Red Clay and his mother. Balto, excited by the noise, wove in and out of the dancers' legs. Reverend Silver Wolf stood with Shaman Quick and helped him shake the bells.

Rafael took my hand and pulled me from my seat. I would have gone with him anyway. We walked together to the bonfire and he dropped my hand. I found a mirror shard glimmering on the ground and picked it up. No matter how loosely I clutched it, the glass drew blood. Maybe it was supposed to.

I've never been a very spiritual person. I don't put much stock into Christianity, and I'm not sure how I feel about God.

Mr. Takes Flight's heart started pumping blood again at the end of November. His physician, confounded, took out his pacemaker and stitched up his chest. Two weeks later and Mr. Takes Flight was back on the farm with his sons, hauling winter squash out of the ground.

These things happen sometimes, Dr. Long Way said. It's just science.

7
Protocol

I looked out on the reservation from my bedroom window. The sun's trajectory was low, weak--exquisite, a silver luminary on every surface. Winter crocuses poked out of the ground, childlike and innocent, frost-purple petals fringed with frost-white edges; they grew with the silver ferns in the shadows of the pines and the mudhills, silver-gray spikes brandished bravely like swords. The oak trees had cast off their ostentatious leaves. Bare, dauntless, and proud, they stood as gray monuments against a flawless, snow-white sky.

Not that there was any snow in Nettlebush. It was sixty degrees.

I rolled out of bed and padded down the stairs.

"Put this on," Granny commanded. She yanked a woolen turtleneck sweater over my head.

Dad had decorated the house with fallen pine branches. He liked the Christmas tree look, but didn't approve of the wholesale slaughter of forests. He'd always argue with the guys at the Christmas tree lots: "A pine tree needs one hundred years to grow to maturity. You're cutting down fifty trees every year. What are you going to do when you've run out of trees? Postpone Christmas for a hundred years?"

I went into the kitchen and found Dad sitting at the scrubbed table, humming carols over his bowl of blue corn mush. I smiled at him and shook my head.

"Good luck on your winter exams, Cubby," Dad said.

I let my tongue loll out of my mouth and rolled my eyes far into the back my head. If there was one thing I disliked more than school, it was tests.

But that's exactly what I spent the morning doing. The

schoolhouse was quiet as Mr. Red Clay walked up and down the rows of tables and handed out thick packets of paper. He set the timer on his stopwatch, stood back against the blackboard, and watched us with eagle eyes. There were no sounds but pencils scratching on paper, pages turning, and the occasional cough. Mr. Red Clay said we could leave as soon as we were finished. Better still, school wouldn't resume until February.

"Aagh!" said Aubrey after school, his hands on his head. "The Dawes Act was 1887. I think I wrote 1881--but I *meant* 1887, maybe he knows that--?"

I'd never been a very good student myself. I don't find dates and numbers all that interesting, and when I read, my mind wanders.

I went with Annie back to her house and we baked big mounds of apple dumplings and almond cookies. "Winter's a very big season for us," Annie said, flour dusting her hair and hands. "We've got the Christmas party and New Year's--that's when we trade presents, you know, homemade things. Then we've got the pauwau with the Paiute and the Bear River anniversary in Idaho. And shinny, of course!"

I was especially looking forward to meeting the Paiute. I'd heard so much about our historic alliance with them.

Joseph trudged into the kitchen in jingling bell bracelets and a headband of twigs. I think he was supposed to be a reindeer.

Annie took one look at him and flared up. "*Lila!*"

"Nope," Grandpa Little Hawk said breezily, his ruddy face smiling. "That one was me."

The farmland out west was blanketed in a gold haze, winter stalks of wheat, rye, and barley ripe and ready for the sickles. I went out to the badlands with a willow basket, slow and vigilant. The unstable terrain out there had me paranoid of landslides; but when I saw how easily Balto navigated the chalk and clay, guided by his coyote blood, no doubt, I felt safer by proxy. I pulled the glasswort from the gullies and dug out the sand hiding beneath the crumbling, blue-gray clay. I ground up the plants and the sand and spent my afternoons making glass ornaments for New Year's gifts: a cat for Dad, because he liked cats; a loom for Granny, who boasted the best knitting skills on the reservation. Aubrey liked orange candy and Annie liked mixed tapes. Rafael liked horrible power metal and I bused out to Paldones and bought him the new Nightwish CD, feeling all the while like I owed Gabriel's eardrums an apology. I mailed Kaya a Christmas card and she sent me back a handmade cornhusk doll. I put the doll on my bedside table next to a photo of Mom and Dad and Rafael's orange caltrop.

Construction of the radio tower was finished by the first week of December. Men and women tromped in and out of the studio and sang the songs their grandparents had taught them, or else they played hand drums or elderberry clapsticks. I went into the studio one morning with little Morgan Stout, Lila's friend. The walls were carpeted to absorb sound, the ceiling insulated for acoustics. We played our plains flutes together until afternoon and managed to make two tapes full of material. The old woman in charge of the airwaves beamed toothily at us as we left.

"Do you think I'll ever be a man, Mr. St. Clair?" Morgan asked me, soulful and solemn. "I want to marry Lila, but I'm young still."

I ruffled his hair and gave him a serious look.

Annie and Aubrey and I went to Rafael's house; Aubrey and Rafael fought over the radio dial in Rafael's room until finally, we heard Mrs. Red Clay's calm, impenetrable voice carrying on a conversation with an anthropology professor from ASU.

"No, sir," Mrs. Red Clay was saying. "Shoshone are descended from the same ancestor as the Aztecs. We did not immigrate to America. We have been here since the dawn of time."

"Ah, isn't this exciting?" Aubrey clamored. "First the internet, now the radio! We're conquering the world!"

We went out to the windmill field, where Dad, Mr. Little Hawk, Mr. Owns Forty, and Mr. Black Day were building a wood stage for the children's Christmas pageant. "I played the Black Bear when I was five," Rafael told us. Families traipsed into the field to set up stalls, booths, and tables while Mr. Red Clay sat on the grass with a delegation of small children, assigning them their roles. Annie handed out bottles of water to the men and they rested beneath the whirring windmill blades.

Dad came over and sat with us on the rim of a stone firepit-- thankfully unlit.

"Cubby," he said awkwardly. "Could I have a word?"

I stood up.

"You too, Rafael," he said.

Oh boy.

Rafael and I followed Dad to the other side of a windmill. I could see the isolated Owns Forty house in the distance. Rafael looked apprehensive.

"Now," Dad started. He stopped. He started again. "Rafael, do you play shinny?"

Rafael grinned shyly. I swear my heart stopped. "Who doesn't?"

"You may find it hard to believe," Dad said, "but when I was your age--how old are you?"

"Seventeen."

"Well, a little younger than you, then. When I was a child, boys couldn't play. Imagine how jealous we were."

"That's lame. Aubrey's the best player we've got and he's a guy."

I never would have singled Aubrey out for sportsmanship. Just goes to show you how people can surprise you.

"You see what I mean, then." Dad went on, a bit constrained, "Maybe we'll play together in February."

Rafael checked at that, suspicious. "Sure..."

Oh, Dad. I couldn't help but smile.

Dad suddenly looked sober. What was that about? He shuffled from one foot to the other, his eyes focused elsewhere. Rafael stuffed his hands into his pockets and hunched over.

I rocked on my heels and swung my arms.

"You'll have to forgive me," Dad said. His mouth was moving very little, a sign that he was tense. "I'm not...familiar with...the protocol. For boys like you. But I..."

I felt my face turning red. No, no, no. Quit while you're ahead, Dad. Please.

"I'm sure you have...urges," Dad went on. "All teenage boys have...urges. I don't know whether you've...tried anything--"

I said please!

"Just as long as you're safe. That's very important. You still have to be safe, even if you're both boys. I don't know what that really...um, entails. You know. How you...do things. I could look it up for you--"

I clapped my hand over Dad's mouth. I took him by his arm, my face burning, and dragged him back to the field.

Come Christmas Eve, the windmill field was transformed. The stalls and stage were decorated with garlands and poinsettias. The air wafted with the heady scents of apple dumplings and corn soup, wild rose blossom and wild onions and baked winter squash, fried, sugared strawberries and mutton wrapped in frybread, almond cookies and almond cakes and honey and marzipan cakes. It was fifty degrees outside and we set fire to the firepits long before evening. The kids put on a play about the Sun and the Winter Winds; the Black Bear and the Gray Bear and Wolf, Spider, and Coyote all made special appearances. Reverend Silver Wolf read passages from the Bible about King Herod and the baby Jesus, and Officer Hargrove and her family showed up midway through the festivities.

I'd never seen Officer Hargrove out of uniform before. She looked cute in her Christmas tree sweater and matching light-up pin. She waved and led her kids to the table where Granny, Dad, and I were sitting with the Little Hawk family.

"I brought cookies," Officer Hargrove said. "Don't worry, they're from the supermarket."

"Don't be ridiculous," said Granny, which was her way of showing kindness.

Officer Hargrove's son stuck his hand out for me to shake, formal and militaristic. He was about twelve years old.

"DeShawn," he said very seriously. "How do you do."

I tried not to laugh. I failed. I shook his hand.

"Mommy," said the little girl, pointing down the table, "what's that?"

Dad quickly hid the calumet from view.

Balto snuggled up to me underneath the table. I rubbed his head between my palms. I looked around the lot until I saw Rafael sitting at a table with Rosa, Mary, Gabriel, and the hospital receptionist. I couldn't hear what they were saying, but it looked like the burden of conversation fell on Rosa's shoulders; Gabriel wasn't looking at Rafael.

"Attention, please!" boomed Mr. At Dawn, standing on the edge of a firepit. "It's time for the warm dance!"

Officer Hargrove's daughter pinched my arm. "What's a warm dance?" she asked.

"Jessica," Officer Hargrove scolded. "What did I tell you about Skylar?"

I didn't mind. I rubbed my hands up and down Jessica's arms.

Jessica giggled. "Warm," she said.

"Many years ago," Dad explained, "we lived in a cold place. We danced the warm dance to send blessings to the animals who needed to brave the cold."

"Sir, your history is fascinating," DeShawn said.

"Thank you."

Granny got up from her seat to join the warm dancers. Dad offered Officer Hargrove a beer.

"No thanks," she said. "I'm driving."

"That's alright, it's only Holsten."

"In that case, gimme!"

I watched the dancers branch into groups, Lila tugging Jessica by her hand. It was a simple dance, sweeping bows and raised arms hailing the heat of the flames. I smothered a laugh when Autumn Rose In Winter lost one of her shoes.

Rafael came over and took Granny's empty seat.

"I hate him," Rafael said passionately.

I knew he was talking about his uncle; and I knew he didn't mean it. I glanced over at the table Rafael had abandoned. Gabriel was shaking his head, his face cradled in his hands. Rosa rubbed his back and talked to him in undertones. She kept sending worrisome looks Rafael's way. I didn't see Mary anywhere.

"He acts like I lied to him about you. I told him to shut up. I told him he's not my dad. He said, 'I raised you. If I'm not your father, what am I?' He's not my father. I hate him. I hate him so much."

Rafael wasn't talking about his uncle after all.

I touched his arm. He nodded. We rose from our seats and went for a walk.

We walked past the windmills and between the pines. The ground sloped downward. I'd only been in this part of the reservation once before; over the summer, when I visited Luke Owns Forty.

Rafael took my hand when the festivities were far behind us. I slid my palm against his and threaded our fingers together, the warmth of his tough skin familiar and nonpareil.

"What should I do?"

I squeezed Rafael's hand.

"It's easy for you," he said acerbically. "You just look at someone and they see the kindness in your eyes. No one could stay mad at you. I'm the type of guy you stay mad at."

I shook my head. I thought he was getting carried away. He must have had arguments with his uncle in the past.

"You're the only one who never gets mad at me," he mumbled. "You know exactly what kind of a person I am. But it's like you don't care. You know, you... I don't know. I don't know what I'm saying. You're so... I feel like I'm always thinking about you. I can't stop. I don't want to. What the hell am I even talking about?"

I couldn't say a word. I wanted to--so many things I wanted to say--but couldn't. My words were a deluge; my mouth was the dam. I let go of his hand. He watched me curiously while I carded my fingers through my hair. I pulled my curls taut.

He took my hand a second time, curling it around his.

"I know," he said. "It's okay."

8
Danny

New Year's Day was a Monday. Dad and Granny and I went around the reservation leaving gifts on our friends' doorsteps. We came home to a sizable pile of presents, woven baskets and homemade confectionaries and a really creepy cat poncho I knew was meant for Dad.

"I feel so old," Dad said dejectedly. He was forty.

"Better old than dead," Granny tossed back at him.

Dad pulled me aside later on and put his hands on my shoulders.

"When you go to the farmland to pick up our winter grain," he said, "take a little extra. You're going to bring it with you to the winter pauwau."

I shook my head in protest. I didn't want to leave Dad by his lonesome again.

"You have to," Dad said. "Our Paiute friends are in a bad way. We have to help them when we can. Besides, I want you to see the Bear River memorial. It's important, Cubby. It's part of who you are."

Granny and I woke up at four in the morning on the day of the pauwau. Groggy and disoriented, I dressed in my regalia and packed a fleece jacket and a change of clothes. I looped my plains flute around my neck and tucked a pen and post-it pad in my jacket pocket. "It's a thirteen hour drive!" Granny shouted up the stairs. I felt immensely sorry for Gabriel and Rosa.

I stumbled down the stairs and into the kitchen, my duffel bag over my shoulder. I climbed into the cellar and stacked wicker baskets full of wheat, sugarcane, barley, and rye. I hit my head on the cellar door on the way out.

"Fool boy," Granny dismissed.

We ate a quick breakfast of eggs. Granny packed a fifth basket with sagebread and cornbread for the road.

We walked arm-in-arm to the reservation parking lot, and Balto followed us.

Poor Balto. I would have loved to take him to Nevada, but I didn't think it was a good idea to keep a wild animal in the car for half a day. I knelt between the cars and rubbed my hands along Balto's muzzle. His small, black eyes were honest, simple, and full of love. I know they say you can't domesticate a wild animal; no amount of training will turn a wolf into a dog. But I don't think a wild animal is any less capable of love than a dog is. Or a human, for that matter.

Stay home, I signed. *With Dad.*

Coywolves understand visual cues a lot better than auditory ones. It was almost prophetic that he and I had become friends.

Balto slipped his head out of my hands. He poked around the asphalt and pretended to have misunderstood me.

I nudged him and signed again. *Stay home with Dad.*

Balto huffed and ran back to the reserve. I watched him sprint down the dirt road until his tail dipped around the bend and he disappeared from view.

"So weird," I heard Mary say.

I stood up with my baskets and smiled, bemused.

Mary grinned at me. She swung an arm around my neck. At least she didn't choke me this time.

"You're a kooky kid," she said. "I like that. I like ya."

Flattered, I tousled my hand through the back of her teased hair.

Granny and I put our baskets in the trunk of the SUV and climbed on board. Mary climbed in after me and I found myself squished between her and Rafael. Rosa was in the passenger seat, sound asleep against the window. Gabriel smiled at me through the rear-view mirror. There wasn't any malice in his eyes, but his mouth was sort of tight.

"Everybody comfortable back there?" he asked. I noticed he'd remembered his overcoat this time. "Catherine? Hilde? How about you, Beth?"

"Boy, this car is huge," I heard Ms. Bright say in the back row. She was a friend of Rosa's, a receptionist at the reservation hospital. "How's my makeup?"

The roads and the sky above them were pitch dark, the highway lights still lit. I couldn't make out much of the desert. I looked sideways at Rafael. He blinked drowsily. He took off his glasses and rubbed his eyes with his fist.

"Screw it," Rafael said. He unbuckled his seatbelt, lay across my lap, and went to sleep.

There might be something in that, I thought. My hand sank into his hair and rested against his scalp. I sat back in my seat and closed my eyes.

I woke some hours later when the car passed over a bump in the road. I squinted at the clock on the dashboard. It was 8:33 in the morning. I leaned past Mary and gazed out the window. I nearly jumped out of my seatbelt. The highway was built clean across a huge canyon. Who the heck would build a highway across a canyon? The great russet walls plunged downward for miles. I didn't want to imagine what might happen if a driver lost control of his car and smashed through the flimsy railing.

The radio hummed with the reedy, airy tunes of a plains flute.

"That's my boy," Granny said proudly.

I grinned. It was cool to think that anyone in Arizona could turn on the radio and listen to our station.

Mary rolled down her window. A blast of cold air gushed into the car. I saw her fish a marble lighter out of her purse. She leaned out the window and tried to ignite a cigarette.

"Mary!" Gabriel burst out.

Rosa snorted and jerked awake. She hit her head on the window.

"My lungs are already rotten, Uncle Gay," Mary said, but relented. She tossed her cigarette down the canyon, pulled her head inside the car, and closed the window.

Rafael hadn't even stirred. My thighs were numb, but I couldn't bring myself to move him. I smiled, resigned. I unhooked his glasses from his eyes; I tucked his braids behind his ears. I really was hopeless. I wanted a name for this feeling, the one that made my heart swell and skip and rendered my head stupid. I didn't have one.

Mary and Rosa passed the time playing Fuzz and I Spy. I looked in the rear-view mirror and saw Granny knitting a wool cap.

I took another short nap and woke around noon. "Welcome to Nevada: The Silver State," read a white-and-blue sign. At least the canyons were gone.

"Where the hell are my glasses?" Rafael grunted, slowly shifting upright.

I slid them slyly over my eyes.

"Dumbass," Rafael said, fighting a grin, and stole them back.

We pulled off the road at a truck stop. I was grateful for the chance to stretch my stiff legs. But I was starting to miss Dad. I missed him even more when we stopped in a cramped, dingy diner for lunch. It was exactly the sort of place Dad and I used to visit for Sunday dinners when we lived in Angel Falls.

We met up with the In Winter family and pushed two big tables together. Autumn Rose In Winter wouldn't stop giggling. She was a very excitable girl.

A middle-aged waitress came over to us with a pen in her mouth and a pad in hand.

"Where all you Indians headed?" she asked.

"Las Vegas," said Gabriel, without missing a beat. "We're showgirls."

Rosa drove the car around to the gas station after lunch, Gabriel curled up in the passenger seat for some much-needed sleep. Rafael and I got out to fill the tank while Mary went into the convenience store to buy snacks. Rafael fumbled with the gas nozzle.

"Could you help me with this damn thing?" he said, aggravated.

I snickered at him and didn't bother to hide it. He retaliated with a very rude hand gesture. I took the hose from him, feigning offense, and squeezed the handle.

"Showoff," he grumbled.

A car pulled up at the filling station next to ours. Zeke Owns Forty threw open the passenger-side door and jumped out. William Sleeping Fox was next out of the car--and then Zeke's father, Luke.

Luke Owns Forty had a lean body, a haggard face, and long, curly hair. I wasn't sure what he did around the reservation. Zeke had let slip once that he was an alcoholic.

Mr. Owns Forty took one look at Rafael and twisted his face in disgust. "Great."

Zeke looked nervous.

I hooked the gas nozzle back at the pump. I wrapped my hand around Rafael's elbow and nodded toward the SUV. He made to move forward, like a shadow.

"Where you going?" Mr. Owns Forty called after him. "Can't stand to look at me?"

Rafael hovered uncertainly. My hand tightened around his elbow. I looked back at Mr. Owns Forty and shook my head.

"Your bastard of a father killed my little girl," Mr. Owns Forty said. "Slit her throat from ear to ear. I'm never allowed to forget it. Don't think I'm going to let you forget it."

"Dad, uh," said Zeke, "maybe not now, maybe..."

"Quiet!"

"What's the matter?"

Rosa had joined us.

Mr. Owns Forty squinted at Rosa, like he'd never seen her before. "Nothing," he said. "Doesn't concern you."

"Please don't yell in front of the children," Rosa said. She stood by the driver-side door with her hands folded in front of her. Her braids, knotted with falcon feathers, tossed in the breeze. "Please don't yell at Rafael. He hasn't done anything."

"Yet," Mr. Owns Forty qualified, and got back into his car, leaving

Zeke--who looked terrified--to fill up their tank.

Rafael pulled open the SUV's door with enough force to dislocate his shoulder. He tossed himself inside without a word.

"Has he been drinking?" Rosa asked Zeke.

"Huh? Uh, yeah..."

"Go find Mr. Red Clay and ask him to drive you," Rosa said to William.

William shrugged and shuffled off.

Rosa and I got into the SUV. Gabriel was still sleeping. And Rafael--hatred poured out of him so thickly, it was tangible. I was pretty sure most of it was intended for himself.

I jostled Rafael's arm lightly. *It wasn't you,* I wanted to tell him. *You didn't hurt those women. You didn't kill them. You're not responsible for anything your father did. None of us can help who our parents are.*

He clenched his jaw. He clenched and unclenched his fist.

I took hold of his fist and uncurled his fingers. I lined his fingers up with mine. When he finally looked at me, it was guarded.

"Maybe I should just get plastic surgery or something."

I think he was being serious, but it was such an outlandish solution, I couldn't keep a small laugh from my lips. He smiled back, and I realized that he had wanted that; he had wanted somebody to laugh with him. It wasn't like the past, when he would seclude himself from human contact and stew in his own misery for days.

Mary climbed into the car and threw candy bars on our laps. I hastily let go of Rafael's hand.

We faced another six hours in the car. Granny, Mrs. Threefold, and Ms. Bright attempted to play bridge with only three participants. Rosa tried to start up another game of Fuzz, but Mary was less interested this time around. She told me instead about how she'd played bass guitar for a little-known band called Crunchy Blood out in Los Portales. I don't think Rafael liked her rock 'n' roll stories; he sat fuming, his arms folded, and gnawed in silence on his chocolate.

"Yeah, that was a bad time for me," Mary said. "Needed me some heavy detox shit. Got hooked on practically everything out there. Coke, meth, X, PCP... It's great at first, but then the highs are shorter and shorter. Soon you're taking a hit just to get through the day. Just to forget."

But forget what?

"Everything," Mary said simply.

"He doesn't wanna hear this," Rafael said.

Mary grinned at him, all her teeth visible at once. "Who doesn't?" she said. "Him? Or you?"

I put my hand on Mary's shoulder and squeezed lightly. She looked at me. Unexpectedly, her gaze softened. Her eyes weren't blue like her brother's. They were hazel.

"Raffy told me you were a good kid," she said. "I thought he was exaggerating, you know, had his head up his ass. I mean, you don't talk. How great can you really be?"

I wiggled my eyebrows and smiled impishly.

"Oops, I gotta take a leak. Rosie! Pull over!"

"Mary!" Rafael said, teeth gritted.

It was evening when we arrived at the Pleasance Reserve. The clouds were a gray-violet where they hung above the last of the sun's scattered, gilded rays. Granny and I got out of the car and unloaded our baskets and duffel bags from the trunk. Rafael tapped me on the arm, a folded pendleton blanket thrown over his shoulder.

"Look over there," he said, and pointed west.

Out west was a broad and winding mountain range, tameless and grand, dark and ominous by sunset. Small wonder there was so little light in the ambient sky: The mountains were blocking the sun.

I felt Rafael's chin on my shoulder, his voice in my ear; his arms around my waist. "That's where we come from," he said. "That's the Sierra Nevada."

My heart rushed. Maybe it was foolish of me. But imagine you're standing in front of the very place where your oldest ancestors once lived. What do you think you would feel? I can only tell you what I felt: a sense of overwhelming homecoming. I thought I could hear the ghostly pounding of the double-skin drums rolling off of the mountain range; and if I strained my eyes, I could see them, the ghosts of our ancestors, traveling down the mountainside with their folded tipis and travois, leaving for the Plains; like a child who leaves his parents, stubborn and resolute, but always knows he can come home again.

"It's owned by the government now," Rafael said. "It's a tourist attraction."

A sickly cold spell brought my heart back down to size.

Granny linked her arm through mine, and we walked up to the open reservation gate. I'd noticed something peculiar already in the lot outside: Ours was the only tribe that had come for the pauwau. Where were the Hopi and the Kiowa? What about the Navajo?

I placed our baskets with the mounds of goods already heaped together by the gate. Men and women knelt and left packets of rose tea and sagebrush tea on the ground. Aubrey's family left bags of basil, mustard, lettuce, and chives. Dad had said that the Paiute were "in a bad way." I'd thought he meant a mild grain shortage, or something along those lines. This didn't look like a grain shortage. This looked like poverty.

Granny and I walked onto the reserve. This *was* poverty. The ground was barren and brown, unsuitable for agriculture. I saw big patches of black soil, dug up for farming, and the dead, wilted stalks of crops that had tried their hardest to grow. The houses shocked me as they loomed into view. Back in Nettlebush, we lived in the sturdy log cabins our fathers and grandfathers had built for us. Here there were only dilapidated cob houses and mobile homes.

This may have been the Pleasance Reserve, I thought, but there was nothing pleasant about it.

I changed my mind when we came upon the town center, big and round. A spitting, crackling bonfire towered amid camping tents. And the Paiute, when they saw us, leapt out of their seats and shouted and waved.

The Paiute wore thin brown buckskins decorated with colored grasses and cliffrose bark. The children wore basket hats on their heads. To look at their smiles, no one would have guessed that they were destitute. For a moment, I forgot it, too. The crowds mingled; I lost sight of Rafael. Granny plucked my elbow and tugged me over to a hunched old woman.

"Skylar," Granny said severely. "This is Cora Tonnu, my sister."

I couldn't be certain that Granny meant "sister" in the traditional sense, because Shoshone also consider their cousins to be their brothers and sisters. I'm serious. A Shoshone will invariably introduce his fifth cousin twice removed as his brother. If I'd known whether Paiute were matrilineal or patrilineal, I could have made a more accurate guess as to the real relationship between Granny and her "sister." The woman looked a lot like Granny, I'll say that. But her hair was shorter--only chest-length--and tied in two braids instead of one. Her eyes, too, were a walnut brown.

"No need to be so formal, Cat." Aunt Cora chuckled at me. "You're Paul's boy, eh? Well, give me a hug."

I put my arms around Aunt Cora and she patted the back of my head with her bony hand. I was all too eager to hug her. I'm sure that sounds kind of pathetic, but I'd spent most of my life not really knowing who my extended family were. I was starved for family, in a way.

The Paiute pauwau wasn't at all like the Hopi pauwau, or even our own. There was very little music and even less dancing. We sat around the bonfire sharing stories and jokes instead.

" 'Paiute,' " said a large Paiute woman, "means 'Water People.' And 'Shoshone' means 'Valley People.' So--in a fight, we win. All we have to do is flood your valley."

Everyone laughed at that.

"Not that we've ever fought!" Mr. At Dawn boomed. "Allies to the end!"

A ten-year-old girl in round eyeglasses came and sat next to me, legs folded on the ground. Her hair was thick and black, her nose as small as a button.

"I saw you hugging Grandma," she whispered. "I think we're cousins. I'm Marilu."

I felt more awake than I had all day. I'd never had a cousin before. Marilu smiled at me and I smiled back broadly.

"What's your name?"

I pointed at the sky.

" 'Up'?"

This is the only part about meeting new people that I don't like. I pointed again.

" 'Finger'?"

I dug around in my duffel bag and tried to find my post-it pad.

"No. Sky!" she finally said. "I win. What do I win?"

I offered her the fresh cornbread from my bag.

"But here's why we're really called Water People," the Paiute storyteller continued. "Before the world began, there was a great big flood. Then the Earth emerged from the water. Then us."

"That's not the whole story," a young man accused. "Tell it like it really is."

"Well, alright," said the woman. "Before us, there was the Old Woman from the Sea. She emerged from the ocean carrying a cloth bag over her shoulder. She walked and walked, but stopped when she became tired. Two brothers offered to carry the bag for her. 'Fine,' she said, 'but don't open it until you reach the middle of America.' The younger brother was a fool and opened the bag right then and there. Suddenly...the Paiute came charging out of the bag! And we all ran west! 'You idiots!' the old woman screamed. 'I meant for the Paiute to live in the very best part of the world. Not the desert!' "

I laughed until my eyes blurred and my sides hurt. I really liked that about the Native spirit, the ability to find humor in adversity.

The Paiute men handed out dinner plates of hominy and honey biscuits when the stars came out. I was deeply embarrassed--they shouldn't have to feed us when they were having problems feeding themselves--but I thought refusing would look rude.

"Where's your mom?" Marilu asked.

She couldn't make it, I wrote on my post-it pad. I was really glad I'd brought it along.

"Mine, too," Marilu said. "Mom works in the city. She's going to get enough money to build us a new house. Do you want to come back and see it when it's finished?"

I smiled, touched. I ruffled Marilu's hair. Marilu crossed her eyes at me, her tongue poking out of her mouth.

By the time the pauwau had ended, it was much too late to drive on to Idaho. Some of us went and spent the night in our Paiute friends' houses while others slept in the camping tents. Aunt Cora invited Granny and me to stay with her and Marilu. I could see why Marilu's mom wanted to build them a new home. The linoleum floor was cracked and collapsing, the paint on the walls worn away. The lights flickered unsteadily; and Aunt Cora needed to stuff the windows and doors with towels to keep the howling winds at bay.

Marilu set up a sleeping bag on her bedroom floor. I thanked her with a pat on the head and went into the bathroom to change. When I came back, I found Marilu sitting on her bed, a photograph in hand.

"This is my best friend," Marilu said, and showed me the photograph. "Every night I say good night to Danny."

I sat next to her and examined the photo. The photograph might have been aged a couple of years; it was crinkled around the edges, and Danny looked a lot younger than ten--and deathly frightened of the camera. His eyes were exotic, an olive green. He was wearing a tan blazer and a tie. A school function, I thought.

Marilu's face crumpled. "I wish he'd come back," she said. "I miss him. A lady came to the bus stop after school and took him away. She won't give him back. Danny's father keeps asking her to, but she won't. I miss him."

I felt frozen from the inside out. I remembered what Dad had told me back in September, how social services got away with kidnapping Indian children when white families felt like adopting them.

It struck me, suddenly, that not a whole lot had changed since the 1800s.

I didn't sleep much that night. Granny crept into Marilu's room early the next morning and shook me awake. It was an eight hour drive to Franklin, she said. I *really* felt sorry for Gabriel and Rosa. I'd never been very interested in cars, but I was starting to think I should learn how to drive one, if only to help them with the commute.

Granny and I ate breakfast with Aunt Cora and Marilu in the kitchen, the refrigerator humming noisily, robins singing outside the window above the sink. Aunt Cora kicked her legs cheerfully under the table and Marilu looked at me plaintively. I wondered whether she was thinking about her friend. I ripped a note off of my sticky pad, wrote down my address, and handed it to her. Just because we lived miles away didn't mean we weren't family. Marilu caught on and did the same.

Quietly, Granny left the rest of her sagebread and cornbread with her sister. We said our goodbyes, and Marilu ran out of the house after us, waving until I couldn't see her anymore.

I wanted to ask Granny why Aunt Cora's family couldn't just come live with us. If I'd had a voice, I would have. As it was, she climbed into the back of Gabriel's SUV without a second glance.

My mood lightened considerably when Rafael boarded the car after me. I hadn't seen him at all during the pauwau, which had proven to be a strangely taxing affair. He grunted and squeezed in at my side. There was a tear in his jeans above the right knee, and his sleeveless blue shirt made prominent the chain tattoo coiling up and down his arm.

"You boys are nutty if you think you'll get away with that," Gabriel said from the driver's seat. "It's freezing where we're going. Put your jackets on."

Rafael and I exchanged a look. Well, alright. Rafael's was more of a scowl.

We dove into our duffel bags and pulled on a couple of winter jackets. I probably should have known better to begin with: I'm always at risk for pneumonia, especially when it's chilly out, because my vocal folds can't close and block foreign pathogens. Rafael wrapped his pendleton blanket around his shoulders and shot the back of Gabriel's head a sullen look. Mrs. Threefold sat next to Granny and they argued about the proper way to cure ham. I didn't know the ham was sick. Ms. Bright snored in the back seat, Rosa sipped coffee from a styrofoam cup, and Mary stumbled into the SUV in clunky black boots. We were on the road again in seconds.

I twisted in my seat and gazed out the back window at the Sierra Nevada. I felt like I was saying goodbye to a long-lost friend.

Rafael prodded me with his knuckles. I turned around and smiled at him.

"I had to sleep in a damn tent with Autumn Rose and Prairie Rose," he said. "Don't know why they weren't with their mom. Or their brother. Or Siobhan. Do you know they asked me if I could paint their nails? The hell makes them think I wanna paint their nails?"

I gave him a simpering look, but it wasn't enough to stave off my grin.

"Be serious," he chastised.

Anyone could see that this was a very serious discussion.

"Anyway, I didn't mean to, but I smudged the stuff all over their fingers while I was painting 'em. So there's that. They both hate me now. Do you still have your candy bar?"

Something told me that this trip was going to feel a lot longer than the last one.

9
Taken Alive

The cold air was biting and bleak. It was the kind of cold that pierced right through your skin and bones: sharp, and oddly wet.

The plains beneath our feet were vast and flat. I thought of the grass dance, how Plains People used to trample over the tall and hindersome stalks to pave the way for unencumbered roaming. I saw low hills in the distance; I heard the gurgling of Bear River and Bear Creek as they merged together behind me.

The noon sun was small and feeble, the pearl-white sky heavy with winter.

I looked around the Cache Valley at hundreds of faces I had never seen before. I huddled underneath my fleece jacket. We were dressed in jeans and wool and fleece, in coats and winter hats, but the terrain was unchanged. The land was timeless; it didn't care who stood on it, whether we were ourselves or our ancestors; we were all the same.

A stone monument rose from the ground, obelisk-shaped. I was too far away to read the writing on the bronze plaque.

Rafael stood at my left side and rubbed his arms vigorously. I guess the wool jacket and the pendleton blanket weren't enough to warm him.

I threw my arm around Rafael and he melted into me. His whole body was shivering. I sympathized greatly. In my entire life, I'd never visited any place as cold as this.

"There you are!" I heard Annie say. She joined us, her voice little more than a whisper. There seemed to be some kind of an unspoken rule about how loud we were allowed to talk--if at all. Where was the commemoration speech? Were we waiting for someone?

Annie grasped my right arm. "I haven't seen you in two days!"

I smiled at her. I knew what she meant. It felt kind of like I'd been missing my left leg.

I craned my head and looked around the historic site. It occurred to me for the first time that those people I didn't recognize were fellow Shoshone. Shoshone who lived in Idaho and Utah and Wyoming.

The crowd parted. Granny hobbled up to the stone monument. I wondered whether I was supposed to follow her. I started to, but Rafael held me back, his hand on my hip.

Granny turned around and faced us, her back to the stone monument. I realized, with a jolt, that she was the speaker we had been waiting for.

"My great-grandmother," she said, "was a survivor of the Bear River Massacre. When I was a girl, she told me her story. She continued to tell us her story until the day of her death. 'Never forget your past,' she always said."

Granny cleared her throat, her hands folded, her face impassive.

"Chief Shoots Running was an intelligent leader," Granny said. "In our language, we called him Washakie. Shortly after the Pony Express War, Washakie had the great foresight to understand that if we continued our nomadic way of life, conflict with the white man would only escalate. Washakie decided that we would get out of their way and make a permanent settlement for ourselves. It was during that time that the majority of Shoshone followed Chief Washakie south. We built our settlement on two major sites: Wind River to the east, and Bear River to the west.

"In those days," Granny went on, "my great-grandmother was called Pretty Eyes. She was a young woman of twelve winters. She had yet to choose a husband. She lived on Bear River with her mother and three little brothers, one of whom was an infant. Her father was recently deceased.

"Today, one hundred and thirty-eight years ago, Pretty Eyes woke at dawn and lit a fire outside her wickiup to cook breakfast for her family. She carried her little brother on her back in his cradleboard and his warm swaddling. Suddenly the snowy ground shook beneath her moccasins. And she looked to the hills--"

Granny turned and pointed at the low-lying hills in the distance. I followed her gaze and swallowed, my throat scorched and dry. The plains transformed in front of my eyes. The stone monument was gone; and so were we. The ground was covered in rolling snow and wooden wickiups, in men and women chipping at the frozen surface of the river to catch the fish underneath. In Granny's place stood a little girl warmly dressed in sheepskin, worry on her face, her brother warbling on her back.

"And she saw horses stampeding on the hills, white soldiers sitting in their saddles. The Mormons had decided they wanted Cache Valley for their own."

My heart was hammering. I wasn't sure I wanted to hear the rest. But I knew I had to.

"Pretty Eyes hastened into her home and woke her mother and her brothers. 'Mother,' she said, 'It's the white men. What should we do?' Her mother, who was called Red Summer, showed no fear. 'Run,' was all she said.

"They did not stop to collect their belongings. Pretty Eyes, her mother, and her brothers ran from their wickiup as fast as they could.

"In running, they came upon the wickiup belonging to a boy named Burns Bright. Burns Bright and Pretty Eyes were close friends. Burns Bright was untying his horse from the post outside his house. He unwrapped the warm winter blankets from around his mare. 'Climb on!' he yelled to Pretty Eyes. 'She will take you to the Eastern Shoshone on Wind River. You must ask them to help us.' Then he took up his battle axe and his bow and arrows and ran bravely to the hills.

"Rather than seize the chance to escape, Pretty Eyes and her mother helped the two oldest boys climb onto the mare's back. The boys were crying. 'Ride east to safety,' said Red Summer. 'Chief Bear Hunter is out there with the Eastern Shoshone. We'll meet you on Wind River.'

"An arrow streaked through the air and pierced the horse's flank. The horse gave out a cry of pain and tumbled in the snow, the boys falling off of her back. Pretty Eyes looked over her shoulder with alarm. She saw only two things: the white men on horseback, rapidly approaching, and the snow stained and swimming with blood.

"What human being can outrun a horse? 'We won't make it,' Pretty Eyes said. 'We have to hide.'

"Burns Bright's wickiup suddenly smashed to the ground. On its ruins stood three stallions, white men sitting on their backs. My God, Pretty Eyes thought. They're going to kill us! A battle axe swung through the air. The blade cleaved through Red Summer's head. The little boys began to scream. 'Run!' Pretty Eyes yelled. In their panic and pain, in their confusion, the brothers ran the wrong way.

" 'Not west!' Pretty Eyes yelled. Still, she could not chase after them. She had to run east and get help. She ran as fast as her legs would take her--faster still--pain coursing through her lungs, pain stitching up her spine. Mother, she thought, resisting her tears. I must find Bear Hunter, she told herself. Bear Hunter will save us. I must run east. The wickiups all around her were shattered. The air was rent with screams so horrible, so raw, it seemed to her that they belonged not to humans, but to suffering beasts. She smelled the fire and blood on the air, thick. Snow began to fall anew. The small baby on Pretty Eyes' back was screaming and crying. Pretty Eyes saw a pile of twine on the ground and decided: I will hide my little brother. Even if they capture me, they can't harm him. She unstrapped the cradleboard from her back and tucked the baby underneath the twine, hiding him from view. Then she pulled his swaddling over his mouth to muffle his screams.

"Something hard and round punctured Pretty Eyes' lower leg. Her knees buckled beneath her. She fell to the wet snow. She examined the wound in panic. It was a bullet wound. She knew of bullets only from the stories her late father had told her, about the war with the Pony Expressmen.

"Her blood swam red and black. She forced herself to her feet, pain splintering through her leg. She came face-to-face with the gunman himself, who sat astride a beautiful horse as white as the snow beneath them. How cold the soldier's face was... As cold as the snow itself. As cold as the ice. The ice! The river was frozen! I'll run across the river, Pretty Eyes thought. The horses can't follow me there. They're too heavy. They'll fall through!

"Pretty Eyes adjusted her course and ran south to the river. A second bullet pierced her. This one struck her shoulderblade. The pain was burning and sharp. Still she ran. Another bullet; again to her injured leg. She could run no more. She cried out, tears of frustration filling her eyes. She fell to the harsh snow.

"The soldier on the beautiful white horse shouted something in English which Pretty Eyes did not understand. He dismounted and approached her. She clutched her leg in pain. He descended on her and reached for her leg. He's going to help me, she thought, incredulous. He wrapped his hand around the bullet wound. He crushed her leg in his hand. She screamed and thrashed with pain.

"Two other soldiers had joined their friend. They, too, dismounted from their horses. They spoke to one another in English. Pretty Eyes tried to crawl away. The butt of a rifle crashed down on her arm, stunning her with pain, paralyzing her in place.

"The men rolled her onto her back. They tore off her clothes and took turns with her on the snow, unmoved by her tears. The snow warmed beneath her with her own blood. Suddenly Pretty Eyes understood that these men were going to kill her when they were finished having fun. Her life was of no value to them. Why would they spare her?

"So clever was the girl that she opened her eyes and lay quite still, unmoving, unblinking. She held her breath and feigned death from her injuries. When the last of the soldiers had had his way with her, he laughed and slapped her cheek. Altogether, the three of them mounted their horses and rode away.

"Snow fell upon her eyelashes and into her pretty eyes, blinding her. Bare-breasted, bleeding, she bit the inside of her mouth to spread warmth to her frozen, tremulous lips. She bit the inside of her mouth until she tasted blood. She longed to close her burning eyes, she longed to seek shelter from the burning cold, but she knew she must lay very still in her bed of snow. Her lungs ached with bursting pain, yet she drew only the shallowest of breaths. She knew she must not visibly move lest the white men realize she was still alive.

"Finally Pretty Eyes could no longer hear the screams and battle cries of her kinsmen. But whether they had been captured and subdued, or had managed to run east to Wind River, Pretty Eyes could not say. Deeming it safe, she blinked the snow from her eyes. Her whole body took up tremors only partially attributed to the cold.

"Numb, in every meaning of the word, Pretty Eyes rose sorely on weak and throbbing legs. She arranged her clothing to the best of her ability so that she might preserve what remained of her modesty. The wickiups were gone. The horses were gone. Her village was gone.

"Pretty Eyes saw fire to the immediate west, rising from a circle of covered wagons. My brothers! she remembered. Her brothers had run west. The white men must have captured them. With protesting limbs and newfound strength, Pretty Eyes started in the direction of the wagons.

"But no...what was all this carnage? The ground was strewn with Indian bodies. Not just the men. Women, too, lay on the ground, shot to death, or else beaten to death. So all-encompassing was the carnage that the snow was more red than white. Pretty Eyes pressed her fist to her mouth to keep from crying out. She knew them. The men, the women--she knew them all. She spotted a friend of hers named Silly Spirit, a woman eight months pregnant. Not so anymore. Silly Spirit lay on the ground with her eyes open. Her stomach was cut open. The little baby pulled from its mother's womb lay naked at her side, frozen to death in the snow.

"What was this? This was not a battle. This was a massacre. Pretty Eyes walked in a stupefied anguish through the maze of the fallen. Here was Burns Bright, her best friend, whose throat and chest were riddled with bullets. His weapons were missing. Here was an old man, cut open from chest to belly. Surely this old man had done nothing to provoke the white men? And there, by the river... No. Pretty Eyes ran, staggering, to the frozen river. The riverbank was lined with the corpses of children. It was there that she found her two brothers, their heads dashed open on the rocky ice.

"What was it that prevented Pretty Eyes from screaming her torment to the heavens? Either it was shock, or else it was self-preservation. She did not know which. She stumbled to the cruel white canvases of the covered wagons. She knelt in the unforgiving snow and gazed through the gap between the wagons.

"She saw the white men with their horses; and also with the Shoshone's horses, and the Shoshone's grain, and the Shoshone's weapons and elkskins and sheepskins, and any number of things which the white men had stolen from the Shoshone. Anger pulsed and pounded throughout her body. Her anger did not end there. For there among the wagons was Chief Bear Hunter himself, the young man's arms and legs bound with biting rope. The white men kicked him and laughed at him. His face was bruised, a congealed mess, and his back ran red with blood where he had been whipped. He did not flinch when the white men kicked him. He did not start when they spat on him. The white men sodomized him with their bayonets. He did not scream. His eyes met Pretty Eyes', but he did nothing to alert the white men to her presence. Finally one of the frustrated soldiers ran his bayonet through Bear Hunter's ears. Still he did not scream--not even in his dying moment.

"Pretty Eyes walked through the ruins of her village. There was frost in her hair and on her skin, her lips and her teeth shuddering with cold. Her mother was dead. Her two young brothers were dead. Her friends were dead and her prince was dead. Only she remained.

"That was when she remembered her infant brother, wrapped in his warm swaddling, whom she had hidden beneath the twine. Her heart started with one last hope. She ran through the snow. Her whole body ached and her lungs were empty and her legs were ready to give up, but she ran. She ran, and she found the pile of twine, and she lifted it off of the ground. And there lay her baby brother, pinned to the ground by a knife."

Granny momentarily paused her recount. The imaginary village was gone. I felt myself returned to my body at last. Granny blinked; twin tears rolled down her face. She wiped the tears away with the back of her veined hand.

I wanted to run to her, but I couldn't move. I couldn't get off the ground. I didn't even remember sitting down.

"My great-grandmother walked without stopping. When she could walk no longer, she crawled. At last, she made it to Wind River. Fifty-three other Western Shoshone had sought refuge there among the Eastern Shoshone. They had had the same idea of crossing the frozen river to safety. From a village of five hundred, only fifty-four had survived."

I looked sideways and saw Rafael with his eyes on the Bear River monument, stony and transfixed.

"The Eastern Shoshone considered a retaliation strike. But we were vastly outnumbered and vastly demoralized. 'Violence begets violence,' Chief Shoots Running said. 'At what point does the violence end?'

"The Shoshone were divided by this singular event. Many of the Eastern Shoshone decided to travel farther south to live in proximity with our friends the Paiute. Perhaps the white men would not deign to follow us to the most arid part of the world. Perhaps they would allow us to keep this small piece of our own land.

"My great-grandmother was not called Pretty Eyes anymore. The Plains Shoshone gave her a new name: Taken Alive. Taken Alive traveled with the Plains Shoshone to Arizona on horseback. It was there that she gave birth to my grandmother, Amelia Looks Over, who was always looking over her shoulder with fear, worried that her father would come back and claim her."

My heart felt heavy and cold. My eyes were burning. I didn't cry; but when I looked around me at the descendants of those victims, I saw tears on many of their faces. I spotted Ms. Siomme dabbing her eyes with her knuckles. I looked at the hills that the Mormons had ridden down when they'd decided to ambush the peaceful settlers. I looked at the river where Taken Alive had found her brothers' little bodies. A wave of grief washed over me and rooted me to the ground. Real people. Real people had died in the most horrific ways imaginable. It wasn't just a story. Their scars were passed down from generation to generation; and the blood they had spilled was the blood running in our veins.

"Come," Granny said, gesturing with her hand to the stone obelisk. "Read the monument the white men constructed in our ancestors' honor. But whatever you feel when you read it, you must remember that feeling from this point forward. Never forget your past."

One by one, the men and women went up to the plaque to read the inscription. I couldn't decipher the expressions on their faces when they turned away.

Rafael, Annie, and I got off the ground. We walked over to the monument to read what it said.

The Battle of Bear River was fought in this vicinity on January 29, 1863. Col. P.E. Connor led 300 California volunteers from Camp Douglas, Utah against Bannock and Shoshone Indians guilty of hostile attacks on emigrants and settlers.

My face was cold to the touch. Every nerve felt numb. I sat at the little brown table in the cafe and listened to the clinking of spoons in teacups, and the murmuring of my friends as they read from the lunch menu.

Rafael slid into the booth at my side. He jostled my shoulder gently. I smiled.

"Stop that," he said. "Don't smile if you don't mean it."

I shrugged, shoulders slouching.

"I know how crappy it feels," he said. "My mom and dad have been bringing me here since I was a baby. I think I was eight or nine before I really understood what it was about."

I looked at him skeptically.

"Alright, ten," he conceded gruffly.

A real smile, or the start of one, found its way to my lips. He smiled back.

Gabriel, Rosa, and Mary sat across the table from us. A frosty window at our side looked out on the small town streets. Granny was elsewhere in the cafe, at a table with her friends. I didn't want to bother her, but I wanted badly to talk to her about the story she had shared with us today. Then I remembered: I can't. I can't talk to anyone. Funny how I still forgot that sometimes.

"Sky, what do you want for lunch?"

I pointed at the eggs on the menu.

The five of us ate in silence, the events of the day still fresh on our minds. Not a whole lot had changed since the 1800s, I thought again. I don't mean to imply that there were massacres out on the street corners everyday. But in a more subtle way, weren't Natives still being oppressed by their own country's government? I thought about the outrageous plaque sitting on top of the Bear River site. I thought about Marilu's missing friend. I thought about how it had taken eleven years to get any justice against Mom's killer. Dad should have been here right now. Bear River was his history as much as mine. Dad didn't deserve to be confined to the reservation for the rest of his life.

My poor Dad, I thought, weighted with sorrow. I couldn't imagine what it must have felt like when he realized that the man who had murdered his wife was his closest friend. It struck me as poignant that Dad had gone to such lengths to avenge Mom even though he and she had been on the brink of divorce. Why had they separated? Dad had loved her dearly. I knew that. Hadn't Mom loved him back? What made people fall out of love? What made people fall into love?

"Try these," Rafael said, and pushed his plate of hash browns at me.

We all gathered outside the cafe after lunch. We met up with Aubrey's family on the sidewalk, Mr. Takes Flight swinging Serafine by her arms. I think the pedestrians were staring at us. Rosa and Gabriel went around the block where they had parked the car. Mary stood chatting with Aubrey's brother, Isaac.

I felt oddly heavy, like the full force of gravity had conspired to pull me between the cracks in the asphalt. We needed a voice. And maybe, if I were a little braver, I would have provided that voice. Except I didn't have a voice to begin with.

"Are you still upset?"

Rafael came and leaned against the brick wall at my side. I smiled wryly at him.

"You're too soft," he said, disgruntled. "That's the problem with you. You'll let it eat away at you and you'll lose sleep. Then you'll get a fever and you'll have to go to the hospital. Again. Do you even know how much that freaks me out?"

I looked sideways at him, affectionate. *I'm sorry*, I signed.

"Yeah, well, don't be. Just take better care of yourself."

Serafine broke free from her grandfather's arms and ran in and out of the crowds of Plains People. Rafael chased after her. I laughed when he caught her around the waist and she tried to climb up his side. He carried her back to her family and said something to her that sounded like a rebuke. She sure didn't look scared of him. And who would be? Once you learned that his dark and hulking exterior belied a gentle heart, it was impossible to fear him. It was impossible not to love that heart. I loved his heart. I loved him.

I loved him.

A dam inside my own heart opened up, and the feelings of heaviness and unease lifted like wind against the winter sky. I loved him. I loved his slow wit and his gruff demeanor and his tender disposition. I loved his endless empathy and his world-weary cynicism and his innocence. I loved that he was a walking, breathing paradox. I loved his lank hair and his iron earring and the tooth missing at the back of his mouth. I loved the way he laughed, music incomparable to any song, and the way he smiled, like you could see the child in him and the animal in him and the man in him all at once. I loved that he listened to crappy music, the kind that made me want to put my head through a wall, and I loved the charcoal stains on his knuckles and the pencils he tucked behind his ears. I loved that he told me to shut up as though I could actually say anything. I loved that he made me feel as though I could. I loved his short fingers and his rough palms and his long legs and his flat belly. I loved that he liked to read Kerouac but didn't know how to pronounce Kerouac. I loved his brown skin and his blue tattoos and his tempestuous blue eyes. I loved that he loved the land. I loved him. I loved him. Oh, God. I loved him.

Something soft and lace-white fluttered on my eyelashes. I tilted my head back and looked up at the sky.

It was snowing.

11
And That's No Tall Tale

Dad and I sat on the front porch together. Dad's rocking chair
creaked as he slit open a thick brown envelope and read my report
card. I watched Balto burrowing for winter mushrooms under the
pinyon pines and laughed fondly.

"You got a few A's," Dad said, sounding astounded.

I was just as confused. In the past, my grades had only ever
averaged between mediocre and lousy. Maybe Mr. Red Clay was
just a really good teacher.

"I think that deserves an ice cream trip," Dad said. He rose from
his seat. He stopped, remembering himself; he bit his lip. He sat
back down.

I frowned at him.

"Well, we'll make our own. I'm sure Dad's recipe is still around
here somewhere. Come on, Cubby."

With interest, I followed Dad into the house. I left the door open
in case Balto got tired of excavating. Usually Dad never talked
about his father. The most I'd heard about Grandpa was from
Granny, who only ever described him as "to be respected" and
"Apache."

Dad led me into the kitchen and opened the cabinets above the
wood-coal stove. "He was a very, very strict man," Dad said. "He
and Mother were...well-suited for each other, to say the least. He
taught us quite a lot about scouting. The Apache take pride in that,
you know, topography skills." Dad pried a fat recipe book out of
the cabinet. "He taught us to play the Apache fiddle, too; Julius
loved..."

I smiled ruefully and cupped Dad's shoulder. Expertly, reticently,
Dad dropped the subject. He flipped through the thick, musty

pages of the old book and stopped on a page catalogued with a strip of blue paper.

"Here we are." Dad smiled very briefly. Most of his smiles were brief. "Let's see... What's a whisk?"

We read Grandpa's recipe together and I climbed down into the cellar to get the sour cream. Dad went nuts trying to find the sugar and the cocoa powder. He really *didn't* know how to whisk. I probably shouldn't make fun of him, considering how clueless I was when I first came to Nettlebush, but he got chocolate goop all over the place; the walls, the counter, my clothes. He managed to look politely dumbfounded while casually destroying the kitchen. I tried to correct his grip twice but gave up when he got the whisk jammed in the wood-coal burners, don't ask me how. I knocked my elbow playfully into his and shook my head. We covered the glass bowl and put it in the cellar to cool.

We sat together on the kitchen floor and waited for the ice cream to harden. Dad surprised me with another smile. "It was rare," he said, "but your grandfather could be very funny. He had this one joke... I don't think I should tell you, it's really not proper..."

Now I had to hear it. I elbowed him again.

"Well, alright. Three old men are sitting in a train station. One is Apache and the other two are white. 'Earl,' says one of the white men, 'where are you going for vacation this summer?' 'Well, Bob, I think I'll go to Arizona,' Earl says. 'What do you want to go to Arizona for?' says Bob. 'There's nothing but a bunch of Indians down there.' 'Where are you going this summer?' Earl says. 'I'm going fishing in Montana,' Bob says. 'You moron,' Earl says, 'there's nothing but a bunch of Indians in Montana.' Finally the Apache man speaks up. 'Why don't you both just go to hell?' he says. 'There aren't any Indians down there.' "

I crammed my hand against my mouth and laughed. I heard Dad's understated chuckle and knew, despite appearances, that he was laughing with me.

"Racine liked that one, too," Dad said.

I shot him a quick look.

Dad looked uncomfortable. "She visited... While you were at the pauwau. It was nice to have some company."

I didn't doubt that. I just hadn't realized that Dad and Officer Hargrove were on a first name basis.

My thoughts carried me away. If Dad and Officer Hargrove started dating... I wasn't one of those proprietary types who can't handle it when his single dad brings home a woman. If he was happy, I was happy.

I'd always thought Dad and Mom were happy together.

"I'm a difficult person to love, Cubby," Dad said grimly. "I'm sure you find it easy, but you have to, you poor kid. You have no choice. I think it was hard for Christine. I think it's hard for anyone raised outside our culture to adjust to a people who prefer to keep their hearts private. Please don't blame your mother for that."

It was one of the few things Dad and Rafael had in common: They always knew what I wanted to say. Each one only had to take a look at me to know what I was feeling. In Dad's case, it was probably that he had known me all my life and grown accustomed to my personality. In Rafael's case... I couldn't explain what it was, because it was instantaneous. I liked that I couldn't explain it.

My stomach churned pleasantly. Rafael had worn his hair in a ponytail at school today. He'd sucked on the lead tip of his pencil while muddling his way through logarithms. Were we really going to need logarithms in real life? I'd thought the pencil thing was kind of gross, and apparently he had, too, because he'd started coughing. I'd rubbed his back and he'd shown me a grateful, unwitting look. One of those "Oops, I don't understand basic safety procedures without trial and error" looks. I liked the feel of his back beneath my hand. I liked that innocent look. I loved that innocent look. I loved him.

So this was what it felt like to fall in love. Stupid and giddy and floating, unfailing, invincible. But mostly stupid.

Dad inspected me in silence. I had the feeling he knew exactly what was going through my mind. There was very little I could hide from him.

Dad checked his wristwatch and stood up. "The ice cream should be ready now," he said.

We retrieved the ice cream from the cellar and sat at the kitchen table. Two spoonfuls in and I was ready to hurl. Dad choked and spat his out. "Oh, God," he said, wiping his mouth. "Did we forget the vanilla?"

"What did you do to my kitchen?!"

Granny was home.

Dad and I cleaned up around the kitchen while Granny supervised, eyeing us distrustfully. I took a quick bath and changed my clothes. I realized I hadn't checked my e-mail in a while; I went into the front room and turned the computer on. Balto had tired of his outdoor excursion and lay curled up by the closet door. I gave him a quick pat on the head.

My first e-mail was from Annie.

From: alilhawk@nettlebush.com
To: stclair@nettlebush.com
Subject: Sales

Hi, Skylar! Guess what? Sales have picked
up. I don't know what did it, really. (Log

in and see for yourself!)

What do you think we should do with the
money now that Mr. Takes Flight is all
better? I suppose we could keep it. It
might be nice to have some pocket cash
without bothering the tribal council. Meet
me at the grotto tonight and I'll give you
your share.

Love,
A

The next was from Kaya, my friend from the Navajo reservation.

From: kaya.tseyi@3suns.net
To: stclair@nettlebush.com
Subject: Re: package

thanks for the cookies. you're a doll.
p.s. do you have mary GL's phone number?

And my most recent e-mail was from Rafael.

From: rgiveslight@nettlebush.com
To: stclair@nettlebush.com
Subject: (no subject)

hey
ok i cant figur ot how this thing woks
wors
works

nhyway the shinny tourament is cokming up
soon and if you're gonna play you need to be

```
on a team

your dad sad somethng about playing togethe
or whatever

ayway i play with holly and daisy ad when we
can get mre people we compete

10 people=team

so you me holly daisy your dad=5
we ned 5 more
aubreys always taken hes the best player
dont ask asnnie she sucks ive seen her play
my grandma coud kick her ass and shes dead

ahwyay yuo should come to the lake tmroeow
tomoreow
tomorrow
fck

this isk stupid im coming over
```

Coming over? Wait. When?

The knock at the front door served as my answer. I looked toward the door, baffled. I turned off the computer monitor, rose from my chair, and opened it.

Rafael was wearing a lightweight gray jacket and black jeans. I liked it when he wore gray. A single, thin braid hung alongside his temple, knotted at the bottom with a dove's feather. His square glasses rested low on the bridge of his nose; he pushed them up with his index finger. The early evening sky was rosy and gold over his shoulder. I took a moment to admire the sky; but mostly I was admiring Rafael. I stepped back and let him inside. I closed the door.

The air crackled with heat. Of course, the hearth was lit. But the way Rafael looked at me, his eyes eddying storms, expressive and all-consuming, I wasn't so sure.

"Your hair's wet," Rafael said.

I don't know which of us reached for the other first. He locked me fiercely in his arms and I buried my fingers in his shirt. I kissed him like my life depended on it. He kissed me back, hard, bruising, his sharp teeth scraping against the inside of my mouth. The feel of him; the taste of him; I drank him up, intoxicating as he was, and my heart thundered and blissfully ached. I kissed him until I couldn't breathe; and when I couldn't breathe, I kissed him still.

My hands rested on his chest where I felt his pulse racing beneath my palms. His lips, hot, rested on my forehead. It was scary, I thought, to love somebody this much. To fall into him so completely, I couldn't remember who I was, unless, in that moment, I was a part of him.

I loved him, I thought. Good thing I could never tell him. I wasn't much for humiliating myself.

The next afternoon was mild and chilly. Dad and I went down to the lake, Balto following, sniffing at the soil, and we met up with Rafael and the At Dawn twins. I don't know if you've ever seen those weird, theatrical Tragedy and Comedy masks--the one mask bawling its eyes out, the other mask cackling at its twin's plight-- but they could have been lifted wholesale off of Holly and Daisy's faces.

"What the hell is she doing here?" Rafael asked.

I'd brought Annie with me.

Annie drew herself up with indignation. "Oh, I'm not wanted, am I?"

I gave Rafael a pleading look. I knew he'd said that Annie wasn't any good at sports, but how was I supposed to tell my best friend to sit on the sidelines and watch? Besides, I didn't know that I was any good at sports, either. I'd never even heard of shinny until a few months ago.

Sulkily, Rafael relented.

"Hi, you guys!" Daisy said brightly. "I've got the tapikolo."

She held up a buckskin sack filled with what I thought were pine nuts.

I'm sure you've heard of hockey before. Well, it turns out the Shoshone have been playing it long before anyone else.

Shinny is a high-speed game played between two teams of ten people. In the days of the buffalo, only women were allowed to play--probably because the Shoshone society used to be so female-oriented--but nowadays anyone of any age can participate. The objective of the game is to get the tapikolo across the enemy team's white line. The first team to succeeds wins. In that regard, it sounds like a simplified form of hockey. But actually, as I learned that afternoon, shinny is much, much harder. A tapikolo doesn't roll like a ball or slide like a puck: It's up to the player to smack it along the ground with little or no traction. The stick you use to hit the tapikolo isn't J-shaped, like a hockey stick, but straight as a ruler, which makes it even harder to strike your target. And if you bust open the tapikolo or knock it into the lake, your whole team loses.

The five of us went into the woods to pick out our sticks--because as it happens, the "stick" you play shinny with is just whatever branch you find lying around on the forest floor. We regrouped by the lake some minutes later and started practicing.

Rafael was right about Annie's skills, or lack thereof. A minute into the game and she whacked the tapikolo up into a tree.

"Is that good?" Annie asked excitedly.

I didn't know for sure, but my gut instinct was, "No." I gave her a thumbs up anyway. I hated to see her disappointed.

Two minutes into the game and the tapikolo splashed into the lake. Dad fished it out of the shallow, muddy bank.

"Maybe you should aim left next time," Dad awkwardly advised Annie.

She did--and the buckskin sack rocketed through the air and slapped Rafael across the face. He staggered. Holly cheered up.

Annie, I signed. *Be gentler with the thing. Pretend it's Joseph and you're trying to get him to go to bed.*

"Are you suggesting that I hit my little brother with a stick?"

The rest of the practice session didn't really deviate. The highlight of the afternoon was when Balto ripped the tapikolo out from under Holly's feet and tore it open, pine nuts spilling on the ground. Holly frowned at him. "He's off the team," she declared.

Daisy clapped her hands when we had finished playing. "Okay!" she said. "That was...good...? But we still need four more people, or we can't compete. Same time tomorrow!"

Annie, Daisy, and Holly split up and went home. Rafael lingered.

"Mr...uh...Looks Over?" Rafael scuffed at the ground with his shoe. "My uncle wants to know if you can look at our basement. He had to pull up the floor and he thinks the joists are rotted."

Dad looked a little surprised. "Of course," he said. "He's home during the afternoons?"

"Yeah, he hunts in the morning. He should be home now."

"I'll pay him a visit, then."

I waved after Dad as he walked through the trees and left us.

Rafael grabbed my arm and leaned over urgently.

"It's bull," he said. "I know my uncle. He just wants to talk about you."

Me? My eyebrows knitted together.

"You and me, dummy."

Well, that made more sense.

"Yeah, so guess what? He sat me down last night and gave me a big talk. He doesn't have a problem with you being a guy. He has a problem with you being you."

It was the last thing I'd expected Rafael to say. I couldn't help but feel a little hurt. I liked Gabriel. I'd assumed he liked me, too.

"Not that," Rafael said. "Just... He thinks it's weird. Because of my dad. And your mom."

Oh, I thought.

No, wait. What did our parents have to do with anything? We weren't our parents. We shouldn't have to carry around their stigmata for the rest of our lives. Especially in deciding who we loved.

I thought: I love Rafael. I don't know that he feels as strongly as I do. He doesn't have to love me back.

Somehow that hurt worse than Gabriel's reproach.

"He's like...'I thought you were just friends.' You *are* my friend. You're my best friend. Why doesn't he get that? Anyway... I think he wants your dad to rally with him. I'm pretty sure he doesn't give a damn about the dry rot in the basement."

I quirked the corner of my mouth dubiously. Dad rallying with Gabriel was pretty unlikely, considering the lengths he had gone to in proving his approval.

Rafael took one look at me, horrified, and I knew we were on the same wavelength. He whispered: "If your dad gives my uncle the safe sex talk..."

I was tempted to run after him and make sure he didn't.

The community gathered around the firepit for dinner as they did every evening. Annie caught my eye and I nodded. I ate quickly and followed her out to the grotto with Rafael and Aubrey, Balto loping after us. The sky was dark, but the cave was darker; we sat in the cave and lit candles. I kept a wary eye over Balto as he strode in and out at his own discretion. Thrusting his curious nose into the middle of a burning flame was exactly the kind of thing the little ditz might do.

Rafael and Annie were feuding. Rafael maintained that Annie was a lousy shinny player and Annie told him, very evenly, where he could shove his shinny stick if he so deigned. Aubrey, bless his heart, was oblivious.

"I got three offers already!" Aubrey jabbered. "I don't know which team to go with this year. Then again, Lorna's built like an ox, she's bound to win--"

"No, she's not," Annie said. Her eyes were sparkling. "I'm going to win."

Oh, Annie. I reached sideways and hugged her.

"Oh?" said Aubrey, rising to the challenge. "Is that so, Miss Little Hawk?"

"Yes, it is, Mr. Takes Flight." She leaned in close. "And you had better watch yourself out there; I won't be giving you any special favors."

Rafael stuck his finger in his mouth, mockingly, but actually wound up gagging.

Shinny fever abounded even at home. Dad had yet to return from his trip to Gabriel's house. Granny took me into the kitchen and showed me how to make ice cream the right way. "Because your father's filled your head with enough nonsense in one lifetime," she said. Happily, the ice cream tasted a lot better with Granny at the helm. Maybe Dad and I really had forgotten the vanilla. We sat by the hearth, chilly as it was outside, and ate together, and Granny told me all about her own forays with shinny.

"When I was a girl," Granny told me, "I was the best player on the reservation." An irritable expression crossed her face. "Second best," she stipulated, rather like the words were poison. "That little Betty Thorn Bush always had to show me up; the nerve of her... Anyway, I could kick the ball from the lake all the way out to the flourmill, and that's no tall tale!"

Talking about the past made me think back to Granny's great-grandmother. The smile slipped slowly from my face. I reached across the rocking chair and squeezed Granny's hand. I meant to lift the burden from her heart, or to provide some solidarity...but Granny wasn't as well-versed in body language as Dad and Rafael were.

"Very well," she said sternly, drawing herself up with magnanimity, a true Indian princess. "I will join your team."

Well, I thought, that's one more player we can stop searching for.

Granny went to bed before me. I brought our bowls into the kitchen and washed up. I could hear the owls outside the window, the coywolves in the trees. I wondered if Balto longed for the family he'd never known, the mother that had rejected his litter and the brothers and sisters who hadn't survived the wild. When I thought about it, I felt terribly sad for him. Maybe I was too sensitive; I don't know. But I couldn't imagine growing up without my father.

A pile of yellow papers on the kitchen table caught my eye. None of my business, I told myself. I started to turn off the oil lamp; but Dad walked in at that moment, looking weary.

Was something the matter? I tilted my head.

"Your boyfriend's uncle," Dad said, "is overcompensating."

He sat down at the kitchen table. I dug the ice cream bowl out of the icebox and passed it to him. I got him a spoon out of the drawer next to the stove.

"Thank you." He gripped the spoon with his pawlike hand. "He'll come around," Dad said. "I imagine he's in a difficult position. He was very young when he started looking out for Rafael. He must feel as though he's got something to prove."

I sat down, elbows on the table, chin in my hands, and smiled gratefully.

Dad dropped his spoon in the bowl and pulled the stack of papers toward him. "I forgot about these. Good thing I didn't just go upstairs..."

I raised my head. Dad took one of the papers from the pile and folded it over neatly, like a booklet. He set it aside. The Shoshone tribal insignia in red ink gleamed off of the back of the yellow paper.

Oh, no. I dropped my head into my hands, exasperated.

"I'm not going to stop helping people into this country just because I can't leave the reservation."

Dad was a "coyote"--a smuggler who specializes in sneaking people into the US. In the old days, when I went to school in Angel Falls, Dad used to trek out to the desert and guide immigrants across the wilderness. He knew all the gaps and weak spots in the border fence by heart. He charged his clients an unusually low fee because, as he always said, "These people don't have much to begin with." But because he took dozens of families across the desert at a time, he made anywhere between $2,000 and $8,000 in a day.

I didn't care about the money. I used to sit in class and stare at the clock on the wall, counting down the hours until the end of the day, sick with worry that Dad might have been shot to death by border patrol.

I looked at Dad beneath my eyebrows.

"I know what you're thinking, Cubby." I didn't doubt that. "But forgery isn't one of the Seven Major Crimes. The FBI can't punish me for mailing fake tribal passports to immigrants. Only the tribal council can do that, and honestly, I'm sure Meredith shares my stance on this."

So he was just going to take his chances? Because the FBI had swarmed in here once before without regard to the law.

"Cubby," Dad said, in his "I'm tired, damn it, don't argue with me" voice. "I don't think you understand what these people go through. The US has a quota, you see. Very few people are allowed to immigrate legally, and when they are, the process takes years. Some families can't afford to wait years when their children are hungry. The government takes 20% of applicants and turns the rest away. What happens to the remaining 80%? Do they just sit at home and watch their children die because they can't find work in their own country?"

Of course I didn't want children to die. When he put it that way, I felt guilty for even questioning him.

"Besides," Dad murmured. "This was my country first. I have the right to decide who lives in it."

Dad, Granny, and I went down to the lake the next day and met up with the At Dawn twins for shinny practice. Rafael and Annie joined us a short while later. Annie had brought Lila with her. Lila gave me a patronizing look.

"We still need two more people," Holly said dully.

"Say no more, 'cause here I am!"

I recognized that voice even before I saw its owner's face. I guess Rafael did, too, because I heard him groan.

Zeke Owns Forty came walking through the trees, a spring to his step. His long hair, combed to one side, hid half of his frantic and giddy smile.

"Zeke volunteered," Daisy said, grinning.

"I'm not playing on the same team as him," Rafael said.

"Never mind that," said Annie, "I'm not playing on the same team as William." She lifted a delicate eyebrow at Zeke. "You *didn't* bring William, did you?"

"Nah," said Zeke, "William can't play shinny without falling asleep." He bounced on his heels and clapped his hands. "When do we start?!"

We practiced batting around the tapikolo for a while, some of us very visibly unenthusiastic about the arrangement. Granny surprised me by showing off how fast she could run: faster than me, for sure, and about twice as fast as Dad. Daisy came up with the strategy of using the speedier players--Granny, Zeke, and me-- to steal the tapikolo from the opposing team and pass it along to the heavy hitters--Dad, Holly, and Rafael. Annie's official job was to "guard the white line," which really just meant that Daisy wanted her out of the way. Lila was more interested in whacking Zeke's posterior with her stick.

"Aubrey's on Shy Lorna's team," Holly reported. "We're going to lose."

"Would you stop being so doom and gloom?" Daisy said. "Brains over brawns!" Then, puzzlingly, she made a muscle with her arm.

"You have no brains," Holly said. "All the brains went to me when we were stuck in the womb together. It was a consolation prize."

"Oh, *that's* why your head's so humongous."

Once the At Dawn twins started bickering, there wasn't any stopping them. Practice was over for the day.

Rafael and I walked down the forest path together. Zeke was at our side, swinging his arms. Dad and Granny had gone to Mr. Marsh's house; Annie and Lila were off in the woods looking for the veined white woodsorrels where the butterflies laid their eggs. I was eager to get home to Balto, especially because he'd developed the habit of leaving dead ferrets on our porch.

I was about to invite Rafael over when Zeke tucked his hair behind his ear, and then I saw it--a huge, purple-black bruise covering the left half of Zeke's face.

"What?" Rafael said. I'd stopped walking.

I think Zeke realized that I had seen something he didn't want me to see. He untucked his hair and muttered quickly that he had to study. He ran down the rest of the path without us.

Zeke studying anything was about as likely as me becoming a butcher.

"The hell was that about?" Rafael asked.

It might have been nothing. Zeke's best friend was a guy who preferred punching to talking. Zeke himself wasn't very different. Maybe they were rough with one another. Maybe it was nothing.

Maybe it was Zeke's father, drunk and angry and wrought with misaimed grief.

The Shoshone ideal is to mind your own business. You don't pry into other people's affairs, and you don't start conflict when it's avoidable.

I watched Zeke's receding back. I wondered how on earth I was supposed to broach the subject with him when it wasn't the lack of vocal cords standing in my way.

12
Lightning and Thunder

My favorite social worker came back for a visit in February.

I heard Balto barking and peeked out the front window. I saw Ms. Whitler standing on the porch, three handbags hanging off of her shoulder. I turned around and waved quickly at Dad. He bolted out of his chair, scooped Balto into his arms, and ran up the stairs to hide.

Granny rose from her rocking chair as I opened the door.

"So nice to see you again!" Ms. Whitler invited herself in. "Brr, isn't it cold outside? It was fifty degrees when I woke up this morning."

Granny said something to me in Shoshone, which I recognized as: "Stall her." She slipped past us and out the door.

I closed the door and gestured Ms. Whitler into the kitchen.

"Ooh, thank you," Ms. Whitler said when I handed her a cup of rose tea.

How was your holiday? I signed.

"Good, good!" Ms. Whitler set her mug down. "We had a big ol' office party on Christmas Eve. What did you do for the holidays?"

I went to a pauwau, I signed. "Pauwau" is one of those words you have to spell out; I don't think anyone invented a sign for it. *And Bear River.*

"Bear River? That's not around here, is it?"

It's in Idaho.

"That must have been fun!"

It was sad, actually. But I saw snow for the first time, and that was
pretty cool.

"Honey, listen, I grew up in West Virginia. I could tell you a thing
or two about snow."

Granny walked into the kitchen, closely followed by Mrs. Red
Clay.

Mrs. Red Clay was a member of the tribal council--more like the
chairwoman, if we're going to be honest--and, as her name might
indicate, Mr. Red Clay's mom. She must have given birth to Mr.
Red Clay at a pretty young age, though; despite her heavy jowls
and her gray-white hair, she was only in her fifties. She had no
sense of humor to speak of, but she was the second coolest person
on the reservation. Granny was the first.

Ms. Whitler's eyes hardened. "Who's this?"

"Miss Whitler," said Mrs. Red Clay, "I regret to inform you that
you are no longer the boy's case worker. I'm afraid you'll have to
leave the reservation."

Ms. Whitler took a sip of her tea. "Who says?"

"I say. I am the boy's attorney."

I sat back in my chair, stunned. Well, I thought, that's kind of neat.
I've never had an attorney before.

Silence stretched among the four of us. Ms. Whitler let out a
plastic, bubbling laugh.

"Oh, alright," she said. She rose from her chair and collected her
handbags. "I know when I'm not wanted. No, really! It's fine!"

Bewildered, I watched her storm out of the kitchen. I listened to
the front door slamming behind her on her way out of the house.

Balto tumbled down the stairs and into the kitchen. He rose on his hind legs and braced me with his paws. I tousled his floppy ears between my hands. I looked to Mrs. Red Clay with a confused frown.

Mrs. Red Clay's face betrayed nothing. "We had better hope the new social worker signs the adoption papers," she said, "or this will have been a waste."

That wasn't very inspiring.

Mrs. Red Clay chatted for a while with Granny. She didn't stay very long. Granny saw her to the font door and sighed when she had gone.

"If I didn't love you so much, I'd let that little hussy take you wherever she wants. She's infuriating!"

I was incredibly flattered.

Granny sat down at her loom. Dad sure was taking long upstairs. I considered running up and retrieving him, but then I remembered that I'd wanted to ask Granny something. I reached over and tapped her wrist.

"Yes?"

I made fists in the air--like gripping a steering wheel--and mimed driving.

Granny raised her eyebrows at me. "You? Learn to drive? Is that such a sensible idea?"

I couldn't see how it wasn't. I wasn't mentally handicapped. Just mute.

A really unsettling thought occurred to me just then. A lot of people--generally people outside of the reserve--treated me like I was a small child when they found out I couldn't talk. I didn't blame them; even now I think it's a natural reaction, if not a very nice one. "Infant," after all, literally means "unable to speak." But what about Granny? She was my grandmother; we'd lived together for almost a year. She didn't really think I had the mental facilities of a small child, did she?

"Fool boy. You're terrible with directions! I don't trust you to navigate a parkway."

I breathed with relief.

The shinny tournament took place on a Sunday. About twenty teams had signed up, and the result was that the whole of Nettlebush came down to the lake to watch the matches. I hadn't realized shinny was so community-centric. Families laid checkered picnic blankets on the ground and ate their lunch in the wide open clearing. Mary jumped up and down and clapped and shouted obscene cheers.

Daisy pulled our team to the side, wincing apologetically. "So, uh, the only other person willing to join the team was Immaculata..."

I looked over at Immaculata. She had a fierce look of competition on her face, her shinny stick resting over her shoulder like a rifle.

I waved at her. She perked up and waved back.

We sat on the grass and watched the first few matches. Rosa's team--mostly made up of nurses and orderlies from the hospital-- got knocked out in the first round. Likewise, Joseph, Jack Nabako, and Morgan Stout lost to a group of fifty-year-old farmers.

"This is prejudice!" Jack screamed.

"Told you he's annoying," Rafael said to me, a smile fighting its way onto his face.

Dad sat at my side, his knees raised and his somber face as

inexpressive as ever. Suddenly he lifted his arm and waved. I followed his gaze, intrigued. I saw Officer Hargrove and her kids coming up the lane.

"I thought you'd gotten lost," Dad said, a muted smile on his lips.

"I know, right? There's no room to park around here," Officer Hargrove joked.

Balto inched his way along the ground, sniffing curiously at the familiar newcomers.

"Puppy!" Jessica said. "Mommy, can I pet him?"

"That doesn't look like any puppy I've ever seen," Officer Hargrove said, eyeing Balto skeptically.

I waved until I got Officer Hargrove's attention. I leaned over and scratched Balto's ears. Officer Hargrove relaxed. "Fine, honey," she said. Jessica keened with laughter and reached for Balto with both hands.

DeShawn squeezed himself in at my side. "I researched this game extensively, for accuracy's sake. Do you play eastern style, or northwestern style?"

Rafael gave him a weird look.

Ms. Siomme and Dr. Stout's team was up against Mr. Red Clay and Mr. Little Hawk's team. Mr. At Dawn drew fresh chalk lines on the soil and stepped back while the teams took positions. Ms. Siomme beckoned for Mr. Red Clay with a crooked finger. Mr. Red Clay pointed toward himself, bemused, for confirmation. Ms. Siomme nodded.

Mr. Red Clay approached the midway line and Ms. Siomme bopped him on the head with an open palm.

Mr. At Dawn blew his whistle. The teams scrimmaged furiously--

but the game was over in seconds, the women victorious. Mr. Little Hawk dropped his stick with disappointment and Ms. Siomme and Dr. Stout high-fived one another. Ms. Siomme shot a wink at Mr. Red Clay over her shoulder. Mr. Red Clay looked ashamed. He had fallen for a lovely woman's guiles, as men of his persuasion are so tragically inclined.

"Next!" Mr. At Dawn boomed.

Granny sat with us and handed out thick stacks of frybread. DeShawn said "Thank you" and Holly said "I'm already fat" and Daisy shushed us while Aubrey's team took the field.

I knew who Lorna was right away. She was a twelfth grader, and as tall as a fully grown man--and a good deal bulkier. I smiled and waved when she looked my way. She blushed. So that's why they called her Shy Lorna.

Aubrey's team was ruthless. Lorna was the brick wall halting her opponents' progress and Aubrey was an impressive combination of lightning and thunder, lightning-fast on long legs, thunder-fierce when he punched the tapikolo past Stuart Stout and clean across the enemy line. My best guess was that years of farmwork had regimented his muscles beyond the immediately evident. He beamed and saluted when we applauded his team's victory. I noticed his glasses were taped to his ears.

"Next!" Mr. At Dawn bellowed.

"That's us!" Daisy hissed.

I picked up the shinny stick lying at my side. The ten of us rose and walked over to the playing field. Zeke was so excited, he was practically vibrating.

We faced our opponents, stalwart, ready for combat. Autumn Rose In Winter giggled and blushed. Prairie Rose rudely wiggled her behind.

"Go get 'em, Raf!" I heard Gabriel shout.

Mr. At Dawn blew his whistle. Daisy and Siobhan Stout scrimmaged for the tapikolo. Daisy whisked the buckskin sack away and passed it to Lila. Lila ran the tapikolo up to the enemy line where Matthew Tall Ridge intercepted. Immaculata barreled at him out of nowhere, forcing him to dive out of her way and abandon the tapikolo.

Was that move even allowed? I looked at Mr. At Dawn. Mr. At Dawn scratched his beard.

I caught the tapikolo on the end of my stick; Prairie Rose charged at me and I lobbed it across the soil to Dad. Dad launched it at the enemy line--but Mrs. In Winter blocked it. Granny shot up the playing field like a bullet--I heard a roar of approval from the audience--she stole the tapikolo from Mrs. In Winter and sent it rocketing toward the far end of the field. The audience cheered. We'd won.

"I just hope we don't play Aubrey's team," said Rafael, a touch surly as we sat down and rested on the grass.

"Oh, I'm counting on it," Annie said, eyes dancing.

Zeke screamed and cheered when his cousin's team played and won. Holly gave him a look of gloom.

I thought: If I'm going to get him to talk, it had better be right now. I reached over and tapped Zeke's shoulder.

"Eh?" He spared me a quick glance, distracted by the game. "What is it?"

I tapped him again to make sure I'd gotten his attention. When he looked at me, I ran my fingers over the left half of my face.

Zeke gulped. "Look, man," he said, "that's none of your business. Why are you prying, anyway?"

I gave him a dry smile. I knew what I would have liked to say. *It's not prying if I'm worried about you. I'm worried about you.*

I couldn't say it--and he didn't give me the chance. He moved over on the grass to sit closer to Immaculata. He ignored me for the rest of the game.

Annie's prediction came true a couple of matches later, and our team was paired against Aubrey's. The ten of us went back to the playing field to face our opponents. Aubrey's brother Isaac dragged his finger across his throat. Annie rolled her eyes.

Mr. At Dawn touched up the chalk lines on the ground. I heard Officer Hargrove clapping and calling my name. I can't describe how that felt. At John J. Calamiere, my old school, the only way to be mute without being bullied was to be invisible, too. Naturally I had never been on a sports team; but even if I had, I'd never had a mother to cheer me on.

Officer Hargrove isn't your mother, I told myself quickly. Just *a* mother.

Holly got ready to scrimmage with Aubrey. Annie shook her head. She pulled Holly aside at the last minute and they traded places.

"Hey!" Daisy shouted. "That's not what we agreed on!"

Mr. At Dawn blew his whistle.

The effect was instantaneous. Aubrey, ever the gentleman, hesitated. Annie tried to swing the tapikolo past him. She almost succeeded, too. Sort of. Okay, she knocked it over his head. I could understand now why Aubrey had taped his glasses to his ears. Zeke jabbered incomprehensibly and ran around Aubrey to collect the tapikolo. Lorna stepped in front of him like a roadblock, grunting, and he fell to the ground.

"Get it! Get it!" Lila shouted.

But nobody was willing to contend with Shy Lorna's brute strength.

I braced myself and dashed forward. I swung my stick at the tapikolo and Lorna, blushing, froze up. The tapikolo skidded across the ground to Granny. Granny passed it to Rafael. Aubrey came out of nowhere and knocked it out of Rafael's reach.

"Dumbass!" Lila shouted.

"Lila!" Annie shouted.

Aubrey ran the tapikolo all the way to our end of the field. He slowed when he noticed Annie running along his side.

"*Aubrey!*" Isaac screeched. "This is not a date!"

Immaculata lunged at Aubrey. Aubrey yelped and rolled to the ground, Annie stepping calmly out of his way. Zeke bopped his mouth and let out a war whoop. Immaculata passed the tapikolo to Granny. It took Granny maybe a split second to shoot the tapikolo across the enemy line.

"And *that*," Ms. Threefold yelled from the audience, "is what makes shinny a woman's game!"

I grinned with disbelief. Never mind that the next team was probably going to cream us. It still felt pretty cool to have beaten the biggest, baddest kids in town. Even if one of those big bad kids was our best friend.

Dad pat Zeke on the back. Annie and Immaculata shook hands, Annie's face glowing and mischievous. Granny and Lila high-fived one another, Granny's ponytail resting over her shoulder, and I laughed to see their camaraderie. I clapped my hand on Rafael's back and he grinned at me, boyish and beautiful.

God, was he beautiful. I thought about how many times he must have missed out on shinny because nobody wanted to play for his team. I felt so inexpressibly happy that he finally had friends. I wanted everyone to know how incredible he was. If I could have shouted it from my rooftop, maybe I would have.

Maybe he knew what I was thinking. Maybe that was why he faltered; why he raised his hand and sifted his fingers through my curls. Maybe that was why he bent down and kissed me in front of the whole crowd.

I can't explain what was going through my mind, because it happened so fast, it was over by the time I processed any of it. My lips felt warm, my stomach heavy with dread. It was one thing to touch each other in private. Privacy was lauded in the Shoshone world. As far as Nettlebush went, I had never seen a boy and a girl kiss in public, let alone two boys.

I looked around the clearing. Nothing had changed. Neighbors were clapping for their friends' kids. Mr. At Dawn was looking for the errant tapikolo, thrust off to parts unknown by Granny's powerful blow. Nobody cared. Nobody cared who I loved or didn't love. It had nothing to do with them. Why should they feel one way or another about it?

Not just loving, but being free to love--I think that's the best feeling on earth.

We lost the next round to the fifty-year-old farmers, who went on to win the title match.

"It's that little Betty Thorn Bush," Granny cursed. "Still showing me up, after all these years!"

You win some, you lose some.

13
Car Crash

"Do you think you'll participate in the sun dance?" Annie asked.

Annie and I sat on the front porch and bundled brown paper around stacks of jewelry and cassette tapes. We'd had another hit on the tribal website.

I don't even know what the sun dance is, I confessed.

Rafael and Aubrey had mentioned the sun dance a couple of times over the summer. From what I'd gathered, it was a week-long spring ritual that took place in the badlands. Unfortunately, that was all I'd gathered.

"Hmm... Well, I don't know much about it myself. It's for men only."

Poor you, I teased.

"Ha, ha," she said humorlessly. "I'm not missing out on much. Women have the full moon ceremony all to themselves. And no, I'm not telling you about it."

I thought back to the isolation tents and Rafael's childhood curiosity. I grinned.

We went to the hospital and dropped off our merchandise in the mail room. Annie linked her arm through mine on the walk back.

Do you think Mr. Owns Forty hits Zeke? I signed.

Annie perused me pensively. "I don't know. Do you?"

Sometimes it was really hard to get a straight answer out of Annie.

Zeke won't tell me.

"I'd imagine not. It's none of your business."

She wasn't being critical. That's just the way Shoshone view familial matters.

I thought: Once familial matters entailed someone getting hurt, they had no business staying private.

I'll tell Dad, I decided. *He can talk to Mr. Owns Forty.*

"But will he?"

I stared at her. I smiled quizzically. Of course he would. Dad wasn't the sort to sit back and let someone else's kid suffer.

Dad said as much when I approached him later on.

He read the sticky note I'd handed him and shook his head. "I don't know whether Luke would hit his boy," he said. "I'll talk to him. The Luke I knew was an attentive father--you had to see him with Naomi--but loss changes people, Cubby. Sometimes it destroys them."

I thought of Rafael's sister and her detox. I thought of Mr. Owns Forty, drunk, Rosa confronting him at the gas station. I didn't understand why people in pain chose to hurt themselves in other ways. Maybe it was a good thing that I couldn't understand it.

I remembered the long drive to Nevada and how sorry I'd felt for Gabriel and Rosa. I reclaimed my post-it pad as Dad sat down at the kitchen table. I wrote a quick note and handed it to him.

Dad read the note, amused. "Mother won't let you drive?"

I pretended to rub the tears from my eyes.

"Well," Dad said, "I'm sure she has her reasons..."

But maybe Dad could talk to her for me and get her to change her mind. I took up the notepad again, but Dad interrupted me faster than I could write.

"No."

I lowered the notepad and regarded him. I didn't understand.

"You have to wait for the adoption to finalize," he explained. "To get a learner's permit, you have to show the DMV your birth certificate. When Mother adopts you, the state will seal your old birth certificate and give you a new one. Odd, I know. Still, you'll have gone to trouble for nothing if you dig up your old birth certificate and it's rendered invalid within a few days."

When he put it that way, I guessed it made sense. But exactly how long was that supposed to take? We still didn't have a new case worker yet.

I went to Rafael's house that evening and helped him clean his room. "Rosa won't get off my back," he offered by way of explanation. I could see why. Rafael's bedroom was more cluttered than a noisy hen coop. Clothes lay on the floor and on the standing radio, most of which I'd never seen Rafael wear, not even once; and there were so many library books on the bed that he'd had to move his pillow and comforter to the floor. I didn't know the library lets you take that many books at a time. Wait, why didn't he just put the books on the floor?

"Shove this in the closet," Rafael said, and stuffed a broken lamp into my arms.

I opened the closet door and found a heap of unwashed bed linens, ancient packages of candy, Rafael's gray regalia, and a bicycle.

I showed Rafael my disapproval with a slow shake of my head.

A knock sounded on the bedroom door. I stuffed the broken lamp in the closet and snapped it closed. Gabriel stuck his head in the doorway.

"Hey," he said, "can I talk to you two for a second?"

A leaden weight settled in my stomach. Rafael looked at me before he followed his uncle out the door.

I followed the two of them to the living room, and we sat at the long window facing the badlands: blue-gray and dreamlike, misty by sunset.

Here it comes, I thought. I steeled myself.

"Would the two of you like to join this year's sun dance?"

What? I stirred.

"Uh," Rafael said.

Gabriel gave us an easygoing, matter-of-fact sort of look. "You're not children anymore," he said. "You're young men now. That means you're old enough for the sun dance. Of course, Skylar, you'd have to clear it with your grandmother, but I thought I should take the time to explain to you what happens during the sun dance. It's not for everyone, so think seriously about this. And remember, it's up to you. Nobody can force you to participate."

I nodded. Rafael shifted uncomfortably in his seat.

"Now," Gabriel said. "A long, long time ago, our ancestors lived on the plains and hunted buffalo. But the buffalo wasn't just a food source. Its skin was used to make clothes and houses. Its bones were used for weapons and fortifications. So you can see how vital the buffalo were to the Plains People's existence."

I sat up, interested.

"There's a balance to the universe," Gabriel said. "The planet is generous when it provides for us. The earliest Plains People recognized that generosity. In their eyes, the buffalo gave itself to us in order for us to survive. It was considered the ultimate act of generosity."

"Is that why we pray whenever we go hunting?" Rafael asked. "I mean, there aren't any buffalo around here, but still."

"Yes, exactly. When we pray just before the hunt, we're thanking the planet for its generosity and promising to honor its sacrifice--and to return it."

Return it? That sounded foreboding.

"The sun dance," Gabriel said, "is how we return the blood we took from the planet. It's how we maintain universal balance. Most importantly, it's how we say 'Thank you.' "

"Blood?" Rafael asked.

"The dancers pierce their chests and backs to draw blood. Very light blood," Gabriel said quickly. "You hardly even feel it. I should know, I've been doing it for fourteen years. We dance in the direction of the sun. The ceremony takes up to a week. We don't eat at all during that time, and we drink very little. We sleep in turns and dance while we're awake. The shaman oversees us to make sure nobody hurts himself. But it's completely optional--so don't feel like you have to participate if you don't want to. You don't have to. Okay?"

"I want to," Rafael said.

I looked at him with surprise.

"What?" he said. "I take from the planet all the time. We all do."

"Skylar?"

The sun dance sure didn't sound like a walk in the park. On the other hand, it was a part of our culture. There was no part of our culture I didn't want to experience.

I nodded my assent. I could always ask Dad about it later on. Maybe he was planning on participating, too.

Rafael nudged me and caught my eye. "I won't let anyone hurt you," he promised. "If you start freaking out, I'll get you out of there."

I grinned widely and nudged him back. When had he ever known me to freak out? I wasn't the one with the explosive temper and the flying fists.

"Shut up," Rafael said, a shy smile at the corner of his mouth.

Gabriel cleared his throat. The grin faded from my face.

"Raf, did you finish cleaning your room?"

"Um, yeah," Rafael muttered.

Gabriel nodded. "Then you should walk Skylar home," he said. "I don't know about you kids, but that's how we did things when I was your age."

Only Rafael's complexion kept him from blushing.

Rafael walked me home just before dusk. My hands swung at my sides, my eyes navigating the dark ground. I half-expected Balto to jump out at us from the trees.

"He's a good guy," Rafael said. "Uncle Gabe."

I smiled at Rafael, though he probably couldn't see it in the low light. I was glad to hear he had reconciled with his uncle. I squeezed his hand and dropped it.

"I mean, he raised me and Mary when Mom died. He didn't have to; he could have dumped us off on someone else's doorstep... You know what?" Rafael said with dawning. "I love him. And Mary.

Even Rosa. I'm lucky to have all of them. They love me. They actually love me. Can you believe that? I'm so lucky."

Me, too, I thought tremulously. I love you, too. You don't even know it. I'll never tell you.

That was my shortcoming: tricking myself into forgetting, even for a second, that Rafael always knew what it was I couldn't say.

In the low light I saw his expression change; his mouth opening, his eyes, blue, widening. My nerves were on fire, and I felt sick, sort of like I could throw up on the spot. I just hoped I didn't throw up on him.

"Sky--"

I don't know what he would have said next. I don't know how I would have responded. Because I saw movement over his shoulder, coming from the direction of my house; and I realized there were two police officers standing on my porch.

I broke free from Rafael's side and ran home, my heart hammering.

Granny and Mrs. Red Clay were on the porch. Granny looked angrier than I had ever seen her. And as I drew near, I heard her yelling at the cops: "This is outrageous! *I* am the boy's custodian!"

I felt like my stomach was inside-out and rising through my throat. I felt like the reservation was swimming, distorting, in front of my eyes.

I felt Rafael's hand on my wrist and realized he had followed me.

One of the cops had noticed me. He turned toward me, his hand on the holster at his waist. "You're Skylar?"

I couldn't even nod.

"I would like to know the specific reason you've decided to reassign my client," Nola said.

"Complaint from his social worker," the officer said. "You guys took him to Idaho in January? He's a ward of the state. You're not allowed to take him to another state without permission."

Oh, God, I thought numbly. Even without a voice, I'd gone and run my mouth off.

"Prove that I took him anywhere!" Granny challenged.

"I don't need to," the cop replied.

"Skylar," said the other cop, "go get your stuff, buddy."

I couldn't have moved my legs even if I'd wanted to. By some unknown force, I found the will to move my head. I shook my head. It wasn't like they could handcuff me.

I saw the taller cop reach for the handcuffs at his waist and realized: Yes, they can.

My legs felt like slabs of ice when I went inside the house. The two cops came in after me, and I think Granny did, too, but I didn't check to see. I was half-delirious with disbelief. This was my home. Why were they taking me from my home? I climbed the staircase to my bedroom. My knees felt like they were shackled to the floor. The cops didn't follow me.

I threw open my bedroom door. I ran my hands through my hair. Okay, I told myself. Calm down and think.

If I climbed out the window, maybe I could evade the police. But Granny had broken some kind of law by taking me with her to Nevada and Idaho. If I ran and hid, would they arrest Granny? Just the thought of Granny in handcuffs filled me with rage. Calm down, I told myself again. That's not going to happen. You'll just have to cooperate.

Cooperate. And get chucked into some stranger's house for who-knows-how-long? I had Mrs. Red Clay as my guardian ad litem. Mrs. Red Clay was one slick lady. Slick enough to help my dad get away with murder. Slick enough to bring me back to Nettlebush? Not slick enough to toss Ms. Whitler off our backs. No. She may have had the upper hand over the FBI, but social services were another story.

So that was it, then. I had to leave Nettlebush, whether I wanted to or not.

I got my duffel bag out of the closet. I packed my cash, my clothes, and my schoolbooks. Maybe whoever got saddled with me would let me keep going to school on the reservation. I had a sudden, wild daydream that Mr. Red Clay or Ms. Siomme would sign on as a foster parent and take me in. I immediately felt ashamed for thinking something so selfish.

I stuffed some of Rafael's drawings into the duffel bag. My plains flute, too--no way was I leaving without that. I hesitated. There was something else I should take with me--something I hadn't even looked at in half a year.

I pulled open the drawer underneath my bedside table. I dug out my dad's beeper and tossed it into the duffel bag.

No use postponing the inevitable, I thought. I swung my bag over my shoulder and turned toward the door.

Dad was in the doorway. The foreign resolve in his immutable eyes scared me.

"This isn't permanent," he promised me. "I'll come get you, and I'll bring you back here."

I shook my head rigorously. I strode across the room and grabbed Dad's shoulders. The minute he left the reservation, he was in bigger trouble than any of us. He couldn't leave. Not for anything.

"Yes, I will," he said. "Don't you tell me what to do, Skylar. I'm the father."

He only ever called me Skylar if it was a really serious situation. Like that time I'd tried to blow up a drinking fountain in fifth grade.

I used to be an angry kid.

"I love you," Dad said. "You remember that."

I loved him, too. I loved him no matter how many secrets he kept, no matter how many people he killed. I guess that's the problem with love. You can't turn it off.

I left Dad in my room and took the stairs two at a time, praying, hoping against hope that he wouldn't come looking for me.

Balto padded out of the kitchen and whimpered. It's amazes me how animals can always pick up on the tension in the air. I knelt down and stroked underneath his muzzle. He liked that best.

"Let's go already," said the cop at the front door.

With one last pat to Balto's head, I stood up. I slipped out the door. Granny stood in the porchlight with the most crestfallen expression I had ever seen on her face. It was so unlike my fearsome Granny that I checked at the sight of it. I squeezed her shoulder. I wrapped my arm around her in a hug. I felt her hand at the nape of my neck, disconsolate.

I trudged down the porch steps and onto the lawn.

"Atta boy," said one of the police officers, his hand on my shoulder. I felt strangely like a convict walking to the gallows.

Something possessed me to look over my shoulder at Nettlebush one last time. I tried to convince myself that it wasn't the last time, that this was just a big misunderstanding and I'd be home in time for spring finals.

My eyes met Rafael's. He stood stock-still, reminding me of an onlooker at the site of a car crash; like someone who can't move away from the wreckage in time because he hasn't finished registering the danger. I don't think I can even name the look I saw on his face. It wasn't an angry look. It wasn't even sad. I think it was lost. He looked lost. He made me think of all those times I'd ventured into the forest and forgotten which way was east and which was west.

I smiled at him. I didn't particularly feel up to smiling, but it wouldn't do to have the two of us looking like wretches.

It felt surreal when I followed the cops to their squad car and climbed into the sticky back seat. The doors on my left and right didn't have handles. The taller of the two cops picked up the radio at the dashboard and spoke into it. I don't remember what he said. Soon--too soon--we were leaving Nettlebush behind, the squeal of tires on asphalt inconceivably cruel.

I guessed I was going to miss the sun dance.

14

Girls Don't Dance with Girls

I climbed the faux marble staircase to the fourth floor. The apartment building had one elevator--I was pretty sure that violated some kind of safety code--and it was broken.

The policemen followed me to Apartment 4B. Tentative, I knocked on the door.

A woman in a bathrobe and curling pins opened the door, her mouth wide open in a yawn. I shifted my duffel bag over my shoulder.

"You're the kid who can't talk," said the woman. "I've had you before."

I remembered her, too. Janet, I thought her name was.

"We'll be in touch," said one of the officers.

Both officers left us pretty quickly after that. I guess they didn't care whether I made a run for it. And I was tempted to try--but then Janet stepped back from the doorway, and she gave me a funny look, and I figured I had better follow her in.

I'd stayed in Janet's apartment once before--almost a year ago, before I went to live with Granny. Back then there had been five of us in the apartment at once: four kids and one Janet.

I squinted, dizzied by darkness. I'd forgotten how dim the apartment was. There was only one flickering, fluorescent light hanging between the squashed living room and the cold and doorless kitchen, the kitchen filled with plastic garbage bags. The carpet was grungy and gray. I couldn't tell whether it was supposed to be gray or had simply deteriorated with age. A spider had made its home on the wall; and sitting on the couch was a teenage girl.

"You're sleeping with Noel," Janet said. "CPS says you're not supposed to room with a girl, so don't tell anyone, or they'll take my check away. And don't get her pregnant."

I balked at Janet's candor. Neither of those was likely to be a problem.

"Eat a TV dinner or something," Janet said, and she went into the kitchen to listen to her compact radio. I saw her pouring wine into her coffee mug.

I cast a look at the teenage girl. I thought I might have gone to school with her in the past--Rumez, or Ramirez, or something like that. No, definitely Rumez. Her hair was crazy, curly--crazier than mine. Her nose was pierced. She opened her mouth when she snapped on her bubblegum, and I saw that her tongue was pierced, too.

"What are *you* looking at?"

I shrugged and sat on the far end of the couch. I unzipped my duffel bag in search of Dad's beeper. With a twinge of remorse, I thought about Balto. I hoped he didn't think he'd been abandoned again.

I took my plains flute out of my bag. I pushed aside Kaya's cornhusk doll.

I felt, before I saw, Noel gawking at me.

"What's that on your neck?" she said.

She reached out with stubby fingers and prodded the rigid red scars on my neck. Her nail polish, bright blue, was peeling and chipped. I tensed, but smiled. Aside from Rafael, I didn't like anyone touching my neck.

Come on, I thought, my head bent over the duffel bag. Where's that beeper?

"Is that a *butterfly*?"

She meant the tattoo on my arm. It was an atlas moth, and all too visible while I was wearing short sleeves.

"You gonna get your punk ass kicked, you walk around with a *butterfly* on your arm."

I think she was being helpful, in an obtuse way. I didn't really feel like thanking her, though.

That night was probably the most disquieting night I'd ever spent. I lay on someone else's bed--no frame, just a mattress and a box spring--and held Dad's beeper over my head, willing it to light up. I'd never felt so alienated from the people I loved, knowing that I couldn't run to them, that my own stupidity had gotten them into trouble.

I fell asleep with the beeper in hand. And I woke up to Noel screaming at me.

"Get up!" she yelled. "School!"

It's not the ideal way to start your day. I jumped awake and fell out of bed, my heart in my throat.

"Come on! School! I'm late again, they'll kick me out!"

My head was killing me. I wished I had Granny's feverfew tea, a great headache remedy.

Noel tore off her pajamas. I shielded my face to give her some privacy. I heard her heels on the floorboard seconds later, fast and heavy, and knew she had run out of the room. I dressed in jeans and a t-shirt. I grabbed a couple of notebooks from my duffel bag. I guessed Janet wasn't going to let me go to school on the reservation.

Janet wasn't even in the apartment. Maybe she'd run out of Lambrusco. I followed Noel into the kitchen and she tossed me a granola bar, cursing, hopping as she tugged her shoes on, snatching up her schoolbag and dashing out the door.

I pulled on my jacket and tugged the sleeves down my arms. Atlas moth or not, I didn't much feel like getting my ass kicked.

John J. Calamiere High School was tall and towering, crammed between a video rental place and a butcher's shop. It's funny, I thought, staring up the length of the building. I went here for two years and I managed just fine. Now I felt nauseous. Kids sat on the cement ledges alongside the front steps and on the wrought iron gates dividing the school from the sidewalk. I kept my head down and followed Noel into the sickening, cream-colored lobby.

I stopped by the principal's office to figure out my class schedule. The principal, a tall and crickety guy with a gray comb-over, wasn't surprised to see me. He and I went pretty far back. "CPS faxed over your records!" he said loudly. He had a way of talking at you, not to you. He'd always struck me as a pretty angry guy. And something else struck me at that moment, too: This wasn't make-believe. This was the law, and the law said I had to go to school without my friends and live without my family. I was here, and for the foreseeable future, I wasn't going anywhere.

I hate to admit how despondent I felt. I felt the way a bull calf must feel when the farmers separate it from its mother. I felt like a southern oak uprooted from its grove and planted among beeches; familiar in only a cursory way, lost otherwise.

I thought about Rafael, how lost he'd looked the other night. I realized how profoundly he'd changed me. He'd given me friendship, he'd given me a voice, and then, when I'd thought he had nothing left to give, he'd taught me how to love someone I didn't have to love. Maybe the most profound and scary way he'd changed me was: I didn't know how to be a Skylar without a Rafael anymore. I was supposed to be with Rafael. I was supposed to make him laugh when he was scowling and quell his stormy moods. Who else was going to remind him of the goodness in his heart whenever he felt dwarfed by his dad's shadow? What was he doing right now? Who was he talking to? At least he still had Aubrey and Annie. In remembering that, I felt happy. If I couldn't look after him myself, at least I knew he wasn't alone.

I was supposed to shadow Noel until the principal fixed my class schedule. I followed her to the first period classroom, where a group of boys were adamantly engaged in an all-out paper airplane war, and heard a couple of kids call my name. Mostly they were jeers along the lines of: "Skylar! Ew, quiet kid's back," and "Wow, I forgot about him."

I retaliated with goofy, exaggerated eyerolls and slid into the empty seat at Noel's side. I opened a notebook, hunched over, and started writing.

I was the master of invisibility. At John J. Calamiere, you don't want to be too different from the herd. Stick out like a black sheep and you become a prime target for weird rumors and gut punches in the locker room. A mute guy tends to stick out just by virtue of being mute. But there's a trick to being invisible: Pretend you're always busy. If you're busy catching up on notes, or frantically scanning the bulletin board, or you've got your head buried in a monster of a textbook, or you're looking for the ever-elusive philosophy professor, nobody's going to walk up to you and start talking; and if they do, you can just wave them away. I always looked busy, even when I wasn't. Consequently, nobody tried to talk to me. Nobody knew me well enough to dislike me. I wasn't even sure they knew I was mute.

Pretending you're busy for seven hours straight is exhausting. I was exhausted by the end of the day. Noel and I walked the streets back to Janet's apartment complex. Noel had this weird compulsion that made her step on all the cracks in the sidewalk. Maybe she was trying to break her mother's back.

"You gonna make a run for it?" she asked me. "My last foster brother ran away. What was his name, Jordan something."

I shook my head. Cooperating sounded like my best bet. I didn't want Granny getting into trouble. I wanted social services to see how compliant Granny and I both were. Maybe then they'd have to let me go back to the reserve.

My spirits lifted. Maybe I'd be back on the reserve by the end of the week.

I wasn't. The teachers at John J. Calamiere lent me battered old textbooks to take back to Janet's place and I found myself studying with Noel for a history test I had no place taking. I was pretty sure I was going to fail it. I fell asleep, miserable, on the bare mattress and box spring, Dad's beeper in hand. I woke in the middle of the night to its faint, clear whistle, the digital screen glowing with a blocky message.

Love you, Cubby.

My chest felt tight and my eyes felt hot. I tucked the beeper under the threadbare pillow and went back to sleep.

On Saturday, I holed myself up in the bedroom and played the plains flute. I was afraid that I'd forget the Native songs if I didn't hear them everyday. It was ridiculous, I knew, considering I'd only been gone from the reservation for a week.

Noel bounced into the bedroom in hoop earrings and a denim miniskirt. She was kind of chubby, I thought, in a cute way.

"I'm gonna get some weed. You wanna come?"

I couldn't tell if she was serious.

"Freak," she said, and flounced from the room.

I had a thought just then. It wasn't a very good thought, but it occurred to me nonetheless. Mary used to take a wide variety drugs. I didn't know whether she still did. I hoped she didn't. But whoever Noel's dealer was--maybe he could get me in touch with Mary.

I hurried out of the building after Noel. I followed her down the sidewalk and across the street. She whistled when she took note of me.

Noel's dealer was a skinny guy in his twenties. He had a weird soul patch, skull cap combo going on. We met with him at the back of a video game arcade, behind a busted pinball machine. I don't mean to imply that I'm the paragon of virtue, but that really pissed me off. There were kids in the arcade. And if the nametag on his shirt--"Dale"--were to be trusted, he was an employee.

I didn't have anything to write with. I'd been in such a hurry to follow Noel that I'd left my post-it pad back in Janet's apartment.

"You buying?" Dale asked me.

I wasn't interested. I've always thought that if you have to poison your body just to have a good time, you've got bigger problems than boredom.

"Skylar?"

I looked up with surprise. It was Officer Hargrove in her plain clothes--it must have been her day off. I saw her kids standing by the whack-a-mole station, Jessica whining softly whenever her mallet missed the mark.

Officer Hargrove's face screwed up with realization. "What the-- Is that weed?"

Dale dropped the bag and darted toward the fire exit. Officer Hargrove was a lot stronger than her small physique suggested; she seized him by his shoulders and threw him into the broken pinball machine. He gasped and buckled with pain. Officer Hargrove put her foot on the marijuana bag and grabbed Dale's wrists, wrenching his arms behind his back.

"DeShawn, honey," she said, "get Mommy's cell phone, would you?"

Five minutes later and Noel and I were sitting on the curb outside the game arcade, Noel shooting sour, acidic looks at me.

The colored lights on top of the squad car flickered. Officer Hargrove waved to whoever was inside as they drove away, Dale in the back seat. She approached Noel and me and literally looked down her nose at us. It wasn't that she was being condescending. It's just that we were on the ground and she was standing.

"What the *hell* were you thinking!"

I tried to keep my face blank. I didn't want to get Noel in trouble.

"And Skylar, what are you doing off the reservation?"

"What reservation?" Noel asked.

Officer Hargrove rubbed her forehead. Maybe she could have used some feverfew tea herself. "Just... Ugh, never mind. Give me your mom's number," she said to Noel.

DeShawn scurried forward and thrust the cell phone into Officer Hargrove's hands.

"I don't know it," Noel said. "She's in jail."

Officer Hargrove looked from Noel to me with dawning. I smiled wryly.

Officer Hargrove drove Noel and me back to the apartment complex. Officer Hargrove told us to wait in the hallway outside the apartment; and then she went inside and started yelling at Janet. I could hear her through the door, thick as it was supposed to be.

Noel suddenly swore. "I'm gonna be expelled!"

I gave her a swift look. No, she wasn't. She hadn't actually bought the marijuana.

"That's terrible," DeShawn said somberly.

"What's expelled?" Jessica said.

I was worried that that was the last I'd be seeing of Officer Hargrove. But she came back the next day when Noel and I were listening to the stereo in our bedroom. She stuck her head inside and gestured to me.

"Let's go, Skylar," she said. "You're staying with me now."

My heart leapt, and for a variety of reasons. The first and most obvious was that Officer Hargrove was in touch with Granny and Dad. By living with Officer Hargrove, I was one step closer to home. And the second... Well, I really liked Officer Hargrove.

"What about me?" Noel said.

I reached over to squeeze her shoulder. She smacked my hand away.

"You're getting a new foster home, too," Officer Hargrove said to her. "I don't like the *atmosphere* of this place."

I collected my belongings and swung my duffel bag over my shoulder. I tried to wave goodbye to Noel, but she wasn't interested. I followed Officer Hargrove out of the room. I heard Janet in the kitchen, screaming about her CPS check.

Officer Hargrove drove me to the other side of town, to a gated black tenement. We went inside.

Officer Hargrove's apartment was small, but cozy. Her refrigerator was covered in her children's schoolwork and Jessica's fanciful crayon drawings. Next to the front door was an evolving height chart. It looked like DeShawn had had a formidable growth spurt in the past six months.

"Thanks, Linda," Officer Hargrove said. A tiny old woman sitting on the couch nodded and shuffled out the door. Jessica was curled up at the end of the sofa with about a dozen different plastic dolls. DeShawn sat businesslike on the armchair, kicking his legs.

Officer Hargrove cleared her throat.

"You're going to have to sleep on the couch," she told me. "I'm sorry. But--"

I shook my head, smiling. There was nothing to apologize about. In fact, I ought to have thanked her--and I would have, if I could figure out a way to do it without words. I touched her arm and hoped that would suffice. She smiled at me fleetingly.

"I'm going to see if I can get in touch with your grandmother," Officer Hargrove said.

She bustled into the kitchen, preoccupied.

"Shawny, let's play dolls," I heard Jessica say.

I left my duffel bag on the floor. I drew closer, curious.

DeShawn sat on the floor at the bottom of the armchair. He sighed. "All your dolls are girls..."

"Let's make them dance."

"Girls don't dance with girls."

I smiled to myself. Something about kids was like magic.

I knelt and unzipped my duffel bag, digging through the wrinkled clothes. I pulled out Kaya's cornhusk doll. I got up off the floor and handed it to Jessica.

Jessica whole face lit up. "A present!" she cried.

DeShawn groaned. "Now I'll never hear the end of it," he said.

"Skylar," Jessica said, "why doesn't she have a face?"

Cornhusk dolls never have faces. The story goes like this. At the beginning of the world, the Three Sisters created corn, beans, and squash for the Plains People to eat. One of the sisters decided to make dolls from the cornhusks for the children to play with. But one of the cornhusk dolls was so beautiful and vain, she didn't want to do anything except stare at her reflection in the pond. Ever since then, Indian dolls don't have faces. After all, we wouldn't want them to jump out of their owners' arms and run for the nearest mirror.

I tickled Jessica's face and she pealed with laughter, slumping over the armrest.

"Kids!" Officer Hargrove yelled from the kitchen, telephone in hand. "What are we having for dinner?"

"French fries!" Jessica shouted.

"Pizza!" DeShawn shouted.

"Too bad," Officer Hargrove said. "I want Chinese."

We sat on the sofa and ate wontons and egg drop soup, Officer Hargrove and Jessica in a heated, one-sided argument with the game show on the television. I smiled, amused. The two of them made me think of Dad, how he liked to listen to baseball scores over the radio and yell at the newscaster when the scores weren't to his liking. I missed him. I tried not to think about that. I tried telling myself that I was going to see him soon.

DeShawn and Jessica went to bed around ten o'clock. Officer Hargrove gave me blankets and a pillow for the couch.

She palmed my head, motherly, comforting, before she turned off the standing lamp and went to her room.

I rummaged around in my duffel bag late at night. By the light of Dad's beeper, I looked through Rafael's drawings.

I smiled. The first was a simple sketch of Aubrey, his Coke bottle glasses taped to his ears. The next greatest fashion trend, no doubt. I rifled through the sketches. The next one was familiar: Mom, her hair in a ponytail, her head bent as she tended to a garden. Rafael had drawn a couple of scenes from his favorite stories, too. I guessed that the woodland monster was Caliban and the girl in the sailor's clothes was Charlotte. Monsters were a recurring theme in Rafael's drawings. He'd drawn the eponymous Beast with long, clawed arms, a gaping maw, and blue eyes. If that wasn't revealing, I didn't know what was. I saw a drawing of Annie with devil's horns, steam coming out of her ears, her faceless subjects cowering in terror. I laughed, long and hard, and I was grateful that my laugh was silent, that I couldn't wake the kids.

My fingers halted between papers. Rafael had drawn me. My pulse missed its rhythm. It wasn't the first time he had drawn me, but nothing ever really prepared me for seeing my face on paper. It looked like he had sketched me while we were in school. My elbow was on the long table, my chin on my fist; my legs were crossed at the ankle and my head was inclined toward my neighbor in conversation, a light smile on my face. There was something softer, more deliberate in those sketchlines that wasn't apparent in his other sketches. I didn't have a name for it.

I missed him. I missed the reservation and everyone on it, but I missed Rafael in a different way. I missed him the way the high tide misses the moon at day. How else is it supposed to ebb and flow? I missed his coarse black hair and his broad arms. I missed his arms around me. I missed his lips on mine.

Great, I thought. I was *that* kind of boyfriend.

15
Buying Back Bear River

I didn't see Noel in school on Monday. I worried about her all
throughout math class. I caught up with the school's ASL teacher
before lunch--a bright, smiling woman with plump cheeks--and
asked her if she knew anything about it.

"No, I don't," she said. "I'll find out for you, okay?"

She never did, though.

In Angel Falls, cops work four ten hour shifts a week; four days
on, three days off. Officer Hargrove usually asked for Saturdays
and Sundays off so her kids weren't home alone. On all other days,
except for Mondays, she worked from seven to five and we didn't
see her at all until dinnertime. Dinner was DeShawn and Jessica's
favorite time of day, and it was endearing to watch them rush at
their mom when she walked through the door, bombarding her
with hugs and tales about their day. Usually she brought takeout
with her; the stove didn't see much use in the Hargrove household.
I decided to remedy that one day. In the morning, I left Officer
Hargrove a note; and in the evening, I made rosemary dumplings
for dinner, a recipe Annie had taught me over the summer. Officer
Hargrove must have liked them, because she put me in charge of
the kitchen from then on.

On Friday, Mrs. Red Clay came for a visit.

I was so happy to see someone--anyone--from the reservation, I
could have hugged her. I didn't, though. I had no way of knowing
how she would react. She sat at the rickety folding table in the
kitchen. Officer Hargrove gave her a cup of coffee, and the two of
us sat down with her.

"To begin with, I would like to thank you on Catherine's behalf for
applying for emergency foster care."

"No need," Officer Hargrove said dismissively. "The kid and I go way back."

She reached for my hair and ruffled it. I winked at her.

"Our next step is to acquire a family court date. Once Skylar's case is in front of a judge, I will lobby for permanent custody to be transferred to Catherine."

"That won't be a problem, will it?"

Mrs. Red Clay's face betrayed none of her thoughts. "When a child is fourteen or older, family court informally deems him competent enough to attest to his own well-being. If Skylar wants to live on the reservation--"

I did. More than anything.

"--a judge will take that into serious consideration."

"But that Whitler witch is fighting this tooth and nail."

"Her whole case hinges on Catherine having taken him out of state without permission. My argument is that Catherine did not take him out of state."

But that was a lie, I thought, alarmed. Ms. Whitler probably wouldn't have a hard time proving it was a lie. All she needed to do was take a look at the calendar on the tribal website. I don't know much about computers; but I've heard it said that once something's out in the World Wide Web, it stays there forever.

"Let me clarify. The Pleasance Reserve belongs to the Paiute Nation. The Shoshone Nation recently put in a bid to buy back the Bear River Massacre site. My argument is that any time Skylar spent on these two sites was not spent in a federally recognized state, but on tribal property. Tribal property does not adhere to state laws."

"Can you do that?" Officer Hargrove asked dubiously.

"It all hinges on whether the US government will sell Bear River to us."

I wondered how likely that was.

"And that Whitler witch?"

"I will argue, as I have argued, that she does not have Skylar's best interests in mind and therefore ought to be dismissed from the case."

"And if the judge won't dismiss her?"

Mrs. Red Clay was silent for a long moment. "I was hoping you would provide testimony, should the need arise."

"Of course I will."

This whole conversation was draining. I felt sorry for the both of them.

Mrs. Red Clay finished her coffee and left the apartment. I wished she had stayed a little longer. I wanted to ask her if the sun dance had started yet, if she knew how Rafael was doing. Of course, I couldn't ask her anything; but that didn't mean I didn't want to.

I liked walking to school every morning with DeShawn and Jessica. The elementary school was close to the apartment tenement, the middle school just beyond it. Every morning I walked the kids to the school gates and waved after them as they ran up the steps to meet with their friends. If DeShawn forgot his lunch on the kitchen counter--and he often did--I ran back to get it. If Jessica's shoelaces came untied, she stuck her foot out and waited for me to tie them again. I held their hands when they crossed the street and invariably, they complained. I'd always wondered whether Mom and Dad might have had more children if Mom's time with us hadn't been cut short. Now I knew the answer: Probably not. But walking DeShawn and Jessica to school, meeting with them at the end of the day... It felt sort of like having siblings of my own.

"What do I do if a bully punches me?" DeShawn asked me one day.

I suspected that might be a recurring problem for him. I didn't know what else to do: I held up my hands and let him practice punching back until my palms were red.

My preliminary court date came mid-March. Mrs. Red Clay picked me up and drove me to the family court building in Pima County.

The lobby was stuffy, sweltering, and jam packed with families. Mrs. Red Clay and I got in line behind a young mother and her two sons. The lobby walls were decorated with murals depicting happy family activities: a father playing catch with his son, a mother tucking her daughter into bed. I'm sure the murals were meant to reassure the families whose lives were about to be ripped apart. The thing is, they were hideous. The faces were grotesque, badly proportioned; the colors, garish, contrasted wildly. Rafael could have drawn better than this. The weird color scheming reminded me of an art technique he'd shown me one day.

"This is called chiaroscuro," Rafael said.

He sat in the church cupola with his back to the wall slat. I sat between his legs, my head against his chest, his notebook on my lap, and he penciled in violent, sinister shading around his sketch, a drawing of the reservation's annual ghost dance.

"I don't know what it means," he said hastily. "So don't ask me."

I laughed, and I was sure he could feel it in my rippling shoulders. He rested his chin on my shoulder, tucked the pencil between my fingers, and guided my hand. The pencil glided across the paper, his fingers entwined with mine, my heart somersaulting in my chest.

"In the old days," he said, "artists sucked at drawing dimensions. They hadn't figured out the secret to 3D yet. You ever notice how really old drawings look flat and childlike? That's what I'm talking about. So when these artists wanted to make something in the drawing stand out, they drew it in ultra-light colors and made the rest of the drawing as dark as they could. It had this weird effect; like...it looked like someone had just turned on a lamp in a badly lit room."

I laughed again at his description. What a way with words.

"You wanna know something really weird? The guy who codified chiaroscuro was called Rafaello Sanzio."

Well, that proved it. It was fate.

"Skylar."

I drew out of my reverie and hurtled back to Earth. For a moment, even, I was disoriented; I couldn't believe I was standing in this foreign building, so far from the people I loved and the comfort of my home.

I cast another look at the murals on the walls. A mother breast feeding her baby.

Mrs. Red Clay drew me over to a row of metal detectors. I jolted. Why metal detectors? The security guard made Mrs. Red Clay set aside her handbag. He made me take off the plains flute hanging from my neck. The handbag and the flute went on a conveyor belt through a box-shaped machine. The guard waved a bulky wand over the both of us, nodded, and sent us through the standing metal detectors one at a time. Mrs. Red Clay collected her handbag; I picked up my flute and draped it again around my neck. My throat felt strangely bare when I wasn't wearing it.

We navigated a maze of elevators and dead-end hallways built on top of a granite floor. Mrs. Red Clay never spoke to me. She led me to an old wooden door with a scratched glass pane, and we went inside.

I had never been in a room as emotionally flooding as this room. Children as young as four or five were sitting on the eroded benches, some with their families, some with elegantly dressed social workers; some completely alone. Court officers stood guarding a swinging door through which I could plainly hear a woman sobbing. The walls were a dull blue-white and laden with inane parenting posters: "It's four o'clock. Do you know where your child is?" Where there weren't posters, there was graffiti. Someone had scribbled "CK YOU" across the farthest wall. I guess the rest of it had worn away.

I sat with Mrs. Red Clay on an old brown bench, the armrest nearest me plastered with wads of chewing gum.

The swinging door banged loudly as two women came through it. One woman launched herself at the other, raw screams tearing out of her throat, punching, hitting whatever she could reach.

"Give me back my daughter!" she screamed.

The court officers pulled the women apart. The shorter woman looked scandalized, grasping her struck face. She bellowed curses at her assailant, who thrashed and struggled in her officer's arms, blindly swinging her arms, begging, crying, tears streaming down her face.

I'd never felt such a blend of sickness and pity.

The rest of the morning was comparatively uneventful. Mrs. Red Clay didn't talk to me, and I felt alone and uncomfortable, stranded in a crowded room. I didn't want to think about what some of these children must have been through already. A little girl sat with glazed eyes on the bench next to mine, dead to the world. Her feet didn't reach the floor. A teenage boy stood hunched against the wall, his hands in his pockets, eyes darting darkly. *Please don't hurt me*, his posture said; but his face said, *You bite me, I'll bite back.*

"St. Clair," a court officer called out, reading from a list of names.

I went with Mrs. Red Clay through the swinging door, and we found ourselves standing in front of a judge's pulpit.

Court wasn't anything like television makes it out to be. To begin with, there weren't any nosy onlookers. There wasn't even a place for us to sit. And there certainly weren't jurors. Just the judge, a couple of court officers, and the stenographer.

"Form 17?" the judge said.

Mrs. Red Clay opened her handbag and handed him a sheet of paper. He skimmed it briefly.

"If I'm to understand," the judge said, "the ward's previous foster mother took him out of state without first alerting his case worker, but you think it's perfectly okay to reinstate her custody."

I kind of wanted to jump up and down and shout, *I have a name!* I wasn't sure the court officers would like that, though, disability aside. One of them, the big guy, kept eyeing me and sneering.

"Catherine Looks Over did not take the boy to another state. She accompanied him to two different tribal residences. Worcester v. Georgia establishes that any land owned by Native American tribes is not subject to the laws of the state surrounding it."

The judge smiled at Mrs. Red Clay under his bushy mustache. "I've heard about you," he said. "Alright, I'll buy it. Still, I understand that one of the properties in question is under ongoing negotiations?"

"That would be the Bear River site in Idaho."

"You finalize that purchase and I'll dismiss these charges."

Mrs. Red Clay paused.

"Ma'am?"

"Sir," Mrs. Red Clay said, "these years are very influential to a child's development. If we are in agreement that the charges are unfounded, I would like to petition for *immediate* transfer of custody. Permanent custody."

The judge rifled through his papers.

"It says here that the boy's case worker disapproved of such an arrangement."

"I have collected various statements attesting to Miss Whitler's unprofessional conduct."

"Well, give them to me."

I couldn't believe how mindnumbing the courtroom process was. It was emotionless and logical. It was like math. I watched the judge and Mrs. Red Clay exchange more papers. I was tempted to start playing the plains flute and see if anyone noticed.

"Very good," the judge said. "Whitler's dismissed from the case. I'll have a new social worker sent to the reservation. Provided that the new case worker likes the living arrangement, the boy goes back to his grandmother on a probationary basis."

"I requested--"

"I know what you requested. You have your version of the law. I have mine. Probationary basis, Mrs. Red Clay. You don't own Bear River just yet."

And then--maybe out of habit--the judge banged his gavel.

16
Wovoka

"Honey, what's wrong?"

Officer Hargrove put her hand on my shoulder. I started and
smiled.

I was supposed to be making dinner. I guess I'd gotten distracted.
I didn't want to hurt Officer Hargrove's feelings; but I wanted to go
home. I hadn't been home in a month. Every day I spent off of the
reservation was unbearable. I didn't know what my friends were
up to. I didn't know who was making deliveries for Granny. I
didn't know whether Dad was behaving himself.

Officer Hargrove looked at the vegetables on the counter. "Forget
this," she said. "We'll order out."

I grasped her shoulder.

I think I was depressed. I didn't feel like doing much of anything--
not eating, not playing the flute, not even looking through Rafael's
drawings. I sat on the floor with my back against the armchair and
smiled when I was spoken to and laughed when it felt appropriate,
all the while aware of how fake I was. I kind of wanted to punch
me in the face.

Officer Hargrove dressed for work after dinner. She leaned down
and shook me gently by the shoulder.

"I've got to work the third shift," she said. "So I won't be home
until late. I'm taking you to visit your family tomorrow. I've been
thinking about it, and nothing says I can't."

I felt like my grin was splitting my face in half. I could have
jumped right off the floor and hugged her. I clutched her hand and
hoped she knew how grateful I was. I think she did; she smiled at
me, in a suspiciously watery way.

It was just DeShawn and Jessica and me when Officer Hargrove left for work.

"I want to play Princess," Jessica said.

DeShawn groaned.

I heard a knock on the door. I figured it was Officer Hargrove, and she had forgotten something for her beat.

It wasn't Officer Hargrove. I opened the door and came face-to-face with a cop I'd never seen before.

"You Skylar?" he asked.

I was too stunned to do anything but nod.

"Come on," he said, and gestured for me to follow him.

I thought: Maybe we had a new social worker already, and I was finally going home. Then I thought: Why wouldn't Mrs. Red Clay tell me that herself? The real problem was that Dad had instilled me from birth with a healthy distrust of the law. I always wanted to know what the authorities were doing and why they were doing it.

Either way, I couldn't leave with this guy. I couldn't leave DeShawn and Jessica. Officer Hargrove didn't get off until three in the morning.

"Sir?" DeShawn asked. He joined me at the door and gazed up at the officer.

I felt my pockets, searching for my post-it pad.

"Pack up," the cop told me, ignoring DeShawn. "Now."

My veins felt filled with ice water. I maneuvered through the room in a daze. I tossed my stray belongings in my duffel bag, my fingers numb. I found my pen and my post-it pad at the bottom of the bag and wrote a quick note. I ripped off the sticky note and handed it to DeShawn.

Call your mom, I'd written. *Don't open the door for anyone.*

DeShawn looked alarmed. "Skylar?"

I tousled his hair and went out the door after the cop.

He led me down to the sidewalk, and from there, his squad car. He was kind of heavyset, I thought; maybe I could outrun him. Don't be a moron, I told myself. All I really wanted was to go home. If I complicated matters by running from the police, what were the odds that they'd happily sign off on returning me to the reservation?

It sucked, I thought, that strangers got to decide where I was allowed to live.

My heart fell into my stomach. We drove right out of Angel Falls and missed the turnpike. We weren't headed to the reservation after all.

I wanted to shout, *Where are we going?* I couldn't throw open the door; the back doors didn't open from the inside. I couldn't roll the window down and climb out. Dad had shown me a trick once, when I was twelve, how to shatter glass just by tapping it with a spark plug. I wished I had a spark plug.

We pulled over at a station alongside a barren, rural road. The police officer opened my door and let me climb out, my duffel bag over my shoulder. By this point I was extremely confused. A county cop in a tan uniform came out of the building, a piece of chewing tobacco in his mouth. "Come on, boy," he said to me.

My spirits sank. I followed him to his car and piled into the back seat. He turned on the country music station and sang along with his radio.

The stars were out when we arrived at our destination, a real ritzy town I had never seen in my entire life. Oh, I thought, I know what's going on. It's a mistake. They're sending the wrong foster kid to the wrong home. I looked much more like my Finnish American mom than my Native American dad. Probably somebody at CPS had gotten his wires crossed and assumed that the Skylar St. Clair who belonged on an Indian reservation couldn't possibly be me.

I dug around in my duffel bag and penned a quick note. The county cop opened the back door and I got out of the car, my legs stiff. I handed him the note.

He chuckled. "No mistake, son," he said, crumpling the note. "This is a real nice home. You'll be lucky if they adopt you."

My heart stopped.

The cop put his hand on my back and pushed me up a flight of steps. I stumbled. My whole body felt like ice. This wasn't happening. This wasn't happening. This wasn't happening--

"Is that him? Ray! He's here!"

The woman in the doorway was extremely blonde. I'm serious; her dye job was so bright, I felt like a brunet. She snatched me into her arms and pulled me to her chest in a crushing hug. I couldn't see the look on my face, but I imagined it was mortified.

The county cop chuckled again. "You two play nice now," he said. He retreated down the steps and into his car.

The blonde lady pulled back and examined me. "Oh," she exclaimed, "I wanted a boy *just* like you! Come in! You'll catch a cold!"

No, I really wouldn't. This was Arizona, not Anchorage.

Whoever this woman was, she didn't possess any of Rafael's empathetic telepathy. She grabbed me by my wrist, jibbering with excitement, and tugged me into her home, kicking the door shut along the way. I kind of resented being manhandled like that. I jerked my hand free from hers and gave her a disbelieving look. The look went right over her head.

"*Ray!*" she shouted. "Our new boy's here! He's Indian, too! He doesn't look it, though!"

A mousy looking guy with a receding hairline came dismally into the foyer. He was much older than his wife. His glasses were big and blocky, and he mumbled something under his breath without looking at either of us.

The woman cleared her throat. She smoothed out the imaginary wrinkles in her pressed gray suit and neatly folded her hands. "How do you do, Skylar?" she said--very slowly. What was that about? "I'm Carla Buthrop. This is my husband, Ray. We're your foster parents."

Except they weren't.

"I think it's just wonderful," Mrs. Buthrop gushed. "You not being able to talk and your dad abandoning you, and us coming along and plucking you out of the gutter. I just think it's so terrific!"

Yeah, lady. Disabilities are a lot of fun.

"I *really* hope you'll be happy here, Skylar," Mrs. Buthrop said. "I can't have kids of my own. But I can make other kids happy..."

However airheaded she may have been, I suddenly felt bad for her. It wasn't her fault that she was kind of...I'm not going to finish that sentence. I patted her arm in a way I meant to be consoling. Bad idea. She crooned and crushed me to her chest again.

"I'm going to make sure your room's ready!"

Mrs. Buthrop tore out of the room like a tornado. Mr. Buthrop coughed and caught my eye.

"Sorry about her," he said.

It didn't matter. I'd made up my mind: With or without the police, I was going home. Granted, I didn't know what city I was in, but I could probably bus it back to Nettlebush. I had cash on me. Maybe not enough cash. Mr. Buthrop drifted out of the foyer and I followed him. I made a cursory sweep of the decadent house around me. A big, open kitchen with a tiled, black-and-white floor. White was a recurring color scheme around here. A cookie jar standing on top of the refrigerator. Now why would it be up there? A vase underneath the living room server table when it should have been on top. Rich people were kind of predictable. And the Buthrops were definitely rich.

Mr. Buthrop sat on the white leather sofa to watch football. Mrs. Buthrop came into the living room, pulling a little boy by his hand.

"And here's your little brother!" she said.

The boy looked terrified. I could tell just by looking at him that he was Native American, but probably not Shoshone. Shoshone eyes tend to have dramatic epicanthic folds. His didn't. Actually, the longer I looked at him, the more I was convinced that I had seen him before. His hair was cut close to his head. His eyes were an olive green, almost gold. And out of nowhere it hit me--

No way, I thought.

It was Danny, Marilu's friend.

I dropped my duffel bag and tried to call his name. I checked myself. It was one of those incredibly rare moments when I'd forgotten I couldn't speak.

"Would you like some cookies, boys?" Mrs. Buthrop asked. She went through the kitchen archway and opened a pantry door.

Danny eyed me uncertainly. I picked up my duffel bag and started toward him.

He darted up the staircase. I heard a door slap shut with finality.

"Here we are!" Mrs. Buthrop sang. She emerged from the kitchen with a package of sugar-free cookies. "I guess Danny isn't hungry..."

I turned my back on her and climbed up the carpeted staircase. I threw open the doors on my left and right until I found Danny on his bed, his mouth open in a soundless yelp.

I closed the door behind me. I searched the contents of my duffel bag for my pen and notepad. Danny backed away from me, his back against the wall.

I scribbled a hasty note and showed it to him.

I'm Marilu's cousin.

He was still, at first, and silent; I wasn't sure whether he had read what I'd written. But he had. He jumped off the bed. His eyes were was big and as wide as saucers.

"You came to take me home," he said. His tone was eager, but his voice was hoarse with neglect.

I couldn't possibly leave without him. I penned a second note.

Yes. But not right now. I need to plan it so we don't get caught.

"Why aren't you talking?"

I hesitated. I didn't want to scare him; but I pulled aside the leather cords hanging around my neck, the plains flute dangling at the end, and showed him the big red scars on my throat. His eyes rounded with understanding.

"Wovoka sent you."

I looked at him, confused.

Danny reached under his bed. His room, I realized, was austere for a little boy. Probably the Buthrops had decorated it themselves. A small TV stood in one corner. The bedspread and carpet were a matching blue. Nothing personal hung on the walls. No God's Eyes or pendleton blankets or spiderweb charms. Nothing to suggest that this room belonged to a Paiute boy. It didn't really belong to him.

Danny pressed a sheet of yellow paper into my hands.

The quality of the drawing was about what you would expect from a ten-year-old. The drawing depicted a snub-nosed man in a Panama hat and flowing trench coat. His muscles were exaggerated in great detail.

"He healed people with his hands and made ice and snow and rain fall from the sky. He turned sunlight into fire. He could talk to people without words. The white men shot him with a shotgun but he didn't bleed."

Oh--the shaman who had started the ghost dance. We called him Wood Cutter back home.

Danny held his drawing to his chest. He peered at me timidly.

I ran my fingers over the back of his head. He shook his head free and scrunched up his face.

I spent the night in the room across the hall from Danny's--just as austere, but decorated in red rather than blue. All that bright red concentrated in one place sort of made me feel jumpy. I didn't really sleep, focused instead on how we were going to escape.

First I needed to figure out where the heck we were. I could have asked Danny, but he was asleep, and the thought hadn't occurred to me while he was awake. I eased open the bedroom door and crept out into the hall. I stole my way down the staircase, blindly groping the banister in the dark. A cordless phone hung on the kitchen wall. I slid it out of its cradle and dialed 411.

"Four-one-one for Heavenly Hills, Arizona," the operator said.

I hung up. It's not like I could have stayed on the line for a chat.

I retreated into the red room and drew maps in my schoolbooks. I thought if I could retrace the route from Angel Falls to Heavenly Hills, only backwards, I could get Danny and me to Nettlebush. The problem with that plan was that I was really bad with directions. An actual road map would have been a lot more helpful. Mr. Buthrop's study didn't have one. I checked while he and his wife were sleeping.

Breakfast the following morning was an uncomfortable affair. The Buthrops had an outlandish dining room with one of those hanging crystal chandeliers. Mrs. Buthrop insisted that we all eat together at least once a day, and it looked like her specialty meal was stale cereal. The happy family pretense irritated me more than anything. Danny kept shooting furtive looks my way. I hoped we weren't too obvious.

"Your wardrobe is horrible," Mrs. Buthrop told me. "I'll take you clothes shopping tomorrow!"

She pinned a note to my shirt--like I was five--and sent Danny and me to the street corner for the schoolbus. I watched Danny get on the bus; I watched the bus pull away from the curb. I ripped the note off of my shirt without reading it and walked into town.

First things first: I found the transit bus stop and copied down the timetable in my notebook. The only route on the timetable I was familiar with was Route 60. My next step was to find a convenience store and buy a road map. Unbelievably, I couldn't find a single convenience store in the entire neighborhood. What did these people do when they wanted to buy gum? I guessed Danny and I would have to fly blind. Alright, I thought. If I could figure out how to get to Route 89, I could still bring us back to Nettlebush. I remembered seeing the 89 road sign on the return trips from the pauwaus.

I spent a couple of hours scoping out Heavenly Hills. Trial and error brought me to a train station to the north. A girl in a fedora and sunglasses stood playing the saxophone between platforms. I wasted time reading the train schedules and made sure one of the ticket tellers saw me.

I walked back to the Buthrops' house around three o'clock. I marched inside and straight up the staircase, pretending I had homework. I searched the bathrooms until I found a bottle of peroxide. I stowed the peroxide away in my duffel bag.

"Dinner!" Mrs. Buthrop sang a few hours later.

Mrs. Buthrop prattled about her yoga class at the dinner table and Mr. Buthrop craned his neck at an awkward angle, trying to catch a glimpse of the television screen in the living room. The canned tomatoes were soggy, the canned peas like mush. Danny didn't eat much. I worried at that, but Mrs. Buthrop never noticed.

At night I listened to the radio in the red bedroom. I turned on the Nettlebush radio station; and the pre-recorded sounds of elderberry clapsticks and the double-skin drum very nearly broke my heart in half. Danny came into the room while I was comparing timetables in one of my notebooks. He climbed up on the red bedspread and folded his legs.

"Do you know my dad?" Danny asked.

I smiled apologetically. I shook my head.

"But you're going to take me to him," Danny said suspiciously. "Right?"

I gave him a solemn nod.

"He's the best dad," Danny said. And then he regaled me with tales of their last summer together, how they'd gone crab fishing up north and worn matching baseball caps, how they'd eaten lunch everyday at a restaurant called Old Country Joe's where the waitresses wore pigtails and if you could finish a jumbo banana split, you got it for free. I listened to his stories with an encouraging smile. I knew what it was like to have a good father. I didn't doubt for a second how much Danny missed his.

Danny fell asleep on my bed that night, his mouth halfway open and his legs dangling over the side. I turned off the radio and righted him on the mattress. I tucked the pillow beneath his head, the blanket over his body. I turned off the lamp and curled up at his side.

I waited until Saturday night to make my move. I stole quietly into Danny's bedroom and shook him awake. He rubbed his eyes and pulled the drawstring on his lamp, light flooding the room.

"Are we leaving?" he whispered wondrously.

I showed him my hand, a sticky note stuck to my palm.

Pack some clothes.

Danny crawled out of bed and inched around the room. I left him to his own devices and treaded quietly down the staircase. I took a little money from the Buthrops' cookie jar, the one on top of the refrigerator, and the vase underneath the server. I felt badly about it; but I didn't know how much money Danny and I were going to need on the run.

"I'm here," Danny whispered hoarsely, plucking my elbow. He had changed out of his pajamas and into a bright orange shirt. His backpack hung from his shoulders, weighted and zipped.

My pulse throbbed loudly in my ears. I grabbed Danny's hand and led him across the foyer. I kept thinking: Any minute now, one of them will wake up and catch us.

The front door clicked softly when I unlocked it; the doorknob hissed when I turned it; the door opened and we crossed the threshold and we were outside, the cold air on our faces, the couple upstairs none the wiser.

I pushed the door shut and we ran.

We were breathless when we arrived at the train station. Danny leaned against the column between platforms and I wrote a quick note on my post-it pad. I was already running out of sticky notes.

"Now what?" Danny asked, his voice scratchy.

I gestured for him to follow me. I got in line at the teller's station and waited, scanning the concourse for cameras.

"Next?" the teller said.

We stepped up to the booth. I smiled at the teller and showed her my note.

Two tickets for Newcastle, Wyoming, please.

She gave me a long, weird look. She glanced at Danny and frowned.

"Here you are," she said at last, and slid the tickets across the counter to me. I paid her for the tickets, picked up Danny's hand, and started through the concourse.

"We're riding a train?" Danny whispered to me.

I shook my head.

There were small black cameras mounted above the platform arches. Cameras like those always have blind spots. In this case, the cameras were poised to catch anyone walking up the concourse; walk against the wall and you were invisible.

I pulled Danny aside, and we walked the wall to the men's restroom.

"I don't have to go," Danny said.

I checked and made sure the stalls were all vacant. I wedged my plains flute in the hinges of the restroom door to jam it shut. I fished the bottle of peroxide from the bottom of my duffel bag and turned on the tap in the sink.

Poor Danny. He yelped when I grabbed him by the scruff of his neck and shoved his head under the cold water.

Danny straightened up and shot me an angry look in the mirror. I pressed my finger to my lips and jiggled the peroxide bottle. I don't think he really knew what I was trying to tell him; but the second time I bent his head over the sink, he showed me less resistance. I uncapped the peroxide bottle and poured its contents over his scalp. I wasn't as careful as I ought to have been; peroxide splashed all over the backs of my hands and stained them stark white.

I shut off the faucet and Danny sat on the cement floor with his head underneath the air dryer. The restroom door rattled, but held strong. "Goddamn door's locked," I heard a man say on the other side.

Danny studied his reflection in the mirror when his hair had finished drying. "Why am I *blond*?" he cried.

I clapped my hand over his mouth, eyes on the door. The door didn't budge. The man must have left. Good, I thought.

I unzipped Danny's backpack and stuffed a new shirt, a blue one, into his arms. I pointed at a bathroom stall and freed my plains flute from the door. Danny grumbled and locked himself in the stall to change clothes. I tugged off my turtleneck and replaced it with a button-down.

It was after midnight when we made our way to the bus stop. We huddled in the shadows of the arching, grated roof until the night bus pulled up to the curb. The bus' doors gushed open and outward, reminding me of a pop-up book. We climbed on board and I left change in the driver's receptacle.

"Cool," Danny said. He charged to the very back of the bus and sat on his knees. I sat next to him and opened my notebook, double-checking the timetable.

So this was it, I thought. I didn't know what would happen once we made our way to Nettlebush. But I knew this: We belonged in our homes. It had taken sixteen years for me to find my home. I didn't care how many times the cops came and dragged me off; I'd run away every time. As for Danny...I only hoped his father knew a lawyer. Maybe Mrs. Red Clay could help them out.

"You can tell Wovoka he sent a good one," Danny said.

He curled up on his seat for a nap. I smiled--though he couldn't see it--and touched his papery blond hair.

17
The Straw That Broke the Camel's Back

There's a split second, I find, between sleeping and waking, where the dream world carries over to the real world and you're not sure which is which.

I felt the battered pillow beneath my head; I felt the starched blanket beneath my back; and immediately I thought, I must be home.

Blearily, I rubbed my eyes. I sat up, smothering a yawn. The events of the previous night came speeding back to me. To begin with, I wasn't home; I was in a roadside motel. I looked to the bottom of the bed and found Danny with a remote control in his hands, his eyes glued to a bulbous television set.

"We're already on TV," he said, his voice characteristically hoarse.

I sat on the edge of the bed and watched the AMBER Alert scroll across the top of the news broadcast.

"Missing: Daniel Patreya; 10; 4'7"; 79 lbs. Hair: Brown; Eyes: Green; Skin: Brown. Last seen wearing: Orange t-shirt and khakis. Missing: Skylar Sinclair; 16; 5'6"; 110 lbs. Hair: Blond; Eyes: Brown; Skin: White. Last seen wearing: Gray turtleneck and jeans."

I kind of thought it was cool that they'd gotten my name wrong.

"I'm hungry," Danny said.

I fished change out of my duffel bag. I was pretty sure I'd seen a vending machine last night in the motel parking lot.

Danny waited in the motel room while I went outside. I wasn't worried about cops coming after us. I thought the cops had a pretty good reason to think I'd jump a train to Wyoming and take Danny with me--specifically that Wyoming was the last place anyone outside of Nettlebush had seen Dad.

I bought cookies and crackers from the vending machine when I heard a crash and a scrape behind me. I turned around to find three guys junking a parked car.

"What you looking at?" one of them spat at me.

I shrugged.

"Yeah, that's right," said the guy, and he and his friends strolled off with a battery, an alternator, and a passenger-side door.

Danny ate his breakfast, and then we made a quick trip to the drugstore, where I bought us a road map. A few minutes later and we boarded our next bus, Danny leaning against the window.

Danny peered at my lap. "What's that?"

I'd taken a spark plug from the car in the parking lot. I knew it was theft, but with the state those guys had left the car in, it wasn't like the original owner could drive it anymore.

"Does Marilu talk about me?"

I gave him a soft look and nodded. *All the time*, I wanted to say; but it would have taken too long to retrieve my notepad, and I was running out of paper.

"She's my best friend," Danny explained, "even if she's a girl. I hope she misses me."

The beeper at the bottom of my duffel bag whistled loudly. My heart jump-started. I'd damn near forgotten about that thing.

Dad, I realized. Dad was calling me.

Frantic, I unzipped my duffel bag. I scooped out bundles of wrinkled clothing until I found the beeper. I pulled it free and read the message scrolling across the screen.

I frowned. Dad had only written one word, not even punctuated.

kilgallen

What was a kilgallen supposed to be? I don't like to admit it; but I was disappointed. Dad must have messaged me while drinking.

We rode the bus to the end of its route and departed in a decrepit town covered in graffiti. It was lunchtime, and we visited the supermarket--which wasn't as super as its name indicated--and bought cold cuts, water bottles, and fruit. The cold cuts were really for Danny; I don't eat meat. We sat on the curb and ate together while I consulted the road map.

There were no outbound buses; we had to leg it. We walked for two miles, Danny complaining of the heat. I lent him one of my shirts to wrap around his head and played the plains flute to pass the time. I played Ring of Fire and thought of Rafael.

We arrived in a town called Tully and I stopped and consulted the map again. Relief washed over me when I realized we could follow Route 60 right down to Route 89. I noticed something else, too, something I hadn't the first time around: Kilgallen was the name of a city.

Was Dad waiting for us in Kilgallen? My stomach lurched. The only place where Dad was safe from the law was Nettlebush.

"I don't feel good," Danny said faintly.

I sat him down on a bench outside of a deli, concerned. I rubbed circles across his back.

He hunched over and vomited water on the sidewalk.

If I wasn't panicking before, I was panicking now. I had never heard of anyone vomiting water before. I didn't know what to do; I couldn't take him to a hospital without the staff alerting social services.

We had to hurry back to Nettlebush. Dr. Stout could take a look at him. Granny or the tribal council could call his father in Nevada. Everything hinged on getting Danny to Nettlebush.

Danny clung to my hand as I led him to the bus stop. We boarded the bus and he slumped against the window when we settled into warm, dusty seats. I crumbled a banana and tried to feed it to him, thinking it might comfort his stomach. He wasn't interested.

We got off the bus in a town called Newfeld, Danny looking wan. It was four o'clock in the afternoon and there were no southbound buses until five. Nor was I up for hitchhiking, having heard horror stories about friendly-old-men-turned-roadside-killers from my dad.

"I'm tired," Danny said wearily.

I felt his forehead with the back of my hand. His skin was burning hot. I wished I had some willow leaves for him to eat. I settled for the next best thing and gave him a bottle of water and a second shirt to wear over his first. If we couldn't kill the fever, we might as well sweat it out.

I brought Danny to a diner to get him out of the sun. He ordered french fries and a root beer float but ate very little. I wanted him to eat. I didn't know what had caused his sudden sickness, but I didn't think an empty stomach was going to dispel it.

As soon as we left the diner, he threw up again--more water.

Maybe the problem was that he was drinking too many liquids. Was that even a real problem? I made him get on my back for the brief walk to the bus stop. He was skinny; but then, so was I. He felt like a brick wall resting on my back. He fell asleep the moment we boarded the bus.

I didn't know what to do. I almost wanted to start praying, except that my belief in God was tenuous at best. I was scared, really scared, that Danny might be dying. In which case, it was wrong of me to drag him down to Nettlebush. I had to get him to a hospital.

One last time, I checked my map. Kilgallen was pretty close. If Dad was in Kilgallen... Even if he wasn't, there had to be some sort of healthcare facility nearby.

I carried Danny off the bus when it rolled to a stop, his head on my shoulder, his backpack hanging off his arm.

Kilgallen was a proper city, tall gray tenements crowded together and narrow streets paved with blackened asphalt. It was oddly quiet, though, like a ghost town, and the whole place smelled faintly of wet, rotted cabbage. It had an open market and a defunct library and some kind of a metro. And I had absolutely no idea where my dad was.

Danny woke up and begged to be put down. My sore back agreed. He held my hand as we scaled the sidewalk. What I really needed was a city map, I thought. Above the skyline I saw a towering complex of gray-white buildings and wondered whether they were the city hospital. It couldn't hurt to find out.

I gripped Danny's hand tightly while we walked through the city. And I started whistling.

You don't need your vocal cords to whistle; it's the same premise as blowing air through a flute. When I was little, Dad and I had developed a system. If we were in two separate areas in the house, and he wanted to find me fast, all he had to do was give me a shout and wait for me to whistle--a low note and a high note, the same every time.

The pedestrians looked at me like I had lost my head. I didn't care. I didn't know how else to find Dad. Danny and I crossed the street.

"Where are we going?" Danny asked groggily.

I stopped walking when I heard a dog barking. That by itself wasn't peculiar; but the barking drew closer and closer; and the closer it drew, the more I thought it sounded familiar.

Balto charged out of the nearest alley. He leapt at me, his paws on my chest, and knocked me to the ground.

I was much too stunned to retaliate. I felt his sandpaper tongue all over my face, wet and scratchy, and his cold, wet nose prodding me, just to make sure I was real. He looked even bigger than I remembered him being. I thought: How the heck did he get here?

I sat up on the pavement, dull pain shooting up my spine. I started to pet Balto when suddenly he ran away. I stood up and Danny frowned at me, like I was hiding something from him.

Balto came running back to me, closely followed by Rafael.

For a moment, I thought he was a mirage. He looked too good to be true, lank, ink-black hair falling down his broad back, blue eyes framed in blue glasses, his arms bare under a black vest. And oh, was he beautiful--the most beautiful thing I'd seen in more than a month.

He walked toward me, slowly at first, like maybe he thought I was a mirage, too. I felt the smile tugging at the corners of my lips. He walked a little faster.

He reached for me, his hands finding my hips; he kissed me, sudden and ravenous, desperate even, and my arms slid around his neck and my hands tangled in his hair, because this was home away from home, because my body, singing with reprieve, begged me to belong to his.

Then, just as sudden, he pulled back and hugged me.

"I love you, too."

I'd heard of the straw that broke the camel's back before, but I'd never understood that phrase until now.

You silly boy, I thought weakly. I smiled against Rafael's shoulder. I closed my eyes, reveling in the feel of him, the feel of his heartbeat, the scent of him. I wondered if it was possible to want something so much that it had to want you back. I felt like it was.

We separated, and I reached for Danny's hand. Danny shook his head and slid to his knees.

I saw the confusion on Rafael's face; and also the worry. "He's sick?"

Rafael didn't wait for a reply. He picked Danny up with one arm and lifted him over his shoulder.

"C'mon," Rafael said to me. "Mary's got the car."

I followed him through the city streets, Balto loping gracefully at my side. I scuffed my fingers across his sandy-and-silver pelt and he responded enthusiastically by showing me his lazy tongue. I know, boy, I thought. I missed you, too.

Gabriel's SUV was parked alongside a bakery. I didn't see Gabriel anywhere, though; or even my dad. Just Mary, leaning against the hood and snacking on a cupcake. Her hair was teased to merciless heights and decorated with delightfully unsettling skull-shaped pins. She grinned devilishly when she saw the four of us approaching.

"My buddy's here!" she said, and pulled me into a crushing hug. I felt like I'd been on the receiving end of a lot of those lately.

"Don't kill him," Rafael said scathingly. "Anyway, we have to hurry back to the reservation. This kid's sick."

Mary took a look at Danny. He peered at her, owlishly, and she felt his forehead with the back of her hand. Her nails were long and red-black.

"Aw, he's not sick. He just needs a cupcake."

"What are you even talking about?"

I rolled my eyes and smiled. Rafael loaded Danny into the back of the SUV and buckled his seatbelt for him. Mary got into the driver's seat and passed a box of cupcakes back to us. I sat in the middle row with Rafael, Rafael digging through the cupcake box, Balto comfortably perched on the floor at my ankles, and we took off.

"You want one?" Rafael asked, offering the cupcakes to Danny.

Danny groaned. "I'll throw up..."

Rafael gave me a dubious look. He offered me a cupcake, but I shook my head. "Who is this kid?"

Danny, I signed. *He's Paiute.*

Rafael took a moment to figure out the fingerspelling. He scowled. "They kidnap him, too?"

I nodded.

"I swear to God..."

I pulled Dad's beeper out of my duffel bag. I showed it to Rafael, my head tilted to one side.

Rafael's face took on an expression of understanding.

"When they first came and took you," he began, "everyone went crazy. Your grandma kept saying, 'It's my fault, it's my fault.' Your dad was angry, but in a cold way. He wouldn't talk to anyone, not even Cyrus At Dawn.

"Then that cop came--she told us you were staying with her. We started to relax, figured it was only a matter of time before you came back to the reservation. Well, alright, I didn't really relax. I couldn't stop thinking about you. I guess the shaman noticed. He pulled me aside during the sun dance, said that I was too distracted, that I was gonna hurt someone, and sent me home. It didn't help, though. I just kept thinking about you.

"Then that cop comes back, tells us you were taken away from her. Your dad goes into overdrive mode. Says he's going to find you and bring you home. I told him not to leave the reserve. I told him you'd be pissed if he got in trouble. I said I'd go looking for you instead. So he showed me how to use that--" He waved his hand, annoyed. "Beepy thing--"

I grinned.

"Shut up," he said, bashful and testy. "Mary and I went to that Angel city place and knocked on pretty much every door. Talked to the kids from your old school, too. We brought Balto along, figured he could help us pick up on your scent. The cops pulled us over at one point." A smile threatened to spread across his face. "Mary told them she was an illegal immigrant running a trafficking ring--"

"Me gusta," Mary said.

"--and they got fed up with her, but then Balto started growling and they kind of backed off, the wusses. Anyway--no luck, so we went to the next city. Mary said I should page you and let you know where we were. I didn't know that it would work. Those damn phones are about as hard to write on as the computers are."

I hid my smile, lest he think I was picking fun at him. I watched the highway sliding past the windows. I watched Danny in the rear-view mirror and saw him fast asleep, wrapped in a spare blanket.

"Where were you?" Rafael asked. "I mean, where did they take you?"

I shot him a teasing smile. I rooted around in my duffel bag for a schoolbook to write in. Something told me this was going to take a while.

The stars were like jewels in the sky, and they shone the brightest over Nettlebush. Or maybe I was so happy to be home, I could only see its beauty.

Mary parked Gabriel's car in the parking lot outside the hospital. Rafael scooped Danny out of the back seat and helped him to the ground. "I can walk," Danny reported. "And I'm hungry now."

"You've gotta get checked out first," Rafael said gruffly.

"I'm gonna go find your dad," Mary told me. She winked, her grin the grin that mothers fear.

Rafael and I walked Danny up the hospital steps. "You should've eaten the cupcakes," Rafael said. We walked through the entry doors and the receptionist, Ms. Bright, gawked at us. Or maybe she was gawking at Balto. It's not everyday a coywolf strolls in for a checkup.

We sat in the waiting room and I rubbed Danny's back, concerned. I tried feeding him an apple from my duffel bag. "No, I want frybread," he said. Balto eyed the apple with interest.

Danny took a paper and crayons from his backpack and sat drawing Wovoka in long and loopy lines.

"You like drawing?" Rafael said.

"Yes."

"Can I show you something?" Rafael ran his fingers through his hair, searching, no doubt, for the colored pencils that always rested behind his ears.

The two of them drew together, Rafael showing Danny a shortcut for sketching faces. A nurse came into the waiting room and called Danny's name.

The nurse, I realized, was Rosa. She dropped her clipboard and took Rafael and me into an emotional hug. Rafael looked flustered. Rosa pat Danny on the head--maybe so he wouldn't feel left out--and sweetly, silently, led us to an exam room. She left us with Dr. Stout, who listened to Danny's vitals and took his blood pressure.

"Water poisoning!" Dr. Stout shouted, much in the same way that a man who has uncovered the secrets of the universe might shout them from the comfort of his home. Unless he's greedy and just wants to keep them to himself.

Rosa slipped back into the examination room. She beckoned for me with a crooked finger.

I looked at Rafael, and he swallowed my hand up in his.

"We're going outside," he told Danny.

"Okay," Danny said. "Bring back frybread."

Rafael and I went out into the tiled hallway, where Dad and Granny awaited us.

Granny wasn't a very affectionate woman. She was kind, in her own way, but strongly reserved. She practically wrote the book on Shoshone reticence.

So it surprised me when she took me at once into her arms, patting my head with a quavering hand.

I hugged her, firmly; because it wasn't her fault, because it was okay now. She started to pull away. I dipped my hand into my duffel bag and pulled out a spindle rolled in silver taffeta. I'd bought it back in Heavenly Hills; I'd thought it made a nice gift, especially for a woman who spent most of her time at the loom.

"Thank you," Granny said curtly, and took the fabric from me with imperial grace.

"I'm gonna see if I can find frybread," Rafael murmured. He edged past us.

"Cubby," Dad said.

I know it's foolish; but suddenly, I felt safe. Dad reached out to hug me, and I leaned into his embrace, and I felt like I was five years old; I felt like I'd felt when I was a small child, when Dad was the biggest thing on the planet and nothing could reach me without contending with him.

Dr. Stout stuck her head through the doorway.

"Any of you know the number for the Paiute tribal office? The kid's asking for his papa."

Dad let go of me reluctantly. "I do," he said.

Dad and Granny and I went to the receptionist's desk, Balto following dutifully. Dad claimed the phone and dialed the number for the Pleasance Reserve, Ms. Bright looking on with annoyance. I took Granny's hand between mine and rubbed it. I swear she almost smiled.

"Skylar!"

Annie burst through the hospital doors, closely followed by Mary. Balto wagged his tail and bent his front legs, ready to pounce. Dad cupped his hand around the mouthpiece of the phone. Annie lunged at me in a hug that would have floored me if she were a foot taller. I caught her and twirled her. Before I knew it, we were dancing, Balto jumping and barking and trying to keep up.

"Outside!" Ms. Bright commanded. "This is a hospital, not a gymnasium!"

We went out onto the ramp outside the hospital just as Rafael came back with a plate of frybread. He nodded in passing and went through the doors to Danny.

"I never, ever thought this would happen to someone on our reservation," Annie said.

I'm just lucky like that, I signed.

Dad and Granny came outside a moment later. Dad leaned down and pet Balto's head.

"Aisling wants to keep Danny for observation," Dad said. "At least until his father gets here."

"I don't understand," Annie said. "Why exactly are they allowed to take us from our homes? For no good reason?"

Dad shook his head helplessly. Annie flared up. Times like these were when she showed her temper.

"We might as well go home," Granny said, and she shuffled down the stone steps without waiting.

"Oh, well, if you must," Annie said. She briefly grasped my hand. "I'll see you tomorrow, Skylar. That is--you are going to school tomorrow, aren't you?"

"He is," Dad answered for me.

Darn. I was hoping I could get out of it.

"You have a good night, Annie," Dad said.

Dad had started down the steps after Granny when I touched his arm, nodding toward the hospital doors.

"Of course," Dad said. "Go say good night to Rafael."

I grinned--was I really that obvious?--and hastened through the sliding glass doors.

Rafael was standing outside an in-patient room--Danny's new room, I guessed--and chewing on a stick of gum. He looked up when he noticed me and started toward me.

"That kid's kinda cool," Rafael said. "I'm glad you kidnapped him."

I rolled my eyes and slugged his elbow.

"You leaving?"

I nodded.

"I'll see you later," Rafael said.

I smiled, bemused. Later? It was already nighttime. Tomorrow was a school day.

"I'll see you later," he said stubbornly.

There was no winning with Rafael. It didn't matter, I guess, because with Rafael, even losing felt like winning. I leaned up and kissed his cheek. He grinned, abashed, and shoved my shoulder.

I dropped in on Danny to wave good night and he waved back, his mouth full of frybread. I left the hospital afterward and found Balto waiting for me on the front steps. I ruffled his ears and we went home together, side-by-side. Even before I walked through the front door, I felt well-rested. My wandering was over. I crossed the threshold and felt the heat of the hearth licking my skin. Dad and Granny and Zeke were sitting in the sitting room, Granny reading a magazine.

Wait a second. I stopped and stared.

"Hi!" Zeke said. "You're back!"

There was a cot set up in front of the fireplace. Zeke was sitting on the floor, legs folded, playing cards in his hand.

I waved, bewildered.

"Zeke is staying with us for a while," Dad said awkwardly, meaningfully. "Just until his father...sorts things out at home."

"Yeah, uh, but I won't be in your way," Zeke said. "Wow, I forgot how blond you are."

I ran my hands through my hair, mussing it up, and smiled.

I wasn't remotely tired when I went to bed that night. To begin with, I was so happy to be back in my own bedroom that I only wanted to sit up and stare at the photos on my closet door and the dreamcatcher above my window, the bags of medicinal herbs at the foot of my bed and the California or Bust poster opposite and drink in every detail. But it was more than that, too. It was paranoia. I was prepared for the police to come take me away again. I was already envisioning my next escape plan; how I would pay for the bus fare, how I would find an Amtrak if I wound up sent to another state. Could they do that? Send me to another state? I knew they'd done it to Danny. It kind of made me mad that Granny wasn't allowed to take me out of state, but a total stranger was.

A beam of light streamed past my window. I sat up, curious. I pushed open my window and peered at the ground, and there I saw Rafael, a flashlight in his hands.

"Told you," he hissed.

I pulled on a fleece jacket and eased myself out the window. I gripped the side of the log cabin and climbed to the ground.

Rafael shut off his flashlight. I felt, more than saw, his eyes on me, raking all over me, and his subtle smile shining through the darkness. And I could only smile at him, like a stupid, stupid fool.

Hi. I am in love with you.

He reached for me, in an almost impatient way, and I yielded, as I'd known I would. His mouth against mine was demanding and needy; my mouth against his was gentle and compliant; and it felt good, it felt better than anything I could remember. I kissed him, an unforgiving staccato, and where my teeth pulverized his bottom lip, my tongue followed in soothing strokes, soothing away the pain. He made a small sound in the back of his throat, a hitched breath; his tongue slid against mine; stars sparked behind my eyes, my hands curving to the contours of his face. The battle broke, and my heart flipped; he kissed me slowly, so slowly, like he was savoring every second, his hands on my waist, my stomach tingling, my temples pounding with dizzying blood.

It was bittersweet when we broke apart, Rafael's forehead pressed against mine.

"Me, too," he mouthed against my lips.

I slid my palm against his--warm, rough--I tangled our fingers together, mine long, his hard. I didn't care about breathing. I just wanted to kiss him again.

"You wanna go somewhere?"

I considered. There was the starfield, where the flowers, blue stars, closed at dusk and opened at dawn. There was the promontory in the badlands, one of Rafael's favorite places--not one of mine, for safety reasons.

I hooked my hand around his. He lumbered after me as I started walking the path to the church.

"The cupola?" he asked, confounded.

I shook my head. I led him around the back of the church to the graveyard gates.

Rafael clicked his flashlight back on. "You're nuts," he accused. "What do you want with a cemetery in the middle of the night?"

I tossed him an amused smile, eyebrows raised. He wasn't afraid, was he?

"Don't be stupid," he said hastily.

He *was* afraid. He jumped when the old, creaking gates swung shut in the wind with a loud bang. I snickered soundlessly.

"If we anger the dead..."

I couldn't believe my ears. I gave Rafael a consoling pat on the shoulder and he took a swing at me, disconcerted. I stole his flashlight and walked along the first row of graves. Rafael scurried after me, glancing over his shoulder.

I found her a few rows back from where I'd expected her to be, which could only mean one thing--she had lived to a very old age. I knelt down and revered her, lost in time.

"Taken Alive. 1851 - 1949. They did not take her spirit."

I touched the weather-worn headstone. I felt I had to thank her, remorseful though her memory was. The suffering she had endured was the only reason my family existed. And to think that this was her burial place, the only place on Earth where she and I could simultaneously coexist... I wanted to talk to her. I wonder how many of us really think about that; the trials our ancestors faced, the stories they passed down to us, lying dormant in our blood.

"Everyone who died in Nettlebush is buried here," Rafael said. "Can I have the flashlight? I wanna find one of my ancestors, too."

At least he wasn't afraid anymore. I stood and handed him the flashlight. "Thanks," he said. I followed him through the blocks of stone.

"There's one of the Takes Flights, damn them, people get our names mixed up all the time. 'Hadrian Gives Light,' never heard of you, sorry buddy... Look, there's my grandma on my dad's side, the one with the nails like claws... Wait, I'm going in the wrong direction..."

He stopped suddenly. He shot me a quick smile over his shoulder and pointed at a headstone.

"Rumilly Gives Light. That's my oldest ancestor. I mean, not my oldest, just the oldest one whose name I know. She would've gone to Carlisle Indian School around the same time as your...great-great-grandmother, or something like that."

I sat down on the ground next to Rafael and smiled, my fist under my chin and my elbow on my knee, encouraging him to talk.

"In Shoshone," he said, " 'Gives Light' is 'Makan Imaa.' Oh, you wanna know something? 'Light' and 'morning' are the same word in Shoshone. So my family doesn't really know whether we're supposed to be called Gives Light, or Gives Morning. Rumilly went with Gives Light, I guess. Uncle Gabriel says she was a candlemaker, so maybe that's why. Plains People named themselves back then. It's not like today when we're stuck with whatever crappy names our parents gave us."

Like Skylar. I wrinkled my face.

"Like Rafael," Rafael corrected distastefully.

I exaggerated my frown. I liked the name Rafael.

"Yeah, well, I don't like it. It makes me sound like I belong stuck to the top of the Sistine Chapel. You can blame my mom for that. She was big on the Christian stuff."

I squeezed Rafael's shoulder. I knew he missed her.

For a moment, there was only the sound of silence. The night wind rustled the leaves hanging from the oak trees, fresh and green, verdant with spring. Rafael tilted his head back and gazed at them appreciatively. He looked at me and showed me a small smile.

"I don't think you're afraid of anything."

Sure I was. I just didn't like people to know about it.

"Well, I'm not afraid of anything," Rafael said. "Not when I'm with you."

19
Lemons and Blueberries

When I woke the next morning, it was unreal, like my body had
yet to realize that we were home. I guessed I had to get used to my
bedroom all over again.

What was even more unreal was finding Zeke Owns Forty in the
kitchen, laughing at a detective story on the radio. He was pretty
messy about it, too; he laughed with his mouth open, blue corn
mush spattering all over the scrubbed table.

"That Jack the Ripper cracks me up!"

I didn't *want* to question his sanity; but I just couldn't help myself.
Granny gave me a bowl of blue corn mush and changed the radio
station.

"Hey!" Zeke complained.

"You will *not* interrupt my soap operas."

Zeke shrugged and slouched over his breakfast bowl.

I probably shouldn't have stayed out so late with Rafael last night.
I was dead tired when I walked to school with Zeke, Zeke
humming obliviously. I'm home, I thought, euphoric. Home, but
tired. The bull and pinyon pines, the dirt paths and log cabins, the
blue, blue sky and blue-gray badlands--they were mine and I was
theirs.

I was bombarded with questions the moment I set foot in the
classroom.

"Where were you?"

"What happened?"

"I saw your name on the news!"

"Were you arrested?"

"Did you go to jail?"

"Did you go to the white house?"

Maybe they'd all simultaneously forgotten I was mute. I returned their inquiries with dull stares and settled into my seat. It wasn't enough to discourage Aubrey, who went on jabbering in my ear--"I knew you'd be back! Said as much, didn't I, Annie? I set aside some artichokes for you, and some mint, of course, are you allergic?"--until the teacher walked into the schoolhouse.

"Alright, everyone," Mr. Red Clay said, rapping his knuckles on the chalkboard. "Let's talk science."

How Mr. Red Clay's lessons usually worked was that the entire school day--four hours--was devoted to one subject. When he addressed the whole room, he spoke about a broad concept. When he went up and down the rows, reviewing with each class individually, he adjusted the topic depending on how old of a child he was talking to. The first graders got the simple versions and the twelfth graders got the more elaborate details.

It was the same today as every day. When he spoke to the smaller kids, he taught them about solids, liquids, and gases. When he spoke to us, he talked about boiling water.

"Boiling is not a heating process, but a cooling process," Mr. Red Clay said. "When you boil water and it produces steam, that's thermal energy being dragged out of the water. Loss of energy, loss of heat. If you could stick your finger in a pot of boiling water and endure the excruciating heat at the surface, you would find that the bottom of the pot is ice cold."

He threw William Sleeping Fox a swift look. "I *don't* advise you to try it."

At the end of the school day, I stuck around to talk to Mr. Red Clay in private.

"Skylar. How may I help you?"

I didn't really know how I should start. *I was in foster care*, I signed. *I had to go to a different school--*

"Yes, I know. Your case worker--" An unpleasant expression ghosted across his face. "--called me at three in the morning for your records."

Oh, jeez. *I'm really sorry about that*, I signed.

"No, no, don't be. So what is it?"

In my other school, I signed, *I took a couple of tests. But the curriculum was different--*

"You failed the tests," Mr. Red Clay surmised.

I was starting to feel sheepish. *Is there any way I can make it up? Extra credit?*

"There's no need," Mr. Red Clay said. "I never intended to count whatever grades they gave you."

Well, that sure surprised me.

Mr. Red Clay smiled; I had the impression it was meant to hide a smirk. "You'll forgive me for saying this," he said, "but I don't put much stock in this country's education system. There's a reason why American schools are ranked twenty-first in the entire world. Let me put it this way, Skylar. There are only three things you need to know in life. Who you are, how the world works, and how you can change it."

I didn't know how to change it. I knew what I would have liked to change--a lot of things--but I didn't know how to change them.

I went to the hospital after school to see how Danny was doing. I found him sitting up in bed and snacking on sweet potatoes. A man I took to be his father sat staunchly at his bedside and wouldn't let go of his hand. Poor guy looked like he'd been crying only minutes ago.

"They adopted him," Mr. Patreya told me. "Without me knowing about it. I kept asking those social workers, 'Where did you take my son?' No one would tell me. That can't be legal, can it? Adopting him without telling me?"

My hands curled at my sides. No, it wasn't legal. But the law didn't seem to concern itself with Native Americans.

I penned a letter to Marilu as soon as I went home. I was sure that Danny would be back in Pleasance long before my letter arrived, but I wanted to tell her about our meeting anyway.

"Hey!" Zeke said, shoving his face in front of mine. "What are you doing?"

Zeke, I'd realized, was kind of a nosy person. I really don't mean that disparagingly; I just can't think of a better way to put it. I showed him my stationery, but he'd already lost interest; he wandered off to the staircase to play percussion on the banisters. I wondered whether he was on ADD meds.

It was five o'clock when I heard a knock on the front door. By itself, that was pretty odd. Everyone knows everyone in Nettlebush, so we tend to just walk into each other's homes whenever we want--provided that it's daytime. Since the serial murders eleven years ago, each house gets padlocked at night.

I got up to answer the door, but Dad beat me to it, looking oddly animated. Small wonder; on the other side was Officer Hargrove.

"Come in," Dad said. "Can I get you anything?"

"No, but thanks. I'm on the beat."

Dad led Officer Hargrove into the sitting room, where she took one look at me and pulled me into a bear hug.

"I'm so sorry," she told me.

Why was everyone convinced it was their fault? I pat her on the back, a little mystified.

"Can they take him away again?" Dad asked.

Officer Hargrove let go of me. "Yeah, but they probably won't," she said. "He's a flight risk. CPS won't bother wasting time and money on someone they know'll just run away again. You got a minute, Paul?"

"Of course."

I wanted to ask Officer Hargrove how DeShawn and Jessica were doing. I kind of missed them, truth be told. I settled for my usual silence, smiling when Dad and Officer Hargrove went into the kitchen for a private chat.

Just before dinner I took Balto out west to the farmland to see the apple trees in bloom. He yipped and pranced, started, then yipped again when he heard coywolves calling back to him from the wilderness. I wondered why he didn't run off to meet with them. I was glad for it, though; I didn't know how I would protect him if his former packmates attacked him. I climbed up an apple tree to pare a few blossoms for Granny. I loved the heady scent of the flowers, dizzying and sweet. I admired the elegant look of them, whorling and flimsy and white, petals dipped in faint persimmon where the receding sunlight scorched them enviously. I loved the fresh grass rolling and rippling in the wind like celebratory sails; I loved how the clouds tugging across the fiery furnace of a red sky were as gray as wet concrete. I sat on a tree branch and watched the sky's inferno quench and dim to a sleepy shade of amethyst, soft as the deliberate strokes of a paintbrush, lethargic clouds cooling into silver. Home. Home. My heart's rhythm spelled the word: Home.

Mrs. Red Clay addressed the community at dinner that night.

"The tribal council has determined to initiate a police force," she said. "Prospective applicants should visit the council building between five o'clock AM and five o'clock PM, Mondays through Saturdays."

I heard confused murmurs traveling on still air. I knew the reason for them. Nettlebush had never had its own police force before. If something horrific happened on the reservation, we were supposed to defer to the FBI. Of course, the FBI couldn't be bothered with us most of the time, so we wound up defaulting to the old ways.

Like blood law.

I'd never liked the idea of an eye for an eye--it just doesn't sit well with me--but I realized that blood law was probably what deterred the majority of crimes from happening in Nettlebush. There was a good reason Rafael's father was the only murderer in the history of the reserve.

"The Shoshone Nation is in the final stages of purchasing the Bear River Massacre site. Once purchased, we will move to have the Cache Valley recognized by Congress as a National Historic Site. The petition sits in the tribal council office and should be signed at your earliest convenience."

Good, I thought. And maybe we could rip that travesty of a plaque out of the ground, too.

The men extinguished the nightly bonfire with a barrel of water and the men and the women carried their pots and their folding chairs home. I carried Granny's loom off the lawn where she had left it and into the house. I couldn't find Balto anywhere, but I wasn't terribly concerned; he liked to stalk small prey in the trees out back, sometimes well into the morning.

I went back to the firepit to say good night to Annie and the guys. Annie had other ideas in mind.

"Why don't you boys come back to my house? We'll make cake."

"Because that won't be a total disaster," Rafael said sourly.

"I would be honored," Aubrey said, with a convincing amount of dignity.

I noticed Zeke lingering by the smoking firepit, trying not to look like he'd been eavesdropping. I felt sorry for him, and I didn't know why. I whistled at him and he jumped. I caught his eye and waved him over.

"Uh, what?" he said.

Annie pressed her lips together. I wondered what the debate looked like inside her head. "Do you want to come over, Zeke? We're making cake."

I saw his face light up, though he hid it quickly behind the half-curtain of his hair. "Sure!" he said. "I mean, I guess so."

Rafael scowled at him. I touched his arm and he relented. I winked.

We went back to Annie's house and she lit the oil lamps in her kitchen. Lila tromped in and out and complained that we were cramping her style. Aubrey got the milk and the butter out of the icebox and Rafael pulled the flour and the sugar down from the tall shelves. Zeke found the blueberries in the cellar and tried not to drop the eggs and Annie and I grated lemon peels into a bowl.

"This is my favorite cake recipe," Annie informed us.

Playfully, I flicked lemon juice at her hair.

"Stop eating all the blueberries," Rafael said to Zeke.

"I wasn't!" Zeke said, and hid his blue fingers behind his back.

The cake was finished in an hour, the floor suspiciously dusty with flour and lemon zest. Rafael buried his head stoically in his dish and didn't surface at all while he ate. He took his sweets very seriously, that Rafael. Neither Aubrey nor Zeke allowed for a moment of silence, one chattier than the next. Joseph came into the kitchen and Annie pulled him onto her lap and fed him with a fork. Sometimes I wondered whether Joseph thought Annie was his mother.

"We should start a rock band," Zeke said.

"I'll play the oboe!" Aubrey said.

"Hell no! You play an oboe and I'll grab it and beat you with it! Hahaha, I'm kidding--"

"The hell is an oboe?" Rafael asked, wiping his mouth with the back of his hand.

Annie sighed. "I need girl friends."

Annie sent each of us home with a piece of cake, which I thought was really nice of her. I gave mine to Granny, along with the apple blossoms I'd collected earlier, and she preened. Zeke said good night to me and tossed himself haphazardly on his cot. He was snoring in seconds.

I started climbing the staircase to my room when I heard a pair of laughs from the kitchen.

I froze on the staircase. It's not that I was worried. I knew at least one of the laughs had to belong to Dad.

But I had never heard him laugh like that in my entire life.

Quietly, I stole my way down the stairs. Zeke was still snoring by the fireplace. I inched over to the kitchen archway and peeked inside.

Dad and Officer Hargrove were at the table together with a couple of Holstens. What shocked me was Officer Hargrove's clothing-- her uniform gone, replaced with a pretty green dress. I had never seen her wear a dress before, not even when I had lived with her. Usually she wore her hair slicked back, too, in a tight, pinned bun; tonight she had left it in its natural state, curly and free.

"There's no way you knew that just by looking at my shoes!"

"Oh, no. I'm Native American," Dad said. "You know how intuitive we all are. Ask anyone."

I crept away from the doorway before either had a chance to notice me. As quietly as I could, I made my way up the staircase and into my bedroom.

Dad and Officer Hargrove were dating. There was no use denying it, or even speculating about it; no one had ever made my dad laugh like that before. At least, not in my lifetime.

I sat on the edge of my bed and touched the picture frame on the nighttable. Mom and Dad were together in the photo, young, their lives yet unsullied by their friend's selfish vices.

If Mom had loved Dad anywhere near as much as I did, I thought, even for a second, she wouldn't mind him seeing other women. After all, he had waited twelve long years.

20

Speaking in Riddles

I went to church with Granny on Sunday, the same as we used to do. I'd never been so happy to see a church in my life. We sat and listened to the Sermon on the Mount, although I didn't understand much of it. I wasted most of the hour by watching Rafael, the picture of brooding unhappiness, who sat sullenly next to a rapt Rosa.

Rafael followed me home at the end of the service. I set up Granny's loom on the lawn and sat on the porch, practicing my plains flute. Rafael sat with me and opened a brand new copybook. I wondered how many notebooks he'd filled with his sketches. Probably dozens.

Rafael took a pencil from behind his ear and tucked his hair back in its place. I caught a flash of his hanging earring and reached over to toy with it.

"You should let me pierce your ear," he said.

Not likely.

I played the Song of the Golden Eagle, one of my favorite pieces. Rafael tossed his head on my lap--like he owned it--and sat sketching characters in his notebook. He loved fables and fairy tales, and he was really big on *The Little Mermaid* lately. I'm pretty sure the titular mermaid wasn't supposed to have fangs and talons, though.

"It's called artistic license," he said harshly.

It's called disturbing, I wanted to retort.

Rafael sketched the sea maiden with flowing, menacing hair. "It was an allegory," he told me, his eyes attentively on the paper. "*The Little Mermaid*, I mean. Hans Christian Andersen loved a guy called Collin something, but Collin didn't love him back.

Collin got married to some rich broad instead. Andersen wrote *The Little Mermaid* as a last love letter to him. Kinda telling that the mermaid kills herself in the end."

Well, that was depressing. I gave Rafael a bland look of horror.

He put his pencil down, suddenly, and mirrored my look.

"I'm eighteen," he said. "I turned eighteen last month."

I almost laughed. What was so terrible about that?

"You're sixteen."

This time I did laugh. He glowered at me, but I ignored it.

I'm seventeen in May, I signed slowly.

"Oh, really?" said a new voice. "Happy early birthday."

Rafael sat up very suddenly. I looked up from the side of the porch.

The man coming toward us was decidedly not Native American. He wore a pepper-gray suit, his facial hair trimmed in a neat goatee. He carried a briefcase at his side and smiled warmly. I returned his smile reluctantly.

"This isn't public property," Rafael said darkly. I guessed he was feeling just as wary as I was.

The man in the suit was not to be deterred. He gave us his hand; I shook it. Rafael shook, too, but only after looking at the guy as though he were a plague.

"My name is Wei Guan," said the man. "I'm your new social worker, Skylar." He added in sign language: *How do you do?*

Granny marched up the steps and onto the porch. "Come, Skylar," she said, opening the front door. "We want to be hospitable."

I got the feeling "hospitable" was a last minute substitute for what Granny really wanted to show this guy. I rose unenthusiastically from the porch floor. I gave Rafael an apologetic look.

"S'alright. Just come to my house when you're done," Rafael said. He tossed a black look at the doorway as Mr. Guan walked through it. He waved his hand at me and went down to the lawn.

Granny and Mr. Guan sat on chairs in the sitting room. I folded up Zeke's cot and stowed it to the side. I sat on the floor, cross-legged.

"So," Mr. Guan said, opening his briefcase, "I understand your previous social worker's been...not so nice."

I grimaced. What an understatement.

"I'll just be honest with the both of you," Mr. Guan said. "A social worker's job is to make sure the house his ward lives in doesn't compromise his safety. I'm telling you right now, I can't see anything wrong with letting Skylar live in this house. Reservations are a blurry area--they're physically a part of the state, but they aren't governed by state laws; are they a part of the state, or not? It's not my job to answer that. It's just my job to make sure Skylar's happy. Skylar, are you happy?"

I nodded, completely caught off guard.

"I had a feeling," Mr. Guan said, smiling.

"Then will you approve my adopting him?" Granny asked.

"Me, personally? Yes. I'll sign off on whatever papers you show me. The problem is that a judge needs to sign off on them, too. And, as I understand, the judge assigned to your case is waiting for your tribe's officials to get back to him...something about a Bear River?"

I wondered whether that judge had had anything to do with me getting sent to the Buthrops' house.

"And if the US refuses to sell Bear River to us?" Granny asked. "This is not the first time we've gathered the funds necessary to purchase the land, only for the government to raise the price."

"Then you'll remain Skylar's custodian on a probationary basis," Mr. Guan said. "But at the end of a six month period, you can reapply for full legal custody."

There wouldn't be much of a point in six months. I'd be nearly eighteen by then.

"I think you'll find this arrangement comfortable enough, though, Mrs. Looks Over," Mr. Guan said. "I sincerely doubt CPS will lobby to remove him from this household a second time. I have a lot of experience with runaway foster children, some as young as six or seven--it's sad, but the agency just can't be bothered looking for them. CPS considers runaways a poor investment. Make no mistake about it, foster care is first and foremost a business."

I don't know whether I'd ever heard anything so disgusting. Granny sighed through her lips. I guess she must have felt the same.

"I would like to take the boy to New Mexico for an upcoming pauwau," Granny said. "Do I have your *permission*? I'm told I can't take my own grandson to celebrate his tribe's history without consulting you people."

"I'm truly sorry you were told that. Of course you can take him to New Mexico. I'll make a note of it in his file."

"And the adoption papers? You may as well sign them while you're here."

"Absolutely," Mr. Guan said. "May I see them?"

Granny got up and swiped a pile of papers off of the mantelpiece. Mr. Guan unbuckled his suitcase and found a pen. Granny offered him the papers and he took them, smiled briefly, and read them over.

He chuckled as he scrawled his signature at the bottom of the sheet.

"What?" Granny asked sharply, eyeing him.

"It's nothing," Mr. Guan assured. "It's just that this is a first. Don't you think?"

I couldn't have been more puzzled had he been speaking in riddles. To be honest, it kind of sounded like a riddle anyway. What was a first? A grandmother adopting her grandson?

"I've never heard of a boy with three birth certificates before."

21

Cynthia Parker

I stared after Mr. Guan. I stared after the door when it clicked shut behind him. I felt cold and foreign in my own skin.

Three birth certificates? What was he talking about?

Granny rose indifferently from her rocking chair.

No. No way was she turning on the Shoshone reticence. I jumped up from my chair and reached for her hand.

"I wouldn't know anything about that," Granny said, and slipped her hand free from mine. "You'll have to discuss it with your father."

I stared helplessly after her as she went into the kitchen to brew a pot of tea.

Dad. Where was Dad?

I bolted up the staircase. I looked through his room and mine. I checked the attic. Nowhere. Dad wasn't home.

I raked my fingers fiercely through my hair, wrapped the curls around my knuckles, and pulled until my scalp stung.

Okay, I thought. Calm down. It doesn't mean anything. It could very well be a clerical error.

Dad would know for sure.

I climbed back down the staircase. My pulse was so loud, I could hear it in my ears. Hurriedly, I went out through the front door. I stood on the lawn below the porch and clapped my hands twice.

Balto dashed out from the pinyon trees.

I knelt on the lawn and rubbed Balto's muzzle. I took an orange peel from my back pocket and offered it to him as a snack. He gobbled it up whole and gazed at me expectantly.

Dad? I signed, my hand spread, my thumb against my forehead.

Coywolves inherited all their ancestors' good genes--the wolf's intelligence, the coyote's affinity with humans--and none of the debilitating ones, like the wolf's shyness or the coyote's spazzy attention span. The attention span probably went to Zeke. Coywolves will even follow your gaze when you point at an object in the distance, something no dog on Earth can do. So you can say that coywolves are really more related to humans; but I'd say they're even smarter. Don't be surprised when they take over the world one day.

Balto's tail wagged with recognition. He sprinted from the lawn to the dirt path. It was all I could do to keep up with him.

We ran down the forest trail and found Dad on the other side of the lake with Mr. Little Hawk and Mr. Black Day, helping to fit a new roof over an aged home. I didn't want to interrupt Dad's work, although he wasn't supposed to be working, anyway; Sunday is a day of rest in Nettlebush. I waited until Dad had climbed down the side of the cabin, drinking from a bottle of water, before I walked over to him and took his arm.

"Cubby," he said, visibly taken aback. "Is everything alright?"

I opened my mouth to tell him exactly what was wrong.

Then I remembered: I can't talk.

I was so frustrated, so on edge, I had to squeeze my eyes shut and clench my jaws. I hadn't even thought to bring a pad of paper.

I felt Dad's hand on my shoulder. I opened my eyes.

"It's okay," he told me. "I'm right here."

You're right here, I thought, but I can't talk to you. There are a million things I've never said to you. I'll never say them.

"Does anyone have a pen?" Dad asked. "Some paper?"

Mr. Little Hawk shook his head slowly, stupefied. Mr. Black Day bent his head and ran his hand through the back of his hair.

"Come on," Dad said gently.

Balto and I followed Dad home. Dad took a notepad and a pencil out of the computer desk and handed them both to me. I wrote quickly and handed him the pad.

How many birth certificates do I have?

I watched Dad's eyes void themselves of expression and knew he was deep within the semantics of his thoughts.

"Two," he finally said, setting the pad aside.

I showed him my bewilderment.

"Your mother and I weren't married when she gave birth to you," he explained. "So my name's not on the original birth certificate. Once we married, we had a new birth certificate made up. The old one was sealed."

That didn't make sense at all. If Dad was my father, why hadn't Mom put his name on the birth certificate to begin with?

And then I thought: Oh.

And I looked at Dad, and I suddenly felt really, really sick--a stranger in my own skin--and he looked back at me, a stranger in familiar clothing, and didn't try to deny it.

"Skylar," he said.

I backed up until I felt the door behind me. It was a knee-jerk reaction.

"It's not like that," Dad went on, his voice strained, advancing. "It's not like that at all. Please calm down, I'll explain--"

No, he wouldn't. I laughed bitterly, soundlessly. Explaining was the last thing anyone in this family liked to do.

"I don't know what you're thinking," Dad said. In all the years that I'd known him, it was the first time he sounded afraid. "Please tell me what you're thinking."

How?

Dad mopped his face with his hands. His face had always reminded me of a sad, flightless hawk's. Now it looked anguished, like he was trapped in a prison cell, serving another man's sentence. In a way, I guess he was.

"Don't blame your mother," Dad said. "It was a long time ago..."

Blame her?

"She was very young. Young people don't always know what they want."

I didn't understand. I didn't understand any of this.

Dad looked me in the eye, much as I thought it pained him to. "I didn't know," he said. "That she was seeing... She waited until you were five to tell me you weren't mine. That's why we were living separately when she...when you were hurt."

Oh.

Oh. I wasn't just someone else's bastard. Mom had actually cheated on him.

I thought: I guess I don't have Dad's nose after all.

I slid against the door and sat on the wooden floorboards. Dad mopped his face again and knelt on the floor. Balto paced around the room, no doubt picking up on the tension between us.

"If you want me to find your real father," Dad said, very slowly, eyes downcast, "then I will. I'll try my best. I don't know him. I know they met in college."

I wanted to scream at him: *You're my real father.*

"Go ahead," Dad said quietly. "Scream if you have to."

I looked at him like he was crazy. Ironically enough, I felt like I was crazy.

So I opened my mouth and screamed.

I could feel the rough air burning my throat. I could feel my clipped nails digging into my palms. And I could hear the silence pouring out of my mouth--deafening--pathetic. I couldn't even scream.

I buried my face against my knees. I wrapped my arms tightly around my legs. I don't know what I was trying to do. I know I wasn't thinking straight.

I heard a soft thump as Dad sat at my side. He put his arm around me and I felt small. Small and sick. I wasn't his son. He didn't owe me comfort. He didn't owe me anything. He didn't have to raise me. Why did he raise me?

Dad laughed without any humor. "I loved that woman," he said. "Even when she was ripping my heart out."

I didn't have to wonder anymore why Dad always looked somber.

I felt the door budge and bump against my spine. Half-aware, I moved over on the floor. Dad stood up. The door swung open, cool, early evening air rushing into the front room.

"Whatcha doing on the floor, Sky-lark?" Zeke greeted jovially.

I smiled at him. I didn't know what else to do.

"Cubby..."

I rose and reached for Dad's hand. I took it and squeezed it; but I didn't look at him. I felt like the impostor who had murdered his real son and usurped his face and name. I had to get away. I couldn't get away. I'd yet to devise a solid strategy for escaping myself.

My legs carried me out the door. My legs felt like they belonged to someone else's body. There was somewhere I was supposed to be right now, wasn't there? I couldn't remember where. I walked indiscriminately, my chest aching.

I wasn't entirely surprised to find myself standing in front of the graveyard.

Mindlessly, I pushed through the gates. I went straight to the last few rows of headstones. I knew where my mom's grave was. I had visited it plenty of times over the summer.

I sat on the dry ground in front of her grave. I read her epitaph for the millionth time.

"Christine St. Clair. 1962 - 1989. Mother and friend."

Mother and friend.

The hollow aching in my chest exploded.

It was stupid of me. I know it was.

My hand balled into a fist. My teeth ground together, pain inching up my jawline.

I punched the epitaph.

The pain splitting through my knuckles was catharsis. It hurt so bad, but at least it was real, and I wasn't real, and I punched the smooth stone again and again. I smashed my fist against my mother's name. I heard the crunching and cracking of bone on stone. It hurt. It hurt so bad. I thought: You hurt my father. You deserve to hurt, too. I didn't know which of us I was addressing.

I leaned back, my hand prickling with alternating numbness and pain. I looked at the blood on Mom's epitaph, the rivulets streaked across her name. And I realized--

Mom was dead. She didn't care that I thought I hated her, in that moment, or that she had humiliated her husband by making him raise someone else's kid. She couldn't care. She was dead. The only person I was hurting was me.

I wouldn't have wanted to hurt her, anyway.

The numbness coursing through my knuckles dissipated, only pain left in its wake. Instantly, the pain intensified, ringing through my knuckles and fingers, swimming hotly in the veins in my wrist. Just the sight of my knuckles was nauseating. The skin had burst open in a bloody mess; the bones beneath had collapsed and sunk in. My fingers were still curled. I tried to uncurl them and they resisted, excruciating. Involuntary tears bit my eyes; to my credit, they never fell. I bit my tongue and tasted blood welling up under my teeth, blinded by crashing waves of pain.

I thought: Great job, genius. You broke your hand.

The blood spilling from my right hand, fresh and stark, mesmerized me. All this blood, and not a drop of it was Dad's. I wasn't my father's son.

I wasn't even Shoshone.

I cleaned my hand at the water pump behind the church. I didn't want Dad to know what a stupid thing I'd done. The blood rinsed weakly off of my skin, the running water stinging and cold. I still couldn't unfold my fist, and the knuckles looked deformed, but as long as I kept my hand at my side, maybe Dad wouldn't notice. Dad, who wasn't my dad. Dad, whom I'd betrayed just by being born. I'm sorry, Dad, I thought. I'm so sorry.

I wished I'd never asked him about those birth certificates.

I looked up at the late afternoon sky, shades of blue losing their saturation as the sun wandered west. Rafael, I remembered. I was supposed to go to Rafael's house hours ago.

It was in a dreamlike state that I traveled north through the reservation. The badlands opened up before me, breathy and blue-gray, milk-white clouds blanketing the canyons. I stopped, for a moment, to watch the view. I loved that view; but now I felt like I was looking at it with someone else's eyes, someone who didn't know how to appreciate it.

"The hell took you so long?"

Rafael came out of the house beneath the southern oak tree. He walked toward me, and I smiled, an automatic response. His face went slack with dread.

"What happened?" he said. "You're white as a sheet."

I shook my head; but it wasn't enough to dissuade him. "Is that blood on your shirt?" he said. "Where are you bleeding?" An expression like a dangerous rainstorm passed over his face. "Who hit you?"

Suddenly I felt tired, like I could go to sleep and stay there for months. I considered turning around and walking home. No, I thought. Home is the last place I want to be right now.

"What the hell did you do to your hand?"

Rafael didn't wait for an answer. He took me by my good hand and led me into his house.

Gabriel and Mary were both in the sitting room, Mary idly plucking the strings of an acoustic guitar. Gabriel looked up from the book he was reading and smiled at me. I'd only just smiled back when Rafael abruptly dragged me into the kitchen.

I'd never been in the Gives Lights' kitchen before, as funny as that might sound. The counters were granite and the walls were the color of packing straw. It was humid in there, the sluggish ceiling fan pushing the same old warm air around in circles. A large array of potted herbs stood between the refrigerator and the walk-in pantry, with the result that the whole room smelled strongly of yaupon and sage.

Rosa stood at the stove in her hospital scrubs and stirred a pot of rosemary elk stew.

"Rosa?"

Rosa spun around calmly. By magnetism--maybe nurses are just hard-wired to zoom in on people's injuries--her eyes landed on my mangled hand. Her forehead puckered in a frown.

"Don't tell Uncle Gabe, okay?"

Rosa's forehead smoothed. She set aside her apron and put the lid on the simmering pot.

"Sit," she said.

Rafael pulled out a chair for me, and we sat at the island in the middle of the kitchen. Rosa pulled open a drawer and took out a pair of scissors. She unearthed a roll of gauze from underneath the kitchen sink. She knelt by the potted herbs and cut the hard, woody stems from the rosemary plants. She ran the faucet and washed and cut the wood into long strips.

She reached across the island, took my hand, and forced it flat.

The pain was agonizing. I squeezed my eyes shut and mouthed a curse. Rosa stuffed a piece of gauze into my open mouth and I bit down, hard. She massaged my palm--incredibly, even that hurt-- and pressed a block of wrapped ice to my knuckles, I guess for the swelling. God, did it hurt. It came as a relief when she eventually took the ice away--but then she spread my fingers and slotted the wooden splints between them, and my vision swam in an unpleasant kaleidoscope of dark colors. Finally she wrapped my whole hand in tight, burning gauze. I was glad I couldn't scream.

Rafael's hand was against my back, soothing, open and broad.

"She's done," he said. "It's okay, Sky."

I spat the gauze into my open palm. I wrenched my eyes open. Rosa was at the stove again, her back to us, her spoon in the pot of stew. Amazing, I thought. It was like she hadn't even done anything.

Apprehensively, I inspected my fractured hand. Wrapped and stiff, it looked alien. The pain, surprisingly, had already started to dull.

"So what happened?"

I looked at Rafael, wondering if I should try sign language or ask him for a book to write in. It hit me: I couldn't do either. My hand was broken. I couldn't sign with it. I couldn't write. I couldn't even play the plains flute. There was no way for me to communicate with anyone.

Man, was I an idiot.

Rafael grabbed my shoulder. His grip was a little hard, but I don't think he was aware of it.

"Did you fight with someone?"

I shook my head.

"You argue with your family?"

I hesitated.

"Yeah, you did," Rafael said. "Don't lie."

I smiled dryly.

"You'll get over it," he said. "I know that sounds rich, coming from me. But they're your family, right? Even when you rail at each other, you're still family."

I looked at him. He couldn't possibly know how close to home he'd hit. Or maybe he could. Why was it that his thoughts were always in tune with mine? There was something there, and I didn't know what it was. I didn't have a word for it. Just something.

I kissed Rafael's cheek. He watched me closely when I pulled back, no doubt culling the unspoken thoughts from my head. He lifted his hand; he faltered; he sank his fingers into my curls. He ran his hand through my hair, his fingertips softly grazing my scalp.

It was amazing to be touched by him. It was like talking without words. How dumb I'd been to think I couldn't talk to him just because my hand was broken. I could always talk to Rafael. He was inside of me, a part of me; and I hoped I was a part of him.

"You know what I like about *The Little Mermaid*?"

A smile spread slowly across my lips. I forgot to shake my head.

"She's mute. She traded her tongue for legs. She can't talk to anyone, even when her sisters come and visit her at the surface of the sea. She can't talk to the guy she loves. But she doesn't need to talk for people to see how good she is. She dances for the prince, even though it causes her pain. She doesn't mind when he marries someone else. She can't bring herself to kill him, even though it's the only way she can go home to her family. She's got the best heart. It doesn't matter that she can't speak. Everybody knows it."

He touched his fingertips to my cheek. To the birthmark on the side of my face.

"Everybody knows it."

I don't know whether I remembered to breathe. I know I couldn't look away.

Rosa sniffed. I looked up and saw that she was crying, her stew abandoned.

Rafael jumped out of his chair. "What's wrong?"

Rosa shook her head. She picked up the corners of her apron and wiped the tears from her eyes. "It was such a nice thing you said."

Rafael dropped his head into his hands.

I left Rafael's house around evening, knowing Dad and Granny would find cause for alarm if I stayed out too late. My footsteps slowed, my hand throbbing at my side. I didn't deserve to go back to their house. Frankly, I wasn't sure I even wanted to. I loved them. I loved them more than anything, and I wasn't their child. I wasn't Shoshone. I wasn't me.

I stepped through the front door. The front room was empty, the computer monitor turned on. The sitting room, too, was empty. I left the front door open in the event that Balto felt like coming inside. I found Dad, Granny, and Zeke in the kitchen, pinyon nut soup boiling on the wood-coal stove.

"There you are!" Granny waved me over. "Don't just stand there!"

I leaned against the counter and got the cornmeal out of the cabinet. I figured I'd make bread.

"Stop," Dad said suddenly.

His voice was unusually cold. I froze.

"Show me your hand."

I raised my left hand and waved it around.

"Skylar."

Exasperated, I turned around.

"Whoa!" Zeke said; I saw admiration on his frantic, giddy face. "Who did *you* punch? He must've had a face like a brick wall."

"Skylar," Dad said.

I shrugged. This wasn't a family that liked to talk. Me, I would have loved to talk. There's got to be someone who finds that funny.

Granny and I made cornbread together while Zeke listened to the Nettlebush radio station. I couldn't believe how clumsy I was without the use of my right hand; I dropped the butter at least twice. Granny sighed at me and ran her hand over the back of my head. It surprised me that she wasn't more severe.

Dinner was quiet and reserved. Most of my soup wound up on my lap. Balto came indoors, no doubt lured by the sweet aroma of the pinyon nuts. I fed him the bread from my bowl. I was the first one up from the table--no accident--and the first one to leave the room.

Dad followed me when I left the house through the back door and knelt at the water pump beside the outhouse. Lathering up soap with one hand proved to be a difficult endeavor.

"Cubby," Dad said.

I took it that he wasn't angry anymore. I looked up at him and smiled blandly.

Dad's expression was unchanging. He looked the way he'd always looked: melancholy and subdued, grounded and resigned, a piece of art you can mull over and contemplate, but never interact with.

He sat with me on the dry, brown grass. I heard the cicadas in the pine trees winding down for the night. It wouldn't be long before the owls called back.

"Has Caias ever taught you kids about a woman named Cynthia Parker?"

I shook my head. I thought Mr. Red Clay had mentioned the name once, but only in passing.

"Let me tell you, then. But first I have to give you a bit of context."

He shifted around, trying to get comfortable on the grass.

"In the 1500s," Dad said, "a large band of Shoshone decided to leave our hunting grounds and live in Texas. Those Shoshone became the tribe we know today as the Comanche tribe. Even now, the Comanche language is practically identical to ours. But the Comanche differ from us in one very notable way. We Shoshone were always peaceful, almost to a fault. The Comanche--they were warriors. In fact, the very word 'Comanche' means 'Enemy.'

"Now," Dad said. He paused. "You know about the pioneers?"

I couldn't keep myself from smiling. *Of course I know about the pioneers.*

"Right, sorry," Dad said sheepishly. "Well, a big group of them built a fort in Texas around the same time that the Comanche were running around down there. As you can imagine, the Comanche and the pioneers clashed very often."

I could imagine.

"Now, the Comanche weren't like us, Cubby. They couldn't just sit down and swallow the way they were treated. So they fought back--often, and vigorously. They massacred hundreds of white settlers. I'm not glorifying this; both sides committed some pretty terrible acts before the final, climactic battle. But the pioneers were no match for the superior Comanche. By the 1800s, the Comanche had completely destroyed the white camp."

I sat up to show him I was listening.

"Here's the thing about Plains People," Dad said. "And I find that this is true no matter which Plains tribe we're talking about. Plains People consider children to have a special wisdom all their own. I mean that very literally. In the Plains culture, harming a child is the most unforgivable act."

Unconsciously, I touched my throat.

"So while the Comanche and the pioneers were waging war, children, naturally, were exempt. And when the bloodshed was over, and the Comanche were victorious, and virtually all of the white men were gone from the camp, the Comanche suddenly found themselves with a fort full of homeless, fatherless children. The Comanche did what any Plains tribe would do: They took them in as their own. One of those children was a little girl named Cynthia Parker. The Comanche called her 'Nadua'--'Keeps Us Warm.' "

Dad looked at me. "So we have a white child growing up with Plains People, learning their ways, living as they live... She even grew up to marry a Comanche man. Their son became the chief of their tribe."

I didn't think I could meet Dad's eyes.

"Do you think the Comanche saw her as anything other than Indian? Do you think she saw them as anything other than her family?"

I hated this. I met Dad's eyes. I wanted to ask him: *How can you stand to look at me?* I wasn't Cynthia Parker. I wasn't just a white kid living with Plains People. I was an embodiment of betrayal and secrecy. Mom had cheated on Dad and I was the result.

"You're my son," Dad said. "I don't need a piece of paper to tell me that. You were my son the moment Christine handed you to me. When you pulled on my hair and stuck your fingers in my mouth, you were mine. When you said your first word at fifteen months, and it was 'Dad'--you were definitely mine."

I looked at Dad carefully. The truth was that I couldn't imagine anyone else as my father. And the best parts of me--I liked to think they had come from him.

"Your grandmother knows," Dad said. His voice was so quiet, I almost didn't hear him. "She's known it as long as I have. But I don't see a reason to bring this up ever again. Do you?"

I guessed I didn't.

Mr. Red Clay was not very pleased when I walked into school on Monday with a broken hand. I grimaced apologetically and took my seat between Annie and Rafael. Annie turned on me at once.

"I'll take notes for you until your hand heals," she offered. "But you owe me."

I knew she was joking; but I felt like I did owe her. After school I went out into the woods and found a skink skull; and I took it home and made it into a necklace. Skink bones look about the same as opals, creamy and white, which is probably why you see them in Native jewelry all the time. I don't mean to imply that I walked around killing lizards for the heck of it. It's just that certain parts of the forest were already littered with their skeletons.

"For me?" said Annie the next day. She took the necklace and tugged it on over her head. "Why, thank you! It's lovely. I don't know how you managed with only one hand."

I pointed at my teeth.

"Is that so? Then I think you should write your notes with your teeth, too."

I pressed my mouth to her cheek and blew raspberries.

We went to the grotto after class, Balto following vigilantly. We sat by the creek, studying for an upcoming test, when Zeke suddenly spoke up.

"Do you guys ever, like, turn your underwear inside-out so you can wear it a second day?"

I stared.

"Well, if I did," Aubrey said gravely, "I wouldn't admit to it."

"You on coke?" Rafael asked.

"I *really* need some girl friends," Annie said.

That sort of discussion was par for the course with Zeke, whose train of thought was both unfathomable and impenetrable. It was rare that we got in any meaningful conversation, though not for lack of trying on Aubrey's part.

"I've seen your father around the reservation, but never your mother," Aubrey said politely, peering at Zeke.

"Yeah, they had a big ol' messy divorce after Naomi--"

Zeke didn't finish. He threw a wary look Rafael's way.

"S'alright," Rafael said. "You can say it. After my dad killed your sister."

"Well, yeah, that," Zeke said, laughing nervously.

"My mother was a hero," Annie said, a fond glow to her eyes. "She was a major in the army. She served in Yemen, after the portside bombing. She threw herself on top of a IED and saved two families."

Aubrey put his arm around Annie's shoulders and Annie smiled at him, fleetingly. But reminiscing didn't last very long, because like many things, it fell under the Shoshone Reticence Rule. Zeke got up to see if he could scale the tallest beech tree and Rafael said he thought he'd left some candy in the cave. That was the end of that.

When I went home that day, I found a pile of letters waiting for me on the computer desk. I sat down and tore them open with my teeth.

The first was from my cousin, Marilu.

Dear Sky,

It's so cool that you met Danny! Thank you for bringing him back here. Everyone's happy, especially his dad, but also me. We talk every night on the phone and Mom yells at me to go to bed.

Mom thinks we'll have the new house by next year so when you come back for the next pauwau I'll show it to you. I want to see your house, too. Please invite me over for the summer! We are learning PEMDAS in math and I'm also learning the violin.

Love,
Marilu

I wondered whether I could type up a response on the computer and print it out. I was a pretty slow typist with two hands, never mind one, but there was no way I could let her letter go without an answer.

My second letter was from Danny.

Greetings to a fellow secret agent of Wovoka from the coniferous one.

I thank you and also your kissing friend and the big-haired sister for rescuing me from the snapping jaws of the secret army (that's what's happening because the white people are actually building a secret army and the bullets are made from Indian brains which have a fourth dimension).

I dreamed about a dinosaur that had sharks for legs. I drew it to show you what I'm talking about (flip over the paper). Keep it a secret we do not want the CIA to know about this.

Danny Patreya

It's pretty sad when the only thought that comes to mind is: Oh my God. I flipped the paper over and my thoughts pretty much remained the same.

The final letter was written in a loopy, childlike scrawl, and I knew at once who had written it.

Hi Skylar,

This is Jessica Hargrove and I miss you. Mommy says she will take me to see you if I make good grades. My doll's name is Jenny and she is my favorite. I will give you a doll too when I see you. From Jessica

It was the shortest of the letters, and no doubt the sweetest. I read it a second time. I couldn't keep the smile off my face. I could see what it was that Plains People respected in children.

I turned on the computer monitor to check the reservation calendar. The mouse didn't want to cooperate with my left hand, and it took ten agitated minutes for me to pull up the tribal website. I scanned the updates slowly. A very interesting one read: "Come burn your computer at the bonfire on Saturday, 7:30 PM." I wondered whether anyone saw the irony in that.

Incidentally, Saturday was also the day of the Navajo pauwau on the Three Suns Reservation.

I'd been looking forward to the Navajo pauwau for months, mostly for the chance to see Kaya again, but also because I was curious about her home. Now, though, I felt weird about going. I knew the truth now--that I wasn't really Native American--and I felt like it would be hypocritical of me, intrusive, even, to show my face.

It's a really haunting feeling, to find out that one of the most basic truths you grew up with--the one that helps define you--is really just a lie.

"You've gotta bring a gift," Rafael said.

We sat together at the picnic table by the nightly bonfire. It was dinnertime, the wafting scent of roasted quail turning my stomach.

"For the Yeibichai, I mean."

Rafael must have seen the confusion on my face. "They're holy people," he said. "You'll know 'em when you see 'em, they walk around wearing weird masks. The Navajo believe that the Yeibichai were the ones who prepared the Earth for them to live on. So when you see one, you've gotta give him a gift. Don't ask me why, that's just the way it is."

He dipped a tin spoon in a bowl of tomato soup. Unlike me, Rafael was left-handed and experienced none of my earlier clumsiness.

"Here," he said, and lifted the spoon to my mouth.

I hadn't been spoon-fed since I was five. Consequently, I felt a little ridiculous. I parted my lips around the spoon and swallowed.

"Don't be like that," Rafael said disgruntledly. "You're my pilot whale."

I stared blankly.

"You know. Pilot whales." His face took on a sheepish undertone. He continued hastily. "Pilot whales travel in pods. They stay together for life. When one pilot whale gets sick or injured, and can't move on, the rest of the pod stays with him. They help each other find the way home. They're the most loyal animal on Earth." He shot a cynical look at Balto lying by the bonfire. "Yeah, more loyal than you, buddy."

First I was a mermaid and now I was a whale. I grinned slowly. Rafael sure liked his ocean analogies.

"Shut up," he said, grinning back. He scooped up a second spoonful of tomato soup.

Pilot whales or not, I didn't think I'd be attending the Navajo pauwau after all. But I suppose admitting we weren't biologically related hadn't turned off Dad's ability to interpret my silences. Dad cornered me that night just before I went to bed.

"Don't you have a friend on the Three Suns Reservation?" he asked mildly.

I wasn't in the mood for an argument. I smiled noncommittally and reached for the doorknob to my bedroom.

"I think you would disappoint your friend if you didn't show up. The Navajo really care about these things, much more than the rest of us do."

I studied him in the darkness of the hallway, moonlight streaming in through the far window. His face was a face I'd known all my life. It didn't look anything like mine. Somehow, I'd never found that suspicious.

Dad's hands rested on my shoulders.

"It's not blood that makes us who we are," Dad said. "It's family. And it's not blood that makes us family. It's love."

There wasn't anyone I loved more than Dad.

Annie and Rafael came to my house on the eve of the pauwau. Annie had me help her bake cookies for the road, although I couldn't really do much except crush the prairie bananas and whisk the cream cheese. Dad and Mr. Little Hawk and Mr. Red Clay set up a folding table in the sitting room and sat playing poker and listening to the radio. It was a boys' night in for those three.

"Did you prepare a gift for the Yeibichai?" Annie asked me.

I nodded. I pulled open a kitchen drawer and took out a seal bag filled with arnica leaves. Arnica's great for cuts and bruises, but it's probably not a good idea to put it in your mouth--which was why I had labeled it "Do Not Eat!!!" in big, loopy letters.

Rafael shoved his head through the kitchen doorway. "Are you riding with us?" he asked Annie.

"Yes, please. And do you have room for one more?"

"Nah, we're stuck with Zeke."

"Then I'd better go see if Dr. Stout can take Joseph, too."

Annie finished wrapping the last box of cookies--I lent her my finger and she tied the ribbon--and she bustled out the door, her briar rose shawl flying around her shoulders.

Rafael took a look at me. "Why aren't you dressed yet?"

I was still in jeans and a t-shirt, and with good reason. I don't know if you've ever seen a men's Plains regalia up close and personal, but it's not the type of outfit you can put on with one hand. It's not just trousers and moccasins; there's a breechclout, a weighted deerhide overcoat, a draping neckpiece--and if you're a dancer, or you belong to a special society, you've got even more craziness to contend with, like fringe, bells, feathers, legging wraps, beaded belts, iron belts, maybe even a warbonnet.

Rafael opened his mouth. He faltered.

"You need help?"

I hoped, really hoped, that my face didn't give away my thoughts. The thought of undressing in front of him was frightening. I'd done it once before, when we went swimming over the summer; but that had been frightening, too.

Discreetly, I looked around. Where the heck was Granny?

"Sky?"

I nodded tersely, before I could talk myself out of it. I slipped out of the kitchen and started up the staircase. Rafael followed me.

In my bedroom I eased open the closet and rummaged around inside. My regalia was hanging on a hook between my schoolbag and fleece jacket, moccasins set aside. I lifted the regalia with my left hand; the soft deerhide slipped through my fingers and fell to the floor. Wordlessly, Rafael picked it up and laid it across the mattress.

We looked at one another. It occurred to me, bizarrely, that he was just as frightened as I was.

My fingers felt numb when I slid them underneath the hem of my shirt. I think Rafael misinterpreted my hesitance as helplessness. Or maybe he didn't. Maybe he knew, just as I did, that I didn't need his help undressing.

If he knew it, he feigned otherwise. He hooked his fingers underneath my shirt. My pulse leapt. He tugged my shirt up over my belly. All I could think to do was raise my arms. He raised my shirt above my chest, above my shoulders and head. He balled it up and tossed it aside.

Cold air hit my skin and I almost flinched. I think I almost flinched for another reason, too. Rafael had one of the worst poker faces known to mankind. He didn't bother pretending he wasn't looking at me.

I wasn't built like Rafael. I was skinny and pale and overall unremarkable. Actually, I thought I was kind of repulsive. Whatever had initially attracted Rafael to me--and I didn't know what it was--it couldn't have been my body.

That was my version of events. His was different. Because when his eyes roamed over the flat, unimpressive expanse of my chest and stomach, my stomach swimming in freckles, he looked so much like a boy tentatively unwrapping a present, something he'd really wanted, and for a really long time, that it frightened me all over again. No one had ever looked at me that way before.

And I liked it.

He was losing track of time. I touched his shoulder, a reminder, and smiled patiently. Quickly, distractedly, he nodded. His tongue darted across his lips--oh, God, that was just about my undoing-- and he unbuckled my pants, fumbling nervously. I laughed a quiet laugh. I sat on the bed and slithered out of my jeans. I reached for the deerhide trousers and stepped into them. That much I could do on my own.

"Here," Rafael muttered. I stood up and he tied the drawstrings for me.

Rafael picked up the breechclout and leveled it in his hands. He wrapped it around my waist, his fingertips tickling my bare skin, and tied it shut at my right hip. He tugged the hanging strips of fabric until they evened themselves out.

He picked up the overcoat on the side of the bed. I lifted my arms, trying to help him.

It was with painstaking caution that Rafael took my broken hand in his. His grasp was light, his touch imperceptible. Careful, devastatingly gentle, he fitted my hand through the sleeve. I heard him breathe with audible relief when my hand came through unharmed and tried not to laugh. He tugged the sleeves down my arms and straightened the dark green seams. He straightened the brocade across my shoulders. The overcoat hung open across my chest.

Rafael's fingers trembled when he raised them to the drawstrings. It struck me so powerfully that I claimed both of his hands in mine and held them still.

His eyes, blue and stormy and vulnerable, met mine. He wanted something, I realized. I was pretty sure I wanted it, too. But I didn't know how to tell him he could have it.

He threaded up my overcoat for me, his fingers unsteady, and fixed the piece that draped across my throat. He looped my plains flute around my neck. I sat on the edge of the bed and he knelt beneath my knees to lace up my moccasins. I watched him with his head bent, his fingers deft, black hair spilling over his shoulders. Something occurred to me just then. I thought: This is how you know somebody loves you. When you can't tie your own shoes and they don't mind tying them for you.

I put my hand on the crown of his head. I reveled in the feel of his hair beneath my palm, coarse and fine-spun, and the warmth of him, a warmth that radiated through my skin.

He lifted his head to gaze at me. He took my hand in his and pressed it to his cheek.

"You're going to be late!" Mr. Red Clay called from down the stairs.

I was the first to laugh. Rafael laughed, too, but in a bashful way. I didn't care what his reason was. I loved his laugh. I would have taken any excuse to hear it.

"M'done," Rafael mumbled. "C'mon."

I got up and followed Rafael down the stairs. I waved goodbye to Dad and his friends. "Ask some cultural questions," Mr. Red Clay counseled us. "I'll quiz you on Monday."

"Great," Rafael said, scowling.

I gathered the wrapped cookies into my arms and went out the door after Rafael and Zeke, Zeke singing a song of his own invention. Granny was on the porch, tossing a piece of bluegill to Balto below.

"Come," Granny beckoned us sternly.

The four of us went out to the parking lot. Gabriel towered over the noisy crowd and waved us over to his car.

"Heeeey," said Mary, decked out in a pair of sunglasses.

"You look dumb," Rafael said.

Annie joined us, and we piled into the car. I was in the back seat between Granny and Rafael.

"We may as well listen to the Navajo station," Gabriel said cheerfully. He turned on the radio as Rosa pulled the car onto the parkway.

The whole trip was pretty short, maybe two hours tops. Mary sang along with the radio in a reedy, grandfatherly voice and Annie raised her eyebrows. Zeke made it worse when he decided to contribute warbling war whoops. Granny and Gabriel talked back and forth about the plan to buy back Bear River: Apparently the US had rejected our bid again, something Granny was particularly incensed about. I guessed I wasn't going to be adopted after all. Rafael pulled a book out from under his seat--aptly titled *Ten Little Indians*--and sat reading and wouldn't talk to anyone. I leaned over the back of Mary's seat in an attempt to see outside the window. "Welcome to New Mexico," read the highway sign. "The Land of Enchantment."

There's also a Plains song called Land of Enchantment; in fact, I had played it for the ghost dance last summer. I wondered what the correlation was. But I could see why New Mexico was called the Land of Enchantment. Bronze and saffron valleys flanked the black tar highway. Gargantuan canyons reached for the sky like God's golden hands. I saw old-fashioned hogans on either side of the road and realized we were already on the reservation. Just how big was this place?

My answer: Very big. We arrived in a huge lot by starlight, cars and RVs parked side-by-side. I climbed out of the SUV with Granny, packages in my arms, and looked around in awe.

There were thousands of us gathered together in one place. I recognized the Pawnee and the Kiowa--Plains tribes, like us--and the Apache and the Hopi. My familiarity ended there. I saw women with pastel blankets tied around their shoulders like cloaks; I saw men in dreadlocks and eagle feathers, their faces tattooed. I spotted a tribe that made me think of Hawaiians, their clothes adorned in sea grasses and seashells. Children dressed in beaded blue spirals and rose shirts, little old men in warbonnets shaped like solar flares--I'd never seen any of these tribes before. I turned to Rafael in confusion.

"You see those guys in the kilts? Those are the Laguna, they're a Pueblo tribe. Or maybe they're the Zuni, I don't know, they always look the same to me. ...Hang on... Yeah, those guys over there, the ones who look Paiute--they're Washoe. Related to the Paiute, but they were mortal enemies. Guess blood isn't really thicker than water. Shut up, I know it's thicker than water, I'm trying to make a joke. Look over there, that's the Timbisha Shoshone tribe. They're basically like us, but they stayed in the desert when the rest of us went to the Plains. And don't let those Chumash guys in the seashells fool you. They don't have traditional regalia. They didn't start wearing clothes until, like, fifty years ago."

"Everybody alright?" Gabriel said.

"I need to use the bathroom," Zeke said, fidgeting.

"Is there a reason you didn't use it before we left?" Annie inquired.

"I didn't need it before we left!"

"Fool boy," Granny said, and pointed out the public restroom stalls.

We waited while Zeke rushed off, Rafael sneaking cream cheese cookies out of the box in my arms. Granny bopped the back of Rafael's head and took the boxes from my arms, eyeing us distrustfully. Aubrey swam through the crowd to us and grabbed Annie's hand. Once Zeke came back, laughing nervously, we left for the pauwau grounds.

I'd never seen a reservation like Three Suns. On our way out of the RV park we passed a chain of motels, a casino, a helicopter runway, and a restaurant with a canyon view. A plashing river cut across the dry grounds, the bank closest to us lined with bright paper luminaries. "That's their clever little trail of breadcrumbs," Gabriel told me with a wink.

The river coursed up the side of a slanted plateau, and at the top was a cozy city, windows twinkling with light. But the city, apparently, wasn't our destination. Entranced by the luminaries, I followed them with my eyes--until they abruptly stopped short. Dizzy, I looked up.

I guessed this was the pauwau site. The grounds were covered in myriads of tribal flags: orange banners emblazoned with dancing eagles, red suns against yellow backdrops, bright flames on royal purple, even the odd turtle or two. Ms. Siomme planted our flag in the ground and smiled at me when I caught her eye. Old men and women sprinkled crushed sage on the soil and muttered blessings. But as far as pauwaus went, the resemblance ended there. The booths bordering the pauwau site, laden with spicy foods and art for sale and dart and milk bottle games, reminded me more of a carnival; and the lights strung up on wooden pikes made an artificial ceiling of artificial stars.

The Navajo tribal council, all twenty members, sat at a long wooden table at the far end of the site. One of the councilors stood up, his blue and silver silks shining under the lights above his head, and spoke into a microphone, conducting the opening prayer. I bowed my head. A pauwau always starts with a prayer; whether you pray to the Wolf or the Great Mystery or Jesus--or no one at all--doesn't make much of a difference.

The councilor sat down when he had finished. A silence traveled through the crowd. I wondered what we were waiting for. Then, out of nowhere, I heard the pounding of a heavy drum. Powerful, high-pitched shrieks rang through the air. Eight women came bounding out of the crowd and into the center of the field. The rest of us stepped back out of respect. The opening ceremony, I realized, had just begun.

The women--the dancers--ranged in age from teenagers to grandmothers. I spotted Kaya among them in scarlet and lavender. Each dancer carried a shield on her arm and a bow in her hand, a quiver full of arrows on her back. The girls looked like warriors ready for a skirmish. The dance, too, resembled a battle. The dancers lunged and ran at each other; they swung their shields with prowess, with synchronicity, such that it always managed to look like the assailant had only just missed her target. The Navajo aren't a Plains tribe; they never counted coup the way Shoshone and Lakota did. Their history instead comprised long and bloody wars. I guessed that this dance was meant to showcase that history. The women ripped the arrows from their backs and swung them like batons, twirling and cutting through the air like windmill blades. They fitted their arrows fluidly into their bows, took aim at the night sky, and released them, all at once, to the final beat of the drum. The arrows clattered noisily to the ground at the end of a lengthy flight. All of the spectators burst into applause.

I could see what Dad had meant when he'd said the Navajo cared greatly about presentation. I didn't think I'd ever seen anything so impressive. I couldn't clap, but I stuck my fingers in my mouth and whistled. Kaya blew a kiss in my direction. Then a Washoe man stepped in front of me, and the crowd converged for the rest of the festivities, and I lost sight of her.

Rafael grabbed my left hand. "I want some ach'ii," he yelled. He sort of had to. It was so loud out there, my ears were ringing.

We walked among the booths until Rafael found his long-coveted sheep intestines. I tried not to heave when he stuffed the intestinal ropes in his mouth and sucked them up like rainwater down a storm drain. I almost lost the battle over my diaphragm when he pulled a half-eaten rope out of his mouth and offered it to me. "Try it," he said. "It's salty." Vigorously, I shook my head. Mercifully, he didn't pursue the matter.

The rest of the wares weren't as gross. A stately looking woman was selling something called Navajo tea, a quaint, mustard-colored beverage with a tiny yellow flower sitting at the bottom of the cup. I bought a cup and it was delicious. A whole booth was dedicated to sandpaintings, incredible portraits made from nothing but differently colored grains of sand arranged methodically behind sheets of glass. One of the sandpaintings depicted a weirdly hilarious scene, a man in the middle of turning into a cat. I didn't question it. I bought it instead. Rafael helped me fit it into my duffel bag. Dad liked cats, and I thought it would make for a funny gift.

The vendor, a tiny old woman, reached across the booth and whacked us on the heads.

"Ow!" Rafael complained. "What the hell?"

"Beware the Skinwalker!" the woman admonished. "For he may steal the form of a cat or a dog; but he may also steal yours. He will cut off your skin and wear it for his own!"

"Yeah, thanks for that," Rafael said, and pulled me away by my hand.

We wove through the crowd in search of someone from our tribe. The area was heavily saturated; we couldn't move an inch in any direction without bumping into strangers, some of them understandably ornery. I spotted a man in a gourd-and-buckskin mask chasing after Jack Nabako and guessed he was the Yeibichai I'd heard so much about. I didn't have time to dig the arnica out of my duffel bag; the Yeibichai tore across the site like a flash flood and never looked back in my direction.

"Did you like my bow and arrow dance?"

I don't know how Kaya had managed to find us. Maybe it was my hair. Blond hair really sticks out when everyone else's is brown and black.

Rafael hunched over. I smiled and waved. Kaya's eyes swept over my other hand. She tsked.

"You need to stop getting into fistfights," she said.

"Huh?" Rafael said.

"It was a joke."

"Oh."

I pointed at the far end of the field. A group of men had gathered in a circle, facing away from one another. Women were marching up to them and dragging them around in a ritualistic dance.

Kaya smiled. "It's the squaw dance," she said. "The man can't stop dancing until he gives the woman a gift."

The Navajo really liked their gifts, I figured.

Rafael was gaping at Kaya. Kaya had noticed. "What?" she asked calmly.

"Did you seriously use that word?"

"What word?"

"You know what word."

"Squaw?"

Rafael stared with disbelief. "Stop it."

I looked between the two of them, perplexed.

"It's a hateful word," Rafael explained to me. "White men used to call Native women--that. That's how they degraded them."

Kaya crossed her arms and straightened her shoulders. "Dine aren't afraid of words," she said casually. "We made it our own."

Rafael had started to scowl. Oh, no, I thought. Damage control time. I really didn't want the two of them to start fighting.

I threw my arms around the both of them and smushed their faces against mine.

The rest of the pauwau was comparatively pleasant. Kaya showed us how to basket dance; she didn't have a basket, so I lent her my duffel bag. We ran and ducked for cover when Gabriel came around with his camera. I found Annie and Aubrey by the ball toss game, Aubrey desperately trying to win Annie a stuffed doll--a lamb, Annie's favorite animal. Granny and Reverend Silver Wolf had joined the squaw dance--I don't know if I should really use that word--and Rosa seemed to have fallen asleep beside a booth selling frybread. How anyone could have fallen asleep with all that racket was beyond me.

It was one in the morning when the celebrations wound down. Granny made her way through the crowd to me and grabbed my arm. "There's church tomorrow," she scolded, like I was the one who had kept us out late. I tucked her hand safely in my arm and we walked along the river, Granny singing a flag dance song beneath her breath. I smiled, endeared. Kaya accompanied us to the RV park to see us off. The weird part, though, was that she spent most of her time by the barbecue pit between caravans, chatting with Rafael's sister. At one point I thought I saw Mary playing with Kaya's hair.

"Everybody ready to go?" Gabriel said. He helped a sleepy Rosa into the passenger side of the SUV. "Where's Raf?"

A shout trilled through the crowd. Waves of Chumash and Mojave men stepped back with alarm. Dread welled up inside of me. Somehow I knew what I was going to find, even before I looked.

Rafael was on the ground, gripping his face. His glasses lay at his side, the wire bent out of shape, the left lens shattered. Mr. Owns Forty must have delivered the blow, because he was approaching Rafael steadily, and he sounded like he was in the middle of a drunken rant.

Zeke, Gabriel, and I moved forward at the same time. The door to the SUV rolled open with a thud and Rosa leapt out, running after us. I knelt on the ground and put myself between Rafael and Mr. Owns Forty. I didn't care what Mr. Owns Forty was doing. My only concern was Rafael.

I winced. Rafael's face looked pretty bad. His lower lip was already beading with dark blood, and the area around his eye was scratched where his glasses lens had shattered. He looked at me in an earnest, shameful way that made me want to throw something at Mr. Owns Forty.

Rosa knelt at my side while I picked the glass shards out of Rafael's face. Rafael hissed through his teeth. I opened my duffel bag and found the arnica. I handed the seal bag to Rosa. Rosa opened the bag for me and pressed and smoothed the leaves to Rafael's face.

"Dad--stop--*stop!*"

I chanced a look over my shoulder. Zeke and Gabriel were holding onto Mr. Owns Forty, Mr. Owns Forty practically foaming at the mouth. Mary suddenly leapt into the fray, screeching, both fists swinging. At least one of them caught Mr. Owns Forty in the jaw. In the midst of all the chaos, I heard the words "my baby brother."

"Mary!"

Gabriel switched his efforts from restraining Mr. Owns Forty to restraining his niece. Mr. Owns Forty saw his chance and took it; he thrust Zeke to the side and Zeke fell, winded; he threw a punch at the side of Gabriel's head. Now that was low, I thought with a stab of anger. Gabriel staggered, caught off guard. Rosa leapt up and ran to him. The arnica leaves fluttered off the side of Rafael's face. Mary threw herself on top of Mr. Owns Forty.

For a nonconfrontational tribe, we sure were feeling confrontational tonight.

Loud sirens blared through the RV park, flashing lights bouncing off the caravans. Someone had called the cops, I realized. I saw Kaya with a cell phone pressed to her ear and wondered if it was her.

The reservation police pulled up in brown squad cars. Four of them jumped out and ran to us; two of them pulled Mary and Mr. Owns Forty apart. Ms. Siomme came running over, concerned, the rest of the tribal council at her heels. Mary started laughing in a way that scared me, because it was low and dangerous and kind of deranged and I wasn't at all certain she was in her right mind. Mr. Owns Forty must have been more drunk than I'd realized: He thrashed and swung his arms until one of the cops had to tase him. I heard Zeke gasp, saw the piteous look on his face, and wished there were something I could do. Immaculata Quick crouched next to him, arms around her knees.

"Really considering that plastic surgery," Rafael muttered.

I smiled wistfully. I picked up his glasses, but didn't bother putting them on his face. They were too broken for that.

I tucked Rafael's glasses in my duffel bag with the arnica leaves. I reached for Rafael's hand and helped him off the ground. He leaned on me, looking out of sorts, and we walked together to the SUV. Granny was standing against the side of the vehicle with Reverend Silver Wolf, their heads bent in conversation.

I let go of Rafael only long enough to slide open the back door. Rafael climbed sluggishly into the SUV. I got in after him and turned his face in my hand. His cheek looked like it was already starting to bruise.

"Gonna add another link," he murmured.

He meant the chain tattoo on his right arm. Every time he felt like hurting someone, he added a new chain link.

Rafael groaned. He must have been in a lot of pain, I thought. With horror, I wondered if Mr. Owns Forty had punched him anywhere else. But if he had, Rafael wasn't saying.

Rafael lay sideways across the seat, his head on my lap. I fished the rest of the arnica leaves out of my duffel bag. I pressed the leaves tenderly against his face.

"I'm sorry my dad's a piece of dirt," Rafael mumbled.

I carded my fingers softly through his hair.

It took nearly an hour before Gabriel and Rosa got into the car. Annie, indignant, wasn't far behind. She sat with her lamb doll on her lap, fuming. "Where did he even get the alcohol?" she demanded to know. "You don't bring alcohol to a pauwau!"

"Uncle Gabe, you okay?" Rafael asked.

"I'm fine, kiddo," Gabriel said. "How are you doing back there?"

"M'sorry about my glasses."

"Don't you be sorry about anything," Gabriel said. "We'll get you a new pair tomorrow."

"Costs too much."

"That's why we have a warranty."

Granny was next into the car; she sat beside Annie in the middle row. Mary arrived after Granny and wouldn't say anything. She sat on Rafael's other side, surveyed the two of us, then looked away.

"Ezekiel will not be coming," Granny said. "He has decided to stay here until his father is released from police custody. Meredith will stay with him."

"Might as well get going, then," Gabriel said, stifling a sigh, and put the car in reverse.

The ride back to Nettlebush was tense and morose. Annie tried to make small talk, but though she was a good actress, she didn't have much to work with. Rafael kept dozing off on my lap. The roads outside the windows were dark and unlit and, honestly, a little creepy. I was relieved once we pulled off the turnpike and into the hospital parking lot. Gabriel parked the car and I climbed out on rubbery legs. All I wanted was to go to bed.

"Thanks for helping him, Skylar," Gabriel said. He went around the SUV and made sure all the doors were locked.

"Night, Sky," Rafael muttered.

"Good night, Skylar," Annie said, and kissed me on the cheek.

I walked home with Granny, my arm looped through hers. The air smelled ashen; I wondered how many computers had burned while the rest of us were away. Balto barked loudly from behind the pine trees and followed us into the cabin. I locked up for the night, the hearth already lit.

"That was an unfortunate experience, Skylar," Granny said sternly. "But all experiences are learning experiences."

I wondered about the meaning of her words. I gazed after her as she hobbled off to bed, her bedroom door snapping shut behind her.

I don't know what time it was when I finally went up to bed. My regalia was comfortable, but heavy, and I was eager to get out of it. I opened my door and Balto padded into the room ahead of me. I stopped.

The lamps were lit. Dad was sitting on the edge of my bed, his head bent, a picture frame in his hands. My heart wrenched. I realized it was the photo of him and Mom when they were young.

The scent of cognac was heavy on the air. Dad had been drinking.

"Cubby?" he said blearily.

I set my duffel bag on the floor and walked toward the bed. Gently, I pried the picture frame from Dad's hands. I placed it face-down on the bedside table.

"My fault," Dad said. "My fault. You used to have a voice..."

One drunk father was enough for one evening. I wrapped my left arm around Dad's back and pulled him off the bed. He leaned against me, much heavier than he looked. I nodded toward the doorway--meaning that I'd help him back to his room--but I don't think he noticed.

Dad mumbled incoherently while we walked down the hall. His breath was rancid, his gait uneven. His door was ajar; I pushed it open with my shoulder. I saw the moonlight spilling across his mattress from the uncurtained window and guided him over to the bed.

"Why Eli thought I'd want you gone... You're my son... Never should've left you..."

I lit the oil lamp on Dad's nighttable and looked around the room for fresh clothes. Before I'd made it to his closet, I stopped short.

The unpainted walls were covered in photographs. The photos looked grainy, like the quality of film you usually find in pictures from the 60's and 70's. But what had really captured my attention was what the photographs depicted. Each photograph was of the same little boy, short-haired and brown-eyed, no older than four or five; smiling, laughing, climbing trees, playing with New Year's presents, playing the Apache fiddle. My uncle Julius was staring back at me from the walls of his old bedroom.

At first I thought it was touching. In her own way, Granny was keeping her son alive. But then I thought: It's not touching. It's morbid. It didn't sit well with me that Dad had to go to sleep every night with his dead little brother reflected on every wall.

I hastened out of Dad's room and into mine. Balto peered at me curiously from atop my mattress. I scooped my duffel bag off the floor and hurried back down the hall. Dad was already asleep by the time I returned to his room, his legs sliding off the bed. I dropped my duffel bag--lightly; I crept across to him and tugged his shoes off his feet. I pushed his legs up on the mattress with one soft shove and pulled the blanket over him. I didn't feel like waking him just to make him change his clothes; and I didn't trust myself to get him dressed with one hand.

I shouldered my duffel bag, and as quietly as I knew how, I went around the room and took the photos off the walls.

I didn't think it was Dad's fault that I'd lost my voice. And it certainly wasn't Rafael's fault that Mr. Owns Forty had lost his daughter. There's really only one person you can blame when something horrible happens. When you spend your time blaming everyone else, you live a little less. You die a little more. Life's already short. It doesn't need our help making it any shorter.

When I had finished taking Uncle Julius off the walls, I hung Dad's sandpainting on one of the empty hooks. I stood back to admire the Skinwalker in the low light from the oil lamps. It really wasn't enough, I thought. There wasn't a gift on earth that could express how grateful I was. This man had raised me. He wasn't obligated to; I didn't have his blood in my veins. But he had loved me anyway. He had loved me when I was a good kid and he had loved me when I was a brat. He had sat with me through doctors' visits when I was sick with pneumonia; he had sat in the hall outside when I spent hours on end with a child psychiatrist. He had taught me how to treat people, how to feel about them, and, against all odds, how to feel about myself. If someone else had raised me...well, I might not have turned out to be me.

Imagine that. Not being you.

I don't think I can.

23
Manna

Rafael didn't come to school on Monday. I figured Gabriel had taken him into town to get his glasses replaced. I sat between Aubrey and Annie at our table while Mr. Red Clay took attendance, frowning over Rafael and Zeke's empty seats.

"Crafts month is coming up," Annie whispered to me.

The Nettlebush Reserve opens itself to the public once a year, usually in May. It's the time of year when tourists come swarming in off the streets and the Shoshone satisfy their curiosity by selling them authentic Native American trinkets--jewelry, pottery, wood carvings, dreamcatchers, even ancient weaponry. It's an important way for the reservation to bring in revenue.

Frowning, I waved my wrapped right hand. Most of the pain had dissipated, but I still couldn't use it for much. I didn't like that I couldn't help Annie.

"Oh, don't worry," Annie reassured. "You can help me crush dyes. We'll go into the woods together."

"I'm sure whatever you're talking about back there is fascinating," Mr. Red Clay said, "but I'd appreciate your eyes up here, please."

I grinned like a demon. Annie blushed.

Mr. Red Clay opened up the lesson with his usual combination of English and sign language. Sign language was a lost Indian art, he always said.

"We're going to talk about a dark period in Shoshone history. This is something most Shoshone don't like to talk about. In fact, once you leave this classroom, you'll probably never hear about this again. But it happened, and to ignore it is to be ignorant."

Mr. Red Clay looked sharply at the student body. "Who can tell me what self-immolation is?"

Boy, this wasn't shaping up to be a peaceful school day.

"Miss Two Eagles?"

"Lighting yourself on fire."

"Why would anyone in his right mind light himself on fire?"

"He wouldn't," William Sleeping Fox said.

"Raise your hand."

William raised his hand.

Mr. Red clay struck himself on the forehead. "Not *now*," he said. "Oh, forget it. Can anyone recall a moment in history when self-immolation was recurrent?"

Aubrey raised his hand.

"Yes?"

"When the Spaniards barged into Colorado in the late 1500s," Aubrey said. "Most of them were hostile. To scare them away without fighting them, the Shoshone men would light themselves on fire."

"Did it work?"

"Well, yes, it was preemptive, wasn't it? 'Get away from me, I'm scary, aagh!' You know--"

"Thank you," said Mr. Red Clay, exasperated. "That will do. But we're not going to talk about the Spanish today. We're going to talk about what those Shoshone men did, and the ramifications it had on our people for a long time afterward."

I thought that sounded kind of foreboding.

"At that time, the Plains Shoshone considered self-immolation a great sacrifice on their warriors' part. The Shoshone men sacrificed themselves so the white men would keep away from their wives, from their children. That's nice. But as a result, the Plains Shoshone suffered a severe shortage of men in the 1600s. Widows were marrying each other to help raise their children. Marriageable girls had to wait years and years for the little boys to grow up. And, perhaps most detrimental of all, the widows were giving birth to baby girls."

Mr. Red Clay perused us, his arms behind his back.

"Infanticide," he said, "is the killing of a baby. And that is what happened in the 1600s. The Shoshone murdered their girl babies in a desperate bid to balance out the population. After all, we Shoshone were always a nonconfrontational tribe. We didn't want the girls to grow up and fight each other when there weren't enough men for all of them to marry."

Everyone must have been transfixed by the story, because it was so quiet in that classroom, I could hear Aubrey breathing on my right.

"Do you know the song--'Rock-a-Bye Baby'? Seems like a pretty grim lullaby to sing to your child, doesn't it? 'Down will come baby, cradle and all.' There's a reason why it's so grim. A white man wrote that song when he witnessed the Shoshone leaving their babies on tree branches to fall to their deaths."

"Why are you saying this?" asked Autumn Rose In Winter. She sounded like she was going to cry.

"Because I don't want you to see the world in black and white. Because I want you to realize that there are good people and bad people everywhere. Some white men are good and some white men are bad. Some Indians are good and some Indians are bad. Every society has its demons. You need to be aware of your demons if you're going to eradicate them."

I was feeling pensive when I left the schoolhouse with Annie and Aubrey. A lot of people on the reserve looked at Rafael like he was some kind of demon that needed to be eradicated. I thought it was getting better, though; like how Zeke and Rafael could finally stand to be in the same room together, or how Rafael hadn't put William Sleeping Fox in the hospital lately. But the fact that Rafael wasn't here today was proof that he was still suffering for something he hadn't done. I wanted people to see him as Rafael, not his father. I just didn't know how to make them see him the way I did.

Annie and I followed Aubrey back to his farm manor for homework. Aubrey's niece Serafine ran in and out of his room, distracting us, and ultimately we abandoned our studies to play tag with her. I was feeling like a regular delinquent when I walked home that afternoon, my neglected books on my back and a smile on my face.

My smile fell with bemusement when I found Granny sitting on the porch with Shaman Quick.

I've said it before, but the shaman very rarely ventured out of the badlands. To see him sitting on my porch in the middle of the day, breechclout and moccasins and all, came as a huge shock. I remembered to smile and waved at him. He shot me a sharp, unimpressed glance.

"Skylar," Granny said importantly. "The shaman is here to talk to you."

Me? I looked to the shaman for confirmation. The shaman narrowed his eyes into squinty little slits. I couldn't imagine what the shaman wanted from me. I couldn't ask him, either; my hand was still broken.

"Tammattsi!" said the shaman.

"Nu kee sakka tsao suwangkunna!" Granny replied harshly.

I showed Granny a pleading look. Granny only sighed, her lips tight. Shaman Quick snapped his fingers; I started.

It is time for your vision quest, the shaman signed.

I looked over my shoulder, just to be sure there wasn't someone standing behind me who also spoke sign language.

"Tammattsi!"

"So'o!"

I rubbed my forehead. I could feel the headache coming on. I sat on the bottom step below the porch.

The shaman signed to me again, looking none too pleased. *All young men and women must perform the vision quest*, he said. *The Wise Wolf tells me it is your turn.*

But I'm not really Shoshone, I wanted to reply. Of course I couldn't. I looked subtly at Granny, wondering why she hadn't told him as much herself.

The shaman snapped his fingers at me a second time. *Do you dare defy the Wise Wolf?*

I shook my head, very solemnly.

Then it is thus. Starting tomorrow you will begin fasting. You will eat only when the sun is down, and at that, nothing more than fruit. You will drink only water. You will not participate in any dances. When I've decided you are ready for more instructions, I will return.

The shaman abruptly rose. Just as abruptly, he stepped off of the porch and walked away. He didn't even bother saying goodbye to Granny.

"I'm proud of you," Granny said. "The vision quest means you're ready to be a man."

I wished I knew what all this was about. Aubrey had told me a little about the vision quest over the summer--a kind of trip to the wilderness that entailed spirits visiting you--but I hadn't given it much mind until now. I wasn't sure whether I believed in spirits to begin with.

Granny dismissed me with a trademark wave of her hand. I went inside to wash up and drop off my schoolbooks. Afterward I stopped by Annie's house and we baked sourdough bread for the nightly bonfire, a surprisingly quick endeavor, mostly because Annie already had the starter sitting in her kitchen cabinet. "Nancy!" Grandpa Little Hawk greeted me. I smiled politely, but I got myself out of there as fast as I could. Grandpa Little Hawk was harmless, but he usually didn't have nice things to say about my masculinity.

It was about four o'clock when I decided to see whether Rafael was home yet. I headed north through the reserve, the gnarled, mossy limbs of the southern oak tree prominent on the spring horizon.

I stood under the southern oak tree and knocked on Gabriel's front door.

Gabriel's smile was sunny when he swung the door open to greet me. If the bloody towel over his shoulder was anything to go by, I'd caught him while he was butchering.

"Hello, Skylar," he said. "What can I do for you?"

I smiled quizzically. As much as I liked Gabriel, there was really only one reason for me to visit his home.

Gabriel seemed to reach the same conclusion, too. The smile slid slowly off of his face.

"He's not with you? Did Rafael not go to school today?"

Alarmed, I couldn't respond. I had assumed--

"I'm going to kill him," Gabriel said.

I don't think he meant to, but he slapped the door shut in my face.

Alright, I thought. If Rafael wasn't with me, and he wasn't with Gabriel, then he had to have gone to one of his hideouts. I looked to the badlands beyond the southern oak. I couldn't see the promontory from here, but I knew it was his favorite place to visit.

Warily, I walked down the sloping terrain to the blue-gray clay. The air around the badlands was cool and swift, green-gray grasses swaying in the wind. The badlands were pretty to the eye, like something out of a child's dream--or nightmare, maybe. Every crevice was in danger of crumbling; all the gorges and gulches were slippery with sand. And don't get me started on the tent rocks, tall, topheavy stacks of stone. I don't know how the mule deer and the prairie dogs eked a living out there.

The promontory loomed in view, and the shadowy figure sitting on top of it. Of course, I thought, shaking my head.

I climbed precariously up the cliffside. Rafael looked up and offered me a candy bar.

I shook my head.

"Not in the mood for people," he said around a mouthful of chocolate.

I sat next to Rafael and inspected him while his eyes were on the horizon. His new glasses were a pretty good match for the old ones; had I been somebody else, and not a person who spent a lot of time staring at him, I never would have known the difference. The cuts around his eye had softened to scratches; the bruise on his cheek was purple and pronounced, but its radius had notably shrunk. Maybe the arnica had helped him a little.

"Do you ever look at me and see my dad?"

I had been subconsciously dreading a question like this. I regarded Rafael carefully. The truth was that I did see his father when I looked at his face. I couldn't help it. Rafael had inherited so many of his father's physical traits. The first time he had kissed me, it had scared me.

Rafael's eyes widened. I never did figure out how to hide my thoughts from him.

"God damn--"

He moved to stand up. I reached for him with my left hand and held on as tightly as I could.

"Even you?"

I pulled on his wrist until he had to sit down.

For a while, Rafael didn't say anything. I could see a nerve working along his jaw, taut and twitching; I guessed he was seconds away from blowing up.

I reached for his hand and took it in mine. He tensed, but didn't fight me. I rubbed my fingers over his knuckles, over the strong skin stretched across the back of his hand. I thought there was something profound in that, that I knew the back of his hand like the back of my mine.

I let go of him. He turned toward me, like he was going to question me, but decided against it, still bitter. I took advantage of his bitterness and slid the glasses from his face. I folded them and set them on his lap.

A flustered, confused expression overtook the bitterness on his face. He opened his mouth--but I don't know what he was going to say; I silenced him, my fingers on his lips. He complied; because for me, he always complied.

I ran the backs of my fingers along the bruise on his face. He tried to follow the movement with his eyes. He gave up after two seconds, his eyes jumping to mine. His eyes were blue, but dark, like the ocean at night, like the night before dawn; his eyes, on mine, felt like electric. I wondered briefly what he saw when he looked at me. Sometimes I longed to see myself through his eyes. Sometimes I wished I could show him what he looked like through mine.

I touched my lips to the scratches on his face. I kissed them, feather-light; I kissed the welt on his lip where the blood had dried. I heard him sigh through his nose--but with tranquility or defeat, I didn't know. He tucked my head against his neck, his arms around me. He wrapped me up in him and held me close, and I belonged there, and I knew it, and he knew it, and maybe that was his solace.

I don't think you always need words to share your heart with another person. Sometimes words are overrated. And that's fortunate for me, I guess. I'm not sure I'd know what to say even if I could say it.

"I was going to punch the shit out of him," he told me. I could feel his voice vibrating against my skin. "Luke. I didn't, though. You know why?"

I'd wondered about that.

"You asked me not to. Last summer. Remember? You gave me that note. 'Stop punching people.' It's the only thing you've ever asked me to do. I can do that much for you. I think I'd do anything for you."

I could feel myself still, in every nerve in my body, in every thought I'd ever had. To have so much power over one person--it was terrifying.

"Am I squishing your hand?"

I pulled back from his embrace, much as I didn't want to, and waved my injured hand, faint smile on my face. I didn't think he was capable of hurting me, not even on accident.

Rafael replaced his eyeglasses. He broke his candy bar in two and handed half to me. We sat and ate together on that cliff, the clouds inching toward us as the sun readied itself for its daily descent. In the back of my head I wondered how long it would be before Gabriel came and found us. He had to have known his nephew's affinity for the badlands.

"You know whether you're gonna start your vision quest yet?"

I looked at Rafael in surprise. It didn't shock me anymore when he read my mind like an open book, but I just couldn't figure out how he had deduced something like that.

He snorted. "The shaman always comes looking for you when you turn seventeen. I don't know why. I think in the old days, the age was twelve. Ask your grandma, she might know."

I smiled lightly. I didn't think she would appreciate me calling her old.

I realized: If seventeen was the vision quest age, then Aubrey must have been fasting back in February. No wonder we'd beaten him at shinny. I realized something else, too. Rafael was eighteen. Rafael had gone through his vision quest already.

He nodded, confirming it. "You're not supposed to tell anyone what happens during your vision quest," he said. "No one except for the shaman."

In that case, I wouldn't badger him for details.

Rafael paused. "Well," he stipulated, "I can tell you this. 'Vision quest' is kind of a misleading name. I mean, yeah, you're gonna have visions, really weird ones, but it's not about the visions. It's about figuring out what direction your life's supposed to take."

Oh. Like an aptitude test? I tried to imagine myself in a business suit.

Rafael grinned bashfully. "You thinking about work? Yeah, that can factor into it. Sometimes. Depends. You can get a message from the spirits, like, 'You are a healer.' So then you interpret it as, 'Oh, I'll be a doctor.' The shaman helps you figure it out. Not like I need him, though. I already know what I'm going to be."

I prodded him in the ribs. He couldn't just leave me hanging like that.

"A speech therapist," he said.

The whole world could have stopped. I wouldn't have noticed.

Rafael gave me an unusually stoic look. "I'm going to get your voice back someday," he said. "I thought that was obvious."

How much can one person give you before he stops giving? Sometimes it felt like Rafael would never stop giving. Sometimes I wondered how I could ever return what he had given me. I wanted to give him everything you could possibly give to a single person. I know that sounds crazy. It must be true when they say that love makes you crazy.

"Rafael, you're grounded!"

Rafael cringed. I winced sympathetically. Gabriel had found us after all.

I've heard it said that the bones in your hand are the most malleable; and maybe that's true. By May the pain in my right hand had vanished. I peeled the cast off and flexed my fingers. They looked a little knobbly to me, but maybe that was just my imagination. I could have cheered with delight. I stood in the front room of my home and practiced all the signs I hadn't been able to use since April. *I am awesome*, I signed, palms facing forward, fingers spread. It was shameless of me, sure. But it's not like anyone in the house would have known what I was saying.

Zeke came back to the reservation around that time. At first I didn't realize it, because he wasn't living with Dad and Granny and me anymore. Instead I found him on Ms. Siomme's ranch one afternoon, helping her to bale out hay. I took it as a bad sign that he wasn't living in his own house. I wondered whether the Navajo had released his father from prison yet.

In the mornings I awoke before Dad and Granny, before the sun had risen, and ate crabapples and prairie bananas to tide me over for the rest of the day. I had thought that fasting was going to be difficult, but it wasn't: I was already accustomed to waking at dawn, and I guess I wasn't a big eater to begin with. Dad invariably woke an hour after me, and he usually left the house right away, without saying much except "Study, Cubby." I figured out what he was up to when I walked back from school with Annie, Aubrey, and Rafael and found the whole reservation lined with empty wooden tables and stalls. Crafts month had officially begun.

The creative energy crackling in the air was practically tangible. Granny had me set up her loom on the lawn and she spent hours out there with her friends, skilfully weaving quilts and pendleton blankets in shocks of red and shades of blue. Ours wasn't the only lawn with a loom on it. I counted seven in one morning and grinned impishly. No one could contest with my Granny, and anyone who tried was in for a world of hurt. I saw women sitting on the ground with wet fingers and spinning wheels, shaping clay pottery with the palms of their hands. I saw men whittling shapes out of wood with their stone knives, bears and elk and eagles with their wings spread. Annie pinched my elbow while I stared.

"Let's go into the woods," she said, eyes sparkling.

I waited outside her house while she went inside and fetched Lila and Joseph. Balto came inching along, curious, and I scratched the scruff of his neck. The five of us went into the forest together; those of us with arms carried wicker baskets. Joseph's job was to collect stones and Lila's was to collect bones. *Skylar, you can collect the dyes*, Annie signed serenely. The signing was really for Joseph's sake. *I'll make the glass. We'll all meet at the grotto in an hour. And remember, stay* away *from the north woods. You don't want to bother the black bears, do you?*

I was smiling when I veered off the woodland path, Balto darting ahead of me. Balto yipped just once, high and clear, and led me to the turmeric scattered across the forest floor. I knelt and picked them; the roots made for a great yellow dye. We walked a little farther and found the lupins, spiral flowers on climbing stalks, and I plucked them carefully. The petals were blue, but the stems produced gray. Wild indigo was a little harder to find--the flowers liked to disguise themselves as lupins--but Balto sniffed at the soil and bit the stalks and I laughed fondly when his teeth turned blue. We followed a small tributary trickling from the lake and I pulled the madder and the bloodroot from the wet ground, my fingers running red. I flaked the bark from the alder trees for orange dye and culled the fanlike, billowing puya for blue-green. I had to wait for walnuts and acacia before I could get black or brown, but Mrs. In Winter was usually nice about lending us some from her garden. And the only way to make a real green was to pick up red onions from Aubrey's farm.

I checked my wristwatch and clapped my hands. Balto dashed after me and we made a race out of running back to the grotto. Balto won by a wide margin. Annie was already by the creek, lighting kindling fires over piles of sand and plant ash. It wasn't long before Lila and Joseph joined us, their hands joined, their baskets swinging.

Found a lot of rocks, Joseph signed.

I tousled his long hair and he hid behind it, like a curtain.

Balto trotted into the cave, no doubt looking for a snack. Lila, Joseph, and I sat with Annie and got to work. I crushed the plants to make the dyes, and as Annie's glassware cooled and hardened, she took whichever colors she wanted from me and discarded the rest. She made windchimes, glass horses and glass butterflies and the most amazing stars you've ever seen, such that the real ones had reason for envy. I took the dyes she didn't need and left them to dry under a patch of sun; when they hardened into ink sticks, we could sell them along with the rest of the crafts. Annie made necklaces out of painted stones and clay beads from the badlands. Lila broke the brittle skink skulls in her fingers and let Annie shape them into rings and bracelets and earrings; Annie let Lila crush the pinecones for their resin and coat the bones to restore their hardiness. We spent so long out by the grotto that Joseph fell asleep, his head on my knee. I stroked the crown of his head and the nape of his neck while Balto helped himself to a dinner of quail.

Rafael and Aubrey joined us at the grotto the next day, long strips of wood and tangled piles of milkweed gathered in their arms.

"We're making bows and arrows!" Aubrey said excitedly.

"Hope somebody shoots himself in the foot," Rafael said sourly.

I noticed Zeke had followed them. I wasn't entirely sure where he stood with us; but he smiled at me, nervously, and twitched his hand in a wave, and there was no way I could let that pass without smiling broadly back.

Now that my hand was healed, I realized, I could go back to playing the plains flute. Aubrey told me that Plains music was always a big seller during crafts month, so I made a quick trip home to borrow Granny's tape recorder; then I went back to the grotto and recorded songs in the cave. I think everybody likes music, although I'm sure we all have our own preferences. But for me, music wasn't just something to listen to. It was the only sound I could make. It was vitally important to me, in the same way that a thirsty man can't help but snatch up the nearest drink of water. When you're standing on the edge of a canyon, and all you want in that moment is to be heard by the person who's standing on the other side, of course you're going to scream.

I emerged from the cave, my flute hanging around my neck, and Lila grabbed my hand like she owned it.

"Hey, daddio," she said. "Break time. You've got to see something cool."

Cooler than you? I signed.

"Let's not get carried away."

She led me away from the grotto and into a part of the woods I'd never visited in the past.

I hope you're not trying to feed me to the bears, I joked.

Lila rolled her eyes. "Your sense of direction sucks."

We crept around the beech trees, Lila tiptoeing across the forest detritus. I couldn't understand why she wanted us to be quiet.

Lila signed: *Look.*

I held my breath. I couldn't help it. The little grove was cluttered with woodsorrels--veined white flowers, delicate and paper-thin. By itself, it was impressive. What rendered it awe-inspiring was the hundreds of butterflies nesting on the tips of the flower petals, their wispy wings aloft and fluttering.

I counted them until my eyes ached; and when I blinked, I lost count. Dusky Emperors with tawny brown wings, spotted Aphrodites in shades of belated autumn gold, Painted Ladies and American Ladies and sleek black Elves, Pale Crescents and Pearl Crescents and the elusive Cattleheart, her wings decorated in shimmering red and pale green. All as different from one another as could be. All eating from the same manna.

Lila sighed. *Isn't it perfect?* she signed. *We could learn a lot from them.*

Crafts month was in full swing by the next day. The tables all over the reservation were stacked with clay jewelry and bone jewelry, timeless ceramics, cornhusk dolls, quilts and pillows in all sizes, wood bowls and wood figurines and glass figurines, bird bone flutes and goatskin hand drums, elkskin tapestries and willow baskets and willow dreamcatchers in every color known to the human eye. And just in time, too--because that was when all the white folks came stampeding in.

I had never seen the reservation this crowded, not even during the summer pauwau. Whole families traipsed through Nettlebush like they were on vacation, sunglasses on their eyes and fanny packs at their waists, their children running amok. Granny guarded her table full of quilts and eyed everyone reproachfully. The weirdest part was that the visitors wanted to take pictures of absolutely everything: The firepit, the log cabins, even the clotheslines and the butter churns. It sort of made me uncomfortable. Not Lila, though. She posed and blew kisses at the cameras.

"Skylar!"

I was helping Granny fold her pendleton blankets--one of the customers had knocked them out of their pile--when I heard my name. I looked up.

The Hargroves were coming up the lane toward our house. Jessica ran ahead of her family, her braids swinging around her head.

I smiled until my face hurt. I stepped out from behind the sales table. Jessica skipped over and wrapped her arms around me in a quick, tight hug. I was all too happy to return it.

"This is for you," Jessica said, and handed me a plastic doll in a pleated pink skirt.

I struggled to keep a straight face. I took the doll graciously and pat Jessica on the head.

Dad came out of the house and put his arm around Officer Hargrove's shoulders. I guessed he wasn't trying to hide it anymore. "Would you kids like a snack?" he asked.

"Yes!"

"Yaaay!"

DeShawn and Jessica ran at him like they were starving. I suppose when you're a kid, you're always starving.

Dad took the kids inside to find them something to eat. Officer Hargrove put her hands on my shoulders, matter-of-factly, and pretended she wasn't looking at me like I was six years old.

"So," she said brusquely. "How ya doing?"

I swallowed a laugh. I gave her a thumbs up.

"Racine," Granny sang. "I set something aside for you, dear--"

Dear? I reached across the table to feel Granny's forehead. Was she sure she didn't have a fever? Granny waved my hand away, annoyed with me.

Granny and Officer Hargrove stood by the table and chatted. I went into the house to find a safe place for Jessica's doll. I could hear spoons clinking in glass bowls from the kitchen; probably Dad had given the kids wojapi. I went back outside to see if Granny needed any more help with her wares.

The shaman was standing on the front porch, a bota bag on his hip, gazing at me through narrow eyes.

Is there something I can do for you? I signed. I tried to ignore the snapping of camera shutters on the lane outside our lawn. I thought it was really rude.

You are ready for the vision quest, Shaman Quick signed. *We will go now.*

Shaman Quick descended the porch steps without waiting for me. I hurried to catch up with him.

I looked over at the table. Granny and Officer Hargrove were exchanging money with a customer; by the looks of it, neither had noticed us. I signed to the shaman, *My grandmother--*

What the spirits posit must not be ignored.

I felt a little foolish as I walked at the shaman's side. A woman in a baseball cap pointed at us and turned to whisper to her husband.

We walked past the firepit and the northern half of the neighborhood. Gabriel's southern oak drew closer in view, and I realized: The shaman was taking me to the badlands. Maybe we were headed back to his place? The shaman lived in a canyon out there, in a house not unlike a wickiup.

He walked across the crumbling clay like it was nothing. I followed him less certainly, apprehension gnawing at the pit of my stomach.

Apparently his house wasn't our destination. We walked past the canyon and the coal seams; the shaman didn't look back. Usually the badlands were cooler than the rest of the reserve, but not today; the sun beating on the crown of my head was so bright, my skull started to ache.

Past the promontory and a grove of southern oaks. Through the green-gray grass and the tent rocks climbing toward the sky like ladders to Heaven. Now I really felt nauseous. I had never been this far out in the badlands before. I was pretty sure that this was coyote territory.

A red-tailed hawk screeched high overhead. A rattlesnake slithered through the cracks in the ground. My shirt was starting to stick to my back with perspiration. I looked over my shoulder. I couldn't see Rafael's promontory anymore. Somehow, that bothered me the most.

"Summi."

The shaman came to a stop; and so did I. I felt clay and sand sliding under my feet. In the far, blurry distance were foreboding trees with woody, leafless limbs. I wondered if the forest looped around to the badlands. I never got to ask. The shaman sat on the flat, slippery ground, facing west, and I sat with him. The air was breathy and warm; and out west were rolling plains of clay flanked by gorges.

The reservation wasn't even visible from here. I wondered how long we had been walking.

You will stay out here for three days, the shaman signed to me.

I nearly jumped. Three days? With the coyotes and the pronghorns? And there wasn't anything to eat out here. There wasn't even grass.

The shaman unfastened the bota bag from his hip. He handed it to me. I heard the water sloshing around inside.

I surveyed him inquisitively, skittish.

Our Father will protect you from the wild, he said. *You must pray. Pray that the Great Mystery fills you with purpose. Empty your mind of everything except for the search for purpose. You will have nothing to eat except for this drink. When it is time for you to come home, I will come back for you.*

I tried to crack a smile; I don't think I succeeded. *Are you sure you won't find my remains?*

The shaman gave me a sharp look, as though to suggest he didn't find me very funny.

One more thing, he signed. *If your spirit guide wishes to make itself known, it will approach you in the form of an animal, which you will not fear.* "Puha," he spoke out loud. But of course I didn't know what "puha" meant.

The shaman rose, as though to leave me. My heart was pounding a mile a minute. I didn't want to be left alone.

I reached for his wrist. To my surprise, he let me take it.

Can you give me my voice back? I said wildly. I was thinking of the prairie chicken dance, of Aubrey's father.

The shaman looked at me with pity. I didn't like that look.

With a heavy sigh, as heavy as a raincloud, Shaman Quick pulled free from my grasp. He started the walk back to the reserve.

Okay, I thought, my heart torching the inside of my chest. I could just follow the shaman home. I mean, what would he do if I tried-- knock me out? There was no real reason I had to stay out here.

I stood up; but my legs were heavy, my skin slicked with sweat, and just as quickly, I sat back down. I untied the bota bag and lifted it to my lips. I felt as though I were dying of thirst. I took a drink of water; it tasted surprisingly sweet.

I wondered whether Dad had performed the vision quest at my age. I felt certain that Granny must have. I knew Rafael had. What had Rafael seen out here? Had the shaman even taken him out here? Maybe the spot the shaman chose depended on the person. I thought the badlands suited Rafael. I felt sure he must have had his vision quest in the badlands. Maybe atop one of those tent rocks, fearlessly daring it to spill over.

I glanced south, the shaman's receding form a smudge on the horizon. In defeat, I thought: People have been going on vision quests since the dawn of time. If it were really so dangerous, no one would do it. I told myself I needed to stop being such a scaredy cat. I took another drink. Man, did it taste good.

An eagle let out a shrill, majestic cry. I tilted my head back to find him, but I only saw the sun, high and full in a sky of endless blue. My eyes watered. I checked the watch on my wrist. My vision was blurry; I couldn't make out the time. I guessed by my shadow that it was a few hours before sunset.

Boredom sank in, and fast. I'm not the kind of guy who can deal with solitude very well. I picked up the plains flute hanging from my neck and thought of Rafael. Rafael had hewn this flute for me almost a year ago. I imagined that I could still feel his hands, rough and brown, whittling the smooth falcon bones. I thought to myself: I'll just play songs until the shaman comes back for me. Then I thought: That's cheating. He told me to pray.

I didn't know how to pray. I'm sure that sounds dumb, but it's true. I'd never prayed a single day in my life. Do you start it like a letter? Do you address it to someone? I didn't know. I closed my eyes--the sun was so bright--and concentrated.

Purpose. Right. I was supposed to find my purpose. Not that I thought I had much of a purpose to begin with, useless lump of flesh that I was. I started to laugh. No, I told myself. Be serious.

I thought about Danny and Mr. Patreya. With any luck, they were getting ready for their next crab fishing trip. I couldn't believe the government just took Indian children from their homes whenever they wanted to. And why? Because white couples wanted to adopt them? A few nights ago I had looked up child protection laws on Granny's computer. I hadn't found anything about the missing Native children--maybe because the government wanted to hush it up--but I had found something else, something called the Indian Child Welfare Act. Basically it was supposed to prevent a disaster like Carlisle Indian School from happening again. Well, it wasn't working.

Uncomfortable, I squirmed. I took another drink of water. I

opened my eyes and found the sun ahead of me, preparing to touch the horizon. An hour until sunset. I could feel the wind on my skin and the sand beneath my thighs.

My pulses danced between my temples. The sweat on my back had started to cool. Gross. Now I wanted to take a bath. I debated taking another drink but decided against it. I tied off the top of the bota bag and set it on my lap. If I was stuck out here for three days, I needed to save what I had. Three days without food. Boy, did that sound nightmarish. At least I had water. Water's more important than food.

A prairie dog poked his chubby head out of the ground. He glanced at me, then burrowed for cover. Fine, I thought. Be that way. I'm just going to take a nap.

I curled up on the ground and tried to get comfortable. I tucked my hand beneath my head to keep the sand from my ears. It wound up in my hair instead. I was starting to feel lightheaded. Stupid sun. Stupid sand. I smothered a yawn. Maybe I could just sleep for three days...

I must have fallen asleep after all. But as for how long, I couldn't possibly say. All I knew was that the ground under my skin felt biting and cold. I figured that meant it was nighttime. I shifted slowly into a sitting position and rubbed the feeling back into my eyes.

My whole body froze.

Alright, I thought. Calm down. Obviously you're dreaming.

And really, it had to be a dream--because it doesn't snow in Arizona, much less in the middle of spring.

I climbed weakly off the ground and stared around. The entire expanse was covered in blankets of untouched snow. The wind howled and licked at my ears, real pain shooting up my temples. My clothes were wet where I had lain in the snow. I touched my fingertips to the frosty dew in my hair and thought: Do dreams usually feel this real? I pinched myself, and it hurt; and I didn't wake up.

Snow drifted from the sky and into my eyes. I pressed my teeth together to keep them from chattering and my skin rose in gooseflesh. I huddled into myself for warmth. It didn't work. Weakly, I thought: Did he drug me? What is this? If I'm asleep, why can't I wake up? If I'm hallucinating, why am I aware of it? And the more I looked around me, the more I realized: I wasn't even in the badlands. The tent rocks and gorges were gone. The sun was invisible behind pregnant winter clouds.

Wake up, I thought desperately. I smacked myself across the face. It hurt like a son of a bitch.

"I wouldn't do that."

I turned around frantically, thinking that the shaman had come back to take me from this--this--whatever it was. But no; it wasn't the shaman. It was a young woman kneeling in the snow, a big wicker basket at her side and an empty cradleboard on her back.

At first I wasn't sure whether she was the one who had spoken to me: Her head was bent, her fingers sifting through the snow. But we were the only two people out here, so who else could it have been? She wore a heavy winter Plains dress made of sheepskin, the soft white pelt still attached to the hide; and her tight leggings and moccasins, beige, looked like they were made from elk. I couldn't think why she was dressed that way unless she was going to a pauwau. She rummaged in the snow and unearthed the hidden rosehips and inkcaps, the mushrooms soft, the berries ripe. She tossed her findings in the basket and stood with it against her hip. And she looked at me, and she had my grandmother's water-gray eyes.

Distantly, I wondered whether she was supposed to be my grandmother, only younger. No, I thought. That's not Granny. Granny's nose was rounder; this woman's nose looked long and straight, like my dad's. Her chin was fuller than either of theirs, which gave the impression that she was squaring it in defiance, even when she wasn't.

Immediately, I knew who it was that my mind had conjured.

"You should say something," Taken Alive said.

"I can't," I said.

I checked at that, bewildered.

Taken Alive thrust her wicker basket into my arms. The wood felt like splinters against my ice-cold hands.

"It's *your* vision quest," she said.

Just like that, she started away from me, the snowshoes attached to her moccasins leaving imprints where she had walked.

Dazed, I shook my head. Please wake up, I thought. Naturally, I didn't wake up. That would have been too easy. Taken Alive walked ahead of me without looking back. Maybe I was supposed to stick with her. I ran to catch up with her, my socks drenched, sneakers leaving trenches in the snow.

"Where are we?" I asked. I stopped walking. I hadn't heard my own voice in twelve years. I laughed breathily against the cold wind, moisture biting my eyes, and touched my throat. The scars were still there. I didn't need to be told how crazy this was. But I could *hear* it when I laughed, soft, and a little deep, definitely not a five-year-old's voice. I wondered whether I could cough, too. I would have tried it, except I didn't know how.

"Keep up with me."

"Oh, sorry," I said. She had outstripped me again.

We stopped on the edge of a bright river cutting through the banks of snow. On either side of the river were tall brown tipis, smoke escaping through the wooden poles at the tops of the canvases. I thought back to history lessons with Mr. Red Clay. The Western Shoshone used wickiups, but the Eastern Shoshone used tipis. We were on Wind River.

Taken Alive knelt in the snow and pushed aside the flaps of a tipi. She took the wicker basket from me and went inside her home. She hadn't told me that I should follow her; but this was my vision quest, as she had said. Wondering at my lunacy, I knelt and followed her inside.

The tipi was a lot roomier on the inside than the outside had suggested. A small firepit filled with rocks burned brightly in the center of the home. My cold skin sang with relief. Hanging from the buffalo hide walls were any variety of tools--a bag of medicine, a bow and arrows, a needle and thread. Taken Alive removed the empty cradleboard from her back and set more stones on the firepit. She took a pot from behind her and filled it with the rosehips.

"Can I help you?" I asked, alarmingly aware that I was asking a figment of my imagination if I could cook with her.

Taken Alive looked analytically at me. She set aside the pot of rosehips, as though a better idea had occurred to her. Or maybe I was annoying her. I don't know whether hallucinations can get annoyed.

"No, you can't," she said. "I've been dead for over fifty years."

I felt a little silly.

Taken Alive thrust the rosehip pot into my hands. "Fill this with snow from outside."

I really couldn't say no to that. I've never been good at saying no.

I pushed aside the entrance of the tipi. I dipped the pot in the deep

snow and filled it to the brim. Finished, I tied the door flaps shut--
it was much too cold out there--and handed the pot to Taken Alive.
She set it over the firepit to boil.

The strangest thing happened to the melting snow. It rose from the
pot in vapors and crystallized in the air. The crystals hung
between us like dangling decorations. My breath escaped my
mouth in a mist.

"Why am I here?" Taken Alive asked.

I smiled faintly. "I was sort of hoping you could tell me."

"That was presumptuous of you."

"I know. Sorry."

It was getting really chilly in that tent. I raised a hand to touch the
ice crystals floating in the air. The moment I touched them, they
cracked and clattered back into the pot.

"Family," said Taken Alive. The word had never sounded so sad
as it did when it came from her lips.

I tried not to stare at the empty cradleboard.

"Family," she said again--this time like it was a breath of fresh air.

"I could tell you about Granny," I offered. "I mean, Catherine.
Your great-granddaughter. She's all grown up now. She speaks
highly about you."

You have lost your mind, I told myself.

Taken Alive looked right through me.

"Or her son," I went on, less certainly. "He's grown up, too."

"You mean your father."

I hesitated.

"What am I? Let's see... Your great-great-great-grandmother."

I started to correct her. "Actually--"

"My daughter had blonde hair, too."

I had to question that. There just wasn't any way my imagination could have provided that sort of detail. Unless Granny had mentioned it once and I'd retained the detail subconsciously.

"We called her Looks Over. You know, in those days--my days--a Shoshone had about twelve different names in her lifetime. My little girl was Looks Over. She had the bad habit of looking over her shoulder all the time. She was a jumpy girl."

I didn't know what to do except smile.

Taken Alive sighed. She removed the pot from the stone firepit. "Then the white men came back for her--took her to that awful school, so far away from me, from my arms--and they called her 'Amelia.' Cut off her beautiful hair, too. You know what that's about, don't you? They're trying to erase us. They're trying to pretend we were never here. Maybe it's guilt. Maybe it's disdain. But we were here first. Everything they've ever laid claim to was on our backs. On our blood."

I was starting to feel a little ill, but for all I knew, it was a reaction to whatever drug the shaman had given me.

"We Shoshone, you know...we never fought back. Maybe it's time for us to fight back."

"But I'm not Shoshone," I said.

Taken Alive pierced me with her gaze. "That's what 'Amelia' said when they sent her back to me."

My stomach felt wrenched and twisted in a thousand coils. I suddenly knew I was going to be sick.

"I'm sorry," I said quickly, and reached for the tent flaps.

"Bring Looks Over back to me. Won't you?"

I wasn't fast enough. I doubled over and threw up.

Water spilled from my mouth and onto the cracked and sandy ground.

I started with panic. My nerves were jumping, my head throbbing. My back was drenched in cold sweat and my throat was chalky and dry.

On my hands and knees, I gazed at the waning, luminous moon in the sky, hanging high above the badlands.

Thank God it was over, I thought deliriously. I shot a mutinous look at the shaman's bota bag. No way was I touching that thing again.

Slowly, my pulse calmed. I sat back on my haunches and wiped the sweat from my brow. I'd never realized how cold the badlands were at night. A shiver trailed down my spine. I could hear the coyotes yowling to one another from the gorges, no doubt getting ready to pair up for the nightly hunt.

Good thing coyotes get along with humans, I thought, unnerved.

I pressed the light-up button on my watch. Eleven o'clock at night. Too bad I wasn't feeling tired. I hugged my knees for warmth. Maybe if I stayed awake long enough I'd get to watch the sun come up. At least I couldn't dream if I didn't sleep.

Man, were the stars bright out here. That is, they were bright all over Nettlebush: That's what happens when most of the community doesn't use electric. But above the badlands they seemed brighter, somehow. Maybe because there was nothing to distract me from the sight of them. No houses. No trees. Nobody but me.

I raised my plains flute to my lips. I stopped. Right, I thought, dispirited. Pray.

"Bring Looks Over back to me"--that didn't make much sense. Amelia Looks Over had died many years ago. Of course it didn't make much sense. It was a hallucination. My purpose. What was my purpose? How could I be sure that people like me even had a purpose?

I checked my watch again. Barely ten minutes had passed.

This was impossible, I thought. I gave up. I started playing the flute.

I played through Heavy Fog, a cheerful flag dance song, and the Song of the Fallen Warrior, mournful but powerful. I tried out the Shoshone love song, simple and sweet, but I liked Morgan Stout's rendition a lot better. I sampled a couple of Paiute pieces I had heard during the winter pauwau, but I didn't know them well enough to play them in their entirety. I was on my third run-through of the Song of the Golden Eagle when a pair of coyotes yipped and cantered over to me, lured by the sounds of the flute. I showed them my hands and they backed away, disappointed to see that I didn't have handouts for them.

By dawn I had exhausted my repertoire of songs. I needed a new distraction. Somehow I got the bright idea that I was going to create a song of my own. I started piecing together different notes in a blind effort to make them fit. It didn't take long before I realized I was a crappy composer.

The sun rose behind me, soothing and cool. Blue ink bled into the black and starry sky, chased away by white-gold sunshine. Sunrise was a beautiful sight to behold, and it captivated me, until I couldn't remember the real reason I was out here. By the time the sun was high and merciless in the sky, the hawks screeching for their morning ascent, I remembered why. My tongue felt as hot as embers. I looked wearily at the shaman's bota bag. I wasn't fooling anyone. I knew I had to take a drink.

The sweet water was a welcome alleviant against my sore throat. I tied up the bota bag and set it on the ground, and immediately I started to dread what I had done. It wouldn't be long now before Taken Alive came back for another bizarre chat. What the heck was in that water, and what ever possessed Plains People to start drinking it?

Around midday the sun was so hot, all I could think to do was take my shirt off and fan myself with it. Soon I was drowsy again. I folded up my shirt and laid it on the ground. I laid my head on my shirt and took another nap.

The second time I awoke, it wasn't to snow, but to a soft carpet. At first I couldn't remember what had happened, why I had fallen asleep, and I hastily put my shirt back on. I stood slowly and looked around.

I recognized this house. There was a closet next to the front door, twin bedrooms to my right. The door at the far end led to an outhouse. The walls were covered in charcoal drawings; when I tried to get a closer look at them, they blurred and distorted before my eyes. I placed my hand against a raw support beam. My eyes followed the light leaking through the ceiling to an east-facing alcove.

"Hello," my mother said.

I couldn't take my eyes off of her. She sat on the window seat in the alcove, her leg tucked beneath her. In a frumpy white dress and a green apron, her teeth poking out of her mouth in a rabbit-like underbite, she was adorable.

I gazed at her in yearning. I couldn't bring myself to take a step closer. I thought it was cruel that my imagination had summoned the one person I'd always wanted to know.

"Are you just going to stand there all day?" Mom asked.

"Well, yeah," I said, sheepish, "that was kind of the intention."

Mom scoffed. "You get that from your father."

My father.

I couldn't help it when dull resentment surged through my being. I took a cautious step closer. "Which one?" I asked, and tried to sound polite.

Mom frowned at me. "The only one you've ever known."

"You really hurt him," I said, the words tumbling haphazardly from my mouth.

"I know."

"He doesn't deserve that."

"I know."

"Then why'd you do it?"

"I'm only human, honey," Mom said. "We're known for our mistakes."

I was too afraid to draw near. I was afraid she'd vanish if I touched her. She wasn't real.

"I'm real," Mom said, her eyebrows dancing. "Just because you imagine something doesn't mean it isn't real. Remember when we used to sit by this window and watch the sun climbing over the pines?"

I swallowed. "I do remember that," I said. It was one of the few things I remembered about her. How young the both of us had been. I realized Mom was little more than a kid when she had had me. And when she died...

"Was it fast?" I asked.

"Yes. It was."

I smiled ruefully. I knew she was telling me what I wanted to hear.

"Come here," Mom said.

I sat tentatively on the window seat with her. Suddenly I wanted to be small again. I wanted those days when I didn't know what fear was, when I didn't have to pretend I knew what my mother's voice sounded like.

Mom reached for me. Maybe she was going to hug me; I don't know. Because my stomach started hurting again, and I knew it was only a matter of time before I threw up. Please don't, I begged my body. I didn't want this to be over, not yet, not now, I wanted to hug my mother--

A wave of sickness pulsed around me. I fell to my knees. My stomach clenched with nausea, sickness and sickly-sweet water pouring out of my mouth.

I drew a deep, gasping breath. My head was about ready to burst, my eyes swimming with tears. The badlands were bright, brutal, the sand under my hands scratching my palms raw. My stomach tightened with hunger. Whether mere hours had passed, or days, I didn't know. I just wanted the shaman to come back. I couldn't take this anymore. I couldn't understand how Plains People went through this with ease.

I wiped my mouth with the back of my hand. I heard a coyote yipping somewhere in the badlands, somewhere south of me. I wondered at that; coyotes, as far as I knew, were mostly nocturnal.

I squinted at the blurry southern horizon. My body felt cooked from the inside out. I wished I had my willow leaves with me, because I was pretty sure this was the start of a fever.

The yips drew closer. The yips turned into barks. That I found odd. A coyote can "bark," I guess, but it doesn't sound anything like a dog's bark. It sounds more like a honking goose. This sounded like a real bark. A wolf's bark.

Balto bounded across the grainy sand. He skidded to a halt at my knees, his sharp nails catching on the clay ground.

I couldn't believe my eyes. A coywolf was definitely better suited to the badlands than a human was, but I had no idea how he'd managed to find me. I sat up on my knees and reached for his muzzle. He dropped a dead ferret at my feet. It was very thoughtful of him.

Home, I signed.

I meant for him to go home--but he must have misinterpreted. He started south, then stopped, his bushy tail held high. He turned his head and gazed back at me expectantly, panting. He wanted me to follow him.

And really, I'd had enough of this. I didn't want to talk to dead relatives anymore. I just wanted to take a bath.

I picked up the shaman's bota bag and started after Balto. He barked, showing me his approval, and took off at breakneck speed. I had no choice but to run if I wanted to keep up.

The badlands were slippery under the soles of my shoes. I tripped more than once, crashing to my knees; Balto was kind enough to circle around until I caught up to him. I wasn't really in the mood to run; my lungs felt like they were about to explode. But soon we came upon the tent rocks; then the southern oak grove; then the promontory. We were halfway home. Balto might have gone on to the reservation; but I wanted to stop by the shaman's house and

return his bota bag. I got down on my knees to collect my breath.
Balto loped back to me, sniffing, bemused. I reached out to stroke
his pelt.

He vanished as soon as I touched him.

I stared, incredulous, blank, at the empty stretch of ground.

Guess the drug was still in my system.

24
Pilot Whale

The shaman scrutinized me from across the little round table.

The shaman's house was antiquated, animal hide walls stretched firmly across a skeletal wooden frame. The house was floorless, the would-be floor nothing more than sand. Sunlight streamed in through the parted leather doorway; otherwise the house was very dim.

A pair of heart-shaped windchimes hung from a pole across the ceiling.

I'm sorry, I began to sign. *But I--*

The shaman stopped me with a raised hand. Resigned, I slumped.

You will tell me what you saw, he said.

I had expected him to be kind of mad at me that I'd cut my vision quest short. Or maybe I hadn't; I don't really know how long I was out there. Either way, the shaman didn't seem to care. Dumbfounded, I signed to him--about my crazy hallucinations-- and he sat up gradually, nodding, cunning eyes bulging. I almost saw a smile on his face. He clapped his hand on his knee the moment I had finished.

A speaker! he signed. *You will speak on behalf of families.*

I stared at him.

What?

That sounds good--it does--but I can't speak.

"Tammattsi!"

I really wished he would stop shouting that at me.

Your spirit guide is the coywolf, he signed to me. *And the coywolf belongs to two worlds. Balance comes from maintaining both worlds. Beware that neither claims you wholly.*

"Toko."

The shaman's granddaughter came into the rustic house, her eyes bulging. Following her was my father.

I stood up so quickly, I was dizzy. Dad stilled me with a hand on the back of my head.

"You really need a bath," he said apologetically.

I smiled at him. I was very aware.

"Aishen," Dad said to the shaman. He took me by the shoulders. "Let's head home, Cubby."

I was exhausted by the time Dad and I returned home. I wanted nothing except to lie down and sleep for hours. Dad had ideas of his own. Sternly--which didn't come easily for him--he sent me out to the outhouse to get cleaned up. My hair was sodden by the time I padded back inside.

"You're going to eat," he said. "I know how strenuous the vision quest can be for your stomach. Trust me, I went through it at your age."

We went into the kitchen together and ate chokecherries from the icebox. It was probably a good thing that Dad had abandoned more intricate culinary endeavors. I sank into a wooden chair, relieved to be out of the hot sun. Dad sat across the table from me, studying me in silence.

"A while ago," Dad said, "you wanted to know about your mother. But I brushed you off, and that was wrong of me."

I swallowed a chokecherry and gazed at him, wondering whether he knew--but how could he know?--what I had seen in the badlands.

"Her family was Finnish. Her father had some English in him, I believe. Her parents divorced when she was very young. Her father walked out on the family and never looked back. Her mother buried herself in her work. For the most part, Christine grew up alone."

I rested my elbow on the table, a frown on my face.

"The mistakes your mother made... You have to understand. She was just trying to fill a void. She wanted love." Dad looked at me meaningfully. "I think that void was filled once we had you."

I ducked my head, embarrassed, and waved at him playfully.

"Sky?"

I looked up from the kitchen table.

Rafael must have let himself into the house. That's just the way it works in Nettlebush. He thrust his head through the kitchen doorway, and when he saw the two of us, he started to nod.

"Immaculata said you were back. I thought she was lying. She kinda does that."

"Come here, Rafael," Dad said. "Have some chokecherries with us."

"Okay. Thanks."

It was oddly relaxing, the three of us together at the same table. Rafael had this really gross habit of spitting his chokecherry pits in the palm of his hand. Dad and Rafael started a contest to see which one of them could spit his pits the farthest. When I finally decided to join in, relenting, and spat my pit out the kitchen window, the both of them called foul play.

"That's just not human," Rafael said disgustedly.

"I saw those landscapes you drew for crafts month," Dad said.

Rafael did this thing with his shoulders, a sort of half-shrug. "They kind of suck..."

"I didn't think so."

"Thanks."

Dad got up to wash his hands at the wash basin. The mention of crafts month had reminded me of something. I pushed my chair back and ran from the room.

"Sky? Where are you going?"

Rafael wasn't the sort of boy who could sit still for very long. He followed me into the front room while I opened the drawers beneath the computer desk. I found what I was looking for and stuffed it into his hands.

He examined it in silence.

"Is that a pilot whale?" he finally said.

It was foolish of me, maybe, but Annie and I had had some glasswort left over. I had looked up the pilot whale on Granny's computer and tried to recreate it out of glass. The finished result was a small blue pendant on the end of a willow string. My rendition was kind of blobby. I probably should have asked for Annie's help.

Rafael's face lit up in an irresistible grin. He wrapped the willow string twice around his wrist.

"Dumbass," he said.

I don't know, I thought, grinning back. Maybe I really was a
dumbass. Everyone needs a pilot whale sooner or later, though.
To show us the way home.

The radio in the sitting room crackled with static. The next thing I
knew, men's smarmy voices were bouncing off of the walls of my
home.

"Come listen to baseball," Dad called.

"Okay," Rafael returned, and padded out of the room.

I lingered in the front room after he had gone. The stack of letters
on the computer desk had caught my eye. I rifled through them
quickly, just to be sure none of them were for me.

One was for me--a letter from the Pleasance Reserve. I slit open
the envelope eagerly and pulled out the paper inside.

Dear Skylar,

*Thank you for the book you sent me. It was really cool. I didn't
know there were that many Indian violinists.*

*Danny is gone. The white couple came to the reserve with a cop
and they took him away. Mr. Patreya was yelling and I think he
was crying and the cop put handcuffs around his wrists. Danny
was crying, too, but I could tell he was trying not to, and the
woman kept yelling at him to stop. Danny even bit her but they
still took him away. Danny told me that if the white family ever
came back for him he would run away, but this time they're
planning on moving very far away and I don't know that he'll be
able to find us. I'm scared. I'm also sad. I don't think I'll see him
again. But I'm glad he came home for a little while. It was so
nice.*

Thank you for everything, and Mom said I can come to Nettlebush this summer, so I will see you in July.

Love,
Marilu

I read and re-read her letter until I was aware of very little else--not the volume in the next room, not the paper beneath my fingers. So it was that easy. It was that simple to take a little boy away from his home.

"--incredible batting average, right after an injury, too--"

The sound in my head clicked back on, the blood rushing to my ears. I gripped Marilu's letter until it wrinkled. I closed my eyes, smothering a sigh.

Little boy, I thought, I hope you find your way home, too.

* * * * *

Thirty-two out of fifty states are abusing the Indian Child Welfare
Act.

The state of South Dakota removes seven hundred Native
American children from their homes every year. Only 3% of the
children removed actually come from abusive homes.

For the state of South Dakota, kidnapping Native American
children is a lucrative business. The federal government grants the
state $150,000 for each Native American child placed in foster
care. An additional $12,000 is granted to the state when the child
is adopted by a white family.

Native American families have been fighting for years for the
return of their missing children. You can join the fight by visiting:

http://lakotalaw.org

* * * * *

* * * * *

Shoshone Glossary

Dosabite - White
Hinni? - What?
Ekkesah - Yawn
Natsugant - Shaman (lit. "Medicine Person")
Kitah - Quick
Tsikkinichi - Chicken
Nukkatun - Dance
Makan - Gives, Giving
Imaa - Light, Morning
Comanche - Corruption of "Kimanttsi" - Enemy
Tammattsi - Fool
Nu kee sakka tsao suwangkunna! - I don't like that!
So'o! - Enough!
Summi - Here
Puha - Spirit Guide (lit. "Power")
Toko - Grandpa (lit. "Mother's Father")
Aishen - Thank You

* * * * *

Made in the USA
Middletown, DE
07 September 2017